PRAISE FO

THE SPY AND

‘A story of a master spy wh ... tury’s most infamous politic ... y secrets’

‘It is unusual for accou ... ibute to history rather than repeating or expand ... oduced an important and very ... ook’

Alan Judd, ... *Spectator*

‘Tim Willasey-Wilsey deftly brings Bill de Ropp to life’

Angus Reilly, *Daily Telegraph*

‘An important piece of intelligence history, hitherto neglected or perhaps deliberately buried’

Sir Richard Dearlove, Chief of MI6 1999–2004

‘A highly informative read on the work of intelligence and the exercise of political judgement at a key and tragic moment in history’

Sir John Scarlett, Chief of MI6 2004–9

‘A fascinating new read… blown my little cotton socks off’

Giles Brown, *Talk Radio* Europe

‘The largely untold story of how Britain on the eve of war was helped by a brave and well-placed MI6 agent with access to Hitler himself deserves to be much better known’

Professor Sir David Omand, former Director of GCHQ and UK Security and Intelligence Co-ordinator

'For the first time, he puts de Ropp into history where he should be. No one will write it better'

Professor Michael Clarke, RUSI and Sky News commentator

'This spy penetrated the heart of the Third Reich and reported valuable information to London which nobody wanted to believe. Tim Willasey-Wilsey has unearthed an agent from the shadows in this captivating book'

Arnaud de la Grange, *Le Figaro*, Paris

'He combines the precision of a scholar with the pace of a seasoned storyteller. His research is impeccable and exhaustive. The result is a deeply rewarding work'

Tilak Devasher, former Member of India's National Security Advisory Board

'"Who is Baron de Ropp?" asked a British journalist in 1954. Seventy years on, this gripping and masterly account by former diplomat Tim Willasey-Wilsey provides the answer'

Dr Andrew Boyd, author and historian, for King's College London

'The story has shades of John Le Carré's enthralling drama, chronological clarity through assiduous research and a message on how governments should utilise intelligence services'

Vappala Balachandran, formerly of India's Cabinet Secretariat

'The incredible story of Wilhelm Von Der Ropp - the high-born chameleon who had Hitler's ear in the build-up to WW2'

***True Spies* podcast**

'An important contribution to our understanding of espionage'

Richard Iron CMG OBE for the Australian Institute of International Affairs

THE SPY AND THE DEVIL

The untold story of the MI6 agent who penetrated Hitler's inner circle

TIM WILLASEY-WILSEY

bl!nk

First published in the UK in 2025 by Blink Publishing
An imprint of Bonnier Books UK
5th Floor, HYLO, 105 Bunhill Row,
London, EC1Y 8LZ

A CIP catalogue record for this book is available from the British Library.

Hardback ISBN: 9781789468670
Trade paperback ISBN: 9781789468687
Paperback ISBN: 9781789468717

Also available as an ebook and an audiobook

1 3 5 7 9 10 8 6 4 2

Design and Typeset by Envy Design Ltd
Printed and bound by CPI Group (UK) Ltd, Croydon CR0 4YY

MIX
Paper | Supporting responsible forestry
FSC® C013604

The authorised representative in the EEA is
Bonnier Books UK (Ireland) Limited.
Registered office address: Block B, The Crescent Building
Northwood, Santry
Dublin 9, D09 C6X8, Ireland
compliance@bonnierbooks.ie

www.bonnierbooks.co.uk

To Ali with all my love and thanks

CONTENTS

Abbreviations xi
Maps xiii
Introduction xvii

1. **'THE HANGMAN'S ROPE'**
   October 1946: The execution of Alfred Rosenberg at Nuremberg 1
2. **'WHAT SHOULD WE DO?'**
   September 1938: MI6 offers a new policy to confront Hitler 7
3. **'WHO IS BARON DE ROPP?'**
   November 1954: The search for a traitor in rural England 23
4. **ANATOMY OF A MASTER SPY**
   1886–1914: Dresden, Lithuania, Australia and London 31
5. **DICING WITH DEATH**
   1914–1918: Surviving artillery, aeroplanes and espionage 45
6. **'EVERY FORM OF OUTRAGE'**
   1919: Bill de Ropp in occupied Berlin 63

7. **'BETWEEN BOCHE AND BOLSHEVIK'**
August 1919: Subversion and subterfuge in Lithuania 73

8. **'MOSCOW ORDERS TO OUR REDS'**
October 1924: Bill de Ropp and the Zinoviev Letter 85

9. **MISSION CREEP**
April to October 1924: From intelligence operation to political conspiracy 97

10. **'THE PRIMITIVE IN US'**
1925–1930: The pressures of spying 109

11. **'STARTLING DISCLOSURES'**
1925–1930: The journalist spy in Berlin 121

12. **'A GENTLEMAN'S AGREEMENT BETWEEN TWO SOLDIERS'**
1931: Bill de Ropp 'gets alongside' Rosenberg and Hitler 133

13. **'THE LIVING EMBODIMENT OF RACE HATRED'**
1931–1933: Triumph and disaster for Rosenberg in London 147

14. **'A BUNCH OF GANGSTERS'**
1934–1937: Extracting secrets from Nazi Berlin 165

15. **'THE LONG KNIVES'**
1934: Blitzkrieg and bloodbath 179

16. **THE NAZIS ARE 'INTENSELY SINCERE'**
1934–1936: The minds of the British people and the royal family 197

17. **'YOUR WONDERFUL FÜHRER'**
1930–1938: Diplomats, journalists and spies in London and Berlin 215

18. **'MADMEN'S DREAMS'**
1932–1939: Nazi plans for the Soviet Union 229

19. **'THE KNOCK-OUT BLOW'**
1934–1938: The race against the Luftwaffe 245

20. **'A RED LIGHT OF PERSONAL WARNING'**
1938–1939: Sex and suspicion on the eve of war 265

21. **'I SUGGEST YOU LEAVE GERMANY'**
1938–1939: Countdown to world war 279

22. **'HEAVY NEW SNOW'**
1939–1940: Bill de Ropp's peace efforts from Switzerland 295

23. **'INFLUENCED BY AGENTS OF THE BRITISH SECRET SERVICE'**
May 1941: The Hess mission to Scotland 311

24. **TWILIGHT OF A MASTER SPY**
1939–1945: Bill de Ropp in wartime Switzerland 327

25. **DOWNFALL**
1945–1946: The defeat of Nazi Germany 347

26. **'ON THE KNEES OF THE OLYMPIAN GODS'**
1945–1973: The players depart 363

27. **THE VERDICT**
How important was the Bill de Ropp case? 373

Postscript 383
Acknowledgements 386
Sources and Bibliography 389
Notes 399
Index 417

ABBREVIATIONS

AA	Auswärtiges Amt (German Foreign Office)
APA	Aussenpolitisches Amt (Rosenberg's Nazi Party Foreign Policy office)
C or CSS	The Chief of MI6
CID	Committee of Imperial Defence
CMG	Companion of St Michael and St George (British civil decoration usually awarded for service overseas)
CPGB	Communist Party of Great Britain
CX	An MI6 intelligence report sent to customers in Whitehall
DSO	Distinguished Service Order (British military decoration)
FO	Foreign Office (British)
GC&CS	Government Code and Cypher School (British)
HMG	His Majesty's Government
IIC	Industrial Intelligence Centre
JIC	Joint Intelligence Committee
MC	Military Cross (British military decoration)
MI5	Security Service (for the internal security of Britain and her colonies)

MI6	Secret Intelligence Service (SIS) for intelligence on external threats
NSDAP	Nationalsozialistische Deutsche Arbeiterpartei (Nazi Party)
OGPU	Soviet Intelligence and Security Service 1923–1934
OKH	Oberkommando des Heeres (German Army High Command)
OKW	Oberkommando der Wehrmacht (Armed Forces High Command)
PCO	Passport Control Office (provided cover for MI6 officers) also Passport Control Officer
PID	Political Intelligence Department (of the British Foreign Office)
PQ	Parliamentary Question
PUS	Permanent Under Secretary (Head of a British government department)
RFC	Royal Flying Corps
RSHA	Reichssicherheitshauptamt (Reich Head Security Office)
SA	Sturmabteilung (Storm Troopers – paramilitary wing of the Nazi Party)
SD	Sicherheitsdienst (Himmler's Security Service)
SIGINT	Signals intelligence
SS	Schutzstaffel (Himmler's paramilitary organisation)
VB	*Völkischer Beobachter* (Nazi Party newspaper)
VC	Victoria Cross (British military decoration)

MAPS

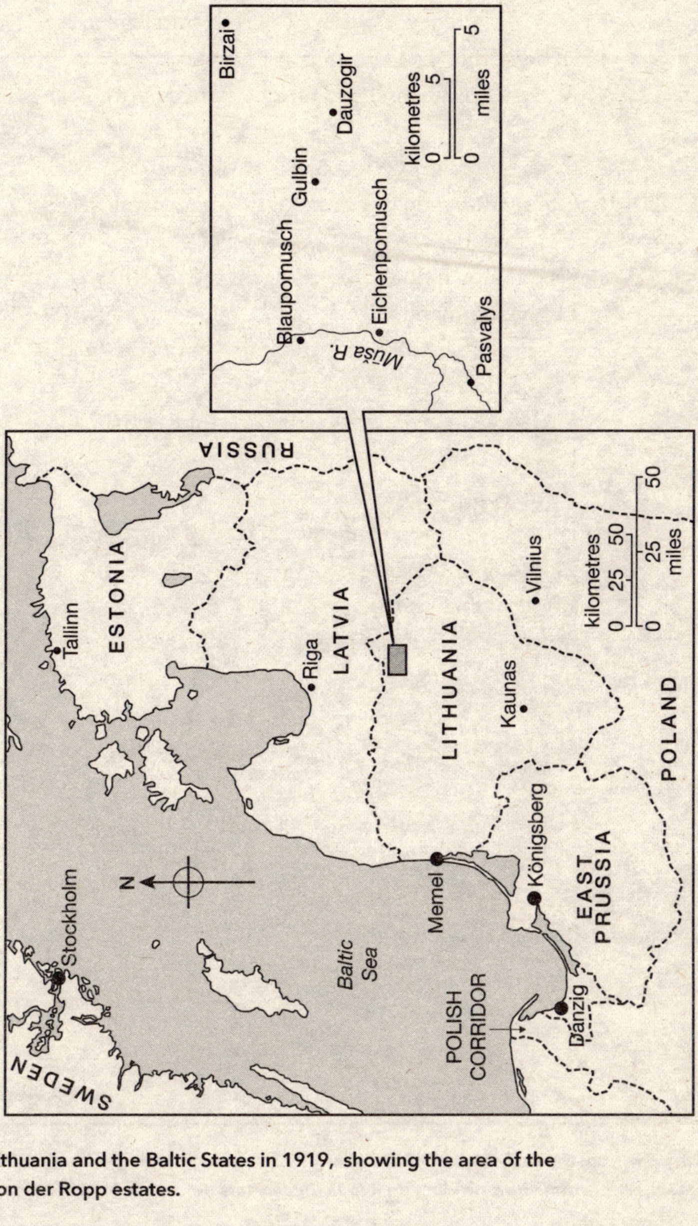

Lithuania and the Baltic States in 1919, showing the area of the von der Ropp estates.

The page from the *Daily Mail* of 28 October 1957, showing the map with Rosenberg's annotations dividing up Russia – nine years before the Nazi invasion.

MAPS

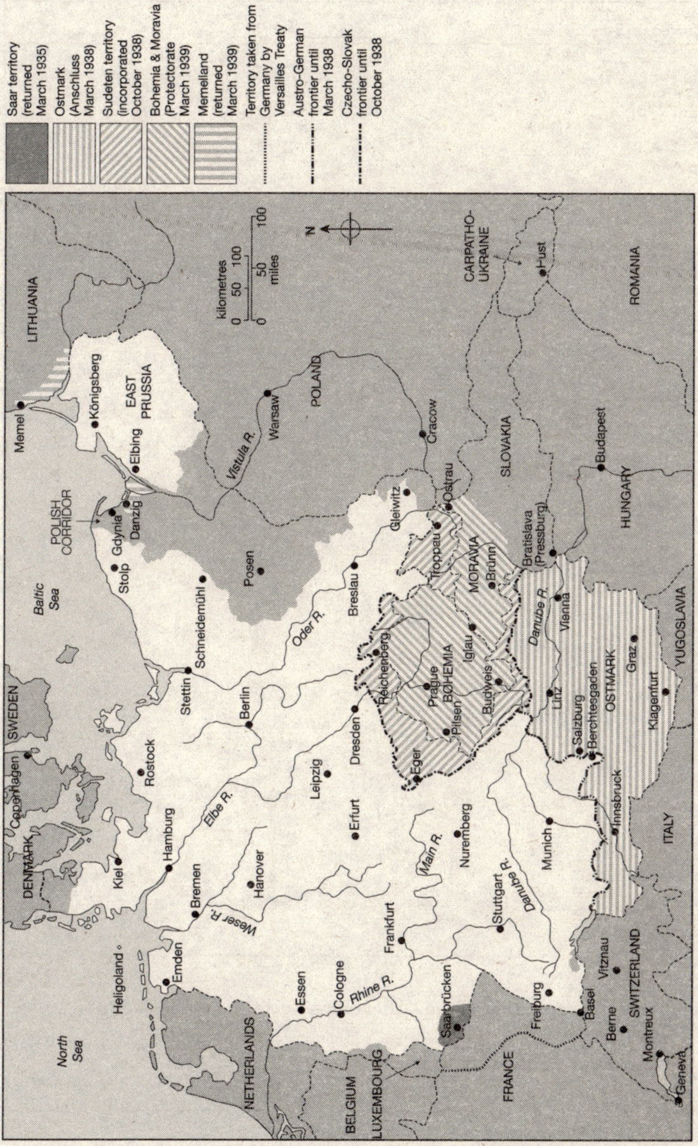

Germany in the late 1930s.

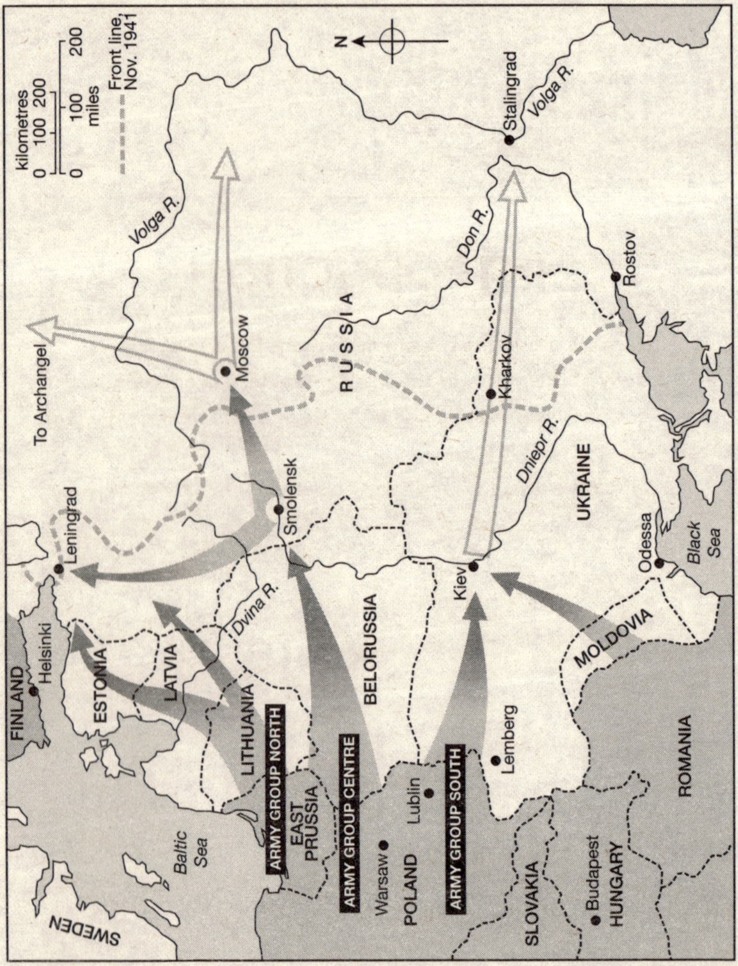

Operation Barbarossa: the Nazi invasion of the Soviet Union, June 1941.

INTRODUCTION

'Here we are in the twentieth century, the age of science, totally at the mercy of the Dark Force. If I were a religious man I suppose I'd call it the Devil.' – Bill de Ropp

'Yet all the time I was Hitler's closest enemy – A spy at his shoulder' – Bill de Ropp

Hardly anybody realises that Britain had a spy with direct access to Adolf Hitler and his inner circle throughout the 1930s. The task of uncovering the story of Baron Bill de Ropp's life was any author's dream. It involved hundreds of hours in archives and extensive overseas travel to find his relatives. To stumble across his key role in the Zinoviev Letter scandal of 1924 was an unexpected bonus. That his older brother was a hyperactive and audacious spy for the German Foreign Ministry only adds to the drama of this astonishing case.

Readers of Professor Keith Jeffery's authorised *MI6: The History of the Secret Intelligence Service, 1909–1949* would have noticed mention of Baron William de Ropp who provided 'at least 70%' of the political intelligence on Hitler's Germany yet only appears on six of the book's 840 pages. In the 1950s the *Daily Mail* had printed five articles about him and a decade later de Ropp was mentioned in three books by

F.W. Winterbotham, a retired senior MI6 officer. Since then historians have tended to overlook and even dismiss the case, deterred, perhaps, by the absence of information about the man.

This has not prevented writers using those scant details and de Ropp's brief Wikipedia page (some of it incorrect) to weave conspiracy theories about Bill de Ropp's loyalties and his alleged role in everything from the British royal family's Nazi sympathies, the death of the Duke of Kent, the alleged financing of Hitler by Shell and Schröders Bank, the flight of Rudolf Hess and even the occult.

The man that emerges from this book was an important and courageous secret agent. It was his bad luck that he operated at a time when the British government had no coherent policy towards Nazi Germany. It was also unfortunate that MI6 was not yet skilled at running an agent near the very top of a hostile party and government. The case represented an important step in MI6's evolution from being a service providing low-level tactical information to the strategic organisation it has since become.

There is the question of how much (and how little) impact a high-level secret agent can make. The Bill de Ropp story should take its place alongside other major cases as an example of how intelligence can only be as good as the policy-makers who use, misuse or ignore the fruits of their labours.

And finally we learn about the huge psychological, personal and family pressures of spying in a country where one mistake can mean arrest, torture and death.

EXPLANATORY NOTE

The MI6 archive remains closed but we know, from the lectures given by the late Professor Keith Jeffery following publication of his history of the service, that the files have been copiously weeded over the decades. Fortunately Jeffery devoted some important pages to the Bill de Ropp case.

In the world of intelligence there are always some evidential gaps. Where I have used words such as 'probable', 'likely', and 'doubtless' it is because I am as sure as I can be and I have included supporting details in the text or in the Notes. Where there was significant doubt about (for example) Bill de Ropp's authorship of an intelligence report, I have preferred to avoid its inclusion altogether rather than risk building a fragile structure upon sand.

I have used 'MI6' throughout because it is the designation by which the British intelligence service is popularly known. Its real name is the Secret Intelligence Service, abbreviated as SIS.

As most of the narrative occurs before 1939, I have usually referred to what we now call the First World War as 'the Great War' or simply 'the war'.

TIM WILLASEY-WILSEY
Somerset 2025

1

'THE HANGMAN'S ROPE'

October 1946: The execution of Alfred Rosenberg at Nuremberg

Alfred Rosenberg seemed to think he could avoid a death sentence at Nuremberg. The man who, more than most, bore responsibility for the worst aspects of the Nazis' racial and educational policies genuinely believed he was a good person.

Someone who worked for him wrote perceptively that 'He had many characteristics that go very ill together. The human kindness, incorruptibility, simplicity and indeed childishness of his nature contrasted with a lack of resolution and courage of his convictions which made him the prisoner of others' disdain . . . He avoided unpleasantness with a timidity that bordered on cowardice . . . His closest collaborators . . . called him the Sphinx on account of the opaqueness of his character and lack of initiative and capacity to express himself clearly.'[1]

This was the curious character who wrote some of the most toxic treatises of Nazism including *The Myth of the Twentieth Century*. It was he who cobbled together a collection of vague and half-understood traditions of Aryan or Nordic mythology into the concept of the Master Race from which other ideas flowed; that the Jews, the communists and the freemasons comprised a global conspiracy. He also gave new oxygen to the fabricated *Protocols of the wise men of Zion* (probably a Tsarist forgery dating from 1905), which claimed that a secret meeting of world Jewry had plotted the destruction of the Gentiles.

Alfred Rosenberg was always one of Adolf Hitler's most eager adherents and yet he was rarely taken seriously by the other members of the Führer's inner circle. Martin Bormann ensured that Rosenberg's access to Hitler was strictly limited. He was seen as a bore who managed to complicate rather than simplify issues. Although his turgid writings were widely ridiculed, his *The Myth of the Twentieth Century* was the second most printed book of the Nazi era after Hitler's own *Mein Kampf*. The Nazis' self-styled philosopher always managed to hang on to his senior position as a Reichsleiter, the second highest rank in Nazi Germany, and continued to be given demanding and important tasks.

The British lawyer Airey Neave met Rosenberg at Nuremberg. Neave, then best-known for having escaped from Colditz Castle, was by that time one of the leading lights in MI9, the agency tasked with helping Allied servicemen escape from enemy territory. He was part of the investigative team at the trials, and later wrote of his experience.

> I knew of Rosenberg as the original Nazi philosopher; anti-Semitic, anti-Church and anti-Slav. He was by far the most boring and pedantic of the accused at Nuremberg . . . [The British Foreign Office official Robert] Vansittart had described him perfectly as 'a ponderous lightweight'. . .[2]
>
> . . . Rosenberg studied me with a pained stare. He seemed set apart from the other defendants and regarded by them as a foreigner. . . He was dark and there seemed nothing very German in his appearance. Most Nazis thought he had Jewish blood and said he must be the only Aryan Rosenberg in the world. He certainly had a Jewish mistress [Lisette Kohlerausch].[3]
>
> But in politics Hitler simply ignored him. Any hopes that

> Rosenberg had of becoming Nazi Foreign Minister were dashed by the clumsy mishandling of his visit to London in May 1933. . . Despite his alleged disapproval of the murderous conduct of the SS in the East there was plenty of evidence to convict Rosenberg on all four counts with which he was charged in the indictment.[4]

The court found Rosenberg an excellent defence counsel in Dr Alfred Thoma. Thoma had been a district judge in Nuremberg since 1926 and a senior district judge since 1935 and he made a serious effort to defend Rosenberg.

He submitted dozens of requests for witnesses, documents and press articles which were intended to demonstrate that Rosenberg had often tried to argue against harsh policies and had expressed himself with increasing temerity against the concentration of power in Party and State. He insisted that he had benign intentions towards the Baltic States. He even tried to prove 'that irrational philosophy has known representatives in other countries too and has a large following'.

Thoma contended that 'Rosenberg had imagined the Jewish question would be solved for Germany and for Europe without force'.[5] He claimed that the atrocities in Ukraine and Russia had been carried out in spite of Rosenberg's protests.

In his final statement to the court, on 30 August 1946, Rosenberg was unrepentant:

> I know my conscience is completely free from any such guilt for any complicity in the murder of peoples . . . I opposed with all my might, as has been proven, every policy of violent measures . . . I was of the opinion that the existing Jewish question would have to be solved by the creation of a minority right, by emigration or by settling the Jews in a national territory over a ten-year period of time . . . I frankly welcome the idea that a crime of genocide

> is to be outlawed by international agreement and placed under the severest penalties . . . National Socialism represented the idea of overcoming a class struggle, which was disintegrating the people, and uniting all classes in a large national community.

The trial did not go well for Rosenberg and he cannot have been surprised by the verdict when it arrived on 1 October. Indeed, of the twenty-one defendants who attended the trials (the twenty-second, Martin Bormann, was tried in absentia), eleven were sentenced to hang,* but only four men were convicted on all four charges: Göring, Ribbentrop, Keitel and Rosenberg. If one adds Hitler, Goebbels, Himmler and Bormann, who were already dead, that placed Rosenberg firmly in the top ten of the Nazi regime, a rank to which he had always desperately aspired and to which he somehow managed to cling.

Joseph Kingsbury Smith of the International News Service was chosen by lot to represent the American press at the executions on 16 October, writing:

> As they went to the gallows most of the ten endeavoured to show courage. Some were defiant and some were resigned and some begged the Almighty for mercy. All except for Rosenberg made brief last-minute statements on the scaffold. . . .
>
> The ten once great men in Hitler's Reich that was to have lasted for a thousand years walked up thirteen wooden steps to a platform eight feet high which also was eight feet square. Ropes were suspended from a crossbeam supported on two posts. A new one was used for each man. When the trap was sprung the victim dropped from sight in the interior of the scaffolding . . . so that no one saw the death struggles of the men dangling with broken necks. . . .
>
> [Von Ribbentrop went first, followed by Keitel and

* And one of them, Göring, committed suicide the night before the executions.

> Kaltenbrunner] . . . Rosenberg was dull and sunken-cheeked as he looked around the court. His complexion was pasty brown but he did not appear nervous and walked with a steady step to and up the gallows. Apart from giving his name and replying 'No' to a question as to whether he had anything to say, he did not utter a word. Despite his avowed atheism he was accompanied by a Protestant chaplain who followed him to the gallows and stood beside him praying. Rosenberg looked at the chaplain once, expressionless. Ninety seconds after, he was swinging from the end of a hangman's rope. His was the swiftest execution of the ten.[6]

Justice was done and seen to be done with one small exception. Rosenberg had asked Thoma to summon two British citizens to appear as witnesses for the defence. *The Scotsman* of 29 November 1945 reported that 'A request by Rosenberg for the attendance of a Baron* de Ropp and Major Winterbotham was refused pending further information about their identity.'

A few weeks later, on 20 December 1945, *The Belfast Newsletter* added that 'Applications on behalf of Rosenberg for the interrogation of Major Winterbotham whose address was given as the Air Ministry, London, and Baron de Ropp of the Savile Club of London were refused. The application said that these witnesses would say that Rosenberg worked for an understanding with Britain and visited London for that purpose.'

So who were Major Winterbotham and Baron de Ropp? And what testimony could they possibly have presented to defend Alfred Rosenberg?

* The document referred to him as 'Baronet', as did subsequent press reports.

2

'WHAT SHOULD WE DO?'

September 1938: MI6 offers a new policy to confront Hitler

Eight years earlier Alexander Cadogan,[7] the head of the British Foreign Office, sat down at his desk in Whitehall and surveyed the wreckage of British foreign policy. After years of appeasing Hitler it was increasingly clear that Germany could not be trusted and that war was almost inevitable. He looked out at the autumnal scene and reached for a sheet of pale blue foolscap drafting paper. If he were to craft a new approach to Germany, he would need to engage the best minds in the FO.

Cadogan may have been clinically depressed. His diary reveals a litany of disconsolate entries. On 14 September he noted, 'Autumn crocuses just coming up! Shall I see them again and what will they portend?' The 20th was an 'awful day'. On the 24th, 'I have never had such a shattering day or been so depressed and dispirited.' The word 'awful' appears on most days.

Although a scion of the enormously wealthy and aristocratic Cadogan family, which owned much of the West End of London, and educated at Eton and Balliol, Alex Cadogan was a quiet, serious and modest man with an eye for detail, shrewd judgement and a diligent nature which made him work excessive hours. He had served in Constantinople and Vienna before a difficult posting to China in the 1930s. After a senior role in London he was appointed Permanent Under Secretary (PUS) in January 1938.

Great Britain was still a great power but the reality felt very different. The nation had the most powerful navy on earth but many of the ships were showing their age. The Royal Air Force still mostly consisted of biplanes. The British economy was recovering from the Great Depression of the early 1930s but was no match for the burgeoning might of the United States' industry.

The British Empire, now increasingly called the British Commonwealth of Nations, might show in red or pink across much of Africa and Asia but the Dominions of Canada, Australia, New Zealand and South Africa had developed an independent streak. Gone were the days when they would slavishly follow the Mother Country into a world war. That concept had died at Gallipoli and the Somme. In future they would need to be convinced by the power of argument and the implications for their own security. The Jewel in the Crown, India, was beset by internal unrest and the desire of both Hindus and Muslims for home rule.

The FO building itself also gave a false impression of power. Completed by Sir Gilbert Scott in 1868 its wide marble staircases and ample corridors spoke of imperial influence. Departmental heads had their own offices behind tall mahogany doors with their own fireplaces tended by liveried servants. The more junior staff huddled three or four to a high-ceilinged room (known as a 'Third Room'), drafting minutes and letters for submission up the long chain to ministers. FO staff were notoriously erudite, and 'drafting' was regarded as the supreme skill.

And yet the FO was not its own master even in the field of foreign policy. Prime ministers always like foreign policy because the royal prerogative gives them substantial freedom from the rough and tumble of Parliamentary procedure. Neville Chamberlain was no exception and his Industrial Adviser in No 10 Downing Street, Sir Horace Wilson, although not a foreign policy specialist, was a significant influence on Chamberlain in favour of appeasement.

The three armed services all had their own foreign interests and their bases overseas. There was also the influential Committee for Imperial Defence (CID) under the vastly experienced Sir Maurice Hankey, which conducted some genuinely strategic thinking about Britain's security around the world. There was the India Office that shared Gilbert Scott's masterpiece which included the Durbar Court where Indian princes were received in suitable style. And finally there were the Colonial Office and the smaller Dominions Office. In crude terms, the former oversaw the black parts of Britain's vast empire and the latter the white.

Even within the FO, Cadogan was not supreme. His boss was the Foreign Secretary Lord Halifax, as tall and languid as Cadogan was small and busy. The two got on well but Cadogan frequently complained to his diary about Halifax's tendency towards appeasement.

Unusually there was also a resident maverick. Cadogan's predecessor as PUS was Sir Robert Vansittart. In a department famous for its caution, reserve and use of nuance, Van (as he was known) was a one-off. He was brazen, impatient, irritable and opinionated. He was quoted as disliking 'Communism, Deutschism and homosexuality'.[8] He preferred to rely on his own sources of information and to face ministers with difficult decisions sometimes presented in a confrontational manner.

Van's career had been stellar with junior postings in France and Persia. He attended the Paris Peace Conference in 1919 before becoming Private Secretary to the Foreign Secretary Lord Curzon and then Private Secretary to Prime Minister Stanley Baldwin. Although he had never served as an ambassador he had been at or near the top of British diplomacy for a decade and a half.

Anthony Eden, Halifax's predecessor as Foreign Secretary, had found Van's style intolerable and arranged for him to be moved sideways to a non-job with the grand title of 'Chief Diplomatic Adviser'. However, the 1939 Foreign Office List shows Vansittart above Cadogan in the pecking order.[9] This was not a reflection of reality, but the fudge enabled Van to continue being interventionist and assertive. The trouble, which Cadogan himself recognised, was that Van's style might be tiresome but his views on the extreme danger of Hitler and Germany were well-founded.

This was the background to Cadogan's choice of contributors for a new policy approach towards Nazi Germany. The need for discretion ruled out Van immediately. He could not risk Van telling everybody that his successor was so devoid of ideas that he was casting about desperately for shreds of intuition.

The first choice was automatic. William Strang was Head of Central Department, which included Germany. He had fought during the Great War with the Worcestershire Regiment and on the staff of the 29th Division before joining the FO. He had postings to Budapest and Moscow and had become something of an expert on the Soviet Union. He was a high-flyer and would become a future PUS himself.

The second was also relatively easy. Laurence Collier was Head of Northern Department, which included the Soviet Union and Scandinavia. The likely Soviet policy position towards Germany and Spain would be key elements in any new policy formulation. He had only had one overseas posting as a junior diplomat in Tokyo just after the Great War.

Frank Ashton-Gwatkin was Cadogan's third pick. He headed up the new Economic Relations Section in the FO and was also an expert on the Far East. He had, however, very recently been catapulted into the German question as a member of the Runciman Mission to mediate the dispute between the Prague government and the Sudeten Germans, a minority grouping within Czechoslovakia.

The fourth was Philip Nichols (often known by his initials

PBB), who had won an MC in the Great War before FO postings in Austria, New Zealand and Italy. He was head of South East Europe Department.

Cadogan would have thought long and hard before writing to his fifth and final contributor. He would have weighed up the pros and cons carefully. It would be very unpopular in the FO, he knew that. He would have recognised, however, that asking four members of the same FO tribe was likely to result in four versions of the same answer albeit with differences of emphasis. So, he took the plunge and asked the Chief of the Secret Service, Admiral Sir Hugh Sinclair, for the view of MI6.*

To modern readers the idea of a country asking its intelligence service for an opinion hardly seems a revolutionary idea, but it truly was. The FO of the 1930s viewed the Secret Service with distaste and disdain. The distaste came from the prevalent view of the ungentlemanly nature of spying and, even worse, having to accept intelligence officers as members of embassies abroad where they might land an ambassador in trouble by being caught suborning an official or even subverting the host nation. The disdain arose from those same secret servants being seen as rather uncouth, not good cocktail party material.

The MI6 counter-viewpoint was that FO diplomats tended to live in an ethereal bubble of polite society detached from the real Hobbesian world of crime, conflict and general brutishness. The FO were seen as thinkers whereas MI6 liked to think of themselves as doers.[10]

There was also some intellectual arrogance involved. In 1930 only one member of MI6 – Frederick Winterbotham, Head of Air Intelligence – was a graduate. Many of the MI6 reports which landed on FO desks were very tactical; a snippet here about a communist

* The service was often known at the time as MI1c or the Secret Service, but MI6 is used here for consistency.

arriving at Harwich from Holland, or a paragraph there about a new model of artillery being developed by a Czech munitions firm. Furthermore, some reports had caused real damage in the past. Everyone remembered the Zinoviev Letter scandal of 1924 which was credited with undermining Labour's electoral chances, and the disastrous ARCOS* raid of 1927 which further weakened relations with the Soviet Union (*see* Chapters 8 and 9).

The FO were able to tolerate tactical MI6 reports about weapons or extremists, but they regarded strategic foreign policy thinking and analysis as exclusively their own domain. Senior officials like George Mounsey or even William Strang would have advised Cadogan (if asked) that letting MI6 opine on policy would establish a dangerous precedent. Moreover they would have doubted that MI6 would have anything valuable to contribute.

Nevertheless, Cadogan had come to both like and trust Sinclair. Sinclair certainly had a winning way with people. He was only the second MI6 Chief (known as C) and like his predecessor he was a former naval officer and possessed a charismatic personality. He had commanded the battle-cruiser HMS *Renown* during the war before becoming increasingly involved in naval intelligence work and finally being chosen to lead MI6. He was a divorcee with a devoted sister, Evelyn, who would accompany him to social events.

Although he had regarded the removal of Van as a disaster, Sinclair committed time and effort to Cadogan and appears surprisingly frequently in Cadogan's diary. For example on 1 February 1938: 'C came round this afternoon with interesting information', and the following day, 'C called and told me of precautions that he had taken'.[11] Cadogan began to appreciate the quality of the advice and the courage of a man who was suffering in silence from the cancer which would kill him the following year.

*ARCOS was the All-Russian Co-operative Society, the Russian trade office based at 49 Moorgate, London. See, for instance: https://www.oxfordreference.com/display/10.1093/oi/authority.20110803095422443.

When Cadogan's letter landed on Sinclair's desk at MI6 headquarters on the fourth floor at 54 Broadway,* opposite St James's Park Underground station, the Admiral would have recognised this as the opportunity of a lifetime. The man he called upon to deliver the MI6 response was Malcolm Woollcombe, predictably known as Woolly.

Woollcombe was Head of Section I† of MI6 responsible for political reporting. He had been born in India, the son of a general. After schooling at Marlborough he had served with the 28th Indian Light Cavalry but had been on leave in England when war broke out. He was briefly aide-de-camp (ADC) to his father before being sent to the Western Front, where he was involved in the Battle of Arras in April 1917, before transferring to intelligence work. His experiences at Arras would stay with Woollcombe for the rest of his life.

After the war he joined the FO in 1921 and was seconded to MI6 the following year. Although not a fully-fledged diplomat he had won the respect of FO heads of department by regularly visiting them and discussing their requirements.[12]

In September 1938 Woollcombe was on his annual 'motoring' holiday in France with his wife and children. They were staying in Chantilly when a telegram arrived from his deputy which read simply 'You must return' – MI6 was not given to flowery rhetoric and telegrams were priced by the word. The family remembered being hurriedly packed into the car and setting off towards the Channel coast and the ferry to England.[13] Woollcombe recognised the gravity of the message and more than once stopped the car to be physically sick by the side of the road to Calais.

The other man Sinclair would have consulted was Colonel Stewart Menzies who would become his successor as C in late 1939. Menzies was head of Section II, responsible for army intelligence collected

* The building is still there, its exterior little changed since 1938. It has been renumbered 50 Broadway.

† All MI6 sections were designated by Roman numerals.

in support of the requirements of the War Office.* His life too had been defined by the war. After Eton, Menzies had joined the 2nd Life Guards and had deployed to France at the outbreak. In October 1914 they went into action near Ypres (in the battle later known as First Ypres) and lost all their officers except Menzies and his brother Keith. For his gallantry he was awarded the DSO. At Second Ypres in May 1915 the 2nd Life Guards were involved again and lost half their men. After fourteen months at the front Menzies was posted to an intelligence role at GHQ.

Menzies and Woollcombe would have conferred in Sinclair's office. All three men knew that they had little to contribute except for one ace up their sleeve; in fact the only ace in a rather depleted pack of cards. This secret agent was known in the office as 12821 or more usually by the shorter format 821: the 12000 meant that the agent worked in Germany. The 800 referred to his case officer, who was the eighth member on Berlin station; and 21 was the agent's own designation. 821 had been recruited by Menzies himself back in 1919 and the colonel had maintained a fatherly interest in his star agent throughout the following decades, occasionally having to mediate disputes between 821's supporters and detractors.

One of MI6's most secret agents, 821 was also one of those at the greatest risk of compromise and execution. Special security measures had been developed to reduce the chance of compromise. He lived in the heart of Berlin under the noses of the three main German security services – the Gestapo, the Abwehr and the SD.† Sinclair, Menzies and Woollcombe knew his real name to be the Baron Wilhelm Sylvester von der Ropp, known to all his British friends as Bill de Ropp.

Woollcombe was doubly fortunate that Bill de Ropp had recently

---

* In the days before the Ministry of Defence was created in 1964 there was the Admiralty (in charge of naval matters), the War Office (for the army) and the Air Ministry (for the air force).

† The Gestapo was the German secret police, the Abwehr was military intelligence, and the SD (Sicherheitsdienst) was the SS's own security service.

returned to London in fear for his life in Germany. He was convinced (rightly as it later transpired) that the Nazis had begun to suspect that he was a British agent. He was under pressure from his MI6 case officers to return to Berlin but, just for the moment, his presence in London was a godsend for Woollcombe, Menzies and Sinclair.

The strong probability is that Woollcombe and de Ropp sat down together in London to write the majority of the paper 'What Should We Do?'[14] This is because the text does not read like an assemblage of observations from past reports. The flow of the commentary suggests that an expert on current German politics was involved in the drafting. Woollcombe himself was knowledgeable but his role also required expertise on Russia, France, Italy, Spain, Japan and Eastern Europe. Whereas Woollcombe had more breadth, Bill de Ropp's intense focus was on Germany.

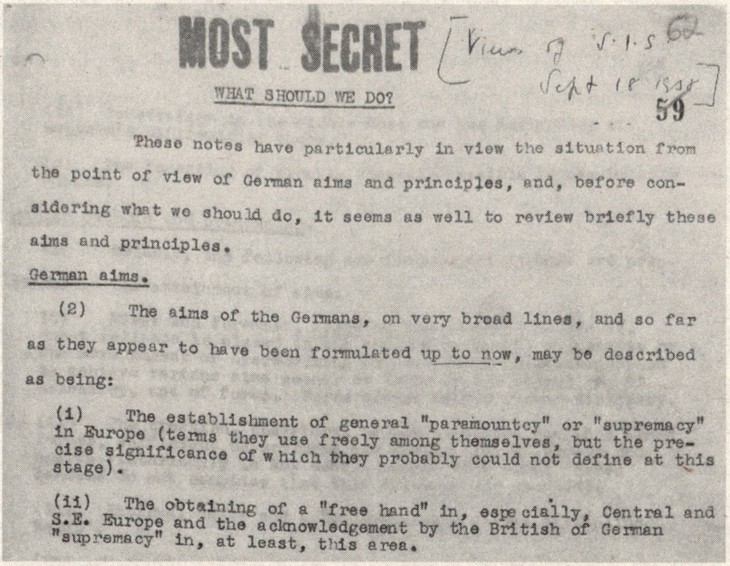

MOST SECRET

59

WHAT SHOULD WE DO?

These notes have particularly in view the situation from the point of view of German aims and principles, and, before considering what we should do, it seems as well to review briefly these aims and principles.

German aims.

(2) The aims of the Germans, on very broad lines, and so far as they appear to have been formulated up to now, may be described as being:

(i) The establishment of general "paramountcy" or "supremacy" in Europe (terms they use freely among themselves, but the precise significance of which they probably could not define at this stage).

(ii) The obtaining of a "free hand" in, especially, Central and S.E. Europe and the acknowledgement by the British of German "supremacy" in, at least, this area.

'What Should We Do?' The MI6 report produced at Cadogan's request in 1938, to which Bill de Ropp contributed. (*The National Archives [TNA]*)

Being an agent and therefore not a staff member of MI6,[15] de Ropp would not have been allowed access to Head Office in Broadway nor would he have been permitted to see reporting from any other agents. Woollcombe would have reserved a room at the nearby St Ermin's Hotel (which was widely, indeed excessively, used by the service) or booked one of the safe houses in West London. De Ropp himself was staying at the Savile Club at 69 Brook Street, Mayfair but too many members of the club had served in the secret services for the Savile to be a safe place to meet.

'What Should We Do?' was produced in just a few days. Wiser civil servants would have advised the authors not to rush. Surely better to let the other four participants submit their ideas first and then cherry-pick the good thoughts and subtly mock the bad ones. But that was not MI6 style. MI6 did not see themselves as civil servants and hated the very concept of 'playing the Whitehall game'. Most of them had served on the Western Front in the war (as indeed had 821) and they saw such diplomatic finesse as un-British. Cadogan had asked a simple question so MI6 would submit an answer with a decidedly utilitarian title. 'What Should We Do?' has a delightfully naïve but honest ring to it.*

How do we know about Bill de Ropp's key role in 'What Should We Do?' Three reasons. Professor Keith Jeffery's magisterial history of MI6, published to celebrate the service's centenary, records that 'in June 1938 Woollcombe estimated that at least 70 per cent of [MI6's] German [political intelligence] came from one very good source [de Ropp] . . . "If for any reason we lose him, he wrote, it is obvious that our supply of political information will . . . be very seriously affected."'[16] Secondly, as we shall see in later chapters, it is relatively easy to identify the views of 821's primary sub-sources in the paper.[17] And, finally, 821's own voice emerges at various points

* The title 'What Should We Do?' was possibly a tongue in cheek reference to Vladimir Lenin's influential political pamphlet of 1902. Lenin in turn took the title from a 1863 book by Nikolai Chernyshevsky.

in the text of this report and the two successor reports which issued from MI6 over the following months.*

The MI6 paper was completed and dispatched on 18 September 1938 and so was available before the Prime Minister's last-gasp attempt to salvage peace at Munich at the end of that month. William Strang signed off his paper in mid-October, Gwatkin and Collier theirs at the end of October, and one other (probably Nichols' contribution) is unsigned and undated. Sinclair may have been naïve in submitting so soon but he seized the moment brilliantly and left the other four papers struggling for relevance.

Cadogan sent his own thoughts to Halifax on 14 October and so was only able to draw on the MI6 and Strang contributions. He then sent all the collated papers together with an additional piece from his private secretary Gladwyn Jebb to Halifax in November with an apology that 'this is all rather diffuse but, if you can find time to read it, it might help you to decide how you would like a single paper drafted'.

There can be no doubt that the MI6 paper was the best of the bunch. At only six pages it is the shortest of all five contributions. It is crisply drafted and well laid out with clear subject headings. The best testament to its strengths is that most of the other contributors filleted it for their own offerings. Above all it made concrete recommendations (some clearly correct, others debatable) whereas the other four papers tended to begin well but lacked both clear direction and destination.

'What Should We Do?' begins with a statement of German aims, which included 'the downfall of the USSR' and a deal with the British by which Germany would accept the survival of the British Empire in return for German supremacy in Europe. It then goes on to assess German methods. 'Great reliance is placed in the ability to attain objectives by the mere threat of overwhelming force.'

The paper next moves on to three immediate policy recommen-

* The other two reports are assessed in Chapter 21.

dations with a breathtakingly frank suggestion that Czechoslovakia should be persuaded to give Germany the Sudetenland. Britain must do more to strengthen its relationship with Italy (but without it being seen as an overt effort to sabotage the Berlin-Rome axis), and a suggestion (which is as controversial today as it was in 1938) to limit the growth of a Jewish state in Palestine to prevent the hostility of the Arab world towards Britain.

Even at this early stage in the paper its readers would have been reeling with shock. This was not the sort of diplomatic nuance for which the FO was renowned. Nowadays we would call it 'positive challenge' but Woollcombe and 821 were not finished yet.

The next paragraph was entitled 'What Should We Do: longer range'. 'We should unremittingly build up our armaments' – here the writers could not resist a dig at the appeasers. 'If we emerge from the crisis without war; we should take the lesson to heart' – one reader (probably Cadogan) has underlined these words in pencil.

On allies 'we cannot really trust any foreign country' but we should bind France as tightly to us as possible. We should attempt to 'weaken the Axis triangle' and, in the case of Japan, 'even at the sacrifice of some principle'. We should do more to strengthen those states particularly in South East Europe which Germany sees as vassals. On Spain, Britain should ensure that it can maintain good relations with whichever side wins the civil war. London should reinforce relations with Turkey and the United States. And finally it should give Germany no pretext for claiming it is being encircled, whilst also making tactical concessions where appropriate to German complaints (for example about colonies).

Some observers have seen 'What Should We Do?' as an example of appeasement but it is no such thing. The message is that Britain has got itself into a desperate fix and needs to use all its skill and cunning to get itself out of a mess of its own making. The key message is that Britain should avoid a war until it has rearmed. Indeed, this was exactly the policy adopted by Neville Chamberlain after Hitler's invasion of Czechoslovakia had destroyed the Munich agreement.

So what impact did 'What Should We Do?' have on British foreign policy? Cadogan's minute to Halifax of 8 November does not show the PUS at his best. It is a rambling eight-page paper which reads like a man thinking aloud. It says something about Halifax's own style that he tolerated this sort of vagueness from his most senior civil servant. One senses Cadogan's mental exhaustion.

Cadogan draws on Woollcombe's thoughts, however – for example, on the German view of power: 'The German technique has been quite simple – to wait until they are strong enough to demand something, then take it', and on Britain's lack of reliable allies, 'We are back in the old lawless Europe and have got to look out for ourselves.' He accepts the MI6 idea that Britain should look at German grievances 'from the point of view of tactics alone'. He fully accepts the sense in cultivating the alliance with Italy and seeing if Mussolini would be willing to act as an intermediary with Berlin. However, he finishes weakly with some diffuse thoughts about disarmament and 'stabilisation of frontiers' which seem almost to shy away from the gravity of the crisis.

The other four contributions delivered some interesting thoughts but without coming to clear conclusions. Strang remarked that 'in our (and France's) dangerous condition of inferiority to Germany in military strength it is difficult to have or pursue a foreign policy'. Collier saw it as essential to prevent a victory by General Franco's Fascists in Spain and he specifically rubbished the notion that Italy could be detached from the Berlin axis. Ashton-Gwatkin, was convinced that the Munich agreement had saved Hitler from being overthrown by a German public which did not want war. Nichols (if the unsigned paper is from him) confined himself to just one thought: that any further concessions must come from a position of strength not weakness.

Cadogan's gratitude for the clarity of MI6's response was

demonstrated by the fact that he asked for it to be entered onto FO files. The system with reports from MI6 was that all intelligence reports should be returned after reading to MI6 headquarters at Broadway. It is fortunate that Cadogan retained it for further consultation because MI6 archives were so severely culled over the next few decades that very few of their reports (known then and now as CX) from the period have survived.

The Woollcombe family still cherish a letter about 'What Should We Do?' from the Treasury Secretary Sir Warren Fisher to Sinclair. Dated 20 September 1938 it reads:

> My Dear Hugh. A most excellent document. There is one implication that could, I think, be usefully made more explicit, i.e. in our own rearmament the vital need for rapid and effective strengthening of our air position. It is air that must 'hold the ring' for us – at all events in the initial months. It is thro' air that the Germans can get at us and had we used the last few years effectively in that arm, the Germans would not have been able to override us as they have this present year. Yrs Warren.[18]

What Warren Fisher did not know was that Bill de Ropp had furnished some of the best intelligence on the German air force over the previous decade and would provide critical insights into German aircraft production and the performance of their aero-engines just one month after 'What Should We Do?'

In mid-1939 Cadogan wrote to Woollcombe on his being awarded the CMG: 'I know something of the work that you have been doing for us for years past and can appreciate its real value.' Gladwyn Jebb added: 'Nobody has helped the Foreign Office more than you have during these last difficult years.' Sir Nevile Bland, a veteran diplomat, commented that he had 'been privileged to observe from the start the admirable way in which you have built up your liaison work with the FO from nothing at all into what it was when I left the office.'[19]

During the Second World War which would engulf the globe only a year later, British intelligence would enjoy its greatest ever successes. Most of those achievements derived from the cracking of the main German encoding and encryption systems, notably Enigma at the now-famous Bletchley Park. That operation known as Ultra allowed Britain to manage its military operations more successfully than would otherwise have been possible.[20] It enabled MI5 to control all the German agents in Britain and to oversee any intelligence that they sent back to Germany.[21] It revolutionised the relationship between intelligence and diplomacy. The new MI6 chief, Menzies, had automatic, often daily, access to the Prime Minister. Diplomats in the decades which followed became much more comfortable in regarding intelligence as an essential tool of their work.

MI6 had already started this revolution in the twelve months before the outbreak of war. The moment Cadogan added Sinclair to his list of contributors to a review of foreign policy options was a turning point, and Woollcombe's paper (the first of three which have survived in the National Archives) seized the half-chance with both hands.

None of this would have been possible without the high-quality material that Woollcombe had at his disposal. Most of this came from Bill de Ropp. So, who was Bill de Ropp and how did he become MI6's star agent in Nazi Berlin?

3

WHO IS BARON DE ROPP?

November 1954: The search for a traitor in rural England

Exactly the same question appeared in the Saturday edition of the *Daily News*[22] on 13 November 1954 with the subtitle 'New riddle in war papers'. The article begins 'Who is the British Baronet [*sic*]* de Ropp? Where is he now?'

During the 1950s there was a spate of war films in the cinemas but few wanted to talk about the war. It was far too recent, and the memories were mostly painful. People wanted to get on with their lives and to suppress recollections which would often disturb their sleep and haunt their dreams.

The problem in 1954 was that almost everybody would have had traumatic stories to tell; from the solicitor who had flown Lancaster bombers over Germany, to the greengrocer whose platoon had been wiped out on D-Day, to the factory worker whose destroyer had been sunk on a Russian convoy, to the conscientious objector who had served as a stretcher-bearer in the Egyptian desert, to the women

* Copying the mistake from the German documents. He was a baron.

who had produced munitions and the middle-aged men who had dug survivors out of buildings in Coventry, Plymouth or Bath.

The journalist who asked the question about the identity of Baron de Ropp was himself a war veteran. Peter Lawrence had been born at the end of the Great War and so was twenty when the Second World War broke out. He joined the 5th Battalion of the Duke of Cornwall's Light Infantry (DCLI) in early 1941 and, after years of training, embarked at Newhaven aboard the SS *Biarritz* for Normandy almost a fortnight after D-Day (D+13).[23]

A few weeks later the grim realities of war descended when they were ordered to take Hill 112 near Caen. The inexperienced DCLI were up against the hardened German 10th SS Panzer Division and within thirty-six hours the 5th Battalion had been reduced to only a hundred men still able to fight. There were 320 casualties of which 93 were buried on the hill. They also lost their twenty-six-year-old CO, their second in a few weeks. The battle would later be described as 'the fiercest and most costly single battalion action of the [Normandy] campaign'.

Peter Lawrence served with the DCLI until Germany's surrender. He did not win a medal nor did he get seriously wounded but he experienced ten months of pure hell; battle after battle with very little time for respite and recovery in between. According to his obituary,[24] 'he regarded each day as a bonus'.

Sitting at his desk at the *News Chronicle* offices in Bouverie Street, just off Fleet Street, in the heart of London's press district, he read, with mounting suspicion, the latest (eighth) volume of *Documents on German Foreign Policy*, which had just been published. The massive project of sifting and then publishing the captured Germany Foreign Ministry records was being conducted by academics from the victorious powers to prevent a narrative developing that Germany had again been 'stabbed in the back'.

Peter's journalistic career was struggling. In 1953 he had penned pieces on an efficient fish factory in Grimsby and on the outpatients' department at a Balham hospital. As 1954 dawned there had been articles on suicides at Oxford University, the appointment of a new police chief for Kenya, polio recovery in Romford and a strike at the Olympia Exhibition Hall. In truth he never landed a big story.

His obituary credited him with the sensitive reporting of the Munich air disaster of 1958 which resulted in the deaths of several Manchester United footballers. In fact, he never covered the Munich crash – this was a confusion with an accident the same year of a Viking transport plane in Southall which killed the crew of three and four people on the ground. Perhaps his journalistic nadir arrived when he reported the ban on wearing fluorescent socks in church. Peter Lawrence was in need of a big break.

The *News Chronicle* had acquired a copy of the thick volume. A junior member of staff was instructed to search for possible stories within its 974 pages. One had already emerged, with the Duke of Windsor denying two statements attributed to him. The former King Edward VIII was reported by a German official 'in 1940 to be dissatisfied with his present post' (the Duke had been a member of the British military mission to the French army command) and also to have spoken in uncomplimentary terms about Neville Chamberlain,[25] and later to have made a much more serious comment regarding a response if Germany should invade Belgium.[26]

The *News Chronicle*'s editorial staff would, however, have realised that a story of such sensitivity would have landed it in serious trouble with the government. Winston Churchill had returned as Prime Minister in 1951 and was known to be annoyed by such revelations from the team working on the *German Documents*. It would take several more decades before the British public would learn of their former monarch's deplorable conduct during the war.

By contrast the 'Baron de Ropp' story seemed to have a lot more promise. There were three references to de Ropp.

The first was dated 25 September 1939, three weeks after the start of the war. The leading Nazi ideologist Alfred Rosenberg reminded

Hitler of a note he had sent him in mid-August that Baron de Ropp was to become adviser on German issues to the British Air Ministry with the rank of Squadron Leader and that he wished to discuss continued contacts between Britain and Germany following the likely fall of Poland.

Two days earlier Rosenberg had received a note from de Ropp in Switzerland suggesting someone from Berlin should be sent to meet him there 'for a private exchange of views' to include the German opinion of Britain and France and, in return, the thoughts of the (British) Air Ministry which had now 'become of extreme importance as a result of the war situation'. Rosenberg added that 'the personalities who are especially close to Chamberlain are fellow club members of Baron de Ropp'. He then asked Hitler for his instructions.[27]

Peter Lawrence then scanned the second document. On 5 October 1939 there was an unsigned note reporting that a member of Rosenberg's Foreign Affairs Bureau (APA) had gone to Montreux and met de Ropp and had invited him to Berlin. 'Surprised by this far-reaching possibility', de Ropp said that he would have to consult 'his Ministry'.

There follows an undated and unsigned note spanning three pages of text which would have had Peter Lawrence on the edge of his seat in excitement.[28] What was this bizarre document? Was it evidence of back-channel negotiations between London and Berlin or was it somebody freelancing, or perhaps even a traitor at work?

The document described de Ropp's second meeting in Switzerland with the APA official. The former alleged that there was a circle in England (known as the 'English Party') who wanted peace with Germany. Once this party was strong enough to gain power over 'the warmongers', de Ropp saw value in the idea of his visiting Berlin.

The 'English Party' did not just consist of the Air Ministry but also the City of London, which feared for the value of sterling. De Ropp proposed a complex arrangement for the Berlin visit by which he would travel 'officially' from London via Holland having been invited to inspect housing arrangements for displaced Baltic Germans on behalf of the Red Cross.[29]

There followed a conversation about German intentions towards the Soviet Union, the Baltic States and Poland before the meeting ended with both men agreeing an elaborate set of codewords for arranging future meetings. In reply to a final question de Ropp insisted that British Union of Fascists (BUF) leader Oswald Mosley had no part to play in the 'English Party'.

Lawrence knew that he was onto one hell of a good story. All he needed to do now was to track down the enigmatic Baron de Ropp. He placed a few phone calls, observing in the *News Chronicle* (13 November 1954) that 'The Air Ministry could not trace him last night. The Foreign Office did not know of him. Reference books do not list him.' So, he set the *News Chronicle*'s own researchers to begin working on the UK phone books and electoral rolls.

Eventually the latter came up trumps. In the 1953 edition of the Electoral Roll,[30] there was a Ruth M. de Ropp living at Lower Park, Vowchurch in Herefordshire. With no other de Ropps in England and no listing in the telephone directory Lawrence thought it worth a punt. He took a cab to Paddington station.

The nearest railway station to Vowchurch was Hereford. The Golden Valley line, which had serviced the village, had closed during the war, so Peter Lawrence was obliged to take a taxi for the eleven-mile journey. At Lower Park, which turned out to be a farm, the owners Jack and Kate Watkins would have told him that Ruth de Ropp, their recent lodger and popular district nurse, had recently bought a house in Peterchurch, the next village just two miles along the valley. Turn left at the Nag's Head pub and continue up Long Lane and you will find Sunnybank, a tiny white cottage on the left. Oh, and yes, the nurse does live with her father, the old Baron.

When he returned to London Peter Lawrence wrote a second article, which appeared on Friday 19 November under the heading 'Baron de Ropp turns up', subheaded, 'He had a secret wartime mission'.

'Yesterday I found the Baron, a slim white-haired man of 68, digging in the garden of a West Country cottage.' In answer to Peter Lawrence's question Bill de Ropp replied:

> I did a special wartime job for the British government on which I cannot comment . . . My family were White Russians but in 1910 I came to Britain . . . Between the wars I lived as a civilian for a time in Berlin. My job was to obtain certain technical information for people connected to the British government. . . It is true that I wrote to Rosenberg, whom I knew well, and arranged meetings with his representatives . . . I could tell you a lot but am not allowed to.

His final plea was 'Please don't publish my address.'

It says a lot for Peter Lawrence's integrity that he did not try to make mischief over the Bill de Ropp story. He could have raised doubts about de Ropp's claim to have worked for the British government and implied that he might have been a German agent. Instead, his hope of a major story ended in disappointment.

In Chapter 22 we shall get to the bottom of de Ropp's extraordinary dialogue with Rosenberg and Hitler in the months after the outbreak of the Second World War. What on earth was he up to? And to what extent were his messages approved by MI6 and by the British government? What truth is there in the suggestion that the Air Ministry had a separate view on the war? Was there really an 'English Party'?

Fortunately, we can now interpret the discussions thanks to the publication of Rosenberg's diaries, which were found cemented behind a wall in a Bavarian castle by American soldiers just before the end of the war. Most of the diary went missing after the Nuremberg war crimes trials but Hans-Gunther Seraphim published the pages for 1934/5 and 1939/40 in German in 1956. The rest of the diary was finally tracked down in 2013 and published two years later.[31]

In February 1957 another journalist, Walter Farr of the *Daily Mail*, phoned Bill de Ropp upon publication of the next volume of *German Documents*.[32] His article on page 6 was headlined 'The Britons who talked with Hitler'.[33] Although de Ropp told him almost nothing, Farr persuaded him to write the series of five articles which appeared in the *Daily Mail* in October 1957.[34]

Farr was a contact of MI6[35] and it is possible that MI6 allowed the articles to be published in the *Daily Mail*. The service had suffered a torrid year in 1956 with the Commander Crabb scandal in which a diver disappeared while inspecting the hull of a Soviet cruiser in Portsmouth Harbour, followed by the ignominious failure of the Suez campaign. A good story about a wartime success was just the ticket.

None of these articles even begins to scratch the surface of Bill de Ropp's incredible life. To understand this extraordinary man and his motivation to become a British spy who not only befriended Rosenberg but also Adolf Hitler himself, we need to travel back in time to the 1880s and a rural estate in Lithuania called Dauzogir.

4

ANATOMY OF A MASTER SPY

1886–1914: Dresden, Lithuania, Australia and London

Great spies don't just happen. They are created by a series of influences in their backgrounds which provide them with the motivation to take unusually big risks in a particular cause or sometimes to fulfil a personal craving or need. With de Ropp we are lucky in having plenty of family sources on his background and we can tick off those factors as we look at his first two decades of life.

Baron Wilhelm Sylvester von der Ropp (later known as Bill de Ropp) was a 'Balt' or more correctly a Baltic German from Dauzogir in Lithuania. Teutonic Knights had settled the Baltic area between the twelfth and fourteenth centuries as part of the *Drang nach Osten* (or 'Eastwards push') of Germans into the Slavic lands, and had established estates in what are now Estonia and Latvia.

A very few held land in northern Lithuania close to the modern Latvian border although most landlords in Lithuania were of Polish origin and Catholic religion. Some branches of the von der Ropps were part of this minority of Lithuanian German Balts. They always described themselves as coming from Courland (which is in fact slightly to the north of the family estates in Lithuania).

In the relatively benign days before the Great War of 1914–18 the Tsarist government tolerated these German landowners, all of whom held Russian nationality and often served in the Russian army but primarily spoke German. The German Balts were Lutheran Protestants living amongst Catholic Lithuanians in a Tsarist Empire which was mostly Russian Orthodox. They ran their estates in much the same way as the Prussian Junkers. They generally did not have tenant farmers but tended the land as *latifundia*, using a large number of poorly paid farm labourers. It was an almost feudal arrangement of servitude. Landowners usually believed they had excellent relations with their farm workers and indoor servants but the truth would emerge during times of unrest or revolution. Between 1905 and 1940 these relationships were to be tested several times beyond breaking point.

Bill de Ropp's father (Guillaume Alexandrowich von der Ropp, known as Wilhelm) was one of these Balts. He pursued a military career in the Russian Corps of Engineers. In 1865 he was posted to the Crimea to strengthen sea defences in the far east of the peninsula at Kerch. There he met the seventeen-year-old Lydia Guriev whose father, General Sylvester Guriev, a former Adjutant General of the Russian army, owned an estate and farm just south of Kerch called Tschurubatse on the edge of the large lake of the same name.*

Upon his retirement from the army as a lieutenant colonel in 1870 Wilhelm was able to buy three estates in Lithuania with the money saved from his military service. These were Dauzogir, Eichenpomusch

* There is now a Churbaske Lake about 5 km south of Kerch and 4 km from the new Kerch Bridge built since Russia's annexation of Crimea in 2014. The estate itself included what is now the town of Eltigen, which was previously known as Nimfeja (and called Nymphe by the family). When one of Lydia Guriev's grandsons visited the area as a German officer in 1942 the estate had disappeared, although there were still some locals who remembered the family.

and Gulbin.* All three properties are close to Birzai† near the Latvian border. Although Eichenpomusch overlooks the river Mūša and has some of the best land Wilhelm decided to live at Dauzogir which had the best house, which he duly enlarged and improved. Lydia found the transition from the almost Mediterranean climate of the Crimea by the Black Sea to this flat and desolate region with its huge dark forests very hard. The winters were extremely cold and travel beyond the immediate neighbourhood was difficult.

Lydia would produce no fewer than eleven children, eight of whom would survive into adulthood. After two of her children had died Lydia travelled to Wiesbaden, the famous spa town on the Rhine, to take the waters and recover. There she came under the influence of a Lutheran pastor of the Missouri Synod.

The Missouri Synod had developed in the United States during the 1840s from Germans migrating from Saxony. Without apparently consulting her husband, who was a thousand miles away at Dauzogir, Lydia converted from the Russian Orthodox Church. For her, as a full Russian-born citizen, not a Baltic German, this was illegal and made her potentially liable to be detained and placed in a Russian monastery on her return to Lithuania. But Lydia went even further by setting up a German Protestant school on the Dauzogir estate and teaching the children German. The family managed to bribe local priests and officials to keep quiet, though these could only be stop-gap measures.

A solution was found in 1886 by obtaining a house in German Saxony. No. 2 Gartenstrasse in Dresden was a substantial town house with a garden, a croquet lawn and a terrace. It was to the north west

* The modern Lithuanian name of Dauzogir is Daudzgiriai. By 2023 the house had almost completely collapsed although some farm buildings have survived. Eichenpomusch, which means 'oak on the banks of the Mūša River', is now known as Ąžuolpamūšė, just off the E67 highway. Gulbin, now Gulbinai, is about 10 km from Birzai just off the 125 road.

† Its German name was Birsen. On 2 August 1941 its entire Jewish population was murdered by the SS and Lithuanian collaborators. (Holocaust Atlas of Lithuania website, accessed 1 November 2023.)

of the city centre in the so-called Swiss quarter and only about six hundred metres from the river Elbe. The family would live in Dresden during the school term-time before returning to Dauzogir for the summer holidays, often travelling by ship from Lübeck or Stettin to Riga but occasionally going overland by train. Bill was born in Dresden shortly after the move.

All the children loved staying with their father at Dauzogir and indulging in rural pursuits: riding horses, visiting neighbours, fishing in the river, boating on the lake, climbing trees and picking wild berries. Writing after the nightmare of the Nazi experience was over Bill's older brother, Friedrich von der Ropp, evoked a rural idyll in his autobiography.[36] Sometimes they were there in winter and watched the convoys of sledges taking the grain to the railway station and the firewood from the forests. At Christmas the von der Ropps entertained the servants. Each would receive a 'blue sugar loaf'. He adds, 'We were four little siblings and three big ones; a little brother joined later.' The little brother was Bill making his only appearance in Friedrich's 256-page memoir. By dint of being the youngest child it seems that Bill was not as closely associated with the family's memories of Dauzogir.

Dauzogir may have been a bucolic paradise, but Dresden was a cultural and intellectual centre; the fourth largest town in Germany, with a population of half a million; and the capital of Saxony. Its opera house was famously associated with Richard Wagner, Carl-Maria Weber and Richard Strauss. For the von der Ropp children the city offered a first-class education, piano and violin lessons, exposure to foreign languages, including French and English, and a social life which would have been unthinkable in Lithuania.

For the four daughters it also provided access to eligible husbands from the German aristocracy whereas the tradition was for Balts to marry into other neighbouring Baltic German families, thereby creating a somewhat inbred population. Maria (known as Marusch) was the eldest and she fell in love with Leopold von Schlözer, a wealthy officer in the elite Kaiser Wilhelm I Hussar Regiment No 7 (1st Rhenish) which was based in Bonn. His family owned a castle at Merano in Italy furnished with some impressive works of art.[37]

Maria's letters to Leo were later published after her death and reveal a fairy-tale life of parties, ball gowns, visiting princesses, military parades, brass bands and foreign travel. Two of her sisters used to visit her in Bonn and they too became drawn into this dream-like existence. Little did any of them know that this whole way of life would be destroyed for ever in the trenches of the western and eastern fronts before descending into an even deeper quagmire of misery and brutality in the years that were to follow.

Margarethe, one of her two sisters, would also marry an aristocrat, Joachim (known as Achim) von Stralendorff, and would live a comfortable life on their estate at Gamehl, near Wismar, close to the Baltic coast of Mecklenburg. She would live long enough to see the Russians arrive in 1945 to evict them from their land, steal their possessions and rape their female workers, before the estate disappeared behind the Iron Curtain for the next forty-five years.

Helene would also wed an aristocrat, Alfred von Reiswitz. Their estate, Podelwitz, would also be swallowed up by the German Democratic Republic (GDR). Much of her family decamped to Chile after the Second World War.

Only one of the four daughters married a neighbouring Balt. This was Gertrud, who wed Bernhard (Benno) von Wildemann. His estate, Blaupomusch, was barely a mile from Eichenpomusch on the western bank of the Mūša.* Benno is one of the family members who plays a significant role in the Bill de Ropp story. Gertrud's mother, Lydia, had resolutely opposed the marriage until two of her sons fronted up to her and insisted on a more reasonable approach. A wedding photograph still exists showing the sophisticated

* To the surprise of the Wildemann family, who thought it had been destroyed, in October 2023, the author found that part of the Blaupomusch house has survived, albeit in an advanced stage of dereliction.

Gertrud with her fresh-faced husband in military uniform looking as if he could be her son.

From the family narratives that have survived, it seems that Lydia's conversion affected the family in different ways. The Missouri Synod is conservative and Lydia became increasingly austere and devout. Friedrich, who would later become a religious zealot himself, approved of his mother's action. 'We experienced what faith means and how the Russian being pushes towards it.'[38]

Young Gertrud, the youngest daughter and the nearest in age to Bill, reacted differently. She was angry at her mother's objections to her marrying Benno. In a very obvious affront to her mother, she secretly converted from Lutheranism to the Russian Orthodox Church. Her daughter Marina later wrote, 'she suffered from the coolness and sobriety of the Protestant faith. The mysticism and solemnity of the Orthodox church suited her much better', before adding 'Grandmother [Bill and Gertrud's mother, Lydia] was fanatical and overly pious as converts often are. So it happened that our grandmother lived most of the time with the children in Dresden where she lived in all freedom and could practise her Lutheran piety.'[39]

In addition to the four daughters there were four sons. Bill de Ropp was the youngest of all the children and appears from time to time in his sisters' letters and memoirs as their cute and lovable little brother who was almost twenty years younger than Marusch. Bill would have seen very little of his two eldest brothers. Alexander was a talented mathematician and inventor. He invented an ingenious underwater device for saving divers from drowning but, in spite of support from the famous Geneva-based bankers Pictet, it failed.[40] This was credited by his family for the mental health problems from which he suffered. He was sent to Bethel Foundation near Bielefeld, an institution originally designed for epilepsy. There he spent the rest of his life until 1944 when he died, apparently of natural causes.*

* There is still some anxiety in the family that he might have been a victim of the Nazi euthanasia programme.

Paul, the second son, inherited the Eichenpomusch estate from his father and farmed it right through until 1940 when the terms of the Ribbentrop-Molotov pact forced him to transfer the property to the Russians. He was provided with land in Warthegau, the Third Reich's province carved out of Poland, but then had to flee the oncoming Russian advance in late 1944 and early 1945.

We have already briefly met Bill's third brother, Friedrich, in his memories of Dauzogir. Friedrich (known as Friedel) was seven years older than Bill and would have a major influence, both positive and negative, during the years that followed. He was educated at the Vitzthum Gymnasium in Dresden before going on to the world-famous Bergakademie at Freiberg (better known now as Freiberg University of Mining and Technology) before he set off for Africa in search of precious metals.

In 1902 the children's beloved father died at Dauzogir at the age of sixty-seven and was buried in the grounds of the house.* Paul inherited Eichenpomusch and Friedrich was given Dauzogir. In Friedrich's absence in Africa, Helene's husband Alfred von Reiswitz looked after the estate while he waited for Podelwitz to become available. There is no indication of what happened to Wilhelm's third estate, Gulbin. Perhaps it was given to Alexander, who was still under treatment at Bethel, or maybe it was inherited by Bill de Ropp.

If Bill de Ropp did own Gulbin he would have had a stark reminder of the fragility of his inheritance when the 1905 Revolution broke out in Russia. In the Baltic States it led to a wave of unrest among agricultural workers, aimed at both the Russian government and the German and Polish landlords. Since the 1863 uprising in Poland there had been a creeping policy of Russification by which the Tsar's government curtailed the use of the Lithuanian language and the power of the Catholic Church. In 1905 came a reaction against these measures, including the creation of the Seimas, a national assembly at Vilnius.

* The grave was still visible in 1990 but has since been swamped by the undergrowth.

The omens were not good for the German landlords who were not seen as an integral part of any future independent Lithuania. Predictably, the instability also led to anti-Semitic incidents directed at the Jewish community.[41] The landlords were furious with Moscow for the slow return of law and order. It felt as if the whole social fabric was beginning to creak or even crumble.

Bill de Ropp said of his childhood:

> I was born the son of a Baltic baron, with large estates in Lithuania and the heir to a substantial income. My mother, who came from an aristocratic south Russian family, did not like living in Lithuania or Russia, so she took me to Dresden where I was sent to a school specially run for German princes and other blue-blooded Europeans. How I hated it! By the time I came into my inheritance I had no feeling that I belonged to any country and no wish to live on the family estates. I wanted to travel.[42]

He was right about the Vitzthum Gymnasium. It was highly academic and elitist. A list of its alumni includes several Dukes of Mecklenburg-Schwerin, ministers in the government of Saxony, Prussian diplomats, a member of the Dutch royal family and numerous big landowners.

Bill was now living alone with his mother in Dresden. After finishing at the Vitzthum Gymnasium in 1904 he may have felt obliged to remain in Dresden with his mother, and enrol in the University (Technische Hochschule) for a degree in electrical engineering. Then, in February 1908 Lydia died, severing his last tie with Dresden.

Bill de Ropp spent the summer after his mother's death on the Baltic coast on the island of Rügen near Rostock with a friend from the Hochschule in Dresden, Colin Sprent. Colin, from Hobart in Tasmania, was nearing his finals in chemistry and would graduate in December.* Their friendship would play an important part in de Ropp's next few years. Their other companion was Bertil von Alfthan, a Finn from Helsinki, who was studying engineering at Dresden.†

Bill de Ropp enrolled at Birmingham University to complete his postgraduate studies in electrical engineering, but he only stayed for six months. Instead, he decided to use some of his inheritance to take a holiday on the continent, travelling in France, Germany and Italy. Colin Sprent was in Paris learning French and living with his fiancée, Ada Genny,[43] who had been having voice training in Dresden. It was doubtless thanks to Ada that Bill de Ropp met Ruth Fisher, also a talented singer.

Ruth was from an eminent Wiltshire family. Her grandfather had been the Canon of Salisbury Cathedral and her cousins included H. A. L. Fisher (the famous historian and politician), William Fisher (who would become an Admiral of the Fleet) and Adeline, who would marry the composer Ralph Vaughan-Williams.

Ruth's own branch of the family was less fortunate. Her father, Bertie, had been a tea planter in Assam (with a particular love of shooting tigers) but had died in 1906, leaving his widow, Edith, their large Georgian home Court Hill House, in Potterne near Devizes. A daughter had died aged three, and their only son, Evelyn Arthur, was clearly unwell and would later be listed as 'mentally deficient'.[44] There were two younger daughters, Dora and Ruth. Fortunately, Edith was comfortably off: her husband had left over £9000 in his will.‡

It was presumably in France that Bill and Ruth hatched their plan

---

* Colin was one of three brothers who had travelled to Europe to study from Tasmania, where their father was Surveyor-General. While Colin enrolled to do chemistry at Dresden, another brother, Malcolm, was at the mining school in Freiberg, while a third, James, was studying medicine at Edinburgh after years in Leipzig and Berlin. (*Hobart Daily Post*, 10 October 1908.)

† Many years later he would become a Nazi. See Wikipedia biography Bertil von Alfthan in Finnish (accessed 2 November 2023).

‡ Oddly, the summary of his will only lists Edith and Dora as beneficiaries but this must be an error.

to visit the Sprent family in Tasmania and to get married there. His studies prevented Colin from travelling to Australia with them but his older brother Malcolm had just returned home from studying at Freiberg. There were also his two sisters. Mabel was a talented writer[45] and Helen (Nel) who had married Judge Herbert Nichols, a future Chief Justice of Tasmania.

The engagement was announced in the *Bath Chronicle* on 14 April 1910. Bill de Ropp was described grandly as 'Baron William Sylvestre von der Ropp younger son of the late Baron von der Ropp (Colonel in the Russian Imperial Army) and of Baroness von der Ropp of Dauzogir, Curland [*sic*], Russia and of Dresden.'[46]

Ruth, travelling alone, arrived in Australia aboard the SS *Orsova* at the end of June.[47] Her mother, Edith, must have worried about letting a single daughter travel half the way around the world to meet a Baltic baron, but fortunately a neighbour from Potterne, Lieutenant Brudenell Hunt Grubbe, was serving aboard HMS *Encounter* as part of the Australia Squadron and was stationed in Melbourne at the time, and may have provided some reassurance.[48]

Bill de Ropp had arrived in Australia before Ruth, travelling from Bremen aboard a German ship. On 6 July he and Ruth were married at an 'extremely quiet wedding' at the Lutheran Church in Melbourne. Mabel Sprent and her brother Malcolm were present. The local paper crooned, 'The youthful bride who . . . is charmingly fair and pretty wore a white cloth tailor-made suit with a large white canvas hat and white ostrich feather boa.' Their honeymoon was in Fiji and Tonga before they returned to Hobart in November for the summer months.[49]

On their return journey from the South Sea Islands in early October the couple suffered a misfortune. They embarked on the German steamer *Scharnhorst* for the short journey from Sydney to Melbourne, and their 'dressing case' was placed in their cabin. They must have then gone up on deck to admire the views of Sydney Harbour. When they returned to their cabin their jewellery had gone.

When they arrived at Melbourne, the police came aboard but could find no sign of the missing items, which included a gold neck-chain, a pearl and amethyst pendant, gold, amethyst and pearl bracelet, gold cufflinks inset with amethyst and pearls, blue enamel watch, two pairs of earrings, a turquoise pendant and a number of valuable brooches.[50] There was extensive coverage of the robbery in the press. 'A Baron victimised,' shrilled the *Adelaide Advertiser*.[51] De Ropp valued the jewellery at £50 (about £7,400 at 2024 prices according to the CPI Inflation Calculator). They were doubtless Ruth's jewels plus some von der Ropp items from Dauzogir. The preponderance of amethyst (not a particularly valuable gem) suggests a Lithuanian connection.[52]

Back in Tasmania the couple rented a house at The Pines in Sandy Bay. Ruth played a lot of golf, coming second at the Ladies' Captain Day at Hobart Golf Club just before Christmas.[53]

Before they left for England there was a succession of leaving parties. Having a real-life baroness to entertain clearly intrigued Tasmanian society. Helen Nicholls hosted a garden party at her house. 'Baroness von der Ropp . . . looked very pretty in a white costume of Anglais broderie. People came in droves.'[54]

Bill and Ruth de Ropp left Australia for Europe in early March 1911 aboard the German ship *Barbarossa*, accompanied by Mabel Sprent.[55] On arriving in England they went to live with Ruth's mother at Court Hill House, her beautiful Georgian home overlooking the Early English village church St Mary the Virgin.[56]

There followed an aimless period in de Ropp's life. His wife, as a baroness, was much in demand to open village fêtes and appear at concerts in Bath. In the three years before the Great War, which would change everything for ever, the couple would spend the summers at Court Hill House and the winters in rented flats in London.

In October, Ruth's sister, Dora, married Captain Arthur Magor of the Wiltshire Regiment in Potterne Church, with de Ropp giving away the bride in the absence of her late father. This is the first time we see him using 'de Ropp' instead of 'von der Ropp.' Anti-German feeling was growing across Britain, partly stoked by spy writers like William Le Queux, while *The Riddle of the Sands* by Erskine Childers, published in 1903, had given the impression that the Germans were up to no good. In that context de Ropp sounded reassuringly French rather than German.*

Bill fancied himself as an inventor in the mould of his brother Alexander and he became one of the founding members of the Institute of Inventors in January 1912.[57] However, nothing came of it apart from some useful society contacts. He then made a short solo visit to Canada, possibly with a view to settling there.

Nothing else having worked for him, de Ropp decided to double-down on his electrical engineering training. After some additional theory at Faraday House, the College of Electrical Engineering in Southampton Row, Bloomsbury, he undertook some practical training at Willans and Robinson in Rugby, working on turbines, diesel engines and 'semi-diesel engines'. The company was one of the principal power-generation firms in the country before it became part of English Electric in 1918.[58] Returning down south he became an Assistant Testing Engineer with the British Electric Transformer Company in Hayes. This was the company that manufactured huge transformers for export.

Quite what Edith Fisher and Ruth de Ropp thought about the Baron messing around in grubby factories in Rugby and Hayes we do not know. Bill clearly had a limit to the number of village flower shows and amateur dramatics he could tolerate. His ability to mix at all levels of society would become a key component of his formidable abilities as a covert operator. He also possessed an extraordinary linguistic ability. He could pass as a Russian, German, Frenchman and Englishman without a trace of a foreign accent in all four languages. This was an innate ability but he also worked hard at

* Interestingly, separate branches of the family, who migrated to the United States, made the same change.

it. His granddaughter would later remark that he was determined to keep up his languages well into his eighties.

Other aspects of this story point to his future as a spy. De Ropp was fascinated by politics and foreign affairs. How could it have been otherwise when the situation in the Baltic States was so fluid and with so many variables: ethnic, religious, doctrinal, economic and national. He also felt somewhat adrift, not sure where he belonged. He must have known that his baronial title was somewhat Ruritanian and so he was always playing a part. He had all the aristocratic charm that you would expect of someone who could mix in the salons of Dresden, but also the realism to know that his inheritance would soon vanish due to political change in Lithuania and that his cash would run out sooner rather than later.

Such was the position in August 1914 when the Germans invaded Belgium and Bill de Ropp at last found a cause.

5

DICING WITH DEATH

1914–1918: Surviving artillery, aeroplanes and espionage

Many people find their true meaning in wartime, and it often defines their lives. Bill de Ropp was one of these. The Great War for Civilisation (as it was known) was appalling and yet it gave his life direction for the first time. It also catapulted him into some real peril; both on the Western Front and due to his brother Friedrich's almost suicidal actions.

The war hit the rural tranquillity of Court Hill House, Potterne like a battering ram. Captain Arthur Magor, who had married Ruth's sister Dora in the village's picturesque church two years earlier, was immediately called back to the colours. He had retired from the Wiltshire Regiment after the wedding and gone to live with Dora at Whitley House at Melksham about eight miles from Potterne. Their first child was on the way.

After a short spell of training at Weymouth, the 2nd Battalion of the Wiltshires arrived in Belgium as part of 21 Brigade. They reached Ypres on 14 October and marched a further six miles east before encountering German cavalry patrols. Arthur was killed almost immediately, and his remains were never found.[59] He must have been near the explosion of an artillery shell. He never saw his baby son.

Barely two months of war had passed, and de Ropp's brother-in-law was dead. For Bill, a twenty-eight-year-old fit and able man, the peer pressure to join up would have been immense. There was, however, the little matter of his nationality. Bill de Ropp, as a Russian citizen, could not join the British army.

De Ropp made his first moves to join up in August 1914, and in early January he visited the Home Office and kicked off the naturalisation process. He arrived with a recommendation from the Commanding Officer of the 5th Battalion of the Wiltshires and an application form with an impressive list of referees:

Brudenell Hunt Grubbe, the naval officer in Australia, was now the Lieutenant Commander of HMS *Panther* (an elderly but fast destroyer operating off the Humber estuary against German minelayers); Colin Sprent, Bill's Tasmanian friend from Dresden, was now living in Kensington; Leonard Raven-Hill was one of the most famous political cartoonists of the day, best known for his illustrations in *Punch* magazine; Clive Bell was one of the Bloomsbury Group and married to Virginia Woolf's sister; Mary Fisher was one of the extended Fisher family, as was Ralph Vaughan Williams, the composer, who had joined the Royal Army Medical Corps (RAMC) at the outbreak of war. [60]

Bill de Ropp's application, with its establishment and society endorsements, sailed through the Home Office in a way that would be unimaginable today. In view of his birth in Dresden, now in enemy territory, the Home Office sent the file to MI5, then called MO5(g), which wanted confirmation from the Russian Consulate that he was indeed Russian. The Consulate duly obliged and Bill de Ropp became a British citizen within a month of first applying.

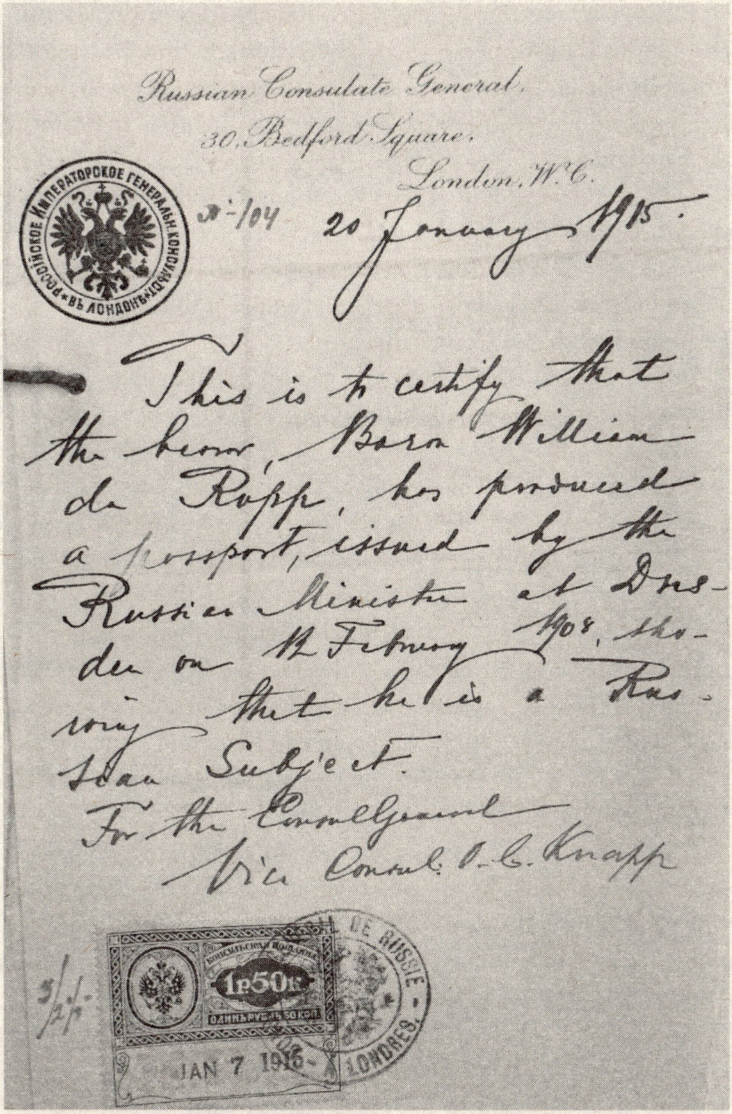

Russian Consulate General.
30, Bedford Square.
London, W.C.

№-104 20 January 1915.

This is to certify that the bearer Baron William de Ropp, has produced a passport, issued by the Russian Minister at Dresden on the February 1908, showing that he is a Russian Subject.

For the Consul General
Vice Consul. O. C. Knapp

1р.50к.
JAN 7 1915
LONDRES.

The Russian Consulate in London confirms that Bill de Ropp is a Russian (and thus not German) citizen, 1915. (*TNA*)

Bill gave as his reason for applying 'a desire to serve in His Majesty's army during the present war and to obtain the right to vote'. His letter from Lieutenant Colonel Brown of the 5th Battalion of the Wiltshire Regiment said he was 'desirous of having [de Ropp] as an officer in the battalion under my command'.

He passed his medical at the end of January and was assigned to the 5th Battalion's training depot at Devizes, just a few miles from Potterne. Its commandant Lieutenant Colonel Reginald Stewart added his plaudits: 'I can thoroughly recommend this gentleman . . . he speaks French and German fluently.'

Bill de Ropp was commissioned in mid-February but, for some reason, did not travel with the battalion when it deployed in June 1915 to take part in the Gallipoli campaign. Instead he was transferred to the 8th Battalion, based at Bovington Camp on Salisbury Plain, part of the 8th Reserve Brigade. This may well have saved his life because the 5th Battalion suffered terrible casualties at Gallipoli and during the subsequent Mesopotamian campaign.[61]

At the end of June 1915 de Ropp applied to his adjutant for a transfer to the Royal Flying Corps, citing his experience as an engineer, thinking it could be applicable to aero engines. Apparently ignoring his technical prowess, the RFC appointed him in mid-September as a Balloon Officer. After training he was sent to France in No 5 Kite Balloon Section of 12th Wing.

Kite balloons were used in the war to direct artillery. Usually two observers would be in the basket at around 5,000 feet, armed with binoculars and a field telephone. They could therefore give the required coordinates to the artillery unit best able to engage the target. They were known as the balloonatics, because of the intense dangers.

An ordinary spherical balloon tends to turn too easily, so the kite balloon was extended with fins to provide stability.[62] It was attached to the ground by a steel hawser about a mile behind the front lines with a tractor and winch so that it could be hauled down and moved when required. That might be when a thunderstorm was approaching (because the hawser served as a lightning conductor, which could set the balloon on fire) or because enemy artillery or aircraft were targeting it.

At such moments of danger the balloonists had a tough decision: to allow the winchmen to wind them down as fast as possible (which was often not fast enough) or to jump out using the relatively new and unreliable Spencer static-line parachute. Much would depend upon whether the balloon was on fire and whether there was enough height for the parachute to open.

German aviators used to target the observers as well as the balloons because the latter were far more easily replaced than the former. In 1915 there were forty British kite balloons along the Western Front. In September alone thirty-three of them had to be replaced, eight due to artillery fire and four damaged by enemy aircraft.[63]

In May 1916 de Ropp's balloon days came to an end due to chronic conjunctivitis. Here again he was amazingly lucky, returning to Folkestone via Boulogne just six weeks before the Battle of the Somme began. 5 Kite Balloon section was assigned to VII Corps under General Thomas Snow and was in the thick of the fighting.[64]

There followed a lengthy succession of visits to a leading ophthalmic surgeon at 24 Cavendish Square[65] and army medical boards but the final ruling was that Bill de Ropp could not tolerate exposure to bright light and that use of binoculars for extended periods would be impossible.[66]

Instead he was sent to the Balloon Training Unit at Roehampton while the eye tests carried on for a full nine months including appointments at Harley Street.[67] In the end it was accepted that he would never be able to return to the front and he duly lost his additional Flying Pay. The training job was not very arduous. The team of officers even had time to have their photograph taken for the society magazine *Tatler*. After de Ropp's departure, they experienced a series of hair-raising accidents including 'an unintended descent into Holborn'.[68]

De Ropp, Ruth and their son, Robert (Bob), were living at 64 Abingdon Villas, Kensington, but he was clearly anxious to be doing something more useful and was putting out feelers across Whitehall. Bob had been born in 1913 and would later claim to recall a moment when:

> . . . my father . . . came home on leave with a package wrapped in dirty newspaper. Opening this he revealed fragments of a Zeppelin* that had been shot down over London. Included in the wreckage was a torn, scorched piece of uniform from one of the crew members. And I could not avoid a sense of astonishment over the satisfaction in my father's voice as he told us that the crew of the Zeppelin was roasted alive in a flaming mass of gas; that Zeppelins were death traps, sitting ducks for anti-aircraft guns; and that their use proved again that the Germans were fundamentally a very stupid people.[69]

Bill de Ropp's ability to seek better employment in the war effort was greatly assisted by his joining the Savile Club in Mayfair. He was proposed as a temporary member in November 1916 and duly elected a few days later, and in January 1917 he became a full member, a status he would retain until he ran out of money for the subscriptions in 1952. His proposer was Robin Legge, a well-known music critic who was also Club Secretary, and his seconders included Everard Hopkins, the illustrator and cartoonist. The Savile was mainly a club for those associated with the arts but it did have some members connected with government and the secret services. Prime amongst these was the writer Compton Mackenzie, who served in MI6 during the Great War, and Sir Paul Dukes, one of the very few MI6 agents (as opposed to officers) to be knighted for their secret work.

* Zeppelins were rigid German airships often used as bombers during the war. It is estimated that some 557 British people were killed during 51 Zeppelin raids. Several were shot down. (H. A. Jones, *The War in the Air*, Oxford, 1928.)

Although numerous musicians such as Sir Edward Elgar and Sir Hubert Parry were members of the Savile, Ralph Vaughan Williams never joined, but Charles Fisher (Ruth's cousin) was a member.[70]

Before we come to de Ropp's next job we should explore a moment of considerable peril caused by his brother Friedrich. We last met Friedrich when he was setting off for Ethiopia in search of precious metals, having graduated from Freiberg Bergakademie, since when he had been in the Belgian Congo and German South-West Africa (now Namibia). He returned to Europe in 1914 with a plan to renovate the house at Dauzogir in Lithuania and resume his father's life as a Baltic landowning baron.

Even when in Ethiopia Friedrich had sparked the suspicion of an observant British official, H. D. E. O'Sullivan, the Kaimakam (an Ottoman title used here for a local official) based at Wad Medani in Blue Nile Province of Sudan. Writing in December 1907 to the Assistant Director of Intelligence in Khartoum, he observed that:

> He is a German, but a Russian subject, and was educated in Germany. Wishes to renationalise as a German but is waiting until no longer liable to military service, having avoided Russian service through a connection of high military rank. . . .
>
> He is in communication with the German legations at Addis Ababa and Cairo and is rendering reports to them on all matters civil and military.[71]

Friedrich von der Ropp's autobiography, *Zwischen Gestern und Morgen* ('Between Yesterday and Tomorrow'), is an extraordinary account of a hyperactive schemer and plotter. It is also a useful historical source, if treated with due caution. We are fortunate that his two letters to the German Foreign Ministry in 1930 and 1931 have survived in the family archive. These letters, which request German citizenship, are completely frank about his long career as a paid agent of the German Foreign Office, the Auswärtiges Amt (AA). In September 1930 he wrote:

> In 1914 I married a native Reich German and was on my estate in Lithuania [Dauzogir] when the war broke out. Not subject to military service in Russia, I was one of the first Germans abroad to make myself available to Germany. Through the intervention of the Vice President of the Reichsbank [Otto] von Glasenapp, who was a friend of mine, I came to Germany and at the end of 1914 I was drawn into politics by the Foreign Office and the Colonial Office (Messrs [Arthur] Zimmermann and [Wilhelm] Solf). I made several trips abroad, especially to America and England to explore the possibilities for peace. The reports on this served as the basis for various studies by the office, including for the Kaiser, the Reich Chancellor and the Admiralty. [Albert] Ballin also took a particular interest in my work at that time since I knew the English and American conditions exactly.[72]

The letters make it perfectly clear that Friedrich became a paid agent of the German Foreign Ministry. His special utility was that he could travel on his Russian passport even though his loyalties were (and were to remain) firmly with Germany.

In his autobiography, he writes, 'I offered my services to the government, since we could go anywhere with our Russian passports, provided that no espionage was expected of me. They gladly responded and asked whether I would be prepared to go to England to study the possibilities for peace.'

In January 1915 he travelled with his wife Elisabeth (Lili) via Stockholm, Bergen and Newcastle to London, where they stayed at the Hyde Park Hotel. He was shocked at the anti-German feelings of the British press and public and by the enthusiasm for the war. To avoid suspicion, in public he and his wife spoke to each other in French. At the end of March they returned to Germany via Newcastle and Oslo and reported to Wilhelm Solf, the Colonial Secretary.

A copy of the report was then sent to Albert Ballin, the General Manager of the Hamburg America Line. Ballin was deeply opposed to the war. He had made a number of attempts to defuse tensions before hostilities began and blamed himself for not having done enough to curtail naval rivalry. It was apparently Ballin who persuaded Friedrich to make a second visit to England via the United States with the ultimate ambition of meeting Sir Edward Grey, the British Foreign Secretary, who Ballin believed to be sympathetic to peace with Germany.[73] The German Foreign Ministry approved the trip but refused to sponsor it.

Friedrich and Lili travelled to New York via Copenhagen and after two months took a Holland America Line ship to Falmouth.

> We landed in Falmouth on November 27th, 1915, and it was immediately obvious that England was different from our first visit. The investigation already showed it: All passengers were gathered in the ship's dining room and – as a new feature – interrogated by interpreters in the language of their passports, that is, we were [questioned] in Russian. I was able to answer the first short question, but I couldn't understand the second. We were saved again by the presence of mind of my wife, who answered in Russian, and our suitcases, in which Ballin's letters of recommendation had been hidden, remained unsearched. If they had been found, it would have been evident that we came from Germany.

Friedrich did not speak fluent Russian but was lucky that his wife, although 'a native Reich German', was from a family (the Stolles) that had established the biggest wine import business in St Petersburg. Indeed, it was Lili's linguistic skill and quick-thinking which had enabled them both to escape from Dauzogir in August 1914 and reach Germany through Russian territory.

After this fortunate start Friedrich and Lili arrived in London and met Baron Heyking from the Russian Consulate. He too was a Balt and so did not denounce the couple to the authorities but recommended they leave as soon as possible. He added that 'England was not thinking of peace, it was now more determined than ever to fight. My wishes for peace are completely hopeless.' Friedrich von der Ropp's next call was on the editor of *The Economist*, Francis Hirst. Although he sensed that Hirst was sympathetic to peace, he 'was very embarrassed because he wasn't even allowed to speak to me because I was from Germany; because any "communication with the enemy was forbidden".'

Incredibly, in spite of these clear warnings, the couple stayed on in London for 'a few more weeks' before returning to Falmouth on 15 December and embarking on the SS *Rotterdam* of the Holland America Line bound for New York. On the way they were stopped by a British destroyer and taken into Kirkwall in the Orkney Islands for passport checks. Friedrich commented that we were 'filled with great concern. I had exposed myself in England; will this have become known to the secret service by now?' They finally reached Berlin in January 1916 and their report to Solf was sent up to the Kaiser. Clearly peace was hopeless. Ballin was bitterly disappointed. Friedrich von der Ropp also met General Erich Ludendorff who was unimpressed by his report and confident that Britain and France would be defeated before America entered the war.

What are we to make of all this? Was this really a hare-brained peace initiative or was it espionage? Logic would suggest the latter. Just by observation of the mood in London, von der Ropp's visit must have been very valuable but, if he was also meeting British contacts, it could have been doubly or triply so.

The key question for us is whether Friedrich met his brother during these two visits to London. At the time of his first visit in early 1915

Bill was busy arranging his naturalisation process and soon afterwards he joined the 5th Battalion of the Wiltshires. Although he was busy training in Devizes he still had his flat in Kensington and a meeting might have been possible sometime between January and March.

Bill returned from the Western Front with his eye problems on 16 May 1916 and was frequently in London from then until the end of the war. However he was away in France during Friedrich and Lili's second visit. We know from Friedrich's private papers that his estrangement from Bill did not occur until 1925. Can we believe therefore that two brothers, brought up together, albeit seven years apart in age, would not have wanted to meet for the first time since Friedrich had set off for Ethiopia in 1905?

On the other hand, Bill had finely tuned political antennae; otherwise, he would not have survived the next thirty years of his life. He would surely have understood the risks. In spite of his Russian passport, Friedrich was essentially German. Bill would probably have known of the case of Karl Lody, the German arrested in October 1914 for espionage and executed at the Tower of London by firing squad.[74] Even more pertinent was the German Karl Müller who travelled on a Russian passport and was executed in June 1915.[75]

The intelligence historian Christopher Andrew writes: 'After the arrest of seven German agents in June 1915 Germany made no further wartime attempts to establish a resident spy ring in Britain. She relied instead on brief visits by bogus commercial travellers from neutral countries who carried as much information as possible in their heads rather than on paper.'[76]

We shall never know if Bill met his brother in London. However, we can conclude that Friedrich and Lili were incredibly lucky. Francis Hirst did not report them to the authorities. He was a liberal who opposed the war even after the German invasion of Belgium. Later on he opposed compulsory conscription. A biographer has written, 'Hirst's outspoken opposition to the war cost him the editorship of *The Economist* in 1916 when Walter Wilson Greg, the most important trustee, lost patience with having to defend the paper's pacifist stance.'[77]

Whoever put von der Ropp in touch with him was clearly well-informed of Hirst's attitudes, but they were hardly secret. So what were the Germans trying to achieve? Surely not to recruit Hirst to the German cause? Possibly to try and get an introduction to Sir Edward Grey, but, if so, it was a crazy idea. More likely it was a second intelligence-gathering trip for the German AA to collect the views of the upper reaches of British society, which would not have been possible using low-level spies like Lody and Müller. The Ballin peace mission provided a thin veneer of cover and for the AA the trip was deniable because they had refused to sponsor it.

MI5 was a new and inexperienced organisation. In August 1914 the service was only five years old and had only nine officers out of a total of nineteen staff. By the end of the war that latter number had grown considerably – to 844.[78] In Friedrich von der Ropp's case, MI5 only started to notice him in March/April 1917 when he was reported by MI6 as being busy in Switzerland trying to sow discord within Russian minority nationalities. Only then did MI5 start to look back at his wartime visits to England. Over the years his MI5 files would become quite extensive as officers tried to work out who Friedrich was and what he was up to.[79]

The ripples of Friedrich's two visits to London did briefly affect Bill, although he remained in blissful ignorance. In June 1917 Major Anson of MI5 asked to see Bill de Ropp's Home Office file on behalf of his Director General, Colonel Vernon Kell,[80] and, in the same month, Major Becke of MI5 wanted to see Bill's military papers.[81] Vernon Kell was the first Director General of MI5. Unlike his MI6 opposite number, Captain Mansfield Cumming, he had extensive service overseas – in fact it was sometimes remarked in semi-jest that the two men had been given the wrong jobs in a typical Whitehall mix-up.

The von der Ropp name would have stirred memories for Kell.

A General Baron von der Ropp had been the Director of Russian Railways in Manchuria when Kell was a Railway Staff Officer in China following his service in the Boxer Rebellion in 1900. In 1902 the General had presented Kell with a silver tray and 'matching table centre' as a souvenir of their collaboration on the railway project.[82] General von der Ropp had later served in Turkestan[83] before being killed in the defence of Port Arthur against the Japanese in 1904. Fortunately for Bill this distant relative had been a Russian and not German.

Whatever the doubts about Friedrich's visits, MI5 appear to have been satisfied with Bill's bona fides because in 1918 he was appointed to the brand-new Directorate of Air Intelligence. The new Air Ministry had been formed in January 1918, based temporarily in the Cecil Hotel on the Strand. Bill de Ropp is listed in the role of AI.1S. AI stands for Air Intelligence and each officer had specific duties. For example Captain Archie Boyle (who we shall encounter later) was AI.1B responsible for 'compilation of all information regarding bomb targets on enemy countries'. Against de Ropp's name are the words 'Special Duties'.

'Special Duties' can mean all sorts of things, some exciting, others mundane. In his case it was a bit of both. He was sent on attachment to Lord Northcliffe's Propaganda Department based in Crewe House in Curzon Street. At long last somebody had had the bright idea of making use of Bill's languages.

Lord Northcliffe was a press baron who controlled several of Britain's newspapers including *The Times* and the *Daily Mail*. He had been a thorn in the side of the Asquith government during the early part of the war and had been partly instrumental in David Lloyd George's elevation to the premiership. Lloyd George repaid the favour by appointing Northcliffe to lead the 'British War Mission' to the United States in May 1917 to confer with US authorities and to win the American public over to the British war aims. Northcliffe grabbed the opportunity with both hands and spent from June to

November 1917 in the USA. For a man widely seen as a troublemaker it was generally a successful visit.[84]

The file in the National Archives shows how Northcliffe, as Director of Enemy Propaganda (but preferring to keep the better title 'British War Mission'), was keen to expand his department with offices on the continent, and drawing on wider government funds including those of the secret service. He caused frequent irritation in Whitehall including to Lord Beaverbrook, who was Minister of Information and his (notional) boss, and the Prime Minister himself,[85] who, at times, regretted his appointment.

However, his work on propaganda was genuinely inventive as one would expect from a man who had been immersed in the newspaper industry. To achieve this he needed people who could interrogate German prisoners. He included £3000 in his 1918 fourth-quarter accounts for 'work among prisoners of war in camps in England and France'. This was Bill's main role. He would write :'Later I took charge of the department dealing with prisoner of war interrogations. It was there that I learnt the delicate art of obtaining information without appearing to seek it.'[86]

The fruits of these interrogations probably arrived too late in the war. The historian of propaganda, Eberhard Demm, comments on Northcliffe's efforts:

> Today the best-known cases of leaflet propaganda are the campaigns of Lord Northcliffe's propaganda office Crewe House against the German and the Austrian fronts in 1918. Whereas it did indeed help to destabilise the Austrian Front at the Piave in spring 1918, it did not produce leaflets for the Germans before 4th September 1918 when the fate of Ludendorff's army was already sealed.[87]

Bill de Ropp became something of an authority on propaganda and was consulted by MI6 on the subject in 1939.

Meanwhile Friedrich von der Ropp had given up on Great Britain and was trying to undermine an altogether larger entity, the Russian Empire. His 1930 letter to the AA continues:

> As a result of the hopelessness of bringing about reconciliation in the West, I then took part in Eastern policy on behalf of the Foreign Minister, organised the Russian League of Foreign Peoples and supported the government in 1916–17 in its attempts to win Poland as an ally . . .
>
> In 1917 and 1918 I was mainly concerned with Lithuania and its becoming a state, in close collaboration with Mr [Adolf] von Maltzan . . . [88] [We] succeeded in bringing Lithuania into being, which without us would undoubtedly have become a Polish province like Eastern Galicia. This work also took me to the main [German military] headquarters and I negotiated with [Field Marshal Paul von] Hindenburg twice.
>
> During all these years I received a monthly allowance of 20,000 marks from the AA and maintained a headquarters in close cooperation with the latter in Switzerland, Sweden, Poland, Vilnius and Berlin. My work at that time extended in all directions and prepared the dissolution of Russia into its national components. With the collapse in 1918, the regular payments were stopped, but I received 50,000 marks from Mr [Rudolf] Nadolny,* then Chancellor of the Reich President, for further work.[89]

Friedrich von der Ropp's work-rate was quite astonishing. He also had a remarkable range of contacts. However, he was less accomplished at building support for his various schemes and he was unable to build trust in his own motives, as we shall later see. Of all the above activities it was his Conference of the Nationalities held in

* Rudolf Nadolny was an exceptionally active German foreign service officer with close links to intelligence. See his *Deutsche Biographie* entry.

Lausanne, Switzerland from 26 to 29 June 1916 which brought him to MI6's notice.

The inclusion amongst the 'oppressed minorities' of Irish and Egyptians inevitably sparked British interest although they were only invited as cover along with the Basques and Catalans. The main focus was on Poles, Finns, Ukrainians, the Baltic States and any other minority that could weaken Russia and help undermine its war effort against Germany.

Friedrich says in his autobiography, 'In general, the participation of the Germans in the foreign peoples' action was kept secret in order not to compromise it as a German action'.[90] He was deluding himself. Everyone could see that the event was sponsored by German money. Indeed the Swiss newspapers queued up to condemn von der Ropp as 'a German propagandist'. Another paper thought it bizarre to hear a Baltic baron defend the oppressed.[91]

The best spies keep a low profile, but Friedrich relished the limelight. An article in the *Morning Post* in November 1916 from Zurich quoted him as saying that 'Hindenburg is now dictator of Germany. He outshines the Emperor [Kaiser] as the sun outshines the moon. William II has become a sort of minor planet revolving around Hindenburg."[92]

The biggest blow to Friedrich was delivered by his own side. Unbeknown to him, the Germans had developed a master plan to undermine the Russian Empire and its will to continue the fight against Germany. The plan was to send Vladimir Lenin and a few fellow Bolshevik revolutionaries in a sealed train from Zurich, across German territory, to Finland and thence to St Petersburg.[93] The plan worked brilliantly in the short term although the long-term consequences were to be disastrous for the future of Europe and Friedrich's beloved Lithuania. The Treaty of Brest-Litovsk between Germany and Russia took Russia out of the war.

Friedrich von der Ropp incurred additional suspicion from MI5 when he approached Herbert White, the *Morning Post*'s correspondent in Switzerland, 'in the guise of an Anglophile Lithuanian'.[94] White reported the approach to the British mission in Geneva in April 1917: Friedrich wished White to communicate an offer of peace to London. Now that the 'Revolutionists' had taken control of Russia it was time for England to sue for peace before all the German armies in the east transferred to the Western Front. His plan was for England and Germany to partition Russia.'[95]

Crazy though this plan sounds, different versions of the idea of partitioning Russia would emerge during the 1930s, as we shall see. Friedrich's problem, however, was that many of his ideas had little preparation. Whilst Germany certainly saw the Russian Revolution as an opportunity to defeat Britain and France before America could deploy sufficient troops to the Western Front, it is doubtful that the partition of Russia had full backing in Berlin.

Northcliffe became involved in designing the final peace settlement with Germany, a role which the British Foreign Office would normally have expected to fulfil. Whether Bill de Ropp contributed to Northcliffe's remarkable article in *The Times* on 4 November 1918 entitled 'From War to Peace', on the future shape of Europe, is unknown but few people in Britain would have had a better understanding of Central Europe.

And so ended Bill de Ropp's war. He had only spent three months in mortal danger suspended over the Western front in a kite balloon. By luck or judgement he had not been compromised by his dangerous brother. And in the last year of the conflict his remarkable talents had finally been discovered.

6

'EVERY FORM OF OUTRAGE'

1919: Bill de Ropp in occupied Berlin

Following the German surrender Lord Northcliffe's interrogation work moved on to the continent. The obvious place for de Ropp to operate was with Major General Neill Malcolm's British Military Mission, which was initially based in Paris before moving into Hindenburg's former headquarters at Spa in Belgium and thence to the German capital, Berlin, where it set up shop in Moltkestrasse.

Malcolm had experienced a somewhat chequered career in the war. He had been much criticised as General Hubert Gough's Chief of Staff to the Fifth Army,[96] but went on to command the 66th Division – and was wounded in action – before leading the 39th and 30th Divisions during the final months of 1918.

In Berlin his duties were described in Parliament by Winston Churchill, the Secretary of State for War, as limited to 'assisting the German Government with shipping arrangements for the repatriation of Russian prisoners of war and continuing the search for missing British prisoners of war'. However, he also said 'Major-General Malcolm also acts as an assistant to His Majesty's chargé d'affaires in Berlin. The latter is concerned with the reduction and surrender of German armament and material under the terms of the Peace Treaty, and is working under a French General, who is President of the whole Commission.'[97]

The chargé d'affaires was Lord Kilmarnock, who arrived in Berlin a few weeks after Malcolm and only had counsellor rank, having been sent as a stop-gap measure while an ambassador was selected. In contrast Malcolm had been a fighting general and was also the Prime Minister's personal representative in Berlin. Little wonder therefore that it was Malcolm and not Kilmarnock who called the shots.

His role inevitably grew in scope as the complexities of post-war Europe became increasingly evident. He started to issue a weekly report on developments in Germany with sub-paragraphs on politics, the military situation and eventually on wider issues such as the economy and health.

The Foreign Office official Lewis Namier of the Political Intelligence Department,* later to become a famous historian, made waspish comments on these (impressive) reports which he presumably saw as invasions into FO diplomatic territory. It is true, nonetheless, that these weekly summaries show signs of haste and a lack of editorial rigour.

For Bill de Ropp these must have been fascinating weeks and months; being back in Germany after such a long absence, watching the misery of a defeated German nation as it teetered on the brink of chaos and communism. To be wearing a British military uniform† must have seemed surreal and must have made contact with the wider von der Ropp family uncomfortable. The experience also reinforced his deep hatred of communism and disorder.

Bill's time with the Mission in Berlin was cruelly interrupted by

* PID was a small department which existed from 1918 to 1920 (and again in 1939–43) to provide intelligence summaries on enemy and allied states. It was not a rival to MI6 in that it collated but did not produce intelligence.

† He had originally been in the RFC but was now an Acting Captain in the new Royal Air Force (RAF).

a family tragedy. His wife Ruth died on 27 March 1919, one of the many victims of the Spanish influenza pandemic which killed more people than the Great War itself. She was only thirty-three, and Bill was left with two young children – Robert aged six, and Ruth who was born on the very day of her mother's death.

Bill's family never recovered from Ruth's death and the trauma, hurt and bitterness would remain until long after he had died half a century later. Robert would later write:

> The Great Plague of the twentieth century . . . killed my mother who had just given birth to my sister. It nearly killed me. I was hustled out of London to my grandmother's house in the country where I quietly began to die . . . But death passed me by. My lungs healed. My health was slowly restored. I was motherless.[98]

Bill was now a widower and he had no job. His official military service ended just one week after Ruth's death. For as long as his mother-in-law, Edith Fisher, remained alive the children could be looked after at Court Hill House where childcare could be easily provided. But Bill had never felt completely comfortable there. Edith may have still resented the wedding in Australia and have suspected it had been planned all along.

This was the moment that Bill got in touch with Stewart Menzies of MI6 (then still called MI1c) and offered his services – he would have been in touch with MI6 as part of his work with Northcliffe both in London and Berlin – the two men met on 30 April and the deal was sealed.[99] Bill became an MI6 agent.

It is worth pausing briefly to imagine the conversation which Menzies must have had with his boss in his office at the very top of Whitehall Court.* The question would have been whether to recruit de Ropp as a salaried officer of the service or as an agent in the field.

* Now the roof space above the Royal Horseguards Hotel. The author was given permission to visit this curious but atmospheric area in 1999.

Two arguments would have swung the decision in favour of the latter course. There would inevitably be some post-war cost-cutting and many officers would lose their jobs. This was not the right time to recruit new officers. Furthermore, Bill's linguistic brilliance would be wasted sitting at a Head Office desk or even out on an overseas station, when he could be more valuable posing as a journalist or businessman without any observable link to the British government and obtaining badly needed intelligence for Whitehall customers.

Menzies's boss, the charismatic first Chief of MI6 Captain Mansfield Cumming, had had a good war. His new service had achieved some remarkable successes, many of them coming on the Western Front where the train-watching system provided General Headquarters (GHQ) with a good view of which German units were facing British troops across the trenches.

The best-known of these networks was 'La Dame Blanche' run by a young MI6 officer from South Africa, Henry Landau. His hard work based in Rotterdam was also rewarded by a stupendous piece of luck when a clerk from the Düsseldorf post office 'walked in' with a copy of the German Field Post Office Directory with 'a complete list of every unit in the German army'.[100] This was the intelligence equivalent of winning the lottery. It answered almost every question and saved thousands of hours of painstaking intelligence collection and analysis.

Once the war was over Cumming gave Landau the job of setting up the new MI6 station in Berlin. 'I was to proceed to Berlin immediately where I was to report to General Malcolm . . . My interview with General Malcolm lasted but a few minutes . . . He was a busy man . . . and exercised tremendous power in Berlin at that time.'[101]

Landau soon fell out of love with the idea of being the MI6 head of station in Berlin. Issuing visas as the Passport Control Officer (PCO) did not match up to the wartime excitement he had enjoyed based in Rotterdam running agents into German-occupied territory. Before he left MI6, however, Landau performed two important services for Cumming. He found an office at No. 17 Tiergartenstrasse which would remain as the MI6 and PCO office in Berlin until war was declared in 1939.* And he found a replacement for himself. 'I promptly departed for Cologne to interview some of my friends in the Intelligence Corps . . . I proposed Captain Foley.'

Frank Foley was from a humble background. His father had been an engine fitter at the vast Swindon railway workshops. He was a small man at five-foot-four and was initially drawn towards the Catholic priesthood. He was teaching in Hamburg when war broke out in 1914 and made a dramatic escape to neutral Holland, at one stage wearing a Prussian military uniform. Back in England he joined the 2/6th North Staffordshire Regiment. In March 1918 he saw action at Écoust where his battalion lost its CO, 22 officers and 586 men. In July that year he joined MI6's train-spotting enterprise where he met both Menzies and Landau.[102].

Frank Foley would become one of MI6's all-time great figures. He is perhaps most famous for the number of Jews he saved by issuing thousands of visas allowing them to travel to both Britain and Palestine.[103] He also ran some of the most important cases in MI6's history. One of these was the agent known as Jonny. Johann de Graff 'walked in' to Foley in 1933 and was run successfully against the Comintern (the organisation of communist parties intended to bring about world revolution) in the Far East, Europe and Latin America until 1939.[104]

Foley would also play a major role in the Bill de Ropp case. Foley was based in Berlin from 1919 until he was withdrawn before the outbreak of the Second World War. From the mid-1930s his focus would be against the Nazis but from 1919 his main role was to work against Bolshevik Russia both unilaterally as MI6 and later in liaison with the German services as they began to recover.

Cumming was having to manage a complete shift of operational focus from Germany to Russia (a transition which would be replicated

* It was later reduced to a pile of rubble by the RAF.

in 1945) whilst at the same time losing many of his best staff and the majority of his wartime budget.

Much of MI6's work was influenced by its cover role for the Passport Control Office (PCO). The FO and ambassadors did not want MI6 officers as members of diplomatic staff and were not willing to give them diplomatic immunity. Following the Great War, however, they reluctantly agreed to give them PCO roles, issuing visas to foreigners who wished to enter British (including colonial) territory. In most posts this amounted to a considerable amount of cover work, often leaving only the evenings and weekends for real espionage. It is true that it did bring MI6 officers face to face with some very interesting foreigners and some good espionage cases resulted; but for every pearl there would be tens of thousands of pebbles.

A PCO office was established at 2 Whitehall Court under Major (soon to be Colonel) Herbert Spencer, reporting to the Home Office. MI6 officers overseas could therefore get professional visa advice promptly. The other department that welcomed MI6's PCO role was MI5, which was the recipient of hundreds of messages from PCOs about suspected communists and their travel plans. There was a danger here in thinking that MI6 was doing a good job by just sending details from visa applications to MI5. The risk was that this routine activity detracted from obtaining real secrets for MI6's most important customers: the FO and the three armed services.[105]

Cumming's main effort against Bolshevik Russia has been brilliantly told by Gordon Brook Shepherd in *Iron Maze*. It was full of glamorous and dangerous events and personalities. Highlights include Paul Dukes (ST25) and his mission to Russia during which he wore several disguises and once famously spent a period living inside a tomb in a cemetery. He was knighted for his work and later recounted his adventures in *The Story of ST25*, one of the great espionage classics. Then there was Augustus Agar of the Royal Navy, on attachment to MI6, who led a small flotilla of Coastal Motor-Boats (CMBs)[106] in raids on Kronstadt harbour and managed to sink the cruiser *Oleg*, disable two battleships and destroy a submarine supply ship. For these actions Agar received a private audience with the King and both a VC and DSO.[107]

Most romantic of all was Sidney Reilly, the so-called Ace of Spies, who travelled into Russia several times. Reilly was really more of a confidence trickster than an agent. MI6 never had him totally under their control and, for all his undoubted brilliance, it is hard to quantify exactly what he achieved. He fell victim to a Soviet trap and received a Soviet bullet in his head.

Indeed there is an inescapable verdict on Cumming's time as Chief of MI6 after the end of the Great War. He loved adventure and excitement but he sometimes lost sight of what we would now call (rather pompously) 'strategic purpose'. The reality is that for all of MI6's work against the Soviets from 1919 to 1925 they enjoyed tactical successes but strategic failure.

If the intention was to depose the Bolshevik government of Vladimir Lenin that certainly failed. If the policy was to help the White Russian armies of Admiral Kolchak and Generals Deniken, Yudenich and Wrangel to win the war against the Bolsheviks that too failed. To be fair to Cumming the British government too was split on how to deal with Russia, with Winston Churchill keen to support White Russian forces but much of the Cabinet determined to concentrate on domestic affairs after a ruinous war and pandemic. There was, however, one notable success: in the Baltic States.

As a Russian speaker it was inevitable that Bill de Ropp would be deployed against the Bolshevik target, and the obvious place for his efforts was the Baltic States. His brother, Friedrich von der Ropp, that inveterate networker, navigated towards General Malcolm like a moth to a naked flame. The Berlin correspondent of the *Oregon Daily Journal* and the *Chicago Daily Tribune* interviewed Friedrich upon the latter's return from Riga. Friedrich laid it on thick. '. . . the town has seethed with murder, looting and every form of outrage . . .' There were 'ferocious starving women' attacking the 'well-to-do'.

He concluded with 'if only the allies would send two or three destroyers there'.

The journalist concludes his piece with, 'The baron's brother whom I know well personally is a staff officer in the British army and at present is working with a British mission on the continent.'[108] This provides useful confirmation that Bill de Ropp returned to Berlin after Ruth's death for a few months to continue his work with General Malcolm's mission still under official military cover but now being paid by MI6.

One of General Malcolm's reports, dated 11 July 1919, contained a section on 'The Bolshevik peril in Lithuania'. It is written in cautious, rather than alarmist, terms. 'Lithuania is in a state of latent anarchy and growing Bolshevism.' It continues, 'The presence of German soldiers has not stopped this development. On the contrary, the systematic looting to which the demoralised soldiers were addicted has increased the universal unrest . . . It is thought that the Poles may wish to march into Northern Lithuania, which would temporarily save the country from Bolshevism but would . . . lead to national risings'. It suggests a solution 'without military intervention, by the appointment of a few suitable officials who would group the orderly and progressive elements in the country around them, reorganise the army and assist the country until it can work out its own salvation'.[109]

This piece is attributed to 'Frederic [*sic*] de Ropp'. However, it was clearly written by Bill. Friedrich never spelt his name Frederic and rarely called himself 'de Ropp' instead of 'von der Ropp'. Furthermore, as we have seen, Friedrich would have taken an entirely different political position, stressing the need to deploy naval and ground forces to the region.

Certainly, Lewis Namier in Whitehall thought Bill was the author. Namier himself came from a Polish Jewish background and could not help but exhibit superiority in his comments on Bill's analysis. 'He belongs by origin to the Lithuanian Junkers. His uncle von der Ropp, a former Bishop of Vilna [Vilnius] and now Archbishop of Mogilev [now in Belarus], is a Polish reactionary jingo. His brother who claims to be a Lithuanian was throughout the war a German agent and now works with the Polish nobility. He himself is the son of a Russian general born, I believe, in this country, knows no Lithuanian at all and knows but comparatively little about the country.'

The future great historian scores half marks for accuracy. Bill was not closely related to the Archbishop of Mogilev. His father was a colonel, not a general, and he was not born in England. But it is true that Bill did not speak Lithuanian and, unlike Friedrich, was not an expert on Lithuania.

It was only a matter of time before Menzies would deploy Bill de Ropp to the Baltic States. The situation there was chaotic and it would need an extraordinary degree of skill to navigate the Byzantine complexities of the politics while also staying alive in a region where over a dozen armed groups were operating in a political vacuum.

7

'BETWEEN BOCHE AND BOLSHEVIK'

August 1919: Subversion and subterfuge in Lithuania

The situation in all three Baltic states was extremely precarious. The German forces that had expelled the Russians from much of the region before the Treaty of Brest-Litovsk in March 1918 had not laid down their arms in November. Their argument was that doing so would allow the Bolsheviks to reoccupy the Baltic region.

Lord Curzon, the British Foreign Secretary, had reluctantly acceded to their request to retain their weapons as 'a necessary evil' under clause XII of the Armistice Treaty which stipulated that 'all German troops at present in territories which before the war formed part of Russia must likewise return to within the frontiers of Germany as above defined, as soon as the Allies shall think the moment suitable, having regard to the internal situation of these territories.'[110]

Meanwhile there were still Bolshevik forces in control of Riga, the capital of the newly independent state of Latvia.

For our purposes the focus must be on Lithuania although it cannot be viewed entirely in isolation. The key players in Lithuania were:

The Soviet Russians and their local Bolshevik supporters who wanted to win Lithuania for world communism. Their hands were full due to the civil war against White Russian forces on several fronts.

The Lithuanian nationalists who desired an independent state free of control from Russia, Germany and Poland.

The Poles who already held Vilnius and had their eyes on denying Lithuania to both the Germans and Russians.

White Russian forces under General Pavel Bermondt-Avalov, whose main aim was to fight the Bolsheviks but who were willing to accept German support. They wanted the three Baltic States to remain as provinces of a future White-led Russia.

The supporters of Juozas Gabrys and Friedrich von der Ropp who wanted German landowners to remain in an independent Lithuania but one closely allied with Germany. Their forces, known as Freikorps, were commanded in Lithuania by Cordt von Brandis. This group often hid their real motives behind a bogus Lithuanian nationalism.

The German troops under General Rüdiger von der Goltz. Many of them were unruly and close to mutiny but others saw the possibility of settling in the Baltic States rather than returning to the chaos and misery of Germany.

The British, who wanted both the Germans and Bolsheviks out of the Baltic States and were cautiously willing to support three independent states but not prepared to deploy any forces (beyond naval vessels) to the region.[111]

The British government's organisation in the Baltic States demonstrated their interest and concern. The FO List for 1920 shows consulates in Kovno (now Kaunas), which was Lithuania's capital until Vilnius was eventually retrieved from Poland, in Reval (now Tallinn) for Estonia, and in Riga (for Latvia). Meanwhile MI6 covered the Baltic states from stations in Reval, Riga and Helsinki.

The Royal Navy sent a squadron of cruisers to operate off the Baltic coast as a deterrent to both the Russians and Germans. General Sir Hubert Gough was appointed Head of the British Military Mission based in Riga with Colonel Stephen Tallents as his Chief of Staff. Lieutenant-Colonel Richard Barrington Ward was Tallents's deputy in Kovno, with the title Assistant Commissioner for the Baltic Provinces. Colonel Ward (as he preferred to be known) sent a monthly report back to Whitehall, similar to Malcolm's missives from Berlin, with paragraphs on the political, military and economic situations.

Meanwhile Brigadier Frank Crozier[112] was recruited by the Lithuanian government, with British approval, to advise on the formation of their army.[113] The British hope was that the three nationalist armies and perhaps the Poles too would expel both the Russians and the Germans. One saying at the time was that the Baltics were caught 'between Boche and Bolshevik'.[114]

There was also Lieutenant-Colonel Harold Alexander (the future Earl Alexander of Tunis), who was sent to liaise with the troops loyal to the Baltic barons.[115] In May 1919 these troops helped Goltz capture Riga from the Bolsheviks. One of their number, Walter von Medem, helped seize the bridge across the Dvina (now Daugava) River and would later play an important part in Bill de Ropp's work against the Nazis.

With the Bolsheviks defeated, the British aim was to get the Germans to lay down their arms. To achieve this objective they put the new German government of Friedrich Ebert under intense pressure. The Germans tried every device to delay their departure but the coercion from London was relentless.

This was the moment when Friedrich von der Ropp and his

supporter Gabrys spotted their last chance to mount a coup in favour of the Baltic barons. They understood that the departure of German troops and the setbacks being suffered by the White Russians would spell the end of the settlers' hopes and that they had to seize the initiative now or never.

The first indication of trouble arrived in Whitehall by enciphered telegram on 2 October. 'Russian and German coup d'etat planned to [capture] Kovno and replace present [Lithuanian government] by Gabrys [and] von de Ropp.' The report initially came from Colonel Ward in Kovno on 30 September but was relayed via Riga two days later.[116]

Rex Leeper, an FO official,* commented:

> Gabrys is a Lithuanian who during the war acted as a simple German agent in Switzerland. He was associated with Baron von der Ropp in Switzerland and probably got his money from him. Von der Ropp is a Baltic baron. His father was a General† in the Russian Army and his mother was a Russian. He himself is simply a German agent and has no claims to call himself Lithuanian. The German-Russian forces are now at Schawli [Šiauliai] in Lithuania and a coup d'état at Kovno [Kaunas] is now quite possible.

The historian Eberhard Demm has written about Friedrich's plot.[117] Drawing on the memoir of Brandis, the leader of the Lithuanian Freikorps, Demm writes.

> On August 31st, [Brandis] was near Bauske in Courland, when Wildemann with three gentlemen, Baron Bistram, a Baron X [Ropp] and a Dr Y [Gabrys], appeared at his place. Baron

* Leeper would serve in Riga in the mid-1920s and would later become the head of black propaganda in the Second World War.

† As remarked earlier, he was a colonel, not a general.

> X described the Lithuanian government in Kovno as almost Bolshevik and stated that he and Dr Y intended a coup.

At this moment Demm provides the first mention of Bill de Ropp being in Lithuania.

> Brandis also mentions X's brother, who met him at Wildemann's estate Blaupomusch and writes that he acquired English citizenship at an early age, worked in the General Staff during the war and is now working as a journalist. This information is confirmed by a letter from Paul Schiemann,[118] which was written to his mother:[119] Ropp's brother, English officer and correspondent for the Northcliffe press, is going to Riga and can probably be very useful to us.

So here we have Bill de Ropp travelling as an MI6 agent in Lithuania under journalistic cover (almost certainly for the *Daily Mail* with the approval of Lord Northcliffe)[120] following his recruitment by Menzies. Quite apart from the coup plotting, the meeting at Blaupomusch with his brother Friedrich and his brother-in-law Benno von Wildemann must have been emotional.

Benno von Wildemann and Bill's brother Paul von der Ropp had evacuated their families to Germany in January 1919. Paul's wife Elizabeth (known as Elli) was the sister of Baron Bistram, one of the coup plotters; the Bistram estate was directly across the river from Blaupomusch, at Rotpomusch. Lithuania was no place for women and children with so many marauding and undisciplined armies and militias in the neighbourhood and with the local peasants ready to loot and pillage baronial estates (and occasionally murder the occupants). Bill's sister Gertrud von Wildemann accompanied her four children to her sister's house at Gamehl near Rostock. Bill's brother Paul also took his family to Mecklenburg but Paul himself had returned to collect payment for the recent harvest.

Even in its current ruinous state one can see that Blaupomusch was a once beautiful house with its gardens leading down the gentle slope to the Mūša River about 150 yards away. It is barely two miles from Eichenpomusch and not more than seven miles from Dauzogir, which Paul was managing on behalf of Friedrich. In a warm early September the discussions may have taken place in chairs on the lawn and later inside the house where two large stuffed bears stood just inside the front door.

Much of the talk would have been about the existential threat facing German landowners in Lithuania. There was doubtless some discomfort about Bill having fought for Britain in the recent war but also great sympathy for the loss of Ruth and interest in his two children. There was also the opportunity for Benno to tell his incredible story.

At the outbreak of war in 1914 Benno had moved his family to St Petersburg and had joined the Russian army, as he was obliged to do as a citizen of a Russian province. Paul and Elli von der Ropp joined them there. All of them were careful to avoid speaking German in public. When the Germans conquered Lithuania, Paul, his family and the von Wildemann children returned home via Norway and Sweden.

Benno and Gertrud stayed on in Russia until the Revolution when, as his daughter Marina narrates,

> . . . the door opened and his adjutant came in and said that a soldiers' council had been formed in the company, that all the officers had been removed and Benno had to hand over his weapon and his officer's insignia to him. Benno became extremely angry and pulled his pistol on the adjutant. If he had been alone, he would definitely have shot. That would have been the end of him because the soldiers were standing in front of the door and watching – all armed. But Gertrud grabbed his arm and said: 'Benno, we have four children.' Benno lowered the weapon and handed it over, along with his epaulettes.

Not for the first time a female von der Ropp's quick thinking had saved her husband. The soldiers' council then gave Benno and Gertrud a horse, a sleigh and two soldiers' uniforms and they set off towards the German lines. They managed to cover a considerable distance in freezing conditions. On one evening they had to take part in a drinking session with revolutionary soldiers. One became suspicious and locked the couple in a railway carriage but Benno had a key which fitted the lock. They escaped in the early morning and crossed over to German lines, an incredibly risky feat. They were able to celebrate Christmas 1917 back at Blaupomusch which, unlike most estates, had not been looted by its workers. [121]

No story could better describe the vulnerability of the Baltic Germans, caught traditionally in between Russia and Germany and now also the Baltic nationalists, Poland and the Bolsheviks. This was a vulnerability which made them rich prey to foreign intelligence services and equally the objects of suspicion. Having heard Benno's amazing story Bill must have realised how lucky he was to have secured his British nationality.

When Russia signed the Treaty of Brest-Litovsk with Germany the family had felt its future in Lithuania was secure. However, the German surrender in November 1918 ended their dreams. As the White Russian armies failed against the Bolsheviks, as the German army gradually disintegrated, and as Lithuanian nationalists became increasingly hostile to the German and Polish landowners their only hope lay in Friedrich's coup.

Having taken his family to safety at Gamehl Benno had returned to form his own Freikorps under Brandis. On 30 August 1919 (at about the same time as attending the plotters' meeting at Blaupomusch) he wrote to Gertrud, 'There's a lot to do. A German-[White] Russian merger may yet occur. I see this as the only salvation for both countries and also for our small homeland.'[122]

Friedrich's coup is best described in a letter to the British Foreign Office from the Lithuanian delegation in Kensington: [123]

> Baron Friedrich Ropp, a Lithuanian landowner and the famous initiator of the idea of a federation of Lithuania and Germany, his brother-in-law [Bernhard] Wildemann and the no less famous Lithuanian politician Gabrys . . . boast that the German government with the exception of Mr Müller, the Foreign Minister and Mr Erzberger, the Minister of Finance, sympathise with them and have even promised to the Gabrys-Ropp government a loan of 300 million marks.

They then add a cautionary note: 'It is not at all certain that the German government are taking this attitude but there is no doubt that the pan-Germans in company with the Barons of Courland and the Russian monarchists living in Berlin are supporting this idea.'[124]

The one aspect the Lithuanians did not mention in their letter was that Friedrich, Gabrys and Wildemann were also conspiring with White Russian generals in Berlin who were loyal to Admiral Alexander Kolchak. However, their forces were bitterly opposed by Lithuanian nationalists. Furthermore Kolchak was reluctant to divert his main focus from defeating the Bolsheviks.

British Military Intelligence suggested another reason why the coup would have failed. 'Without an arrangement with Poland, the Russo-German troops would only be a few days or at the most a few weeks in possession of Kovno, after which they would be completely annihilated by the Poles, as this would just give the latter the chance they need.'[125]

They were right. Friedrich, as usual, had been astonishingly active and resourceful but had not read the politics correctly. There was no way that a defeated and destitute Germany could support a coup against British and French interests in the Baltics. At last Berlin ordered General Rüdiger von der Goltz to pack up and come home. Many Baltic barons recognised that this was the end and they left too. Benno von Wildemann paid a sad farewell to Blaupomusch for ever.

In 1922 Lithuania issued a Land Reform Law prohibiting the

foreign ownership of more than 80 hectares. The Baltic barons could therefore keep their houses but not enough land to sustain (and heat) them. In 1929 the law was modified to permit 150 hectares.[126] Paul von der Ropp stayed on heroically until 1940 when all the Baltic barons had to leave under the terms of the Molotov-Ribbentrop Pact.

The result had been an unexpected victory for British foreign policy. To remove the Germans and Soviets with a minimal deployment of force and effort was one of the most impressive diplomatic examples of making bricks without straw.

It is hard to measure Bill's contribution to this success; however, he had clearly done a good job. At a time when MI6 was short of funds and laying off officers and agents he was retained as a highly deployable agent. In fact he was thought worth the time and expense of fitting out with more robust cover.

In June 1920 the Anglo-Baltic Merchants Ltd published its prospectus with three directors: the Hon. Bernard Francis Rollo of 131 Victoria Street, London SW; the Hon. Gilbert de St Croix Rollo of The Hope, Moffat, Dumfriesshire, and Baron William Sylvester de Ropp of the Savile Club, 107 Piccadilly,* London W1. Bill is described as 'Baron of the Russian Empire. Flying Officer RAF (retired)'. He certainly knew how to make an impact. In September 1920 he was appointed 'Managing Director outside the United Kingdom'.

Bernard Rollo was probably an MI6 contact recruited by Cumming himself. In his diary Cumming wrote, 'I have however found one man, a Scotchman, who occupies a position which will give him exceptional opportunities of knowing if anything in the nature of war is impending.' Against this entry he has written the word 'Rollo'.[127] Bernard Rollo was Director of the British Overseas Bank. He was also the owner of 9 Eaton Terrace, London SW1 and Keltie Castle,

* The Savile Club moved from Piccadilly to Brook Street in 1927.

Dunning, Perthshire. He had been Manager of the Egyptian National Bank in Alexandria at the turn of the century before running the bank's London branch and becoming a partner in the brokers Steer, Lawford and Co.[128]

His younger brother Gilbert had served in the Royal Naval Air Service (RNAS) during the war and had later become a major in the RAF. Both brothers held 500 shares each in Anglo-Baltic Merchants and Bill 100. The other 9,000 shares were held by members of Steer, Lawford and Co. Whether these shares had anything more than a notional value is unclear.[129] After all, the company was principally a vehicle for Bill de Ropp's overseas travel. It had 'an office' (probably little more than a brass plate) at 4 Bishopsgate and later at Room 285, Winchester House, Old Broad Street, London EC2.[130] Room 285 played host to dozens of companies.[131]

Bill continued to live between the Baltics, London and Potterne. The 1921 census shows him staying at 79 Cheyne Court in Chelsea. His landlord was Henry Howard Piggott an Assistant Secretary in the Ministry of Transport. He was the man who five years earlier had pushed Bill's application for British citizenship through the Home Office system. Bill's children were still in Wiltshire with their grandmother.

When we look back at this period there is one unavoidable question that must be asked. Did Bill de Ropp betray his brother's coup? He had actually sat with the plotters and almost exactly a month later the enciphered telegram had arrived in London. As a man with excellent political instincts Bill must have seen the flaws in Friedrich's plot. The fact that the German Foreign and Finance Ministers had not signed up to the idea would surely have registered with him. The idea of a bankrupt Germany spending 300 million marks on such a crackpot scheme was too improbable to take seriously. Furthermore, Bill did not have the same emotional links to Lithuania as Friedrich and Benno.

Fortunately for him, the coup idea was known to many others.

Rüdiger von der Goltz was aware, as were Brandis and Bermondt-Avalov, who was an absurdly unreliable character. The coup planning would have leaked eventually.

Bill gave up being a Director of Anglo-Baltic Merchants at the end of 1922. Menzies and he probably realised that commercial cover might be very good for concealing identity but was hopeless for asking searching political questions. In future Bill de Ropp would use journalistic cover for most of his work but employ commercial cover when technical intelligence was required.

His next contribution to British intelligence history would see him using an entirely different and more ambitious guise.

8

'MOSCOW ORDERS TO OUR REDS'

October 1924: Bill de Ropp and the Zinoviev Letter

Bill de Ropp played a central role in the Zinoviev Letter, one of the great scandals of the twentieth century, credited with changing the outcome of the October 1924 General Election. His name has never been mentioned in any of the numerous books and articles about the affair. Furthermore, his involvement requires a reassessment of the timeline and of the purpose of the famous letter. This chapter will outline the new discoveries and Chapter 9 will examine what this might mean for historical interpretation of the scandal.

On 25 October 1924 the *Daily Mail* published the text of a letter which had allegedly been sent by the Soviet Chairman of the Communist International (Comintern) Grigory Zinoviev to the Communist Party of Great Britain (CPGB). The first five of the seven banner headlines read:

CIVIL WAR PLOT BY SOCIALISTS' MASTERS
MOSCOW ORDERS TO OUR REDS
GREAT PLOT DISCLOSED YESTERDAY

'PARALYSE THE ARMY AND NAVY'
and
MR MACDONALD WOULD LEND
RUSSIA OUR MONEY

The most incendiary parts concerned a desire by Moscow to stimulate greater radicalisation in the British armed forces. 'It is evident that agitation-propaganda work in the army is weak, in the navy a very little better.'

It is now generally agreed that the Zinoviev Letter was a forgery, but the secret of its success was that its contents were credible. Even a senior Soviet official was quoted as thinking so.[132] British intelligence had intercepted previous messages from the Comintern and the themes had been broadly similar.[133]

Ramsay MacDonald's Labour government had been seen as soft on Russia. It had negotiated two Anglo-Soviet Trade Treaties, one of which involved relieving the Soviet debt burden. The government also withdrew from prosecuting a Scottish communist, John Ross Campbell, who had called on soldiers to refuse to go to war.[134]

What ignited the *Daily Mail* article into a political scandal was its proximity to the second General Election of 1924, due to be held just four days later. The letter is often credited with damaging the Labour Party's chances of re-election on 29 October 1924, after which Ramsay MacDonald's government was replaced by a Conservative administration under Stanley Baldwin. In fact, the Tories would almost certainly have won anyway but with a smaller majority. Nonetheless the Zinoviev Letter has passed into legend as an Establishment plot against Socialism in general and the Labour Party in particular. Both the Wilson and Blair governments, on coming to power, requested enquiries into the government's papers on the affair.

MI6 found itself front and centre of the scandal because it was the MI6 station in Riga which sent a translation of the Zinoviev Letter to London on 2 October. MI6 Head Office did not

CIVIL WAR PLOT BY SOCIALISTS' MASTERS.

MOSCOW ORDERS TO OUR REDS.

GREAT PLOT DISCLOSED YESTERDAY.

"PARALYSE THE ARMY AND NAVY."

AND MR. MACDONALD WOULD LEND RUSSIA OUR MONEY!

DOCUMENT ISSUED BY FOREIGN OFFICE

AFTER "DAILY MAIL" HAD SPREAD THE NEWS.

THE BRITISH RED ARMY.

OUR COMMUNISTS TOLD TO FIND GENERAL STAFF.

ARMED INSURRECTION.

A CLASS WAR.

FOREIGN OFFICE PROTEST.

£5,000 OR £5 A WEEK FOR LIFE.

"DAILY MAIL" ELECTION COMPETITION.

POST FORMS NOW.

21 DEATHS MYSTERY.

THE MASTER ASSASSIN.

LATEST NEWS

DE VALERA ARRESTED.

ULSTER POLICE ACTION.

YOUR VOTE.

HANGED IN PAIRS.

PEKING CHANGES HANDS.

COUP WHILE CITY SLEPT.

GATES OPENED BY PLOTTERS.

The Daily Mail's Zinoviev Letter article of 25 October 1924 (*University of Warwick*).

acknowledge receipt until the 9th, which was the day before it was sent to Whitehall customers with a covering note from Malcolm Woollcombe[135] that included the sentence 'The authenticity of the document is undoubted.'[136]

In her role as the Foreign Office historian, Gill Bennett was given the job of writing the most recent (1999) official report and she was permitted access to the MI6 archives.[137] She also paid a visit to Moscow during that short period when the KGB archives were more accessible to Westerners than ever before. However, in the absence of any definitive evidence, her four main conclusions were understandably tentative. She concluded that the Zinoviev Letter was a forgery but that it was still impossible to identify the forger. It was still not clear whether the MI6 station in Riga knew it was a forgery or whether they sent it to London in good faith. The same was true of MI6 Head Office although they clearly made a mistake in testifying to its authenticity without sufficient evidence, and a group of right-wing figures was determined to make the most of the letter, whether it was forged or not.[138]

Almost twenty years after writing her official report Gill Bennett authored a book entitled *The Zinoviev Letter: The Conspiracy that Never Dies* which has become the gold standard on the scandal. With more than double the number of pages of her 1999 report Bennett had the space to examine the numerous theories put forward over the past century, some of them compelling and others less so.

Bennett was clearly intrigued by the explanation of one of her hosts during her 1998 visit to the KGB archives in Moscow. Oleg Tsarev pointed a finger at a man named Pokrovsky as the forger. Indeed, Bennett gave Tsarev 'the final word' in her official report. In her subsequent book she examined the Tsarev angle in more detail. It concerned not only Pokrovsky but also a British Intelligence officer, Captain Black, and a Russian with British nationality, General Korniyev.

There are now five versions of the Black, Korniyev, Pokrovsky story.

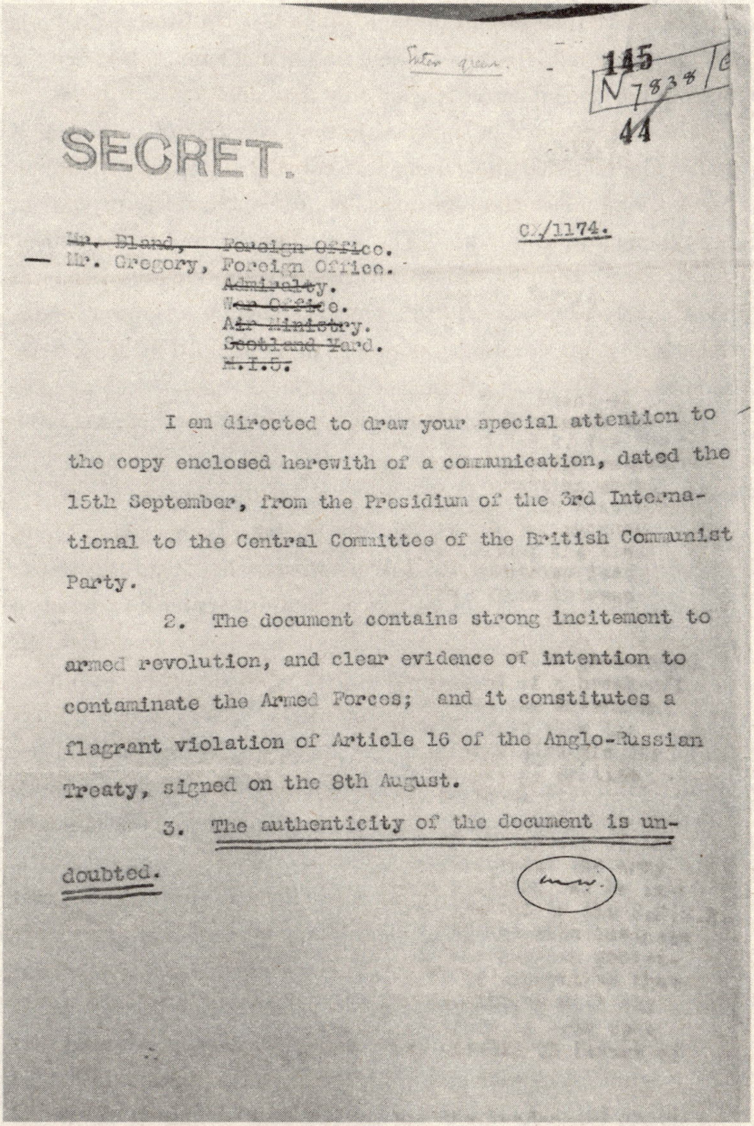

SECRET.

CX/1174.

~~Mr. Bland, Foreign Office.~~
Mr. Gregory, Foreign Office.
~~Admiralty.~~
~~War Office.~~
~~Air Ministry.~~
~~Scotland Yard.~~
~~M.I.5.~~

I am directed to draw your special attention to the copy enclosed herewith of a communication, dated the 15th September, from the Presidium of the 3rd International to the Central Committee of the British Communist Party.

2. The document contains strong incitement to armed revolution, and clear evidence of intention to contaminate the Armed Forces; and it constitutes a flagrant violation of Article 16 of the Anglo-Russian Treaty, signed on the 8th August.

3. The authenticity of the document is undoubted.

Woollcombe's initials (*circled*) under the note that accompanied the Zinoviev Letter to Whitehall customers. (*TNA*)

They all have their origins in the KGB archives in Moscow;* so it is the same story told five times. There are some differences between the five but the general narrative is broadly the same.

The first appeared in an article in the *Daily Herald* on 25 March 1929. The fact that the *Herald* was edited by a William Norman Ewer, a communist who later turned out to be a Soviet agent, adds an extra dimension to this story. The second was relayed to Bennett by Tsarev during her 1998 visit to Moscow. The third is from Bennett's book, which draws on all the other four. The fourth is Gordon Brook-Shepherd in *The Iron Maze*, quoting an unpublished 'History of State Security Organs', an in-house record of Soviet intelligence passed to him privately. And the final references are to be found in *The Crown Jewels* written by Nigel West and the same Oleg Tsarev who met Bennett in Moscow.

The combined narrative is that the Zinoviev Letter was forged in Riga by an ex-Russian Imperial Army officer called [Ivan] Pokrovsky who was urged by certain British interests to produce material to compromise the Labour Party. Pokrovsky was linked to a notorious White Russian forger in Berlin, Vladimir Orlov. The man who approached Pokrovsky in Riga was a Captain Black of MI6. Black was the alias of a Russian officer called General Korniyev who had been granted British citizenship during the Great War. Both Pokrovsky and Black were paid £500 for their services and advised to decamp to South America.

The biggest problem with this whole line of investigation is that nobody has ever been able to identify any General Korniyev either under his own name or under his MI6 alias, Captain Black. As Bennett makes clear this is a crucial piece of evidence which is lacking.

Anyone who has read thus far may already have surmised that Korniyev and Black were both aliases of Bill de Ropp. Could Bill pass as a British MI6 captain? Yes, in fact he was an acting captain in the

* In 1924 the Soviet security and intelligence service was known as the OGPU.

Royal Air Force (formerly Royal Flying Corps) until 1919. Could Bill pose as a White Russian general? Yes, he spoke perfect, accent-less Russian. At thirty-eight years old he was perhaps a little young to be a general but he had known the forty-two-year-old General Pavel Bermondt-Avalov in 1919; and General Pyotr Wrangel, a fellow Baltic German, was only forty-two when he became Chief of White Forces in Crimea. And, of course, it is true that Bill had obtained British nationality at the start of the Great War.

But what about South America? This detail alone does not fit. Pokrovsky certainly went to Brazil and was later in both Argentina and Uruguay. One of the five versions has Black telling Pokrovsky that he too was going to Brazil.[139] Bill de Ropp was doubtless misleading Pokrovsky. There is no merit in trusting members of a forgery ring and Bill had no desire to meet an OGPU assassin on the beach in Rio de Janeiro.

Instead, on 2 October 1924 Bill de Ropp embarked at Tilbury aboard the British India ship SS *Madura* bound for Mombasa in Kenya.[140] He described himself as a thirty-seven-year-old retired man and gave his address as the Savile Club, Piccadilly. This was the very day that Riga station sent the Zinoviev Letter to London. This too is of significance because it shows that much of the plan took place in September and possibly earlier.

De Ropp family folklore tells us that Bill went out to Kenya to profit from the 'coffee boom'.[141] His son, Robert, later wrote, 'He tried to make his fortune in Kenya . . . and only succeeded in losing what little money he had.'[142] Neither of these explanations makes any sense. The coffee boom in Kenya took place in the 1930s not the 1920s. Furthermore, Bill was the only passenger on his page of the ship's manifest who made it clear that he was not planning to live or settle in East Africa but intended to return to England.

An alternative but intriguingly bogus explanation for his trip is provided in a letter dated 28 July 1926 from Gerard Clauson of the Colonial Office to Vernon Kell of MI5 quoting his Minister

William Ormsby-Gore* that Bill 'assisted with the Secretariat work of the Governors' Conference'.[143]

Ormsby-Gore was referring to the East African Governors' Conference, which took place at Government House, Nairobi between 26 January and 11 February 1926. It was a highly significant event, the first time the British Governors of Kenya, Northern Rhodesia, Nyasaland, Uganda and Tanganyika had come together to discuss common issues. Representatives of the colonial administrations of Zanzibar and Sudan also attended. They discussed railways, air-mail services, land and labour policies, 'native taxation', medical research, minor frontier adjustments, economic crops and the King's African Rifles.

Much of the preparatory work was done in advance at the Colonial Office in London and it is simply not credible that Bill would have been sent out to Africa fifteen months in advance. The Secretariat was managed by Colonel C. W. G. Walker DSO and he doubtless had several assistants because there was a certain amount of complaint at the conference about the Secretariat costs and their apportionment.[144] However, Bill is not mentioned once in the many conference papers retained at the National Archives at Kew.

Ormsby-Gore had led his own East Africa Commission to the region when he was out of office during the term of the 1924 Labour government. The Commission consisted of one MP from each major party. Major Archibald Church (Labour),† Frederick Linfield (Liberal) and Ormsby-Gore himself for the Conservatives.[145] Their programme began in Cape Town on 1 September 1924 and ended when they embarked on the SS *Madura* on 1 December at Mombasa.

This was *Madura* making its return journey. Bill met up with the Ormsby-Gore mission in Africa in mid-November. He would later develop a productive relationship with the Labour MP Church,

* Ormsby Gore was Under Secretary of State. The Secretary of State was Leo Amery.

† Ironically, both Church and Linfield lost their seats in the October 1924 General Election which took place during their absence in Africa.

whom he met at Livingstone, the border town between Northern and Southern Rhodesia* and the site of the Victoria Falls.[146] He also became friendly with Eric Dutton, Private Secretary to the Governor of Kenya. Both Church and Dutton would visit de Ropp in Berlin during the 1920s and 1930s.

Dutton, who had been badly wounded at Gallipoli, had been a member of the Savile Club since 1918. Elspeth Huxley would later write of him, 'Gusto . . . was one of Eric's qualities. He enjoyed his particular kind of life, with its variety and the contacts it brought him, especially with those in high places; he was a lover of intrigues, of anecdotes, of the quirks and foibles of mankind.'[147]

Dutton was known for his acerbic tongue but even he found merit in the work of the Ormsby-Gore Commission which tried to reconcile the views of the colonial settlers with those of the African population. Their report also tackled some of the most sensitive issues such as land reform, labour, education and medical services.

There being minimal evidence of input from de Ropp into either the Ormsby-Gore Commission or the Governor's Conference it is hard to escape the conclusion that his period in Africa was intended to get him out of the way. There were no active intelligence requirements on Africa – there would be later when the Nazi Party in Germany would demand the return of Tanganyika; but not as early as 1924. And, anyway, the colonial territories were part of MI5's responsibilities, not MI6's.

Bill was sent to Africa to be shielded from danger. This happens sometimes when an agent gets blown to his or her target and has to be relocated, perhaps to Australia or Canada, with a new identity. Occasionally even a case officer may be sent to, say, Quito, Kathmandu or Lusaka on a three-year posting out of reach of a terrorist group. In Bill's case he was being protected from the anticipated aftermath of the Zinoviev Letter.

---

* Now Zambia and Zimbabwe. The town is still called Livingstone. According to Church Bill de Ropp was travelling with 'a German Jew'.

It is telling that Ormsby-Gore gave Vernon Kell, of all people, an explanation which he and Kell knew to be false for Bill's absence in Africa. This suggests that he knew the real reason for Bill's period of exile. This is not entirely surprising since Ormsby-Gore had been an intelligence officer during the Great War. In fact the very same letter shows that he knew the de Ropps (as he called them) rather well.

> There are three de Ropp brothers, Baltic Barons in origin. The eldest [Paul] lives on the family property in Lithuania and has become a Lithuanian citizen. Frederick, the next brother . . . is now one of the Honorary Secretaries of the German Colonial Gesellschaft*. The youngest, William, is a naturalised British subject who served in the British army during the war and subsequently in Lord Northcliffe's Enemy Propaganda Department. You probably know all about him. All three brothers are by tradition High Tories, and hate Bolshevism and, in fact, Russia and the Russians.[148]

The sentence 'You probably know all about him' is clearly a reference to Bill de Ropp's secret role for MI6. Ormsby-Gore would have felt it safe making this somewhat indiscreet remark to Kell, the Director General of MI5.

The evidence points to at least one MI5 officer being aware of (and possibly involved in) the Zinoviev Letter conspiracy as early as April 1924. Joseph Ball was not just a senior MI5 officer (the head of B Branch), he was also a qualified barrister and a devoted adherent of the Conservative Party. Three years after the Zinoviev Letter he would become deputy head of Conservative Central Office's publicity department. He was an enthusiastic member of the Savile Club, his name appearing as a proposer or seconder of several candidate members.

---

* Gesellschaft translates as Society or Organisation.

He knew Bill de Ropp both from the Savile and as a former interrogator of German prisoners towards the end of the Great War. He wrote a note about Bill on Friedrich's MI5 file on 23 April 1924. 'I know personally the Captain Baron William Sylvester de Ropp (formerly a GSO [General Staff Officer]). He is a very able and patriotic person who served well in the British army during the war. He is not identical with the suspect [Friedrich] and I think separate files should be made at once.'[149]

During April and May 1924 Ball and Stewart Menzies tried to exclude Friedrich von der Ropp from Britain. Why was this thought so important as to warrant two senior officers' time? Although Friedrich had come and gone from Britain numerous times he had been refused a visa in 1920 because of concerns that he was a German spy.

In early April 1924 the PCO in Berlin (Frank Foley himself) sent in Friedrich's new application for a visa to London with a recommendation that it would not be detrimental to the public interest.[150] A few days later Menzies wrote to Ball to say that MI6 still wanted a 1920 exclusion order against Friedrich to remain in place.[151] Ball replied a month later indicating that 'our information would hardly justify a military objection . . . we are anxious to assist you but our information is poor . . . We are holding up the Home Office file . . . until we have your reply.'[152] Menzies replied 'de Ropp's brother [Bill] in a private letter advised his only being granted a single visa, which certainly shows that the family has not a very high opinion of this gentleman's activities.'[153]

This objection was not sufficiently strong and so Friedrich was allowed entry into Britain. Earlier in April a British businessman and retired naval officer Stanley Benbow Hebbert had called at the Home Office to support Friedrich's application. He said that he hoped to introduce him to financiers to help him raise a loan for the Pomeranian Farmers' Cooperative Union. Hebbert added that he (Hebbert) and his associate Guy Scrase Dickins were now press agents for Conservative Central Office.[154]

Later (in 1926) MI5 would get worried about Hebbert's activities. They were monitoring the telephone calls between a German journalist suspected of being a spy, Wilhelm von Kries, Hebbert and Friedrich. At one meeting Hebbert told MI5 that Friedrich had little role to play on behalf of Pomeranian Farmers and, for good measure, denounced him both as a spy and (absurdly) for having 'Bolshevik tendencies'.[155]

If the Zinoviev Letter plot began in early 1924 (as will be argued in the next chapter) one can see why both Menzies and Ball would have seen Friedrich, a suspected German spy, as a liability and wanted him kept out of Britain. They would have worried about Friedrich's family connection to Bill de Ropp and his link to Hebbert, Scrase Dickins and Conservative Central Office. Friedrich even gave Scrase Dickins's house at 91 Kinnerton Street as his contact address.

Bill de Ropp's role in the Zinoviev Letter is important, but equally significant is that it demonstrates that the plot was not hatched hurriedly to scupper the chances of Labour in the October 1924 election. Its origins were somewhat different.

9

MISSION CREEP

April to October 1924: From intelligence operation to political conspiracy

The revelation of Bill de Ropp's key role in the Zinoviev Letter affair provides a significant contribution to the ongoing debate about the Zinoviev Letter, which has fascinated historians and politicians for exactly one hundred years.

This is not the place to try to solve the whole mystery, not least because there are still several pieces missing from the jigsaw, which, in all likelihood, will never be found. So what does Bill de Ropp's involvement tell us?

Firstly the longer timescale enables us to see that the Zinoviev Letter initially had a different purpose. It was not intended to coincide with the October 1924 General Election. In fact the origins probably lie in a request made by the Labour Home Secretary Arthur Henderson.

In late January 1924 the first Labour government assumed office under Prime Minister Ramsay MacDonald. It was a salient moment in British political history and Whitehall was intensely nervous. MacDonald, a working-class man from Lossiemouth, and other members of his cabinet were cut from a very different cloth to previous, Conservative and Liberal administrations.

For MI5 and MI6 which had been working against Russia and the Comintern ever since the victory over Germany there was an added concern about links between Labour, the Trade Unions, the Communist Party of Great Britain (CPGB) and Moscow. However, the reality of Labour government soon calmed the nerves. In many ways MacDonald himself was a conservative man. He became his own Foreign Secretary, with Arthur Henderson taking over at the Home Office.

Whitehall soon found that it was business as usual. There were no red flags, no barricades, no bombs, just the familiar old Whitehall routine with bowler hats, rolled umbrellas, the commuter trains from Godalming or Woking and the interminable chain of paperwork as ministers received advice from officials.

MI5 and MI6 were not particularly happy that their ministers preferred to keep them at arm's length. However, the matter that really bothered them was the constant agitation of the Comintern in Moscow and its links to the CPGB. Both services also disliked the normalisation of relations with the Soviet Union, although this trend had started under the previous government.

MI6 and the Government Code and Cypher School (later GCHQ) continued to intercept Comintern messages and some were passed to the Special Branch of the Metropolitan Police, which used to provide the government with a regular update on activities entitled 'General Communist Activities'. On 7 April the Comintern had sent a letter to the CPGB calling for 'mass demonstrations' on 1 May.[156]

Arthur Henderson's attention was drawn to one of these reports and at his request his Permanent Secretary, Sir John Anderson, wrote a letter (dated 3 May 1924) to MacDonald, drawing his attention to a paragraph about Comintern money being sent to the CPGB for propaganda purposes. Henderson asked for the report to be verified as genuine and, subject to there being no threat to the source, he thought the government should ask the Soviet chargé d'affaires, Khristian Rakovsky, for an explanation.[157]

There followed some internal minuting within the FO. Henry Maxse of Northern Department thought a protest would be counter-productive. He questioned the authenticity of the Comintern message and observed, 'The Soviet Government is a past-master in the art of supplying forged documents to Foreign Intelligence Services.'

George Mounsey, Head of the FO's Treaty Department, added that he favoured placing the onus on the Home Office itself to find malpractice by the Soviets in London rather than relying on innately dubious documents.

However, Sir Eyre Crowe (the PUS) asserted, 'It is practically certain that the letter quoted is genuine.' He then added, 'It is only on . . . evidence obtained *in this country* that we could hope to take effective action against those inculpated.' Finally he judged: 'If we had intercepted it in the post addressed to the Communist headquarters in England, the value of the letter would be vastly increased.' MacDonald noted in conclusion that 'these minutes are very sensible.'[158]

As they read these minutes at the MI6 Head Office in Melbury Road, Kensington, one could forgive Sinclair and Menzies for interpreting them as akin to 'Who would rid me of this meddlesome priest?' Rather like Henry II's expression of frustration at his Archbishop of Canterbury, Thomas à Becket, the wording was open to various interpretations.

Sir Eyre Crowe, judging by his strident acceptance of the authenticity of the document, may have discussed the documents with Sinclair. What Crowe wanted was firm evidence that the FO could use to protest to the Soviet government. This evidence could not come from the ether or from an overseas source. It needed to be found in England (most probably London). And crucially it must not come from a source who could be compromised by its use in a protest to the Soviets.

Neither Crowe nor Sinclair may have discussed the idea but

it is not a huge logical leap to conclude that a forgery would best serve that purpose. The decision to commission a forgery was the first of several tipping points which would turn a perfectly justifiable intelligence operation by degrees into a tawdry political conspiracy.

So the origin of the Zinoviev Letter most likely began in April and May 1924 at the very same time that Menzies and Ball were discussing how to exclude Friedrich von der Ropp from Britain.

What was the intention of the conspiracy? Was it a surgical operation to undermine the links between the CPGB and the Comintern (as Henderson clearly wished)? Or was it a wider plan to damage UK-Soviet relations, which many in MI5 and MI6 disliked and distrusted? The second of these options could also impact the British government's foreign policy objectives, whether Conservative, Liberal or Labour.

The probability is that the first objective gradually morphed into the second and that those people tasked to implement the operation (including Bill de Ropp) would not really have acknowledged or even noticed the difference between the two. Bill de Ropp had no time for the Soviet Union, the Comintern, Bolshevism, the CPGB or communism. He would have regarded any subtle policy distinctions between the two objectives as an act of self-delusion.

Indeed Bill de Ropp and some of his anti-Bolshevik colleagues may not even have worried when actions intended to damage Soviet Communism became entangled in a question of UK domestic politics.

Sinclair and Menzies as government officials would surely have drawn a distinction between an act designed to weaken a foreign power and its offshoots and one in which a domestic political party would be impacted. However, by October, they may have been past caring. MacDonald's decision not to prosecute the communist John Ross Campbell for urging soldiers to refuse orders would have appalled the senior leadership of both MI5 and MI6 so soon after the Great War in which they had all served. Furthermore Ramsay MacDonald had kept MI6 at arm's length and there were even members of Labour who wanted to see MI5 and MI6 abolished.[159]

The second important policy and moral line was crossed on the evening of 9 October or early morning of the 10th when MI6 sent the Letter into the Whitehall machine regardless of the fact that Ramsay MacDonald had announced a General Election the previous day.* The alternative course of action would have been to abort the whole operation – but the prospect of abandoning so much hard work would have been deeply unattractive. The chances of reconstituting it at some future date would have seemed minimal, especially following the departure of Pokrovsky to Brazil and de Ropp to Kenya.

So the involvement of Bill de Ropp gives credence to the idea of the Zinoviev Letter being a classic example of 'mission creep'. An operation initially designed to support a government objective gradually became a broader attack on UK-Soviet relations before finally being used against the Labour party itself. This rings true to anyone who has served in Whitehall where conspiracies are vanishingly rare and cock-ups are legion.

Secondly Bill de Ropp's appearance as both General Korniyev and Captain Black gives a considerable boost to the Russian version of events, namely the explanation given to Gill Bennett during her 1998 visit to Moscow, based on the OGPU files which also furnished the evidence used by the *Daily Herald* back in 1929, Gordon Brook-Shepherd and Oleg Tsarev. This version not only includes Korniyev and Black but also places Ivan Pokrovsky as the forger. This also tallies with the testimony of the Latvian political police.

The MI6 officer John Nicholson was posted to Riga in 1934 and quoted the sinister Head of Latvian Political Police, Artur Shmidkoff, as being convinced that the forger was a British MI6 agent based in Riga:

---

* The covering note, held at the National Archives, was signed by Malcolm Woollcombe who always insisted the Zinoviev Letter was genuine; so it is just possible that the Letter was sent to Whitehall on a routine basis without the involvement of Sinclair, Menzies or Morton.

> He said that, with a squad of men, he had raided the flat of a known ex-British agent and had discovered carbon copies of what he described as 'the original Zinoviev letter'. These carbon copies had certainly been produced on the agent's typewriter which was found in the flat ... He personally was convinced that the man was indeed the originator of the letter and he implied that it had been fabricated and passed to a 'British organisation' for financial gain. He thought that the letter certainly had been forged and then, knowingly or unknowingly, been used for political purposes. I [Nicholson] sent the story back to London but never received an acknowledgement.[160]

With this new evidence some of the other Zinoviev Letter theories can be abandoned. The involvement of a Madame Bellegarde (suggested by the *Sunday Times* Insight team) is one such, as are the various efforts to place Sidney Reilly at the scene of the crime.

Thirdly, and most importantly, Bill de Ropp's involvement provides some tantalising new clues as to who else was implicated in the operation which became a conspiracy.

Bill de Ropp was an agent of MI6. His recruiter and case officer was Stewart Menzies. All his Baltic reports would have been handled by Desmond Morton (who was in charge of Production, known as Prod) and Malcolm Woollcombe who was head of the Political Section. Of these three men Gill Bennett has already pointed to Desmond Morton and Stewart Menzies as MI6 officers with close links to the Conservative Party. Within MI5 Joseph Ball was both closer to the Tories and less principled than both Menzies and Morton. Bennett even quotes Morton writing enigmatically to Ball in July, 'I will not capitulate what it is we are out to do, as I think my description on the telephone must have made it quite clear to you.'[161]

In theory this does not necessarily mean that MI6 was institutionally involved from the outset. Malcolm Woollcombe swore to his dying day that the Letter was genuine and it is quite possible that

Morton and Menzies kept him in the dark. The MI6 head of station in Riga, Rafael Farina, must have known because Ivan Pokrovsky was his agent and would have told him about the forgery. The Zinoviev Letter was attributed to an agent designated FR3/K, a genuine agent who continued to provide good intelligence until 1931.[162] We know that Farina himself ran him because FR stood for Farina Riga.* Farina had worked for Joseph Ball at MI5 before transferring to MI6. Indeed one wonders if his transfer to MI6 and then Riga was entirely coincidental.[163]

What is notable about Bill de Ropp during this period was how close his relations were with men who had served in Russia and the Baltic States in 1919 and 1920 and members of the Savile Club. A Venn Diagram would show a marked overlap between the two groups. Not all of them were involved in the Zinoviev Letter but several were, including Henry Maxse, 'Don' Gregory, William Blennerhassett and Donald Im Thurn.

There was a curious twist to the Zinoviev Letter story in a subsequent corruption case involving 'Don' Gregory (John Duncan Gregory), the FO's head of Northern Department. The unproven implication was that Gregory's female friend Aminta Bradley Dyne had tried to make money out of the Baltics or the Zinoviev Letter or both. One of the people involved was William Blennerhassett.[164] He was a fluent Russian speaker who had served in the Intelligence Corps during the war before attachments to the FO and to MI6. He won the DSO while serving at Murmansk in 1919.[165] Bill would have known Blennerhassett when he was Vice Consul in Kovno (Kaunas) for much of 1920 until May 1921.[166] Bill also seconded Blennerhassett's proposal of a Dutch candidate to join the Savile Club in April 1922.[167]

Donald Im Thurn, who was close to the Conservative Party,

---

* There were three phases of designation. For example, one agent was H16 in the 1910s (where H stood for Holland), then TR16 in the early 1920s (where T was his case officer Tinsley and R was for Rotterdam), and finally 33016 from the later 1920s where 33000 stood for Holland; 16 meant he was sixteenth on the station's list of agents

had served in MI5 during the war and, in 1924, was a director of the London Steamship and Trading Corporation. He used to have lunch regularly with Major William Alexander who worked at MI5 for Joseph Ball. Wealthy and well-connected to those with interests in north-east Europe, it appears that Im Thurn was responsible for raising the money to pay Pokrovsky to relocate to South America. At a lunch party in 1928, neither the Conservative Party Leader Stanley Baldwin nor the Chairman J. C. C. Davidson seemed at all surprised when Im Thurn raised the subject of the forgery except to express amazement that he had 'kept [his] mouth shut all these years'.[168]

Ormsby-Gore may or may not have known of the conspiracy at the time but he was more than happy to protect Bill's cover by attesting to his notional role for the East African Governors' Conference. Finally, Bill would be well known to Thomas Marlowe of the *Daily Mail* from his time working in and reporting from the Baltic States in 1919.

Whether or not MI6 was institutionally involved from the outset, the fact remains that it certainly became involved from the moment Woollcombe sent the Letter, received from Riga, into the Whitehall machine. The inclusion in Woollcombe's covering note of the words 'The authenticity of the document is undoubted' was a serious error and could be explained by Woollcombe being unaware of the forgery.

Bill de Ropp's involvement was bittersweet. His son was nearing the end of his time at Cheam Preparatory School and he could not afford the fees to send him on to one of the great public schools. Following his success in the Baltic States after the war Bill de Ropp had resigned from the Anglo-Baltic Merchants in October 1922, which suggests that MI6 no longer had any further Baltic tasking for him.[169]

His motives were not purely financial. He was proud of his British nationality and war service. He enjoyed being British and revelled in the Savile Club and being a member of the ruling class. His son would later write: 'My . . . father settled in England, became naturalised, married an Englishwoman, fought in the British army in

World War One . . . He imitated the English in everything including sleeping with the windows open even when the outside temperature was below zero . . . He was what Turgenev called Anglophile.'[170]

Furthermore, Bill de Ropp was able to play three of the roles needed for the plan to work. He had been a propagandist in Lord Northcliffe's department at the end of the war and he was fluent in Russian, which would be helpful in producing a Russian text of a notional letter from Zinoviev from which he could make an English translation.[171] He could also pose as Black and Korniyev.

The only problem with using Bill de Ropp was his brother, a suspected agent of the German government. This may explain the correspondence between Menzies and Ball to try to keep Friedrich von der Ropp out of the country. The normal MI6 correspondent with MI5 was Valentine Vivian, as head of counter-intelligence, and so Menzies's involvement was unusual and suggests a particular operational need. When the attempt to keep Friedrich out of Britain failed, MI6 decided to go ahead with Bill de Ropp regardless. After all, agents who can pose as White Russian Generals do not grow on trees.

Bill de Ropp would probably have travelled to Riga in early September. There were numerous sailings from British ports (London, Hull, Dundee, Aberdeen and Belfast) to Riga each week, which was more discreet than going by rail through Germany where he risked being recognised. Alternatively, with Sinclair's assistance, he could have travelled aboard one of the many Royal Navy ships operating in the Baltic.

The date on the Zinoviev Letter of 15 September may well have been the actual date that Pokrovsky passed the completed forgery to Bill de Ropp posing as Black. The same or following day he would have given it to Farina. This gave Bill de Ropp a fortnight to return to London, bid farewell to his mother-in-law and two children before making his way to Tilbury to settle into his first-class cabin on the SS *Madura* which sailed on 2 October, the very day that Farina sent the telegraphic copy to London.

It is not clear whether de Ropp received any financial reward. Pokrovsky was certainly paid; the Soviets thought he received £500. However, in 1928 Donald Im Thurn was allegedly paid the considerable (and improbable) sum of £5000* by Conservative Central Office for passing on to a man referred to as X who was on his way to Argentina.[172] X was doubtless Pokrovsky who did move from Brazil to Argentina with a new identity and an Argentine passport.[173]

It seems most unlikely that Bill de Ropp received anything like £5000. He certainly had little money from 1924 to 1928 and he failed to find the money to send Bob to public school. He does appear to have come into some funds in 1928 when he moved to Berlin and took a comfortable, but not opulent, flat in Kurfürstendamm and sent his son to Australia. Perhaps because he returned to England only a few months after the Zinoviev Letter, he was deemed to have forfeited a sum which was intended to compensate him for a life in exile.

The Zinoviev Letter saga only ran into trouble after the SS *Madura* had set sail. A remaining mystery is why no posted copies of the Letter addressed to the CPGB at 16 King Street, Covent Garden and to the Soviet legation in Chesham Place, Belgravia were ever intercepted by the Post Office or the Metropolitan Police. Had Bill de Ropp, Rafael Farina or Ivan Pokrovsky failed to post them in Riga? Or had the Latvians intercepted them? There is no evidence that either the CPGB or the Soviet Embassy ever received their copies. This meant that the MI6 copy was the only one available for leaking to the press.

There was no shortage of volunteers to take the Letter to Thomas Marlowe, the editor of the *Daily Mail*. Colonel Freddie Browning, the popular former deputy head of MI6 (then MI1c) under Cumming and now a Director of the Savoy Hotel was one. A second was Admiral Sir Reginald 'Blinker' Hall, the legendary Director of Naval Intelligence (DNI) who played such a significant role in Room 40 of the Admiralty which had broken the German naval codes in

* Equivalent to some £381,000 in 2024. CPI inflation calculator.

the Great War. On retirement from the Royal Navy, he became the Conservative MP for Eastbourne. Hall was a natural activist and he founded 'National Propaganda' which campaigned to prevent the subversion of the free market.[174]

One can imagine Bill de Ropp's mixture of excitement and anxiety as the daily news reports were posted on the ship's noticeboard by the radio operator. He was lucky in two ways. Although the Soviets soon found out that Black and Korniyev were the same person they never identified either alias as Bill de Ropp. He had probably been to Riga in his own name, as a *Daily Mail* correspondent, in 1919, so he had needed to stay in Riga for as short a time as possible and avoid meeting anyone he knew. In this he succeeded.

The Soviets also knew the Letter was a forgery. There was one fortunate aspect to this, which MI6 had not considered. Gill Bennett was told that the OGPU did not even initiate a leak investigation. Why would they? Their only interest was in tracing the forger and the customer. This they did with ease thanks to two of their own sources.[175]

Bill de Ropp and his controllers in Broadway had expected a witch-hunt but of the OGPU variety. In fact the investigation came in the form of a feeble official enquiry led by Sir Maurice Hankey, which concluded that there was nothing to see here; and a more muscular one from Labour Party activists and some elements of the press. Doubtless Sinclair, Morton and Menzies were relieved that Bill de Ropp was abroad for the next few uncomfortable months, but he was able to return after only six months away.

Friedrich von der Ropp dates his estrangement from his brother to 1925. Did he discover that Bill had been briefing against his being granted British visas? Or did Friedrich, that arch-conspirator, resent being excluded from one of greatest plots of the twentieth century? Or did Friedrich get wind of the intrigue and inform the AA? It is quite possible that Germany knew of the plot through its own coverage of Orlov. At the time Germany and Russia were enjoying a rapprochement following the 1922 Treaty of Rapallo. Germany would probably not have informed the Russians but would have sat back and enjoyed the damage being done to Anglo-Russian relations.

The Zinoviev Letter was one of the least admirable episodes in MI6's history. The fact that the Conservative Party became involved not only inflicted moral damage on MI6 but the service lost control of its 'restrictive security'. Suddenly a tight-knit group, all bound by the Official Secrets Act and all used to keeping secrets, was joined by a list of Conservative Party officials and hangers-on.

In a strategic sense, however, it was curiously successful. The CPGB never became more than a minor irritant, unlike many of the communist parties on the continent, and thereafter the Labour Party recognised that the Soviet Union was its Achilles heel. Apart from a brief period during Harold Wilson's premiership the relationship between the Labour party and the security and intelligence services has been positive and professional.

The former Labour leader, Neil Kinnock agrees.

> I have never had any doubt that the Tsarists who probably composed the letter did it with the contrivance of some helpers in the Security Services and the ready assistance of the *Daily Mail*. [However] the Labour Governments, certainly after the departure of Harold Wilson, and operationally even when he was PM, worked satisfactorily with the Security Services. The majority [Labour] feeling about the Communist superpower was always characterised by distrust and opposition to Soviet treatment of dissidents, trade unions, artistic expression and civil liberties and to Soviet imperialism. There was deep resentment against the way in which the Soviet perversion of Socialism distorted perceptions of Labour's democratic socialism at home and abroad. George Orwell's output (always widely read by Labour people) further strengthened dislike for and distrust of Communism.[176]

10

'THE PRIMITIVE IN US'

1925–1930: The pressures of spying

It is remarkable that Bill de Ropp escaped exposure over the Zinoviev Letter and it is testament to how well he played his cover roles as Black and Korniyev, and to the discretion of his various colleagues and contacts (such as Ormsby-Gore). He was clearly a skilful operator but also a lucky one because, after a period of near-destitution, he placed a bet on Germany becoming the next big headache for MI6.

Bill de Ropp returned to England early in 1925 barely six months after having left. The Zinoviev Letter furore had died down although it would flare up from time to time during the later 1920s. Bill was of little use to MI6, which must have judged that he was now comprehensively blown to the Soviet target, the service's overwhelming priority. They kept Bill on the books though, because he was an effective agent and perhaps also because they needed to keep him onside given what he knew of recent events. The tasking and pay were now occasional and so he would need additional sources of income.

When in Kenya Bill de Ropp had got to know Roy Truscott, the Editor-in-Chief of the *East African Standard* newspaper. Bill had probably been looking for journalistic work. Truscott had fought in France with the 16th Battalion of the Sherwood Foresters from 1914 right through to 1919, both in the trenches and at GHQ, reaching the rank of lieutenant colonel aged only twenty.[177] He was awarded the OBE and won two Mentions in Despatches. He was also General Manager of his family's printing and stationery firm, which is how he came to know his business associate and mistress Gertrude Woodman Hunter, whose American husband, Robert Hunter, had died in 1924.[178]

In February 1925, soon after his return to England, Bill married Gertrude's younger sister at a registry office on the Isle of Wight. She was Marie Winifred Woodman, known as Jimmy, who was living at Nettlestone. She was twenty-five years old, small, dark-haired and strikingly attractive. She was also very strong-willed and would become a major support to Bill during his years in Berlin and something of a trial later in life. She had served in the Red Cross towards the end of the war, for long enough to have earned the Victory and War medals.

The Woodman women were no shrinking violets. Jimmy's father had run the family's large bookbinding business at Herne Hill, South London. He had served in the RFC during the war. He married a German woman, Catherine Hensman, and their eldest daughter Gertrude was sent to Dulwich High School and then to a college in Brunswick. At the outbreak of war she managed to get home to London thanks to the intervention of 'friends in high military places'.[179] When their father died in 1923 Gertrude displaced her brother as General Manager of the family business and became well known as one of the few female Chief Executives in the country.

Jimmy was made of similar stuff. She was clearly taken with the idea of being a baroness and made greater use of her title than Bill, who was more modest by nature. She was also not keen to begin married life by having to look after Bill's two children. Robert (known as Bob) was now twelve at Cheam Preparatory School in Hampshire.* Ruth was only six and staying with her grandmother, Edith Fisher, in Potterne. Cheam had a reputation for sending boys on to Eton, Harrow or Winchester, but public-school fees were way beyond Bill's financial means. And while Jimmy doubtless had shares in the family bookbinding company there was little ready cash.

Family problems were building up relentlessly. Edith Fisher was ailing and the house in Potterne was too big for her. In 1925 she moved to Crane Lodge in Salisbury with a lawn running down to the south bank of the Avon. She could have her grandchildren to visit occasionally but increasingly called on the assistance of her daughter Dora, the widow of Arthur Magor. Dora had since married a Colonel Frank Spencer (formerly of the Lincolnshire Regiment) who lived at Hungerton Hall, near Grantham. Bob would describe him as a 'purple-faced colonel who kept a stable of hunters and rode to hounds'.[180] Edith, Dora and Frank must have been unimpressed by Jimmy's reluctance to shoulder the duties of a step-mother.

In September 1925 Bill arranged for his friend, Major Archibald Church, the former Labour MP for Leyton East,† to spend ten days in Germany. With the help of Friedrich he arranged for Church to meet Walter de Haas who was head of the British Empire section of the German Foreign Ministry, Theodore Seitz, the former Governor of South West Africa, Heinrich Schnee, the former Governor of Tanganyika, Hjalmar Schacht, President of the Reichsbank, and various other senior German officials. This launched Church as one of the best-informed British MPs on German and colonial issues until the early 1930s when the advent of the Nazis removed his best sources of access. Like Friedrich his best contacts would be the centrist politicians Heinrich Brüning and Gottfried Treviranus.

---

* The records at Cheam suggest that Bob was there between 1924 and 1928 but both dates look like errors. The records were retyped some years ago. The correct dates should be 1921 or 1922 to 1925.

† He had lost his seat in the October 1924 General Election.

Church's diary of his visit provides a fascinating insight into Friedrich, Lili and Bill, who acted as his hosts throughout.[181] Jimmy seems to have been there but is barely mentioned. With Bill there were already signs of a semi-covert relationship with Church. One evening when Friedrich was away Bill took him to the Bohemia night club. Church noted, 'Met Foley of Passport Office and wife – curious sidelight on Berlin's fallen angels. Very little room to dance. Very expensive show too. Then at 2am to Foley's beautiful flat. Danced again. Back to Eden [Hotel] at 3.45. Interesting interlude.' It was unlikely to have been a coincidence that Bill introduced Church to Foley.

On his penultimate day Church recorded, 'Bill came along a few minutes later while I was shaving to take me along for a talk. [We] had lunch and then a walk through Tiergarten where we made our parting vows and exchanged mutual aspirations.'

Earlier Bill had expressed his concerns about German involvement in the Shannon Power Scheme, the huge hydroelectric project being undertaken by the newly independent government of the Irish Free State. Siemens had submitted a project proposal and Bill was doubtless responding to MI6 tasking to see if there was a political dimension to the project.[182] Feelings were still raw in London about perceived Irish Republican connections to Germany during the latter stages of the war and about German intentions towards the newly formed Irish Free State.

However, it was Lili who stole the show. At Grünheide (her family's estate near Berlin) and in Berlin she bowled over Church with her charm. Although pretending to accompany him *comme mère* there seemed to be little that was motherly about her cultivation of a man who was actually three years older than her. Church noted down some of her more memorable quotes. 'You are on the threshold, my little boy, of a mighty career'. 'Think of me always as a source of strength and not of weakness'. 'Whatever befalls you, let me know. I shall understand'. 'You and I will each keep a corner sacred to each other.' 'We Balts are so different from you. There is so much of the primitive in us in spite of our external refinements.'

Given that this was happening right under Friedrich's nose, and even aiming off for the permissive mores of post-war Germany, it is hard to believe that Lili's motives were romantic or sexual. She was presumably cultivating Church as another source for Friedrich's work for the AA. Church had a budding career in the Labour party and might have gone far had it not been for the split caused by MacDonald joining the National Government in 1931. Church sided with MacDonald. Later his reputation was somewhat sullied by his espousal of eugenics.

Church had been thinking of making another trip to Africa with Bill but Lili urged him to take Friedrich with him instead. Here may be another clue to the impending rift between the two brothers.

Bill's lack of a firm home and job may have been the origin of the somewhat desperate idea of going to live at Dauzogir. Friedrich owned the property but was making no use of it. Paul was living nearby at Eichenpomusch. In his dark and brooding autobiography, Bob would give the impression that he was abandoned at Dauzogir on his own for two years:

> I found myself transported, a timid boy of twelve, straight from the ordered life of my English prep school. It was my father's plan, aided and abetted by his second wife, to house me in this ruin until he could ship me off to Australia, a convenient dumping ground for unwanted offspring . . .
>
> [He continued] He and his wife managed to scrape up some money from somewhere and departed soon after my arrival for Berlin where they lived in style in an apartment on the Kurfürstendamm.[183]

Bob evokes a nightmare existence at Dauzogir, alone in the huge but dilapidated house which had been damaged by shellfire during the Great War. He shared the house with Latvian servants who lived below stairs. Hunger and cold were constant companions as were rats, and Bob lived in terror of ghosts.[184] He added to the horror by mounting a battle-damaged human skull on a pole outside his window.

If Bob's account is true then Bill was criminally negligent in leaving a twelve-year-old boy alone at Dauzogir for so long. But the facts do not wholly support Bob's account. There are family photographs of Bob and his sister Ruth enjoying life at Grünheide and at Gamehl (the von Stralendorffs' castle near Rostock) in 1926 and 1927. It seems that the extended von der Ropp family helped look after the children. When Edith Fisher died in 1928 half of her wealth went to the children, held in trust but giving Bill and Jimmy as their guardians a degree of latitude over how to spend the money.[185]

These funds enabled Bill to enrol Bob on the Australian Big Brother programme, a youth migration system, begun in 1924, which matched a young migrant, known as a Little Brother (in this case Bob) with a Big Brother in Australia who could provide advice and companionship whilst they were taught about farming at a government-run training farm.[186] In identifying Australia for Bob's future Bill was doubtless recalling his own visit down under nearly two decades earlier.

Bob arrived in Perth aboard the SS *Largs Bay* on 22 February 1929. The local newspaper reported 'Mr Robert de Ropp, son of Baron de Ropp, a former wealthy landowner of Lithuania, whose estates were confiscated during the wartime revolution. He is proceeding to South Australia and is the only Little Brother for that state among a party travelling on the boat under the auspices of the Big Brother movement.'[187]

In his account of the next two years Bob conjures up a period of despair and misery to compare with the time he spent at Dauzogir. He found himself at a farm near Broken Hill 'My father had dumped me in a dying land . . . The rains did not fall. Dust was everywhere . . . The sheep were dying.'[188] Eventually he abandoned the farm because the farmer could not afford to feed him. He lived in a ruined warehouse at Port Adelaide and considered suicide before deciding to return to England.

The Australian newspapers paint a different, if equally depressing, picture. Bob was enrolled at Roseworthy Agricultural College (some thirty miles north of Adelaide) and won a prize for 'Identification of Farm Seeds' in January 1930 when his first full college year ended. The principal's annual report referred to the drought conditions and the depression. This is exactly what Bob experienced during his work on a farm prior to the start of the next academic year.

It was at the end of his second year that things went horribly wrong. Bob was arrested by police for staging an armed robbery. He was carrying a loaded and unregistered revolver and a knife. The headlines were 'Son of Russian Baron. Arrested at night.'[189] Later police found a black mask and it emerged that Bob was addicted to drugs. He was duly deported back to England aboard the Orient Lines' SS *Oronsay*, which docked at Tilbury on 22 April 1931.[190]

His father was not there to greet him. Instead, he sent a Universal Aunt* with a letter expressing his disappointment that Bob 'had failed to avail [himself] of the great opportunities in that young country'. Bob eventually found refuge with Ralph and Adeline Vaughan-Williams at their house, White Gates, in Dorking. Adeline was one of his many aunts and she and the great composer looked after Bob for the next few years and paid for his education at the Royal College of Sciences. This launched him on a successful career as a scientist.

None of this reflects well on Bill and Jimmy, but they too had their burdens to bear. Some money had come in during the later 1920s. Whether this was a belated payment from Joseph Ball for the Zinoviev Letter or whether the couple dipped into Bob and Ruth's legacy is not clear but Bill and Jimmy started to enjoy life in Berlin.

* A company founded in 1921 that provides personal care services to its clients. See the Universal Aunts website. (Accessed December 2023.)

This was the period when Berlin lived on the edge, with social turmoil matched by the excesses of the nightlife.

Bill de Ropp's move to Berlin must have been predicated on a reassessment that he had not been burnt (or 'blown' in MI6 terminology) in his real name as a result of the Zinoviev Letter affair. To be an identified enemy of the Soviet Union in the 1920s and 1930s carried real risks. Robert Vansittart mentioned the cases of Kutyepov and Miller in his autobiography *The Mist Procession*:

> A White Russian leader in Paris, General Kutyepov, went into the street and was seen no more. Disappearance always fascinates . . . The Head of our Secret Service [Sinclair], a man equal to Blinker Hall in natural genius for the game told me that the General had been hustled into a taxi, gagged, injected and run to the north where a Soviet ship hovered. His colleague, General Miller, soon vanished too. These impudent abductions caused the terror that was intended.[191]

The real story was even more shocking than Vansittart related. Alexander Kutyepov, a close friend and official contact of Biffy Dunderdale, MI6's talented and suave Head of Station in Paris, was the commander of the White Russian opposition following the death of General Wrangel in 1928. His kidnapping took place in January 1930. According to the KGB assassin Pavel Sudoplatov:

> This job in 1930 was done by Yakov Serebryansky, assisted by his wife and an agent in the French police. Dressed in French police uniforms, they stopped Kutyepov on the street on the pretext of questioning him and put him in a car. Kutyepov resisted the kidnapping, and during the struggle, he had a heart attack and died, Serebryansky told me. They buried Kutyepov near the home of one of our agents near the outskirts of Paris.[192]

The Yevgeny Miller story would have registered even more strongly with Bill de Ropp because Miller was a Baltic German from Latvia. In September 1937 he too was kidnapped but he was suspicious and left a note in his office:

> I have a rendezvous at half-past twelve today at the corner of the Rue Jasmin and Rue Raffet, in Auteuil, close to Bois de Boulogne, with General Skoblin, who is arranging a meeting for me with a German officer, Mr Strohmann, military attaché with a neighbouring power, and an official of the Embassy, Mr Werner. Both speak Russian fluently. Perhaps it is a trap.[193]

There was another angle, as recorded by the British Trotskyist writer Hugo Dewar:

> On the evening of the day of Miller's disappearance the Soviet freighter *Mariya Ulyanova* was reported to have left Le Havre before her scheduled time and without having fully completed the normal harbour formalities. This unusual haste was, in the circumstances, suspicious. Even more telling was the fact that shortly before its departure a van belonging to, or hired by, the Soviet Embassy in Paris had been observed on the quayside, and customs officials had noted that a large trunk had been taken from this van and carried aboard the Soviet vessel.[194]

While Bill and Jimmy were reinventing themselves in Berlin, living in an apartment on the bustling and vibrant Kurfürstendamm, Friedrich was busy working for the German Foreign Ministry (AA) in England. His letter to the AA in 1930 in which he seeks German citizenship provides some detail of his activities on their behalf.

> I returned in February 1923 to work exclusively for the Foreign Ministry thanks to [Carl] von Schubert, at that time head of the

English department. I was given a monthly stipend of £150 and worked on the relationship between Germany and England; to start with helped by my brother, who had English citizenship, from whom I severed ties for various reasons after cooperating for two years.

My work in England began at a time when it was very difficult for Germans to penetrate there and I was a pioneer in many circles, for which my statelessness helped. My work was carried out in such a manner, that, having been provided with guidelines and preconditions concerning German politics, I was prepared to have these accepted in the authoritative circles in London. In this way I was able to help bring about quietly the most important results for German politics.

At the instigation of the government office, I also took on assignments for the German Colonial Society and prepared for the return migration of Germans to Africa, brought together His Excellency [Theodor] Seitz with Amery and Ormsby-Gore and I am also today seen as a trustworthy person of German colonial interests.

I repeatedly informed the Foreign Ministry [AA] with assessment reports of the political situation and continue to operate mainly [in] English authoritative circles. Notably, I have directed English attention to the eastern border and thereby prepared for the future. So, I undertook with Major Church (now member of the Labour government) a thorough tour of the Eastern German border and his report of this attracted the biggest furore in the Foreign Office that both he and I were requested to refrain from publication. The family retains a German language copy of this report while a copy has been received by the Foreign Ministry and could still be important for the future.

In London I was personally particularly friendly with Sir Eyre Crowe through whom I became acquainted with

Lord [William] Tyrell and other gentlemen of the Foreign Office,* relationships which I continue to nurture. I also have many other personal friendships there.

Thanks to these connections, in the summer of 1928 I was able to bring Dr Brüning and Treviranus to London,† who had the opportunity to discuss the situation of Germany and especially the problem of our eastern border with the leaders of the Conservative Party and the Government in the house of Sir Henry Page Croft [the Conservative MP for Bournemouth]. I also introduced these gentlemen to other circles. I also have personal relationships with the Labour Party and its leaders but have placed the greatest emphasis on the Conservatives and those close to them, as foreign policy is still primarily under their influence. I often use my Berlin office to bring foreign visitors together with important Germans.

During my frequent visits to London, I became aware that a great influence on England could be exerted purely spiritually and so I established relationships with church and Christian circles and found great interest in the point of view that the downfall of our era can be traced back to the decline of Christianity. I am known in England as a leader in the Christian renewal movement.[195]

Neither MI5 nor MI6 would have relished the description of Friedrich working in England 'helped by my brother'. In fact, MI5 were constantly confused by the brothers. In June 1926 Major Alexander wrote sarcastically, 'The two brothers were supposed not to be on speaking terms, but I observe . . . that Frederick

* Sir Eyre Crowe was Permanent Under Secretary at the FO 1920–25; William Tyrrell (later Lord Tyrrell) followed him in that role from 1925 to 1928.

† Dr Heinrich Brüning, German centrist politician who would become Chancellor during the Weimar Republic 1930–32, and Gottfried Treviranus, a politician from the Conservative People's Party, who later served in Brüning's cabinet.

took William's child over to Berlin with him on 9.6.26. Perhaps he is a kidnapper!'[196]

Many years later both MI5 and MI6 took to describing Bill as 'the good baron' and Friedrich as 'the bad baron'. In March 1939 Major Vivian of MI6 wrote to Jane Sissmore[197] of MI5, 'I rather gathered the impression that, if the bad baron were immersed in boiling oil, our friend would be only too happy.'[198]

It is worth pondering whether this fraternal animosity was real or confected. Friedrich dates the estrangement to 1925 but he was still taking Bill's children to Germany for the summer holidays in 1926 and 1927. Furthermore, in Berlin the two brothers must have bumped into each other on occasions. Bill's flat in Kurfürstendamm and Friedrich's office cum apartment at 107 Kurfürstenstrasse can only have been half a mile apart. The brothers also shared many of the same friends and contacts, such as Brüning, Treviranus, Seitz and Church.

Bill had every reason to appear to distance himself from a man who was widely suspected of being a German agent. And yet it does seem that the split was genuine. Bill did not go to Friedrich's daughter's wedding in 1939 (which was awash with guests in German army uniforms) or to Friedrich's funeral in 1964. Indeed the family never even thought to inform Bill of Friedrich's death.[199]

Maybe it was because the brothers were too similar. They both lived secret lives. Friedrich was clearly the wealthier,* the more extrovert and self-confident. His ability to get alongside key targets was astonishing, as was his sheer energy. However, his projects had a high failure rate. Bill was more cautious and reflective. He liked to take his time and make sure that his plans would work.

As the Nazi era dawned the brothers would be pulled even further apart.

* He had been successful as a miner in Africa, and his wife Lili came from a prosperous family.

11

'STARTLING DISCLOSURES'

1925–1930: The journalist spy in Berlin

Encouraged by the lack of a dependable salary from MI6, Bill launched himself into journalism. He was already well connected with the *Daily Mail* from his Baltic days, and in Berlin he was even closer to *The Times* team. He had taken Archibald Church to dinner with H. G. Daniels, the Bureau Chief, and his assistant Norman Ebbutt in September 1925 and had invited the Daniels out to Grünheide for lunch.

At the Savile Club Bill had also met John Balderston, an American who had been a war correspondent in Europe and was now a budding playwright in London. From 1920 he had also been Editor of the magazine *Outlook*. He invited Bill to write three articles on Africa, based on his recent travels in Kenya and visits to Tanganyika and Mozambique.

The articles, all published during 1926, are conservative in tone but also reformist in that they seek better relations with the African population – though they are, of course, 'of their time'. Bill was quick to identify the flaws of German rule in Tanganyika and of Portuguese colonial practices in Mozambique, which he contrasted with what he saw as the more equitable system of the British. The articles also drew on the findings of the Ormsby-Gore Commission and the East Africa Governors' Conference.[200]

Balderston's influence and the genuine quality of Bill's writing procured him further commissions from *Outlook* credited to 'Our Berlin correspondent'. Their importance for our purposes is that they chronicle how Bill's expertise on Germany finally persuaded MI6 (since 1926 based at their new head office in Broadway opposite St James's Park underground station) to re-engage him as a full-time and well-paid agent.

His first piece on 'Germany inside the League' following Berlin's entry to the League of Nations in Geneva demonstrates Bill's ability as a political analyst as well as his excellent written English. He focuses on Germany's collective depression since the war and the desire to see the removal of the Allied armies from occupied areas. It concludes with some thoughts about the dangers of Russia's possible entry into the League. 'No mention is made of the Soviet's subversive propaganda which would receive a new stimulus . . . Geneva would serve as a most useful platform for the dissemination of the Soviet's World Revolutionary ideas.'[201]

Writing for journals, even in the 1920s, did not pay the bills – 1926 was also the year when Bill became a representative in Germany for the Bristol Aeroplane Company. The company, founded in 1910 by Sir George White, was based at Filton and was famous for having produced the Bristol Fighter, one of the most successful aircraft of the Great War. Since the war their focus had been on engine manufacture. In 1919 Bristol acquired Cosmos Engineering and its chief engineer, Roy Fedden, who had invented the Jupiter radial engine. Roy Fedden and Bristol's Sales Director Ken Bartlett would become close companions of Bill's in the years ahead as German military aviation became the top intelligence priority of the British government.[202]

The timing was no coincidence. In May 1925 MI6's Air Section had decided that it needed to be 'well-informed about all aeronautical development'. It also specifically identified civil aviation as a way for agents to 'obtain military information of great value'.[203]

The strong probability is that Bill's new role was fixed up by a young officer called John Darwin. Darwin had fought in France with the Coldstream Guards and had been wounded before transferring to the RFC where he formed 87 Squadron and won the DSO. In April 1923 he was appointed to the Air Ministry Department of Intelligence where he increasingly began to work for Quex (Hugh) Sinclair who became C in the same year.[204] This was an area of cooperation between MI6 and the Air Ministry which we shall see proliferate in later chapters. The relationship between the Bristol Aeroplane Company, the Air Ministry and MI6 also dates to this period. It would later get much closer and develop real significance.

In February 1926 Benbow Hebbert (*see* pp.95–6) reported to MI5 that he was aware of a conference in Berlin attended by 'a number of Germans, de Ropp, his brother and an officer named Darwin of the British air intelligence service . . . to discuss the means of obtaining aeroplanes for Germany.'[205] He added that the Germans 'were aware of Darwin's identity and consequently no business resulted'. Hebbert said he had obtained this information from Wilhelm von Kries, the London-based journalist whom MI5 suspected of being a German spy, and added that he thought Bill de Ropp was 'still attached' to the British intelligence service. Hebbert's account was distrusted by MI5, not least because his brother was serving with British Intelligence and may have been the real source of his information.[206]

The terms of the Versailles Treaty had been particularly harsh on German aviation. Germany was only allowed to maintain one hundred seaplanes or flying boats. Staffing was limited to one thousand men and Germany was not permitted to maintain an air force. A long game of cat-and-mouse ensued as Germany tried to hide aircraft and engines in factories, rural barns and even private houses. However, the Allies were in no mood to compromise and by the end of 1921 15,714 aircraft and 27,757 engines had been found and destroyed.[207]

Even the construction of civil aircraft was restricted until 1922 but thereafter the civilian aviation sector expanded rapidly. Naturally enough the Germans sought ways to exploit civil aviation for future military requirements.

Bill authored a two-part article for *Outlook* on 'German Flying Progress' for publication in November 1926.[208] Earlier that year several German airlines had been consolidated into Lufthansa, and Bill marvelled at how the German airline industry had developed so fast in spite of the restrictions imposed by Versailles. The second part of the article, published one week later, was more discerning as Bill, the inveterate spy, focused on areas of particular interest.[209] The first was German night-flying capabilities, learnt during the war, and now being used on international routes to Copenhagen, Stockholm and Malmö. He then switched to what clearly concerned him the most, flights to the East.

'The foundation of the Russo-German Air Traffic Co., the Deruluft, whose capital was subscribed in equal parts by the Deutsche Aero Lloyd and the Soviet Government marked a most important development in commercial aviation in Eastern Europe. The Deruluft was granted the monopoly for the airline [route] Berlin–Konigsberg–Moscow the only rapid mode of communication between Western Europe and the Bolshevik capital.' It is typical that Bill used the word Bolshevik rather than Russian. He then continues, 'Specially constructed Fokker machines fitted with 360hp Rolls Royce engines were selected for the long flight from Königsberg to Moscow.' Plans were afoot to extend the route to Peking using three-engine Junkers aircraft.

The aircraft with the Rolls-Royce Eagle engines was the Dutch-built Fokker F.III but some later variants used the Bristol Jupiter VI.

The three-engined aircraft was the Junkers G-24.[210] A later variant (G-31) would also be powered by the Bristol Jupiter. As late as 1929 foreign engines dominated the German market, especially the Napier Lion (made in London), and the Bristol Jupiter made under licence by Siemens as the SAM22B.[211]

The Bristol business model involved engine manufacture at their factory in Filton, near Bristol, but demand for the Jupiter was so great that they reached licensing agreements for local production with several countries including Italy (Alfa Romeo), Sweden, Poland, France (Gnome et Rhone), Russia, Japan (Nakajima) and Germany.

Siemens and Halske were based at Siemensstadt, their company suburb, outside Berlin. They already had experience building radial engines and were soon producing the Jupiter in large numbers including for the Dornier X flying boat, a vast aircraft which required no fewer than twelve Jupiters. Designed in 1925, it made its first flight on Lake Constance in 1929.

Bill de Ropp had a three-fold reason for his interest in German aviation: selling Bristol engines for civil aircraft, watching out for the potential military use of civil aviation, and tracking the expansion of Russo-German relations since the Rapallo Treaty of 1922.

Two CX reports survive in the National Archives dating from 1928. which describe the nature and depth of Russo-German cooperation on aviation training, and even the exchange of intelligence – for example on recent Polish military manoeuvres.[212]

Whitehall was barely interested in developments in Germany, however, not even in the use of civil aviation as a cover for building an air force. Much of the governing class still believed that France had obliged the Allies to be too harsh on Germany in the Treaty of Versailles and that some infringements of the rules should be tolerated. The focus in London remained on the domestic British economy, industrial relations and disarmament.

There is nothing more dispiriting than producing good intelligence for it to be ignored by government because it is inconvenient and would require significant and burdensome changes in policy. This is when intelligence can sometimes be leaked to newspapers at moments of maximum leverage.

This may be what happened in the case of the various articles that appeared on the main news page of the *Manchester Guardian* on 3 December 1926. This was the very day that British Foreign Secretary Sir Austen Chamberlain arrived in Paris to continue disarmament talks with his opposite number Aristide Briand before going on to Geneva to meet the German Foreign Minister Dr Gustav Stresemann. The timing was theoretically perfect to ensure that Chamberlain and Briand would ask Stresemann some difficult questions and to ensure that Stresemann (who was not pro-Russian) would bring an end to this covert cooperation.

The *Guardian*'s headlines read:

CARGOES OF MUNITIONS FROM RUSSIA TO GERMANY
Secret plan between Reichswehr officers and the Soviet
STARTLING DISCLOSURES
Military intrigues to be stopped by German government

The page contains two articles by the *Guardian*'s Berlin correspondent, Frederick Voigt,[213] but the real meat comes from an anonymous source described as 'a correspondent'. It begins, 'I am able to substantiate the surmise of your Berlin correspondent that Russia is involved in the trouble that has recently arisen over the secret activities of the Reichswehr.' The writer then goes on to allege, correctly, that Junkers had established a factory in Russia, that the construction of a poison gas plant was under way and that weapons were being secretly smuggled to Germany from Russia, and then continues, 'officers of the Reichswehr have travelled to and from Russia with false papers visaed by the Russian authorities. General von Seekht, until recently

Commander in Chief of the Reichswehr, was on the best of terms with the Russians.'[214] The correspondent finally quotes from a dispatch from the Russian ambassador in Berlin about 'how much the resignation of von Seekht was to be regretted'.

The writer was correct. Following the Treaty of Rapallo in 1922 with the Soviet Union the German aircraft manufacturer Junkers set up a factory at Fili near Moscow in 1923 and two years later the Reichswehr established a fighter training school at Lipetsk, deliberately chosen for its remoteness, 275 miles south-east of Moscow.

If the plan was to cause uproar in Germany against this covert collaboration, it failed. The *Berliner Tageblatt* was unapologetic: 'These industrial relations began in 1922 and were known to all German Chancellors and Foreign Ministers.'[215] The semi-covert cooperation would continue until September 1933 when the German airbase at Lipetsk finally closed.

There is no conclusive evidence that the anonymous source was Bill de Ropp. All we can do is point to several powerful circumstantial indicators.

The article was published just one week after the second of Bill's two pieces on aviation, which would have followed a period of research particularly focused on civil German-Russian cooperation. The writer was almost certainly based in Berlin and had cooperated with Voigt on the other two pieces on the same page. Words like 'surmise' and 'foundered' and constructions like 'not unaware' suggest he was a fluent English speaker.

The tone is much more censorious of the Soviets than of the Germans. The article mentions a communication from the Russian ambassador in Berlin to his government in Moscow, which suggests a remarkable level of access, unusual for a journalist but less so for an intelligence agent. De Ropp later told MI6 that the information had been leaked by Soviet sources to embarrass the emerging Nazi party.[216] Bill could have published it in *The Times*, where he was well known and regarded as a member of their Berlin team but could not have done so anonymously. Finally, Voigt was, for many years, in close touch with MI6.[217]

If Bill was the anonymous source one can only speculate whether he had sent his report through his case officer to Head Office, which had then suggested he leak it to a newspaper because politicians were taking no notice of CX. Or did he go solo, knowing that the penalty would be no worse than a sharp reprimand? Having already been part of a conspiracy involving MI6, Bill may have learnt some bad habits.

In October 1926 Bill wrote about 'Business revival in Germany'. Much of it is upbeat, welcoming a business rapprochement with France and the disillusion amongst Social Democrats in Marxist economics but, as usual, Bill's worry was about Russia and Bolshevism:

> The German banks and industries have granted a loan of three hundred million marks to the Soviet. Thus the materialistic forces of Russian Communism are beginning to ally themselves with the materialistic forces of Central Europe . . . The danger must not be overlooked that this policy must inevitably strengthen the position of the Bolshevik power in the East. [218]

At the end of November 1926 Bill published an article on 'Airships' in *Outlook*.[219] Apart from being a fascinating read, its main significance is to confirm that it was always Bill de Ropp behind the byline of 'Our Berlin Correspondent'. The detail on the use of wartime balloons (including kite balloons) and the perils of the 'incendiary bullet' for any craft filled with inflammable gas fits neatly with what we know of Bill's wartime experience. Others also wrote on German affairs, including the historian Sir Charles Petrie (who was attracted by Mussolini's achievements in Italy) and Sanford Griffith of the *New York Herald Tribune*. They used their own names and lesser-known authors were described as 'A Berlin correspondent' not 'Our Berlin correspondent'.

Outlook gave every impression of flourishing. Vera Brittain wrote on women's issues, Lady Curzon on lifestyle subjects, Hilaire Belloc on Literature, Phyllis Satterthwaite (twice a Wimbledon finalist) on tennis, and Commander J. M. Kenworthy, the Labour MP for Hull, on military affairs.

In April 1927 Bill wrote 'Political cross-currents in Germany'.[220] He examines the far left, far right and centrists. Of the former he remarks on their 'discipline probably due to the strong influence exerted by Moscow . . . It is said that Russian Red Army instructors are lent to the *Roter Frontkämpferbund* (Alliance of Red Front Fighters) in order to inculcate the Communist youth with fighting spirit and the blind obedience demanded of Russia's Red troops.'

On the right Bill identifies the Stahlhelm (the veterans' association) with its eight thousand local branches as crucial. As we shall see, Bill would become close to one of the leaders of this organisation. He observes that the National Socialists under Hitler and Ludendorff had been the most important group on the right until their failed coup (the Beer Hall Putsch of November 1923). He concludes that National Associations 'preach the need for keeping the German race free from the incursions of Slav and Semitic elements' and that 'the idea of a rapprochement between the English-speaking nations and Germany is being seriously discussed in German Nationalist quarters.' Little did he realise that he would be discussing these very issues with Adolf Hitler himself only four years later.

It must have been a shock to Bill when *Outlook* suddenly collapsed in June 1928. A prestigious magazine which had begun in 1898 folded so quickly that its final edition did not even mention its imminent demise. Balderston's biographical notes in the New York Public Library give us a clue as to why.

> [At the end of the war] I bought a failing six-penny weekly in London, called *The Outlook*, so took it over lock, stock and barrel, hoping to do something to straighten out the mess,

> a considerable ambition for a youth of thirty, but I plugged away at it for several years until all the money was gone.[221]

One of Bill's last articles for *Outlook* was entitled 'Religious revival in Germany' and must have reminded him of the religious strife in his own family after his mother's conversion to Missouri Lutheranism. He foresees trouble ahead because 'the growth of Communism among the working class, the dominating position held by Jewish finance, and the intense spiritual restlessness of the younger generation of Germany gravely imperil the power of both the Protestant and Catholic churches.'[222]

It took the British government a long time to recognise that Germany might pose a threat in the future. Maurice Hankey, Chairman of the Committee of Imperial Defence (CID), was the British government's best strategic thinker, helped by his longevity in the role. As early as 1929 he realised that the Ten-Year Rule needed to be rescinded. This was the rule introduced in 1919 which assumed that there would be no major wars for ten years. This fed through into budgetary decisions about naval and military strength. In 1919 nobody could conceive of fighting another war after the slaughter in Flanders. The Great War had surely been 'the war to end all wars'.

Rather like stopping an oil tanker at sea, it took until 1933 before the Ten-Year rule was (de facto) repealed. But 1930 was the moment when realisation dawned for a perceptive few. In December 1929 the British occupation force was withdrawn from Germany. Far from being greeted with enthusiasm, the move 'produced an upsurge of xenophobia in Germany'[223] with President Hindenburg putting forward additional demands. In September 1930 the NSDAP (Nazi Party) polled 6.5 million votes and increased its representation in the Reichstag from 12 to 107 seats. Hankey 'saw all the secret intelligence reports which showed that undercover rearmament was being carried out on a wide scale in Germany'.[224] He, Vansittart and Sir Horace

Rumbold, the British ambassador in Berlin, were among the very first to realise that Germany had the potential to involve Britain in a second world war.

What Britain needed more than anything else was good intelligence on German capabilities and intentions, including the political and foreign policy aspirations of the vociferous parties of the extreme right. This was to be Bill de Ropp's big chance.

12

'A GENTLEMAN'S AGREEMENT BETWEEN TWO SOLDIERS'

1931: Bill de Ropp 'gets alongside' Rosenberg and Hitler

Bill de Ropp's cultivations of Alfred Rosenberg and of Adolf Hitler were a masterclass in espionage, demonstrating that Bill possessed innate skills as a spy. Within months he transformed himself from a utility agent, capable of running a variety of tasks for his occasional controllers at Broadway, to a deep-cover spy reporting from the heart of Germany. At the same time he morphed from being a jobbing operator being paid occasional tranches of £50 to a fully salaried source who eventually earned £1,000 per annum, making him one of MI6's best-paid agents worldwide.[225]

It would be reassuring to think that this was all part of a carefully crafted process by Menzies and Woollcombe. In an ideal world they would have booked a conference room at Head Office with a blackboard and plenty of coloured chalks for a brainstorming session with a thermos of black coffee on a trolley in the corner. One would have expected at least two officers from Berlin station to be present including Frank Foley himself. Woollcombe would have placed a dot in the centre of the blackboard signifying Hitler and then two concentric circles. He would have stressed that the service was not trying to recruit a top Nazi at this stage. Instead they were attempting to identify the best source of intelligence for Bill de Ropp.

Around the first of the rings would be the names of Hitler's 'inner circle'. In 1930 this would have included men like Hermann Göring, Rudolf Hess, Joseph Goebbels, Alfred Rosenberg, Ernst Röhm and Gregor Strasser. On the edge of the second circle would be less well-known figures who might have particular reasons for inclusion; for example Ernst Bohle who had been born in Bradford or the fun-loving 'Putzi' Hanfstaengl who was half-American.

Hitler himself would have been only briefly discussed. It would be difficult for Bill de Ropp to get access to the Nazi leader without the fact coming to the attention of observers who might seek to make trouble either for Hitler or for de Ropp. There was no getting away from the fact that Bill was a British citizen who had fought with the British army during the Great War. Some people might also recall that he had interrogated German prisoners for Lord Northcliffe's Propaganda Ministry and had been based in Berlin whilst serving under Major General Neill Malcolm, Chief of the British Military Mission, in 1919. Nobody, it was to be hoped, knew that he had subsequently been recruited by MI6 – but the possibility was hardly an enormous imaginative stretch.

By contrast, Hitler's inner circle would have provided plenty of scope for discussion. Göring, the corpulent and extrovert former Great War flying ace, would have merited a lengthy conversation. Socially he was a few cuts above the other Nazis and would surely have ridiculed them in private to his friends and family. As we shall see, Wing Commander Grahame Christie invested a lot of time in Göring to good effect. He produced some impressive reporting for Vansittart and might have mined real secrets if the relationship had been professionally handled by MI6 instead of by Christie himself, a well-meaning but amateur sleuth. Göring was committed fully to the Nazi regime and remained loyal to it even in the dock at Nuremberg in 1946, but he did have his disagreements with Hitler and particularly with Himmler and Goebbels and was not shy in talking about them.

Rudolf Hess would also have been worth lengthy consideration. He had been brought up in a middle-class setting in British-administered Alexandria in Egypt. He too may have thought himself a few rungs better than his colleagues. He was also introverted, thoughtful and solitary but was also Hitler's closest confidant. MI6 would later become very familiar indeed with Hess after he flew to Britain in May 1941, and would discover the extent of the mental problems that would have made him such a difficult source to evaluate. It is possible that Hess feigned some of his bizarre behaviour after discovering the extent of his blunder in 1941 but the same peculiarities surfaced in Nuremberg in 1946 and during his long detention in Spandau prison.

Amongst the other names discussed Rosenberg would have been the most prominent. He too was different from the other Nazis. He was well educated to university level. He was a Baltic German from Estonia and therefore would have felt less sure of his German heritage. He had spent time in Russia and had been there during the 1917 Revolution before moving back to Estonia and then Germany after the end of the Great War. There were some Nazi mutterings that he was a French agent because of a holiday spent in Paris in 1914 or even a Jew because of his name. However, Hitler remained loyal to him. Rosenberg had written some bizarre books about Aryan supremacy but he saw himself as the Nazis' foreign affairs guru and as their future Foreign Minister. That fact alone would place him high on MI6's target list.

Ernst Röhm would have been seen as too thuggish, and Joseph Goebbels as too zealous. Gregor Strasser was too socialist and thus unlikely to survive in the NSDAP. In the end Rosenberg would probably have been the choice – less high-profile than Göring and Hess and therefore more accessible.

The meeting in Broadway, however, never happened. Brainstorming was not a concept in 1930 and MI6 simply did not think of 'targeting' future sources in that way. In the twenty-one years since its creation MI6 had mostly recruited agents who had either offered their services or become available in some other way.

From time to time MI6 officers stationed abroad recruited good agents but almost always from people they had met in the course of their duties as PCOs (Passport Control Officers; *see* p.68). The concept of targeting as a professional exercise was more than a decade and a half in the future and would become standard during the long years of the Cold War against the Soviet Union. Those who served in Broadway during the 1950s, before the service moved to Century House in Lambeth, cannot even remember a conference room.[226]

Furthermore, even in 1930, nobody thought that Hitler would become Chancellor of Germany, still less the Führer whose very existence would dominate and transform Europe for the next fifteen years, leading to the most destructive war in human history. One file in the National Archives, known as the 'Adolf Hitler scrapbook' kept by War Office officials, reveals how little was known about Hitler and his inner circle by 1930.[227]

In 1930 MI6's main target was still the Soviet Union but Head Office at Broadway had decided, quite rightly, that Hitler's electoral success in 1930 did now merit a more thorough effort to understand the NSDAP and its leader. This meant a step-change from using Bill de Ropp as an occasional source under journalistic cover. The incentive was offered of a reliable monthly salary in exchange for well-sourced secret intelligence from insiders within the party itself. This was not to be business as usual.

Bill de Ropp got the message. Fortunately we know exactly how he went about this task because he explained it in his *Daily Mail* articles in October 1957. He started with an ambitious plan. 'I should make friends with Hitler while he was no more than the leader of a minority, if boisterous, party and stay with him as his friend if he rose to power.'[228]

This may sound like hubris but it makes perfect sense. Once they become prime ministers or presidents it becomes extremely hard to meet world leaders. They soon have an outer office with a chief of staff and a diary secretary who control access to their boss. New political leaders, however, do tend to stay loyal to the friends and contacts who supported them during the tough times in opposition.

Bill then pondered his 'plan of action'. He could use his existing journalistic cover to request an interview but reckoned he would just receive the party line in return. He could join the NSDAP party and become an enthusiastic Nazi but risked coming under suspicion because of his British nationality. The third way, which he chose, was to gradually navigate towards Hitler 'posing as a sympathetic Britisher'.[229]

He began with his old friend Baron Walter von Medem whom we last encountered in 1919 recapturing Riga from the Bolshevik forces. The von Medems were also Balts and had owned large estates in Courland, which became part of Latvia. Since the failure of Friedrich's coup Walter had become a journalist on the conservative newspaper *Der Tag* while also being a member of the Stahlhelm (The Steel Helmet), the organisation for German war veterans. The Stahlhelm had become a right-wing militia although it did not formally join the Nazis until 1934.

Von Medem introduced de Ropp to a Major Hans Berthold, a veteran of the war against the British in South-West Africa, who was also in the Stahlhelm but increasingly frustrated by its relative inactivity. It was he who put Bill in touch with a serious Nazi official, Arno Schickedanz, the Berlin correspondent of the Nazis' Munich-based newspaper *Völkischer Beobachter* (*VB*). Schickedanz was also a fellow Balt from Riga. He was not a Baltic aristocrat but Bill had the social skills to get on with people of all backgrounds.

Birmingham University, Australia and the Royal Flying Corps had taught Bill how to mix beyond his social milieu. Like all good spies Bill was a good listener.

> I invited him to a real Russian dinner at a Russian restaurant, complete with zakouski and vodka. Young Arno turned out to be a merry lad with a strong and irreverent sense of humour. Those were lean and hungry days for the Nazis and he made no secret of the fact that he enjoyed our meals as much as my company.[230]

Bill too enjoyed the good things of life and his expenses became a bone of contention at Broadway, which was run on a very tight budget by Commander Percy Sykes, known as 'Pay'. In the years ahead Bill would make effective use of the numerous cafés and restaurants near his flat on Kurfürstendamm.[231] Café Kranzler, of which there was also a branch in Unter den Linden, was a favourite; Kakadu (Cockatoo) was popular and often had a cabaret; Romanisches Café was artistic with a large Jewish clientele; the Zigeunerkeller was owned by the famous restaurateur Karl Kutschera and served Hungarian cuisine in its 'gypsy cellar'. As the years went by, the Zigeunerkeller and Kutschera's Café Wien would attract increasing Nazi scrutiny and hostility.

It was only a matter of time before Schickedanz suggested that Bill should meet his boss and old friend, the editor of *VB*, Alfred Rosenberg. It was Arno who set up the slightly awkward meeting for Bill at the Anhalter Station in Berlin where Rosenberg was waiting for a train to Munich. As Bill remarked of Rosenberg, 'Austere and deadly serious, he was not an easy person to make contact with. But he too was a Balt, so again my ancestry came in useful. Indeed he knew more about my family than I did.'[232] With Rosenberg's train about to depart they agreed to meet for tea on the K'damm on his next trip to Berlin.

> Our next meeting was a huge success. Our conversation roamed from politics to Nietzsche, from Hinduism to Taoism, from Britain to Bolshevism. Rosenberg, although a mediocre public speaker, was a most interesting talker in company which he found congenial and when the subjects under discussion interested him.[233]

So began the most important MI6 operation against pre-war Nazi Germany. Although it produced some good analysis of Nazi attitudes and broad intentions it also had significant limitations and they are to be found in the character of one of the most disturbing men of the twentieth century.

Rosenberg was born in 1893 in Reval (now Tallinn) in Estonia into a middle-class German family. His father was a director of a local German company. His mother died when he was young. After school in Reval he went on to study architecture at the Technical University in Riga. There he joined the Rubonia Club where he first met Arno Schickedanz. In the summer of 1914 he visited Paris with his girlfriend Hilda whom he married the following year. At the outbreak of the Great War the university moved to Moscow.

The Russian Revolution took place while he was there but he completed his course before returning to Reval. Perhaps appropriately, the design he submitted for his diploma was for a crematorium. At the end of November 1918 he moved to Germany only weeks after its catastrophic defeat in the war.[234]

Rosenberg will be a key character in the chapters that follow. In many ways he was the ideal contact for Bill de Ropp. He had few friends and was widely denigrated by the likes of Goebbels. He craved acceptance, particularly from Hitler. His so-called philosophical ideas bored most Nazis (including Hitler) and in Bill de Ropp he found someone who was prepared to listen. He may never have realised that Bill only took an interest because he was being paid by MI6 to obtain intelligence.

Bill de Ropp continues his narrative. One day he 'casually mentioned' to Rosenberg that he and his wife would be spending a week or two at Garmisch, the winter resort close to Munich where Rosenberg and Hitler were still based. Rosenberg took the bait: 'Would you like to meet Hitler while you are there?'

It was early in 1931 that Bill and Jimmy travelled to Garmisch. Bill would have left Jimmy for the day at their chalet and taken the train back to Munich from Garmisch-Partenkirchen station. It was under ninety minutes to Munich on the newly electrified single-track line with its views of Lake Starnberg on the right-hand side. Bill would have been tense and smoking heavily. A lot was riding on this meeting going well. Indeed if it went badly he might find himself frozen out from all contact with the Nazi hierarchy. He may have pondered whether he should not have been satisfied with Rosenberg. Perhaps Hitler was a step too far.

On arrival at Munich Hauptbahnhof Bill would have walked the five blocks to the offices of the *VB* at 39/41 Schellingstrasse. He and Rosenberg – who was editor from 1923 to 1938 – had settled into armchairs in the editor's cramped office when Hitler 'burst in. He was dressed in an old trench-coat and an ill-fitting reach me down suit.'[235] Hitler did not waste time with any formalities but plunged into his first question: 'What do the English think about my movement?' In particular he wanted to know what 'well-intentioned politicians' say.

Bill played a very straight bat. 'They say that a great deal of what you preach is justified but that you are too radical.' This set Hitler off into a long 'harangue' about the Treaty of Versailles, the confiscation of Germany's colonies, the Jews and the 'stab in the back' at the end of the war.[236] Bill might have reflected on the irony that it was his old boss, General Malcolm, who had given this name to the fiction of Germany's betrayal in November 1918.*

---

* General Malcolm had used this term during dinner with the defeated German General von Ludendorff in February 1919. It was later used by Ludendorff to explain Germany's defeat and then taken up as a wider conspiracy theory.

Hitler then asked about the Jewish question. Here we must be sceptical of Bill's claimed response: 'It seems to me rather absurd to condemn an entire race. Many of our Jews fought with distinction in our army and the same must have been the case in the German forces.'[237] He then claims to have added, 'I personally know some Jews whom I like very much.' This sent Hitler into a rage and he shouted at the top of his voice, 'I shall annihilate the Jews.' Suddenly his rage ended and he talked calmly about the colonies before he abruptly left the room.

Bill had the walk back to Munich station and then the train journey to Garmisch to rake over the embers of a seemingly disastrous meeting. Rosenberg had gently chided him, 'Dear friend, Hitler hates the Jews as much as I do and he detests smoke.' Only then did Bill realise that he had chain-smoked throughout the meeting. He also recalled that Hitler had been extremely abrupt, calling him 'Herr' instead of 'Herr Baron' or 'Liebe Herr' or 'Herr de Ropp'. He saw this as a studied insult.

Back at their chalet Bill told Jimmy about the meeting, describing Hitler as a lunatic. However he also pondered how to manage similar situations in the future in the unlikely event that there would be further meetings. He decided on a plan which had some merits but would have far-reaching consequences. In future, he would adopt the strategy that he personally agreed with Hitler but that his influential friends in England did not. Bill would calibrate the views of his 'influential friends' to provoke future indiscretions such as his comment about annihilating the Jews.

Two days later, and to Bill's astonishment, Hitler requested Rosenberg to set up another meeting. Rosenberg suggested they should drive to Garmisch to have tea with Bill and Jimmy but neither of them 'wanted this stormy petrel invading our peaceful Garmisch where we had many highly respectable friends'.[238] Thinking quickly on his feet he said that he had to go into Munich to collect some books and so they agreed to meet again at Rosenberg's *VB* office.

This time Hitler was in a more amiable mood and he soon explained why he had requested this second meeting. He said that his supporters 'are too inclined to tell me what they think I want to hear. If you could keep me informed of what, in your opinion, the English really think, you will not only render me a service but it would be to the advantage of your country . . .' He added, 'It goes without saying that this is a gentleman's agreement between two soldiers and I shall never expect you to give me any information that you should not give to a foreigner.'[239]

Bill de Ropp returned to Garmisch for a second time in a more buoyant mood. 'Here was exactly what I needed . . . Considering how garrulous he was, I could expect a good deal of useful information.'

We should pause at this point and assess what had just happened. Perhaps Menzies and Woollcombe did the same at 54 Broadway when they received Bill's report.

First was the excellent news that Bill de Ropp was now 'alongside' (MI6 still uses such naval terms, thanks to its heritage) both Rosenberg and Hitler. The prospects for future intelligence were good, although Woollcombe would have understood the need to sort out the real intelligence from any special pleading by Hitler.

Secondly Bill had been completely up-front about his Britishness. It was far better to be blatant about it than to attempt to conceal or downplay the fact. In spite of his friendship with Rosenberg, Hitler was normally suspicious of Balts. He once said, 'I often find it difficult to get on with our Baltic families; they seem to possess a negative sort of quality and at the same time to assume an air of superiority.'[240]

Thirdly Rosenberg would be delighted with the outcome because it would win him Hitler's approval, secure him more access to his leader and buy him additional credibility as a future foreign policy chief. It would also enable Bill to see a lot more of Rosenberg.

Fourthly Hitler's line about both being soldiers was important. There was a bond between men who had fought in the Great War; something that would always make Rosenberg feel inferior.

Bill's terrifying days in a kite balloon moored over the Western Front might pay interest at last.

But two aspects should have given pause for thought. Bill's decision to portray himself as a sympathiser was fine as a tactical ploy but would need careful monitoring. It could lead to Bill producing intelligence for London that was skewed. When speaking to a sympathiser people tend to skip over some of the negative issues which a sceptic might be better able to elicit.

Secondly Hitler's request that Bill become his confidential adviser on British matters also carried potential risk. It might encourage Bill, over time, to divulge confidential insights obtained in London in the hope of obtaining additional intelligence from Hitler. This would require Menzies and Woollcombe to remain constantly aware of the cost–benefit equation.

We should also consider Hitler's threat to annihilate the Jews. While there is good reason to be doubtful about Bill's own comments on Jews (not least because anti-Semitism was so rife amongst the upper classes of most European nations in the 1930s) there is no reason to dispute Hitler's statement.

We shall never know if MI6 sent any of Hitler's comments to Whitehall as a CX report because almost all the CX of that period has been destroyed.[241] If they did produce a CX report, the contents would not have surprised anybody – Hitler is not explicit in *Mein Kampf* about wanting to kill Jews but his venom towards them is so extreme and irrational as not to rule out thoughts of genocide. [242] At one point he wrote, 'if twelve or fifteen thousand of these Jews who were corrupting the nation had been forced to submit to poison gas' then the millions of deaths at the front 'would not have been in vain'.[243]

Even assuming that Bill de Ropp remembered Hitler's words (or general meaning) correctly twenty-seven years later (which is not impossible given the clarity of what Hitler allegedly said), would a CX report distributed around key Whitehall departments have made any difference? After all, Hitler was just a loud-mouthed populist with little chance (or so it seemed at the time) of getting into power. And what would Whitehall have done? In the years to come they would frequently disparage Hitler's comments about Jews but without backing their criticism with any practical sanctions.

Woollcombe might also have judged that the wild threat to annihilate the Jews was too significant to report without some form of corroborating reporting, either from another source or from a future meeting between Hitler and Bill de Ropp. The prospect of German Jews fleeing to Palestine from a real or imagined future pogrom in Germany would have alarmed the British government. Britain administered Palestine under a League of Nations mandate and was desperately trying to balance Palestinian rights against an influx of Jewish migrants with overly high expectations following the 1917 Balfour Declaration, which spoke of 'a national home for the Jewish people' but also that 'nothing should be done to prejudice the civil and religious rights of existing non-Jewish communities in Palestine.'[244]

However, Menzies and Woollcombe would surely have recognised one particular aspect of Bill de Ropp's brilliant crab-like approach to Hitler and its five stages: von Medem–Berthold–Schickedanz–Rosenberg–Hitler. The crab simile is apt because Bill de Ropp always moved sideways; only at the first stage did he ask to be put in touch with the Nazis. At every other stage it was his interlocutor who suggested meeting his boss.

Later in the 1930s Bill would come under very real suspicion of being a British spy. If the SD, Gestapo or Abwehr had ever ordered a drains-up investigation into the case they would have asked the killer question of any espionage investigation: 'Who made the first move?' Of Rosenberg they would have asked: 'Did Bill de Ropp ask you for an introduction to Hitler' and the truthful answer would have been: 'No, it was my idea.'

MI6 was not as clueless in the 1930s as some observers* have

* Notably Hugh Trevor-Roper who served briefly in MI6 during the war, and Kim Philby, whose motives were malign.

claimed but it is possible and even likely that nobody had these difficult thoughts following Bill de Ropp's successful second meeting with Hitler. Certainly, no one had any idea how complicated life would become having an agent in direct contact with the world's most dangerous man.

We do not know how often Hitler and Bill de Ropp met over the next eight years although there is evidence of at least a dozen meetings. The importance of the relationship was not just in the intelligence it produced but in that it gave Rosenberg top-cover for maintaining his friendship with de Ropp and it served as a warning to the likes of Canaris, Himmler and Heydrich, who may have harboured suspicions, to direct their inquisitive attentions elsewhere.

13

'THE LIVING EMBODIMENT OF RACE HATRED'

1931–1933: Triumph and disaster for Rosenberg in London

Following the success of Bill de Ropp's approach to Hitler in January 1931 the relationship with Rosenberg flourished:

> I used to meet Rosenberg every week, either in his office or in his home where I spent many fascinating evenings talking Nazi politics and philosophy, collecting news and gossip. I often dined with Rosenberg. The food at his dinner table was execrable: generally stewed veal, damp vegetables and soggy pudding but the Burgundy was always excellent. His butler would be dressed in full SS uniform and in winter there would be a large log fire crackling.[245]

After a few months Bill had the idea of inviting Alfred Rosenberg to visit London. If Rosenberg were ever to become Germany's Foreign Minister, the role to which he aspired more than any other, he needed both to have high-level contacts in London and to be seen by his Nazi peers to be capable of operating at that altitude.

For MI6 this was an ambitious idea. The service was more used to lower-level activity, with communist agents, arms suppliers, and forgers. To arrange for an agent to bring his high-level contact to meet politicians, editors and society figures would require careful handling to avoid political repercussions, and also needed a certain degree of audacity.

Fortunately there was a new recruit at Broadway in the form of Squadron Leader Fred Winterbotham. A tall, good-looking man, he had served as a fighter pilot in the war and had been shot down, spending over a year in German captivity. Following the war he went up to Oxford to study law at Christ Church but then decided to go into farming, first in Gloucestershire and Scotland and later in Rhodesia (Zimbabwe). When he joined MI6 in 1930 he was brimming with self-confidence and exuberance. He was assigned to the post of Head of Air Intelligence, Section IV, with a cover role at the Air Ministry at Adastral House on Kingsway (where the Air Ministry had moved to after a period at the Cecil Hotel in the Strand).

In his book *The Nazi Connection*, he provides a good description of his arrival at Broadway:

> We entered the portals of what looked like a rather down at heel office building and were escorted up four flights in a large, slow lift by a blue-uniformed government messenger. There we were met by a smartly dressed type, obviously ex-service, who, unbeknown to me at the time, carried a revolver in his belt. We were guided along a richly carpeted passage to a thickly padded door, beyond which lay the office of the Chief of the British Secret Service, Admiral Sir Hugh Sinclair . . . As the Admiral got up from behind his large carved mahogany desk to greet me I saw a rather short stocky figure with the welcoming smile of a benign uncle. His handshake was as gentle as his voice and only the very alert dark eyes gave a hint of the tough personality that lay beneath the mild exterior.[246]

Winterbotham was joining a service with a stellar public reputation. Hugh Trevor-Roper, the future great historian, became an MI6 officer in 1941, and he provides an insight into both its reputation and his view of the reality. For the latter one must aim off for the author who Guy Liddell of MI5 labelled (with commendable understatement) 'something of an intellectual snob'. . .

> So I found myself in the Secret Service, that mysterious and powerful organisation of which in my boyhood I had read, admittedly in the form of novels . . . It had a myth about it in those days, a myth of ubiquity, infallibility, colourful exploits, dark doings, brilliant results. A myth moreover accepted abroad where its very name inspired awe and emulation . . . Foreign intelligence services envied the British Secret Services: it was their idealised model . . . The Soviet government, seeing conspiracies all around it, imagined the British Secret Service as their universal organiser.[247]

Trevor-Roper's biographer, Adam Sisman, writes:

> Hugh's boyhood illusions about SIS did not survive his first visit . . . He came to see the SIS as an example of a closed inward-looking society, recruiting by patronage, feeding on fantasy and self-perpetuating illusions and increasingly isolated from reality. Its members, he felt, tended to come from one of two unimpressive groups: rich men of limited intellect whose egos were boosted by membership of a secretive organisation with a romantic past; or retired officers of the Indian Police whose experience had been limited to harassing innocent Indians suspected of communist leanings. On the one hand, empty-headed members of the upper class, clubland habitués; on the other, unimaginative policemen whose brains had been scorched by the Indian sun.[248]

Patrick Reilly spent two years working at MI6 for Menzies and firmly rebutted this view. He only knew of three MI6 officers who frequented clubland and only two Indian policemen. 'My strong impression was that they (MI6) were a devoted body of men, loyal, discreet, with a strong esprit de corps, content to work hard in obscurity for little reward. What however is certainly true is that the pre-war SIS was small, poor and, to put it mildly, intellectually undistinguished.'[249]

Winterbotham was exactly the sort of new blood that MI6 needed. However, when taking over the role that Darwin had previously occupied, he soon realised that it was going to be tough to obtain genuinely secret intelligence on foreign aviation capabilities. The Air Ministry had made clear that it could obtain all the overt intelligence required. Air displays, magazine articles and reports from defence attachés overseas would bring in lots of material.

Sir Cyril Newall, the Deputy Chief of Air Staff, had told Winterbotham that 'a small amount of accurate information was worth far more than a large amount of nonsense.' The problem was where to start, and in his search for agents Winterbotham was not helped by the fact that the budget available to him was minuscule.

Casting around desperately for ideas, Winterbotham was impressed by some CX reports coming in from Germany about the Nazi party.

> I therefore asked whether the agent who had been reporting on the Hitler antics could be brought to London so that I might have a talk with him. I looked him up in our records and found that he was a man of about forty years of age, a Baltic Baron who had been dispossessed of his lands by the Bolsheviks. He was now resident in Berlin and was acting as a political correspondent of *The Times* newspaper . . . I arranged to meet Bill de Ropp . . . in the lounge of an hotel not far from our office where we normally entertained agents

> from overseas as it was obviously undesirable to have them at Head Office.[250]

This was St Ermin's Hotel barely a couple of hundred yards from Broadway. It was another sign of a rather young and naive service that it used to meet its agents so close to the office and all in the same place. MI6 would later pay a heavy price for this sort of carelessness, which hostile services, like the future KGB, would exploit.

When Winterbotham finally met Bill de Ropp:

> I must say that I was a little surprised to find a perfectly normal Englishman about 5 foot 10 with fair hair, a slightly reddish moustache and blue eyes dressed in a good English suit. As he got up to shake hands he greeted me in perfect English without any trace of an accent . . . He told me about his life in Berlin as a journalist and as a keen observer of the German political scene. He and his English wife had a small flat in the Kurfürstendamm.
>
> As our luncheon progressed it was clear to me that de Ropp was highly intelligent and had a spontaneous, neat sense of humour; there was nothing cumbersome about his talk or his thinking. He would obviously be able to make decisions quickly and he seemed from his conversation to be a good judge of character.

Bill then started to tell Winterbotham about his relationship with Rosenberg. 'Although Bill had been very calm and matter-of-fact when he was telling me about Rosenberg and the apparent aims of the Nazis, I scented an underlying excitement which I myself felt at the prospect of the upsurge of this new party; if it came off, and there seemed every reason to believe that it would, it would be a political time-bomb.'[251]

Given how Hitler would become one of the most important

intelligence targets of the twentieth century it is interesting that Woollcombe was willing to share his star political source with the head of the Air Section, especially as the Rosenberg and Hitler relationships were still new and not fully established.

There are two probable reasons. First, Hitler was not yet a big enough figure to warrant more than the occasional report. Second, Bill had already established a track record for reporting on civil aviation. His three reports for *Outlook* and his probable anonymous report for the *Manchester Guardian* were doubtless supplemented by CX reports for MI6.

Winterbotham asked Bill de Ropp how to approach the problem of obtaining aviation secrets. After a few weeks back in Germany, Bill contacted Winterbotham. 'He had talked to Rosenberg since he returned and that there was every prospect that he, Bill, might be put on the Nazi payroll as their English contact, a fully paid agent whose job would be to interpret the articles in *The Times* for Rosenberg: to try to influence Dawson, the paper's editor in London, to be sympathetic towards the Nazis; and to do everything possible to make important British contacts for the Nazis in England.' If Bill could introduce Rosenberg around London, he thought, there was a good chance that Winterbotham would be invited to Germany.

Winterbotham would have discussed the contents of Bill's message with both Woollcombe and Menzies. It is never desirable for an agent to be paid by a potentially hostile entity because that leads to a loss of control and the danger that the balance of advantage could shift over time. Obviously, it was good that Bill told MI6. Not to have done so would have been a serious cause for concern if ever discovered. However, in this case they probably calculated that the term 'English agent' did not mean secret agent. Rosenberg wanted him as his private consultant on British affairs. Rosenberg was not involved with the SD, the Abwehr or the Gestapo. He just wanted someone to help massage his image with the foreign press.

Sinclair consulted Vansittart at the FO, and gave Winterbotham the go-ahead to invite Rosenberg with the two provisos that it must be kept low-key and be presented as a private rather than an official visit. He added that if Winterbotham 'made a mess of it' his job would be in serious danger.

Winterbotham wrote of a 'glorious autumn day' – in fact, it was December (1931):*

> . . . when I met Bill and Rosenberg off the Harwich boat train at Liverpool Street Station. In Rosenberg I saw a reasonably well-built man of about my own age, some 5 foot 11, with dark hair, hard, somewhat roundish face and a blob of a nose. He had a pleasant smile and a firm handshake and was well dressed in a perfectly reasonable suit which, for some reason I never understood, still managed to proclaim he had come from the continent even though Bill had probably vetted his outfit. He seemed at first meeting intelligent and cheerful.

MI5 noticed Rosenberg's arrival although it could not identify 'Roth' (clearly a misspelling of Ropp). Vernon Kell, the Director General, wrote to the FO adding, 'I understand SIS have and are giving you a good deal of information about [Rosenberg].'[252] The other member of Rosenberg's party was Dr Hans Thost, who was the *VB* correspondent in London, albeit one with a semi-secret role to promote Rosenberg's reputation and to increase his understanding of Britain. MI5 were suspicious about Thost and opened his mail. In one letter in April 1932 Rosenberg advised him not to go beyond the bounds of his profession as a newspaper reporter and begged him to 'exercise great discretion and avoid friction in future'.[253] Rosenberg never fully trusted Thost and did not want him to foul up relations with Britain.

The key meeting of the visit for Rosenberg and Bill de Ropp was with *The Times*. Bill de Ropp had set up a lunch with the editor,

* He wrote from memory and his timings are often slightly awry.

Geoffrey Dawson. The session went well. Rosenberg was pleased to have met the editor of Britain's most influential newspaper, and Dawson felt he got across the message that the press in Britain was free from government control.

Bill had known Dawson during his Northcliffe days and Dawson was a witting collaborator in maintaining his cover, and content for Bill to tell people that he worked for *The Times*. It is interesting that Dawson did not refer to the lunch in his diary, doubtless because of the secrecy surrounding Bill's role. Research of *The Times* employment records in 2023 has shown that Bill was never an actual employee and he never filed a story under his own name. One other journalist on *The Times*, however, was aware of Bill's true role.

A. L. Kennedy (who sometimes wrote the foreign leaders) noted in his diary on 22 April 1933:

> I had luncheon the other day with Baron de Ropp, the one political spy I know who seems well worth his keep. He is just back from Germany and was v interesting about the internal affairs of the Nazi Party. A struggle is beginning between Göring and Goebbels, the extremists, against Hitler, backed by Rosenberg who are moderates. None of them really knows the world outside Germany, except that Rosenberg knows Russia and the Baltic states well. De R told me they study TT [*The Times*] minutely themselves but do not let its views percolate through the German press because they are too candid . . .
>
> De R said that the Nazis had got their knife into [Norman] Ebbutt [by now *The Times* senior Berlin correspondent] metaphorically speaking owing to his opposition to their movement. He said they would not dare do him any outward visible damage – but that if they were given the chance they would certainly get him run over by a motor car or otherwise accidentally done in. I must warn Ebbutt but carefully because the poor fellow is already much shaken by his experiences.[254]

Fortunately Ebbutt was not murdered but he was expelled in 1937. He was deeply anti-Nazi and one of his greatest frustrations was that his copy was altered back in Printing House Square. Under Dawson *The Times* was widely seen as an instrument of the appeasers, and he himself wrote as late as 1937, 'Personally I am, and always have been, anxious that we should "explore every avenue" in the search for a reasonable understanding with Germany . . . The more personal contact between the two nations the better.'[255]

Even more damaging was his leaked comment that 'I did my utmost, night after night, to keep out of the paper anything that might hurt their [Nazi] susceptibilities.'[256] However, Dawson's defenders point out that 'Never once was admiration expressed for Nazi Germany, although that it had made some positive achievements was neither denied nor begrudged.'[257] Furthermore *The Times* 'consistently urged the necessity for armaments'.[258]

The paper was seen in foreign capitals as 'the official spokesman for the British government'. This was a burden that Dawson had to bear but it was perfect for cementing Bill de Ropp's relationship with the Nazis.

One must ask whether Bill de Ropp had any effect on *The Times* editorial policy or indeed the expulsion of Ebbutt. In the latter case it was Goebbels and Ribbentrop who ensured that Ebbutt was removed. By 1937 Rosenberg had lost any influence in the fields of propaganda and (Western) foreign policy. As for the former there is no correspondence from Bill de Ropp in the Dawson archives at the Bodleian nor apparently any mention of him in his (almost illegible) diaries.

Fred Winterbotham padded out the Rosenberg visit with some other events. He relied entirely on memory in writing his books forty-five years later and there are some obvious errors. But there was a lunch with Rosenberg, Bill de Ropp and Winterbotham at which Rosenberg outlined some of his ideas for Germany's recovery and future dominance. They sounded sufficiently absurd that both Fred and Bill had to suppress smiles. Little did they know! Winterbotham spent a day driving Rosenberg and Bill around the Surrey countryside including a visit to his old school, Charterhouse.

He also arranged a cocktail party for Rosenberg at the RAF Club with some well-connected friends and colleagues. Archie Boyle (his notional boss at the Air Ministry) was a key guest as he helped reinforce Winterbotham's cover role. Allen Bathurst, Lord Apsley had been in the army and at university with Winterbotham. He was a former Minister of Transport in the Baldwin government with a distinguished war record. Bobby Perkins was the Conservative MP for Stroud. Nigel Norman was the principal organiser of private flying clubs in England and an expert in aviation who would later be involved with airborne troops in the Second World War. These were well-chosen guests by Winterbotham at a time when Rosenberg craved acceptance by the British establishment and insight into British aviation circles.*

The following day they had lunch with Oliver Locker-Lampson. Winterbotham claims to have set up the lunch, but Bill de Ropp would have known of Lampson's remarkable exploits. He had become a Conservative MP in 1910 but, in 1915, he was sent to Archangel with his naval armoured car squadron to form the Russian Armoured Car Division. After some extraordinary adventures he was withdrawn at the outbreak of the Russian Revolution but, by then, had developed close links to Russia and would doubtless have come into contact with MI6.

His anti-communism led him to found the Blue Shirts, the 'Sentinels of Empire', but his flirtation with fascism did not last long and he later tried to ban the wearing of political uniforms and introduced a bill in Parliament to give British citizenship to Jewish refugees. In 1930 Rosenberg just saw a fellow fascist in him, and on his return to Germany sent him a gold cigarette case which Lampson

* Ironically both Apsley and Norman would be killed in air crashes in the coming conflict against Rosenberg's Nazi regime.

promptly returned.[259]

Winterbotham waved Rosenberg and Bill de Ropp off at Liverpool Station on a cold, foggy December morning. The trip had been a great success in cementing the Rosenberg relationship with Bill de Ropp and there was every chance that Winterbotham would be invited to Germany.

Furthermore there had been very little press coverage and barely any criticism. *The Graphic* of 12 December 1931 sported the headline 'Scouting for Hitler':

> Alert and intelligent looking, smart in his English cut clothes, Dr Alfred Rosenberg has been walking about the streets of London . . . Dr Rosenberg is expected to be Foreign Minister in any potential Hitler cabinet and he may have wished to prepare himself for his task by visiting the country which his party, for some mysterious reason, expects to take the most favourable attitude if it reaches power.[260]

A historian of the early Nazi Party, Konrad Heiden, wrote in 1944:

> In December 1931 when Alfred Rosenberg went to London and became celebrated as 'one of the best dressed Germans' he spoke to English questioners almost as to friends. 'I admire the calm and assurance with which the English nation is combating its difficulties,' he said. 'The nation has no nerves and in this it is setting the world an example.' Germany, he said, expected the support of England in her demands both for the cancellation of reparations and an international adjustment of armaments. England, he declared, has a strong sense of justice.[261]

Rosenberg long harboured the notion that Great Britain was a natural ally of Nazi Germany. Bill de Ropp helped foster the idea, and kept it alive in Rosenberg's consciousness for many years to come.

By contrast Hitler was much more realistic. Heiden quotes Hitler as saying as early as 1924 that England 'had the single desire to Balkanise Europe in order to create a balance of power on the continent and prevent her world position from being threatened. She is not basically an enemy of Germany . . . France however is Germany's explicit enemy. As England requires the Balkanisation of Europe France requires the Balkanisation of Germany.'[262]

Hitler's view had not changed eight years later when he had a long discussion about Foreign Policy with Rosenberg's friend Kurt Lüdecke in September 1932. Even aiming off for Lüdecke exaggerating the stridency and fluency of his own arguments it was a fascinating exchange of views.[263] Lüdecke (writing in 1937) claims to have said:

> Would it be possible, even probable, that England could be induced to join a Nazi dictatorship in a crusade against Soviet Russia? Why should England help to Germanise Eastern Europe as far as the Urals? . . . Why should he [an Englishman] ally himself with an anti-Jewish, anti-Christian juggernaut to bring all of Central Europe and parts of Soviet Russia under Nazi control, make Germany the most formidable power in Europe and build up thereby a direct threat to himself? Absurd to expect such a step from democratic England, from jealous perfidious Albion . . . No use to cherish the hope that England would voluntarily surrender any part of her colonies to meet the legitimate German need for expansion.

Hitler listened intently and replied:

> What if I were to be attacked by Italy, France and England, and Stalin should betray me . . . what then? For that very reason it would be better to align myself with Italy and Japan and play along with England even if I can't get her friendship . . . The economic power of the Versailles States is so enormous that

> I can't risk antagonising them at the very outset . . . No I've got to play ball with capitalism and keep the Versailles Powers in line by holding aloft the bogey of Bolshevism – make them believe that a Nazi Germany is the last bulwark against the Red flood. That's the only way to come through the danger period, to get rid of Versailles and re-arm. I can talk peace but mean war.

Bill de Ropp picked up this last point when he made one of his final ventures into journalism around this time. He penned an article for the *English Review* February 1932 edition entitled 'The New German Nationalism'. Many of the old contributors to *Outlook* seem to have migrated to the *English Review* including Sir Charles Petrie, Hilaire Belloc and Francis Yeats-Brown. It is an interesting piece in that Bill remains loyal to his democratic instincts and supportive of Brüning's centrist government. It is noteworthy that he did not see the need to sell his soul to the devil and support the Nazi party just for the sake of his cultivation of Rosenberg and Hitler. He calculated, correctly, that even extremists have respect for people who retain their integrity.

He does, however, argue that reparations need to be cancelled in view of the economic crisis and attendant hardship. The article concludes:

> It seems by no means improbable that Adolf Hitler, the leader of by far the most important Nationalist party, will, in the near future, control German affairs . . . Will National Socialism bring internal peace to Germany and an end to the present suicidal party strife or will it, inspired by intolerance and a desire for retaliation, plunge Germany into chaos and threaten the security of Europe? The question will probably be answered by the end of the year.[264]

He was not far wrong. Hitler became Chancellor of Germany on 30 January 1933, although he had to wait another year until the death of President Hindenburg in August 1934 before he became the overall Führer by combining the two roles of Chancellor and President. Three months after becoming Chancellor, Hitler confirmed Baron von Neurath as Foreign Minister in charge of a ministry still full of aristocrats.

Hitler tried to assuage Rosenberg's disappointment by appointing him Head of the NSDAP's Foreign Office (APA), which was set up in a wing of the Hotel Adlon on the corner of Unter den Linden and Wilhelmstrasse. A few weeks later Rosenberg was appointed as one of only sixteen Reichsleiters (Reich leaders) at the very apogee of the Nazi Party and junior only to Hitler himself.

The Reichstag fire of February 1933 was an event which the Nazis put to good use in their quest for power. There is a curious angle which deserves a brief mention. In the voluminous German investigation files into the affair is a six-by-four-inch postcard addressed to the Reich's Justice Ministry.[265] On 2 March 1933 a Baron von der Ropp humbly petitioned the President of the Supreme Court 'to instruct the Public Prosecutor to put on record the names of the real incendiaries. At the moment these men are still employed in Göring's Residence, whence they carried the incendiary material into the underground passage. It would be an irreparable loss to future German historians who are kept in ignorance of the names of the real incendiaries.'[266]

The writer of the postcard does not appear to have been Bill de Ropp. The handwriting is not his, nor is it Friedrich's. The writer also uses the full 'von der Ropp', not the amended 'de Ropp'. Whoever wrote it was taking a big risk by indirectly accusing Göring of complicity. In fact, one wonders if it was a provocateur trying to denounce one of the Barons von der Ropp as a communist or anti-Nazi. The strong probability is that all the Barons von der Ropp, including Bill, would have received visits from Göring's Gestapo in the same month.*

In May 1933 Rosenberg paid a second visit to London. This

* Göring ceded control of the Gestapo to Himmler the following year.

one was very different from the first. A low profile was no longer possible and Rosenberg carried personal responsibility for Nazi party policies. Furthermore it was no longer for Bill de Ropp and Fred Winterbotham to arrange the programme. The German Embassy in London managed some of the appointments and probably did not try too hard to make the visit a success. Dr Thost, the correspondent in London of Rosenberg's *Völkischer Beobachter* (*VB*) newspaper, again accompanied his boss for much of the visit.

Rosenberg's friend Kurt Lüdecke begged Rosenberg not to go, in none too diplomatic language as he recalled, saying,

> 'I don't like this . . . It's beyond me your willingness to risk a trip to London when you ought to be here on the spot every minute. You're not sitting in the saddle yet . . .' He didn't know the British; the international situation was against him; he couldn't possibly bring back a conspicuous success, and his enemies would do their best to make it appear a fiasco. Hitler might find it a welcome excuse for dropping him. And he was leaving Göring behind his back – Göring who didn't like him. 'You can't speak even a word of English! You haven't got one decently fitting suit to wear. Your evening clothes are impossible.'[267]

We don't know what Bill de Ropp advised but, although he was in London throughout, he wisely kept his head down and did not suffer any collateral damage from the disaster that ensued. Rosenberg had meetings with the Foreign Secretary Sir John Simon; the Minister of War Lord Hailsham; Sir Robert Vansittart and Norman Davis, who was United States ambassador-at-large visiting London at the time. All four meetings were uncomfortable for Rosenberg. Lord Hailsham stressed the need for Germany to abide by the Versailles Treaty on disarmament and Davis made a similar point. The discussion with Davis was described as 'an outspoken exchange in which cards were laid on the table'.[268]

Rosenberg's hopes of being granted an audience with Prime Minister Ramsay MacDonald were dashed. This was one area where Bill might have tried to help through his acquaintance with Alan Barlow, the fellow Savile member who was MacDonald's private secretary in 1933. Barlow and MacDonald did not get on well together and Barlow lasted in the role for barely a year. In the event, the German Embassy did not even request a call on the Prime Minister, and so Rosenberg would have had little reason to blame Bill de Ropp for the failure.

One of the still unresolved mysteries was whether Rosenberg called on the Chairman of the Royal Dutch Shell Group, Sir Henri Deterding, at his house at Buckhurst Park near Windsor. The programme for the visit seemed to have a lot of days of 'motoring' in the countryside. On Saturday he spent the afternoon 'motoring with Dr and Mrs Thost. Motored to Dorking and had tea at the Deerhurst Hotel. Returned via Epsom which Dr Rosenberg wanted to see.' On Sunday, 'Went motoring and lunched in the country with German friends of Dr Thost.'[269]

Reynold's (a popular, illustrated, weekly, centre-left, newspaper dating back to 1850) claimed that Rosenberg had seen Deterding and that the issue discussed was the Baku oilfields which both Shell and Germany wished to wrest back from the Soviet Union.[270] This whole subject has become a fertile area for conspiracy theorists but it is worth noting that the breaking up of the Soviet Union and the creation of a Ukraine allied to Germany was an obsession of Rosenberg's and access to the oilfields in the Caucasus was a fundamental German necessity in the event of a war.

The most memorable moment of the visit was when Rosenberg laid a wreath bearing a swastika at the Cenotaph in Whitehall. A passerby picked it up and threw it in the Thames. Looking back on the visit the leader in *The Scotsman* commented:

Dr Rosenberg's visit has been marred by his tactlessness in

> depositing a wreath with party elements at the Cenotaph but that is a trifling incident arising from good intentions unguided by imagination and would have been best ignored. There will be ample compensation for it if he tells his leader frankly . . . how [the visit] has aroused the uneasiness of the national leaders, while the ill treatment of the Jews and others has forfeited the goodwill of the sections of opinion that were disposed to be most sympathetic to German claims.[271]

On his departure from Liverpool Street Station there was a demonstration with people shouting, 'Down with Hitler!', 'Down with fascism!' Before he left, Rosenberg told the British press, 'I've enjoyed my visit and especially a trip I had into your beautiful English country yesterday.' This hardly sounded convincing. A *Daily Herald* reporter who travelled with Rosenberg from Liverpool Street described him as 'tired out and depressed beyond description, yawning constantly, with his face lined and unshaven, and his manner nerveless [*sic*]'.[272]

On 15th May *The Times* delivered the coup de grâce:

> The Special Nazi envoy to England, Herr Rosenberg, left London yesterday thus cutting short his stay in this country by two days. His visit will hardly be regarded as a success even by those who were responsible for it . . . He had little previous knowledge of our country, could speak no English, and was palpably unacquainted with the British temperament . . . Before talking about good will abroad it would be best to stop the teaching of hatred at home.[273]

Heiden wrote about this second visit:

> Alfred Rosenberg went to London on May 1st. Rosenberg then looked like the future Foreign Minister of Germany. Rosenberg's trip to London was in a sense a test of his diplomatic gifts and

> its outcome was deplorable. The sight of this morose figure, the living embodiment of national socialist race hatred, did much to intensify English mistrust of the new Germany. From right to left Rosenberg found a hostile press; public incidents made his stay in England almost unbearable and he soon departed. England's response to Hitler's private envoy was broadly this: we can deal with Germany but not with National Socialism.[274]

Looking at the two visits MI6 must have felt reasonably satisfied. Bill and Fred Winterbotham earned a lot of credit for the first and suffered virtually no damage from the second. On the other hand, Rosenberg's second trip opened him up to attack from his many enemies; particularly Göring, Goebbels and Ribbentrop. MI6 must have realised that their star subsource was holed below the waterline. He was never going to be Foreign Minister. But would it still be possible to extract valuable intelligence from him and use his senior position as a Reichsleiter to develop new forms of access?

14

'A BUNCH OF GANGSTERS'

1934–1937: Extracting secrets from Nazi Berlin

Bill de Ropp would have realised that Rosenberg's prospects had been damaged by his second trip to London and that his enemies in the party would be circling, sensing blood in the water. Kurt Lüdecke was Rosenberg's adviser on United States politics just as Bill was his adviser on Great Britain. Unlike Bill de Ropp, Lüdecke was wealthy, a genuine Nazi and rashly outspoken about his views on Nazi party mistakes. When Göring had him arrested (twice) he assumed that Rosenberg would come to his rescue.

Rosenberg was a weak personality and in a fragile position compared to the big emerging beasts of Himmler and Goebbels. He did not lift a finger to help his long-time friend. Bill witnessed this betrayal at close quarters and would have reassessed his own position. Far better to keep a low profile, milk Rosenberg for intelligence while he still could and watch out for new opportunities.

We are helped in tracking Bill's activities because Rosenberg started writing a diary in May 1934. Bill is frequently mentioned and we can observe the master spy using every opportunity and manufacturing others to call on Rosenberg and discuss the issues of the day.

An example is May 1934. On the 17th Rosenberg wrote:

> Ropp complains about the [German] Propaganda Ministry which he says is spoiling the mood in England again with new forceful speeches about Jews . . . Great agitation on account of Lithuania [alleging that Gauleiter Erich] Koch would plan attack on Memel . . . Query from [Alan] Barlow on behalf of [Ramsay] MacDonald asking where things really stand. I will send Ropp to Königsberg; he wants to know the entire settlement plan in detail so that he can report on our positive restructuring programme to counter-balance the lies invented to produce a certain effect which also comes from the FO . . . Ropp confirms once again that *The Times* article was inspired jointly by the FO and [the German ambassador in London Leopold von] Hoesch or his advisers. [275]

On 22 May, 'Ropp turns up, complaining again: MacDonald's office is asking me again for "clarification" about a Nazi campaign against "petty critics and spoilers".'[276] On the 29th: 'Today Ropp informs me of a message from London saying that it would not be possible for State Secretary [Erhard] Milch to be received by either a Minister or the Permanent Under Secretary at the Air Ministry. The reason: the no-holds-barred speech by Dr Goebbels in the Sportpalast!'[277]

Bill de Ropp was equally active in March 1935. On 14 March Rosenberg notes, 'Ropp came the day before yesterday furious about <u>his</u> (that is, the British) Foreign Office. He said that his Foreign Office and a small clique in the War Office repeatedly spoiled all reasonable attempts at a German-English rapprochement.' Later the same day, 'He [Ropp] is coming again today: message from the [British] Air Ministry. [Foreign Secretary Sir John] Simon has approached them to inquire whether they have a definite opinion about how one can best negotiate in Berlin! Obviously, people in the Foreign Office no longer have full confidence in their own assessment of present-day German mentality . . . Ropp requested the strictest discretion.'[278]

One can see what Bill de Ropp was doing here. Not only was he seizing every half-chance for a meeting but he was also playing to Rosenberg's prejudices. Given Rosenberg's own responsibility for anti-Jewish sentiment in the Nazi party it seems incongruous that Bill could complain to him about Goebbels's anti-Semitic speeches, but Rosenberg's dislike of Goebbels trumped all other factors. Blaming von Hoesch for an article in *The Times* is another example.

By raising the Memel issue Bill de Ropp then gets assigned by Rosenberg to travel to Königsberg and find out from the Gauleiter Erich Koch what his true intentions were towards Memel, East Prussia and the Baltic States. This would make instant CX for Woollcombe to send to senior Whitehall customers.

Meanwhile Bill de Ropp was using his acquaintance from the Savile Club Alan Barlow, Ramsay MacDonald's Private Secretary, to give every appearance of being able to relay messages to and from No. 10 Downing Street. He was almost certainly exaggerating his influence in No. 10 although he would have met Barlow at the Savile on his trips to London.

And finally, Bill was exploiting the tensions between the FO and the War Office to give the impression that Berlin could exert more influence in Whitehall if only it played its cards better. At the same time he was deliberately belittling the role of the (non-Nazi) German ambassador in London von Hoesch. The same would apply to Konstantin von Neurath and all the non-Nazi aristocrats in the AA.

In doing this Bill was relying on Rosenberg's child-like naivety. He might easily have told Bill that it was his job to stop *The Times* being influenced by von Hoesch. In fact there is no evidence that the ambassador had this level of influence with Dawson. Rosenberg always took Bill's allegations and assurances as the unvarnished truth without, it seems, ever checking them out.

There are dangers in playing these games, of course. In later chapters we shall see that Bill de Ropp had built up in the minds of Rosenberg and Hitler a picture that the tensions between the FO and the British Air Ministry represented a fundamental fault-line in British attitudes towards Germany. This would later have serious consequences because it may have been one of the factors that persuaded Hitler that Britain under Neville Chamberlain would never be able to unify behind a declaration of war against Germany.

If the CX produced by Bill de Ropp had survived the various culls in MI6's archives they would have shown that Rosenberg was by far his most productive source. Indeed we saw the Rosenberg connection behind some of the judgements in 'What Should We Do?' and they are even more discernible from the two other surviving strategic reports in the National Archives from 1938 assessed in Chapter 21.

Even as Rosenberg lost influence, he still received the *Reichsleiter Dienst*, which was a summary (always marked Secret) of internal party and national news issued by Goebbels's department. Rosenberg's APA also produced a regular service of foreign news and intelligence for the other Reichsleiters.[279] So there was always a rich vein of intelligence for Bill to mine even if the biggest secrets of the Reich were confined to a small inner circle around the Führer.

The other advantage of being close to Rosenberg was that Bill de Ropp had the trust of the officials of the APA. Of these the most significant was Arno Schickedanz, who was particularly knowledgeable about Romania. There was also Horst Obermüller, the other heavyweight operator on Rosenberg's team.

Bill de Ropp had other valuable sources. In his *Daily Mail* articles in October 1957 Bill wrote, 'I spied on Adolf Hitler, Alfred Rosenberg, Head of the Department on Foreign Politics [APA], on [Reinhard] Heydrich, deputy head of the Gestapo, on General von Epp, Governor-General of Bavaria, on Erich Koch, Ober-President and Gauleiter of East Prussia, and Ernst Röhm, head of the SA and many more top Nazis.'[280]

Bill would also have met General Franz Ritter von Epp through

Rosenberg because von Epp partly funded the purchase of the *VB* newspaper. He already had a dark stain on his character for his involvement in the Herero genocide of 1904–8, when tens of thousands of Herero and Nama tribesmen and women were killed by colonists in German South-West Africa (now Namibia).

In spite of his title Von Epp was not an aristocrat. He had earned his knighthood for valour in the war. He was the hardest of hard men and a committed Nazi whereas Bill was fundamentally gentle and politically centre-right. But the job of a spy is to mould himself or herself to the shape of the target. This was Bill de Ropp's remarkable talent.

Bill wrote, 'Von Epp, a retired regular officer of good family, was much respected by Hitler. He enjoyed Wagner and three times I endured the excruciating agony of listening with him to Siegfried in the Royal Box at the Munich Opera House hoping that, at the supper which I knew would follow, I might obtain some useful information. I generally did.'[281]

Von Epp played a key role in two aspects of the Nazis' rise to power and so his CX must have been fascinating for Whitehall customers. He exercised considerable influence on Bavarian politics not least by his decisive armed interventions. On 9 March 1933 he seized power in Munich from the regional government. He also helped persuade the Reichswehr to persevere with Hitler at the time when Hindenburg looked upon the 'Bohemian corporal' with contempt.

Heiden writes, 'a committee [was formed] for the sole purpose of influencing a dozen generals and colonels of the Reichswehr staff. The leader Franz von Epp, the man who in bygone times had helped invent Hitler, was assigned to influence Hindenburg himself. The Military Political Bureau was going to make the old generals understand why there had to be a National Socialist movement; to win the spiritual domination of the people [and] to penetrate the soul of the proletariat'[282] as only the SA had hitherto achieved.

Von Epp, as an old Africa hand, was also tasked by Hitler to draw up his plan for the continent. It involved persuading Britain to return Tanganyika, paying Belgium to give up much of the Congo, and Portugal to cede Angola thereby creating a huge German colony straddling Africa from East to West. Hitler then told Bill that he would import Chinese labour because Africans were 'indolent and stupid'.[283] As Bill de Ropp later observed, the idea sounded ridiculous at the time but future Nazi policies in other areas were even more insane but still implemented.

An MI6 report dated February 1938 describes a later German idea of demanding 'one large compact area yielding tropical produce' in preference to distinct unconnected parts of Africa. The proposed area would stretch 'from the Gold Coast [modern Ghana] to Gabon'. The AA had added a comment that 'If we become strong enough to induce England and France to accede to our demands, we shall get colonies.'[284]

His wider family did not provide rich pickings for Bill de Ropp's reporting. His brothers and sisters were now too old to have any relevance and their children were too young to have reached any rank of importance. However, his brother-in-law Achim von Stralendorff worked in the household of Friedrich-Franz, the heir to the now abolished Dukedom of Mecklenburg-Schwerin.[285] The Duke had been four years ahead of Bill at the Vitzthum Gymnasium in Dresden. Much to his disgust his eldest son joined the Waffen SS in 1931 and was later associated with Werner Best, who would be convicted of war crimes. Friedrich-Franz and his son provided Bill de Ropp with one of his few channels of insight into Himmler's elite force. Achim von Stralendorff's son would also join the German army and would later brand Bill de Ropp 'a traitor'.

Bill de Ropp's claim to have spied on Heydrich is more tenuous. He describes a terrifying moment when he found himself seated next to the tall, fair-haired SD chief at an SS dinner organised by Himmler during the September 1937 Party Day celebrations at Nuremberg.

> Himmler presided and what a bunch of gangsters was gathered there that night in a macabre setting of skull and cross-bone

emblems and gruesome jackbooted SS leaders . . . I had just started on my dinner when I heard a voice behind me say, 'Permit me, my name is Heydrich.'

At this dinner were any number of important guests including the British and French ambassadors. Why had he chosen to sit next to me, a man of absolutely no political significance? A sinister symptom? But this was not the moment to give way to panic so I said 'Delighted to meet you Herr Heydrich'. . . It shocked me to find that a mass murderer of his calibre should look so entirely normal . . . Our conversation soon narrowed down to one subject, Anglo-German co-existence. Germany would guarantee the continued existence of the British Empire; on the other hand England would give Germany a free hand in Eastern Europe. I had heard the same theme over and over again from Hitler and Rosenberg.[286]

Following this unexpected meeting Bill suggested to Broadway that he develop Heydrich as yet another sub-source. His idea was to open up a discussion with Heydrich about 'Bolshevik personalities and intrigues'. It was an odd proposal given that Bill was rightly scared of Heydrich and it may signify that Bill was still under pressure to produce more intelligence to justify his costs of £1000 per annum. Valentine Vivian was having none of it. He minuted: 'I would have nothing to do with this tortuous scheme. ACHTUNG!'[287]

We are fortunate in having another stream of Bill de Ropp's reporting to London. Occasionally MI5 retained CX reports in their files on Nazi suspects. These show Bill de Ropp's more tactical contributions but they also reveal something of his methods. A prime habit of his was to frequent the lobby and bars of the Kaiserhof Hotel, which the Nazis used as a meeting place and canteen with much the same carelessness as MI6 used St Ermin's Hotel.

The Kaiserhof on Wilhelmplatz played a significant part in Nazi history. Lüdecke wrote (about 1932) that 'the famous Kaiserhof hotel near the Chancellery [was] only a few steps from the Palais of the President of the Reich. Here for decades past ambassadors, foreign ministers and kings had stayed; here Bismarck made friends with Disraeli, and here Hitler had established his headquarters in Berlin.' By 1934 the Nazis had moved into the various government offices but still used the Kaiserhof as a rendezvous. An outsider would be viewed with suspicion but Bill de Ropp was not an outsider.

On the MI5 file on Dr Thost (the *VB* correspondent who had accompanied Rosenberg on both his trips to London) there is a memo dated 26 November 1935 that is clearly from Bill de Ropp. 'About a fortnight ago I sat in the bar of the hotel Kaiserhof with Erich Koch when Thost suddenly bounded into the room. He greeted me with his usual effusion and introduced himself to Koch who was not interested and showed it. So Thost departed after a short time. He did not mention his precipitate departure from England.'[288]

In fact, Thost had been expelled from London by the FO at MI5's suggestion. Bill de Ropp then goes on to provide a little more context:

> Rosenberg, the editor in chief of the *VB*, had observed that the recall of Thost had been contemplated for some time as it was felt that he was not the right man for London. It is most regrettable that Thost was forced to leave in disgrace and so much publicity was given to his departure. According to Thost his association with Count Pallavicini* is probably the reason for his expulsion ... Pallavicini also told Thost that Sir Philip Sassoon† was secretly arranging a large credit for the Italians in cooperation with a group in the City.

* Pallavicini was a noble Italian family of the former Austro-Hungarian empire. Marquess Alphonse Pallavicini was Counsellor at the Hungarian Legation in London and a close friend of Lord Londonderry, the Secretary of State for Air and prominent appeaser. Not to be confused with Carl Paravicini, the Swiss Minister in London.

† Philip Sassoon was Under Secretary of State for Air 1931–7.

Top left: Baron Guillaume Alexandrowich von der Ropp, Bill de Ropp's father, who served in the Tsarist army as a Colonel of Engineers. *(© Dagmar von Stralendorff)*

Top right: Lydia von der Ropp (née Guriev), whose conversion to Missouri Lutheranism would have far-reaching consequences for the family. *(© Christoph Böttcher)*

Bottom: The von der Ropp family on the terrace in Dresden in about 1892. From left to right, Friedrich, Gertrud, Bill, Margarethe and their mother Lydia *(© Christoph Böttcher)*

Left: Bill de Ropp (far right) with his father, mother, sister and Friedrich in Dresden, circa 1893. *(© Fritz Böttcher)*

Right: Bill de Ropp photographed with his pet dachshund in Dresden in about 1902. *(© James de Ropp)*

Dauzogir, the von der Ropp family estate in northern Lithuania. Vestiges of the house remained in 1990 but have since collapsed. *(© James de Ropp)*

Top left: Friedrich von der Ropp in his heyday when he was working as a paid confidential agent for the German Foreign Ministry. *(© Fritz Böttcher)*

Top right: The youthful Bernhard (Benno) von Wildemann married Gertrud von der Ropp in 1906. She would save his life during the Russian Revolution in 1917. *(© Gundula Konold)*

Bottom: Schloss Gamehl, near Rostock, where Bill de Ropp's sister, Margarethe von Stralendorff, provided refuge for her Baltic relatives. *(© author)*

Above: Bill de Ropp (back row, second left) as a member of the Royal Flying Corps kite-balloon training team based at Roehampton in 1917. *(© Tatler)*

Right: 54 Broadway, London SW1, MI6's headquarters from 1926 until 1964. Although dark and decrepit inside, it provided easy access to central government. Despite being renumbered 50 Broadway, the building (shown here in 2024) has changed very little externally. *(© author)*

Left: St Ermin's Hotel near 54 Broadway, which was used by MI6 to meet and accommodate visiting agents. *(© author)*

Below left: Admiral Sir Hugh Sinclair, known as Quex, was the second Chief of MI6. He followed the Bill de Ropp case closely and laid down strict rules for its secure handling. *(© National Portrait Gallery [NPG])*

Below right: Colonel (later Major-General Sir) Stewart Menzies, the third Chief of MI6. He recruited Bill de Ropp in 1919 and maintained a paternal interest in the case. *(© NPG)*

Malcolm Woollcombe, the head of MI6's political section, who was responsible for Bill de Ropp's political reporting and circulating it in Whitehall. He was highly regarded by successive heads of the Foreign Office.

(© Tamsyn Woollcombe)

Fred Winterbotham, the dynamic head of MI6's Air Section whom Bill de Ropp introduced to Alfred Rosenberg and Adolf Hitler.

(© Sally Maitland)

Cecil Insall, one of Frank Foley's station officers in Berlin who was tasked to receive secret reports from Bill de Ropp in the late 1930s. *(© Lynn Insall)*

Frank Foley, the veteran head of MI6's station in Berlin with whom Bill de Ropp kept close but cautious local contact. *(© Michael Smith)*

Bill de Ropp's two children, Bob and Ruth, on holiday in Germany in the mid-1920s.

(© James de Ropp)

Grünheide just outside Berlin, which belonged to Friedrich von der Ropp's wife, Lili. Here they entertained Archibald Church and were eventually evicted by the Gestapo in 1945.

(© Fritz Böttcher)

> Dr Bömer [of the APA] said that Thost had shown a talent amounting almost to genius for saying the wrong thing and making friends with the wrong people. His departure is not regretted by anyone wishing to make National Socialism popular in England. It is probable that Dr Seibert will be appointed as his successor. Von Chappuis of the English Department of the APA made no secret of his relief that Thost had been removed. Colonel Wenninger with whom I lunched about a fortnight ago said that Thost's departure had been accepted with complete equanimity by the German Embassy in London.[289]

This was not the sort of report that Woollcombe would have circulated to Whitehall. It would have fallen to Vivian, as MI6's head of counter-intelligence, to share it only with MI5, for whom such detail was bread and butter for their work. Vivian (stretching the point only slightly) described the source as 'a very reliable Nazi source.'[290] Not only did it provide valuable feedback on Thost's expulsion and how it had been greeted in Berlin, but it also provided the name of his successor.[291]

After the war Thost was interrogated and mentioned that Pallavicini, who claimed to be both Hungarian and Italian, had offered him secrets about relations between Rome and London in return for money. Pallavicini then suggested Thost should meet two British intelligence agents.[292] Shortly afterwards Thost was expelled, clearly thinking he had been set up. He was thrown out partly in retaliation for the German expulsion of the British Vice Consul in Hanover, Captain Werner Aue.* Aue was accused of sending military information to the British Embassy in Berlin. [293]

Bill's aristocratic background made it easy for him to cultivate contacts in the AA. This was the ministry that was most resistant to Nazism. Many German diplomats were aristocrats themselves and

* This was Captain W.C.R. Aue formerly of the Black Watch who ran a book-binding company and may have been connected to the Woodman family business.

COPY.

SECRET

Dr. THOST.

About a fortnight ago I sat in the bar of the Hotel Kaiserho[f] with Erich KOCH when THOST suddenly bounded into the room. He greeted me with his usual effusion and introduced himself to KOCH who was not interested and showed it. So THOST departed after a short time. He did not mention his precipitate departure from England.

The reaction in Nazi circles best acquainted with THOST's activities in London appears to be a mixture of official indignation and unofficial releaf. I have heard the following opinions expressed:-

ROSENBERG, Editor in Chief of the "Voelkischer Beobachter": The recall of THOST had been contemplated for some time as it was felt that he was not the right man for London. It is most regrettable that THOST was forced to leave in disgrace and that so much publicity was given to his departure. It was debated in Berlin for some time whether THOST's involuntary exit was to be made the subject of a press campaign, but it was decided that it might be as well to let sleeping dogs lie as nobody in Berlin really knows the reasons for the action of the British authorities.

According to THOST his association with a Count PALLAVICINI is probably the reason for his expulsion. PALLAVICINI, according to THOST, acted as agent provocateur and gave him information which in THOST's official capacity as newspaper correspondent was compromising to receive.

PALLAVICINI told THOST that a firm in London was engaged in illegal dealings in German Marks on a large scale; the name of the firm was given. PALLAVICINI also told THOST that Sir Philip Sassoon was secretly arranging a large credit for the Italians in cooperation with a group in the City. The possession of this knowledge was according to THOST the reason for his expulsion. ROSENBERG thinks that there may be other reasons, one of which is retaliation, for certain actions undertaken against British officials in Germany. In any case it has been decided to say nothing more about it unless some British journalist makes himself unpopular in Germany.

Dr. BOEMER said that THOST had shown a talent amounting almost to genius for saying the wrong thing and making friends with the wrong people. His departure is not regretted by anyone wishing to make National Socialism popular in England. It is probable that a Dr. SEIBERT will be appointed as his successor. I understood from BOEMER's remarks that SEIBERT is already in London in a different journalistic job.

Von CHAPPUIS of the English Department of the A.P.A. made no secret of his relief that THOST had been removed.

Colonel WENNINGER with whom I lunched about a fortnight ago, said that THOST's departure had been accepted with complete equanimity by the German Embassy in London.

26.11.35.

Bill de Ropp's report, dated 26 November 1935, on Dr Thost following the latter's expulsion from London. (*TNA*) affected a disdain for the Nazis. This attitude gradually changed, however, as it became ever clearer that the prospects for advancement required both joining the party and carrying out the Nazis' policies. Historians have increasingly begun to challenge the myth that AA officials were not among those responsible for the crimes of the Nazi period. One of the most honest appraisals can be found on the von Richthofen family website.[294]

Bill knew Herbert von Richthofen, who was brought up in a quintessential Prussian military family of ardent monarchists and was a relative of the famous fighter ace. He was sent away to a harsh Prussian boarding school before joining the AA in 1904. After postings to Cairo and Sofia, he and his wife, Rosine, retired to his villa in Garmisch where they would meet Bill and Jimmy de Ropp during their winter vacations.

Persuaded to return to the AA he became ambassador to Denmark (1930–36) where his valet accused him of making derogatory comments about Hitler. He survived and was sent to Brussels for two years where he joined the Nazi party in 1938 before being sent again to Sofia as ambassador, where he played a role in bringing Bulgaria into the tripartite alliance with Germany, Italy and Japan.[295]

A schoolfriend from Dresden provided Bill de Ropp with another entré into the German Foreign Ministry (AA). This was Ernst Woermann who had gone on to study law at Heidelberg, Munich, Freiberg and Leipzig before military service in the war. He joined the AA in 1919 and attended the Paris Peace Conference. Subsequently he served in Paris and Vienna but he met Bill de Ropp again when he was posted at the London embassy from 1936 to 1938. Unlike many AA officials he became a supporter of Ribbentrop and joined the Nazi party in 1937 and became Political Director of the AA in April the following year.[296] (He later offered only equivocal support for the Indian revolutionary leader Subhas Chandra Bose who travelled to Berlin in 1941 to seek Hitler's endorsement for his plans to mount an insurgency into British India.)

A third contact in the AA was Herbert von Dirksen, the last German ambassador in London before the Second World War. He would have known Friedrich von der Ropp, as they were both in Africa before the First Word War.[297] Dirksen had postings to Poland and Japan before being sent to London to replace Ribbentrop. In spite of being an anti-Semite and a party member as early as 1936, Dirksen fell out of love with the Nazis during his time in London (1938–9). A problematic CX report, probably from Bill de Ropp, of von Dirksen complaining about events in Berlin survives in the National Archives as we shall see in Chapter 21.[298]

Dirksen was 'vain and pompous' but nowhere near as unpleasant as another of Bill's regular AA contacts, Carl Theo von Zeitschel, who had joined the Propaganda Ministry in 1935 before moving to the AA in 1937. As an official in the Political Department he was a natural interlocutor for Bill de Ropp. He joined the SS in 1940 and in June he was posted to France where he played a key role in the deportation of the Jewish population. He died in the Allied bombing of Berlin in 1945.

With sources such as these, one can see why Bill de Ropp was MI6's top agent in pre-war Nazi Germany and the best producer of strategic political intelligence whilst also providing MI5 with low-level personality reporting. There is enough evidence to see that Bill was a highly inventive operator, always looking for a means to expand his range of contacts.

On the other hand the Rosenberg connection denied him the proximity he needed to the immediate decision-making circle around Hitler: Himmler, Goebbels and Göring. To have abandoned Rosenberg in favour of one of his rivals would have been too risky and almost guaranteed to fail. We shall see in Chapter 21 how the Rosenberg connection skewed his reporting towards the minority Rosenberg view. There were also, arguably, too many AA sources. The AA was never fully trusted by Hitler and was only rarely kept in the loop as to Hitler's real thinking.

What Bill de Ropp needed were more sources in Germany's armed forces, especially the army and nascent air force. This was the background to the extraordinary events of 1934.

15

'THE LONG KNIVES'

1934: Blitzkrieg and bloodbath

Bill de Ropp's array of sources provided just enough CX for Woollcombe to be able to justify his salary and expenses to Admiral Sinclair and the parsimonious Percy Sykes. However, the involvement of Fred Winterbotham in the case added a significant dimension of both risk and opportunity. By portraying Winterbotham as a senior officer in the British Air Ministry, Bill de Ropp was able to engineer new high-level military access. Not only did this provide MI6 contact with key figures in the German army and embryonic air force, such as General von Reichenau and General Kesselring, but it also pleased Rosenberg who now had the locus to talk to his Führer about military and air force matters, much to the irritation of Hermann Göring.

In early 1934 Fred Winterbotham finally received his invitation from Rosenberg to visit Germany. Rosenberg had clearly had to negotiate this with Göring, as head of the German air force, and with Hitler himself. Winterbotham managed to obtain approval from Sinclair and Vansittart on the understanding that he was notionally going in a private capacity, 'on leave', and yet would also keep the

British ambassador, Sir Eric Phipps, informed through the air attaché at the British Embassy in Berlin.

He travelled by train and was astonished by the formal reception on arrival at Berlin where he was met by Rosenberg, a red carpet, a phalanx of SS guards and a motorcade of black Mercedes limousines. For an MI6 officer, even one as self-confident as Winterbotham, this was an unusual moment. This sort of ceremony is ten-a-penny to ambassadors but intelligence officers are more accustomed to making low-key entrances usually by the back door where cameras are less likely to intrude. It was therefore something of a relief to reach Bill de Ropp's flat.[299]

> I stayed with Bill and his wife in their flat on the Kurfürstendamm. They put me on a divan in the sitting room. The flat was fairly high and looked out over the back which was lucky because the Kurfürstendamm was the most fashionable street in Berlin, a bit noisy both by day and by night . . . Bill's flat was both central and comfortable . . . I wanted time to see something of Berlin while I was there. Although Bill's wife Jimmy was an excellent cook we usually only had breakfast in the flat and then took our other meals when and where we could.[300]

Before starting his round of meetings Winterbotham had an important discussion with Bill de Ropp on methods. He agreed to pretend that he spoke little German in spite of his time as a prisoner of war. Bill would do the translating and Winterbotham would have more time to think and study his interlocutors. Bill also urged him not to use the Nazi salute. 'Far better, [Bill] advised, to behave in a completely British manner, for the Nazis respected this attitude which was most unlike that of some of their other hangers-on who would give the *Heil Hitler* salute whenever possible.' The only time Bill gave the salute was in a crowd when there was a high chance of getting 'roughed up'.[301]

Rosenberg mentions the visit in his diary. 'Major Winterbotham had been here on "leave" from February 27th to March 6th. I brought him together with Reichenau, [Bruno] Loerzer, Hess, two commodores and then to the Führer . . . The conversation took a very satisfactory course and W submitted a splendid report in London.'[302] It is interesting that Rosenberg puts 'leave' inside quotation marks. He either guessed or was told by Bill that Winterbotham was not permitted by Whitehall to portray the visit as official.

His mention of Winterbotham's 'splendid report' caused some post-war embarrassment for Winterbotham who invented a complex story about submitting a critical report to Whitehall and a fake positive one for Rosenberg. The truth is that most British visitors to Berlin in 1934 were amazed by the achievements of the Nazis. Winterbotham was no different. In the 1980s he admitted in his oral interviews with the Imperial War Museum that he was impressed by Hitler both for the clarity of his ideas and the depth of his knowledge of international affairs. 'An extraordinary man' was his conclusion. It was only in 1936–7 that doubts began to develop for many and then predominate in 1938–9.

There are some errors in Winterbotham's recollection of the trip and of his meetings. For example, he quotes Hitler as being critical of the visit by British Foreign Secretary Sir John Simon and his deputy Anthony Eden, whereas that meeting took place a year later, in March 1935. Nonetheless most of Winterbotham's memories tend to be broadly accurate albeit with a tendency to accord himself an enhanced role in proceedings. The intelligence historian Christopher Andrew, who met Winterbotham, regarded him as 'generally reliable but exuberant'.[303]

Winterbotham met Adolf Hitler at Bismarck's Old Chancellery in the presence of Rosenberg and de Ropp. Understandably for Winterbotham this was one of the most remarkable moments of his life and he devotes many pages of his three autobiographies to the event. For our purposes the most important discussion was about the German air force which is covered in Chapter 19. Hitler also spoke of his hostile intentions towards Russia. Otherwise, Winterbotham did not make particularly good use of his hour with Hitler beyond stimulating a rant about communism.[304] There followed a short meeting with Rudolf Hess who was one of Rosenberg's few friends within the party.

The most important achievement was to obtain Hitler's blessing to have discussions with the Führer's officials and military officers. This 'green light' also allowed Rosenberg to rebuff firmly the enquiries of Putzi Hanfstaengl who asked what Winterbotham was doing in the Chancellery.

The highlight of Winterbotham's meetings was with the pro-Nazi General Walter von Reichenau, Chief of the Ministerial Office of the Reichswehr Ministry. He would be one of the instigators behind the Night of the Long Knives just three months later. He was also the general who, along with his boss, the Minister Werner von Blomberg, would require the Reichswehr (renamed the Wehrmacht in 1935) to take an oath of allegiance to Adolf Hitler. At a stroke this had turned the German national army into the military arm of the Nazi Party, a truly fatal move and one which many officers would live to regret.

Hanfstaengl, who defected from the Nazis in 1937, would have us believe that von Reichenau possessed a conscience and that he harboured doubts about Hitler.[305] If so he must join Rosenberg as someone with a vast distance between their conscience and their actions. In the coming war he would be responsible for some monstrous war crimes.

Von Reichenau had been instructed by Hitler to brief Winterbotham on his early planning ideas for a future invasion of the Soviet Union. It was one of those events where circumstances coalesce to produce the right atmosphere for the spilling of secrets. The location was important:

> Horcher's [wrote Winterbotham] was a magnificent restaurant with dark oak panelling and a resplendently Victorian red plush décor. In the great dining room stood a vast table with a snow-white cloth bearing up manfully beneath the heavy array of silver and shining glass. There was something too very splendid about the traditional German waiters in their black knee breeches, white stockings, red waistcoats and white aprons. The room, the décor and the waiters all conjured up an aura of sumptuous luxury.[306]

Another lucky component, which made this lunch so remarkable, was that Göring sent his regrets. In Göring's presence von Reichenau might have been more cautious. In his place Göring sent two air commodores:* Ralph Wenninger and Albert Kesselring. The first would become Air Attaché in London and the second one of Germany's most important commanders during the Second World War. Loerzer was also there. He was a First World War fighter ace who, in 1934, was notionally a civilian before 'rejoining' the Luftwaffe the following year.

Winterbotham explained:

> The seating arrangement at the table was that Rosenberg sat at the head; on his right was the General; I came next to him with Loerzer on my right and opposite were the two Air Commodores on Rosenberg's left and then Bill de Ropp. As we sat down I glanced across at Bill and saw that his eyebrows were twitching a little bit. It suggested to me that he thought that this was going to be a very important meeting. I don't think Bill ever knew about this habit of his when excited but it always alerted me.[307]

* They were in fact brigadier generals although they would not formally have this rank until the Luftwaffe was officially acknowledged in February 1935. Winterbotham was using their RAF equivalent ranks.

Reichenau's description of his plans, in perfect English, was truly remarkable. A successful invasion of the Soviet Union would be based on speed and surprise. The weather window for the operation was 'between the melting of the snows in the spring and the arrival of the frost in the autumn'. Three large spearheads of tanks would be launched into Russia covering some 200 kilometres each day. Each spearhead would be like an arrow which would fan out at the base. Artillery would defend the flanks of each spearhead.

Following the tank columns would be motorised infantry equipped only with their weapons. Their personal equipment would follow by air with other supplies. Engineers would accompany each spearhead, building aerodromes as they went and ensuring that each aerodrome was equipped with fuel, ammunition and mechanical workshops. These facilities would be available to all pilots who would not need to worry about finding their own squadron's workshops.[308] Long-range bombers would support the advance. Winterbotham continued:

> As the conversation was entirely in English Rosenberg didn't understand it and he sat stolidly at the head of the table. Wenninger, who did understand English, was looking more and more astonished while Bill, who I saw fleetingly out of the corner of my eye, was almost jumping up and down in his seat with his mouth half open. There was no question of this being a rehearsed bit of propaganda.
>
> I didn't want the General to stop here so I began to look a bit puzzled and suggested to him that such warfare might be difficult in Russia with its great areas of marsh and woodland. At this point he put his left hand on the tablecloth with the three middle fingers stretched fairly wide and pushed them across towards the silver candlesticks in the middle saying that fortunately Russia was a very large place so the German tank spearheads would be able to go round the marshes and woodlands and not through them.[309]

The one question that Winterbotham dared not ask was about communications. The speed of the advance would make the laying of landlines impractical and so there would have to be enciphered radio comms. At this stage Britain knew very little about Germany's Enigma machine, although the Poles had made significant progress in researching its mode of operation.

The concepts that Winterbotham had been hearing amounted to what the British would later call 'Blitzkrieg'. This was not a word used by the German military in the 1930s but the fundamentals rested on a combination of close air–land integration (especially incorporating dive-bomber support), fast-moving armoured forces of combined arms (tanks, motorised infantry, artillery and engineers) and, above all, agile decision-making by commanders placed well forward. Both Guderian and Rommel exemplified this leadership style. Guderian would write in 1950 that he had first conceived of the idea in 1929 but it did not become widely known until publication of his 1937 book *Achtung Panzer*.[310]

> I became convinced that tanks working on their own or in conjunction with infantry could never achieve decisive importance. My historical studies, the exercises carried out in England and our own experience with mock-ups had persuaded me that the tanks would never be able to produce their full effect until the other weapons, on whose support they must inevitably rely, were brought up to their standard of speed and of cross-country performance. In such formation of all arms, the tanks must play primary role, the other weapons being subordinated to the requirements of the armour. It would be wrong to include tanks in infantry divisions; what was needed were armoured divisions which would include all the supporting arms needed to allow the tanks to fight with full effect.[311]

As Winterbotham walked back to the Kurfürstendamm with Bill de Ropp he asked why Reichenau had been so loquacious. Was he really speaking out of turn or was the purpose to reassure Britain that Hitler's warlike intentions were uniquely directed against the Soviet Union? Bill de Ropp explained that 'Nazi plans necessitated a neutral Britain. A neutral America was much more within their grasp, with its large German population and an already established Nazi Bund; but they needed to turn Britain to their favour. "That," said Bill, "is why you have been invited to Germany."'[312]

De Ropp insisted to Winterbotham that von Reichenau 'had certainly not been putting on an act. His zealous ardour went far beyond prepared propaganda.' Kesselring had told Rosenberg about the discussion and the latter was sufficiently concerned to hope aloud to Winterbotham, 'I'm sure it's not necessary to ask you not to pass any information on to the Communists.'[313]

It was a remarkable insight into the detail of Germany's military planning even if Hitler's long-term intention to attack Russia had been mentioned in *Mein Kampf*. The attack in June 1941 (over two months late by Reichenau's own timetable) broadly matched Reichenau's description.

The British ambassador Eric Phipps was irritated that Winterbotham should have spent an hour and a half with the German Chancellor without informing him. Winterbotham had rather casually told the air attaché about his meeting, and then wondered why he had incurred the ambassador's wrath. Such seems to have been the naivety of MI6 in the 1930s. However, Phipps was delighted when Winterbotham (still notionally on leave) visited the British Embassy at 70 Wilhelmstrasse to brief him, and drafted a telegram there and then to the Foreign Secretary, copied to the Cabinet and Buckingham Palace.[314]

Winterbotham expected plaudits when he returned to London after his epic trip, but Samuel Hoare, the Foreign Secretary, was furious and told Sinclair that Winterbotham should not travel to Germany again. Hoare was heartily disliked both by the FO and MI6 (in which he had served) and Sinclair buoyed a dispirited Winterbotham by suggesting that Hoare would not be there much longer. Hoare was forced to resign over the Abyssinian crisis in December of the following year.[315]

The War Office was no more positive. They dismissed Reichenau's plans for Russia as 'a lot of nonsense' – according to Winterbotham they were still busy working out how to win a repeat of the 1914–18 war.[316]

The biggest disappointment came from Winterbotham's many friends at the Air Ministry. They were fascinated by the Reichenau lunch but explained how the continuing trend towards disarmament meant that the Ministry could take no responsive action. They arranged for Winterbotham to see Lord Londonderry, the Minister, and Philip Sassoon, his deputy.[317] Both men were sympathetic but their hands were tied by government policy. No reports on these responses to Winterbotham's visit have survived in the National Archives and it is doubtful that much, if anything, has been retained in MI6's much-weeded records. So we are dependent on Winterbotham's passable, but not infallible, memory.

Winterbotham recounts how Desmond Morton in MI6 would often have Sunday lunch with his neighbour Winston Churchill at Chartwell. On the Friday evening before each lunch Morton would come into Winterbotham's office in Broadway and receive a verbal download on recent intelligence about the German air force. On the Monday morning Churchill (who was on the backbenches in his 'Wilderness Years', from 1929 to 1939) would submit a Parliamentary Question. Shortly thereafter Winterbotham would receive a request from the Air Ministry to contribute to the government's answer to the PQ.

Sinclair became exasperated that the government would repeatedly deny that Germany was rearming even though it was in receipt of intelligence to the contrary.[318] He finally made use of his direct access to the Prime Minister to remonstrate. Stanley Baldwin explained that he could not go into a General Election with a rearmament policy or he would lose heavily to the Labour Party. This conversation must have happened in June 1935 when Baldwin succeeded Ramsay MacDonald as head of the National Government. In November of the same year the General Election was held.

Baldwin did agree, however, to convene a committee to look into the question of German rearmament. The special cabinet committee was held in July 1935 to examine the air parity question. Winterbotham provided a colourful description of the event, giving the impression that he was the central figure in the proceedings. 'The figure of 1,500 German first-line aircraft by 1937 was adopted as the standard* and the committee warned that the situation must be carefully watched and urged that extra funds be provided for MI6.'[319] In the car on the way back to Broadway Sinclair told Winterbotham, 'You put your career on the line.'

The Winterbotham–Bill de Ropp double-act had got off to an impressive start. The von Reichenau lunch was one of those events which only happens a few times in an intelligence officer's career; a moment of sublime revelation when he or she does not want to do or say anything that might cause the flood of information to stop.

The failure of the War Office to take the reporting seriously detracted considerably from its value; another reminder that intelligence is only worth anything if it is assessed and then understood. Winterbotham would make future trips to Berlin but usually as part of a wider delegation. These visits always gave Bill de Ropp the opportunity to broaden his sphere of contacts. Of these Erich Koch, the Gauleiter of East Prussia, would be the most important.

No sooner had Winterbotham departed than Bill de Ropp returned to his existing sources to track the seismic developments inside Germany. One of his principal contacts was Hans Berthold,

* For the background to such statistics see Chapter 19.

who had introduced him to Arno Schickedanz and into Rosenberg's circle. Like von Reichenau, Berthold was a tough character. As a young man he had travelled to German South-West Africa where he became a journalist for the colonial magazine *Kolonie und Heimat*.[320] These were pioneering days for the colonists with the exploitation of the mineral resources, especially diamonds.[321]

At the outbreak of war Berthold seems to have joined the German colonial forces which were defeated by South African troops in July 1915. He would have been held as a prisoner of war at the camp at Aus in the very south of the colony from where he would have been repatriated to Germany at the end of the war.[322] South-West Africa then ceased to be a German colony and was governed by South Africa under a League of Nations mandate.

On his return to Germany Berthold joined the Stahlhelm but quickly became disillusioned with the lack of activity. He took part in Wolfgang Kapp's putsch in Berlin in 1920 which failed to overthrow the Weimar government. In 1930 he joined the Nazi Party and was a sympathiser of Walter Stennes, the SA leader who mounted a couple of half-hearted coups that same year against Hitler's leadership. When they failed, Stennes was forced into exile in China, and Hitler called upon Ernst Röhm to lead the SA.

Bill de Ropp also made friends with Röhm who was close to Rosenberg's American adviser, Kurt Lüdecke, and worked for von Epp. Röhm also earned the unlikely admiration of Anthony Eden who described him as flamboyant, scarred, scented, intelligent and brave.[323] Röhm had just returned from Bolivia where he had spent five years training the Bolivian army. He was homosexual and surprisingly open about his liaisons. He was also disillusioned by his lack of advancement in the party. From his viewpoint he had saved Hitler on several occasions during the 1920s and since his return from La Paz his stormtroopers had provided the party with the muscle which had got them to power. He wanted to be made Minister of Defence in place of the Reichswehr's General Werner von Blomberg.

Röhm viewed the Reichswehr as full of aristocrats who were not sufficiently committed to the Nazi vision. Meanwhile Himmler's SS was increasingly becoming a rival to the SA. Röhm was very slow to work out what was happening. Hitler's plans for conquest would require organised military power and an existing army was a better bet than a body of stormtroopers led by a man with overweening political ambitions.

Hitler was urged to take bold action by Göring, Goebbels and Himmler and the result was the Night of the Long Knives at the very end of June 1934. Röhm was the most prominent victim of a purge which probably killed around a hundred supposed renegades within the Nazi party. Gregor Strasser, one of the earliest Nazi leaders, was among the dead as was General Kurt von Schleicher, Hitler's immediate predecessor as Chancellor of Germany. Hans Berthold was never heard of again and was presumably one of the many undocumented victims.

Rosenberg was never in serious danger of being purged. Neither Himmler nor Goebbels saw him as a sufficiently serious threat, but Rosenberg himself was undoubtedly nervous. His friend Kurt Lüdecke would have been purged if he had not escaped to Czechoslovakia and thence to Canada. The von der Ropp family's friend Gottfried Treviranus, a former minister under Brüning, had a lucky escape while playing tennis and he courageously tried to save Schleicher (who had already been killed), before managing to flee to England[324] allegedly with the help of Archibald Church,* who allowed Treviranus to cross the border into Holland on his passport.[325] Treviranus would be helpful to the British and Canadian security authorities in their work against the Nazis.[326]

By chance Bill de Ropp was in London during the purge. He spent seven nights at the Savile Club from 28 June.[327] He would have travelled to London by train via Hook of Holland and Harwich

* MI6 considered recruiting Church in 1940. (NA KV 2/344/2 Folio 19)

to accompany Horst Obermüller of the APA to the Hendon air show, where, on Saturday the 30th, Winterbotham took them to see the aerobatics display by the RAF. It was a remarkable day with a crowd of 180,000. The Prince of Wales arrived in his own aircraft before watching while three RAF Bristol Bulldogs staged a mock attack on two Boulton Paul Overstrand bombers (the last biplane bombers). The message was that the RAF could defend the country against enemy bombers. In the subsequent aerobatics by a squadron of nine Bulldogs one aircraft crashed and the pilot was killed. The show went on regardless, with the demonstration of an Autogiro and the shooting down of a balloon, which must have made Bill de Ropp wince.[328]

On leaving the airfield Winterbotham saw a newspaper boy with a banner headline announcing the shooting of Röhm. He showed it to Obermüller who remarked, 'Thank God, we got him before they got us', a remark which suggests he was not entirely surprised. Winterbotham added that Obermüller left that evening for Berlin where he transferred from Rosenberg's APA to become 'head of an intelligence unit at Hamburg which worked against England. I had news of his inefficiency from time to time.'[329] In fact, the Hamburg office of the Abwehr was the principal site for espionage against Britain and would score some significant successes against MI6.

Röhm should have seen the coup coming. General Blomberg's leading article on the front page of the *VB* on 28 June had declared that the army's role in the Third Reich was clear and unequivocal. Hitler had also omitted Röhm's name from the 'National Union of German officers.' Either Röhm was not concentrating while he was on holiday at the Bavarian lakes at Wiessee or he felt he was fireproof having only recently declared that 'The Storm Troops are ready to die for the ideal of the Swastika.'[330]

Rosenberg's diary includes a lengthy entry on the purge,[331] and one can sense his relief. He implies that the British had advance notice:

> Messages about a putsch had come from all sides, to the APA as well.* [Ramsay] MacDonald in a very intimate circle had said to the violinist [Fritz] Kreisler, 'Now in the next few weeks things in Germany will indeed be forcibly changed.' Kreisler's wife – a non-Jew – passed that on in confidence and thus we also learned of it. In addition [Viktor] Lutze, a decent fellow, had warned the Führer.†

One wonders from where MacDonald received his advance notice and whether he was talking about a putative putsch by Röhm or about Hitler's counter-strike. If it was from Bill de Ropp via MI6 it would have been somewhat unnerving for Bill to see it boomerang back so quickly.

There is a particular irony in Rosenberg's comments on Strasser who was one of his earliest colleagues in the party:

> Gregor Strasser turned out to be half a man. Could not stand the hostility of Dr Goebbels who had started labelling Strasser's mother a Jewess . . . As a result he lost confidence in the steadiness and dependability of the Führer and suffered in 1932 from a substantially exaggerated opinion of himself.

Rosenberg himself had a Jewish mistress, the 'beautiful red-haired Lisette Kohlerausch', who had been arrested by the Gestapo but released at Rosenberg's request by Göring.[332] Rosenberg constantly worried about the hostility of Goebbels and Hitler's loyalty.

Bill and Jimmy felt less than confident about returning to Berlin. They knew that Rosenberg could not offer them much protection if somebody were to make mischief from Bill's past friendship with both Röhm and Berthold. So they booked a holiday in Lisbon, leaving

* Rosenberg here means a supposed putsch by Röhm.

† Lutze would replace Röhm as the head of the SA.

Hamburg on 21 July on the small Hansa Line steamer *Lahneck*, only returning to Berlin when certain that the coast was clear.

As a result of this dangerous year Bill spent several nights at his beloved Savile Club. A recent chairman of the club has pondered . . .

> . . . the interesting question of the extent of pro-German sentiment in Clubland in the 1930s. The Athenaeum . . . had a definite problem. Not only was the German Embassy in Carlton House Terrace just yards away but also, under their rules, the German ambassador Joachim von Ribbentrop was automatically granted honorary membership in 1936 . . . There he could find himself in the company of the appeaser Lord Londonderry and the wealthy and openly Fascist George Pitt-Rivers, amongst others.[333]

At the Savile there was:

> John Collings ('Jack') Squire a journalist, poet and critic who was one of the founders on 1st January 1934 of The January Club, a dining club discussion group formed ostensibly 'for the study of modern methods of government and particularly for the study of some adaptation of Fascism to suit British conditions' that supported (though it was not officially associated with) the British Union of Fascists until it dissolved about eighteen months later. In May 1934 Squire chaired 'The Black Shirt Dinner' for 250 members and guests at The Savoy at which he was photographed in *The Tatler* (in white tie) sitting next-but-one to Sir Oswald Mosley's mother Maud. Among the guests were Mr W. Joyce (later 'Lord Haw-Haw') in black-shirt.[334]

None of this need surprise us too much; 1934 was close to the apogee of British conservative admiration for Hitler. The Night of the Long Knives was one of many events over the next five years which would reduce the number of admirers. Bill de Ropp knew Squire well but the Savile was no hotbed of fascism. A Committee Meeting on 31 January 1934 recorded, 'It was unanimously and of course rightly decided that we don't reject people merely because they are non-Aryan.'[335] Many Savile members went on to have distinguished war records and indeed many died in the process.

Bill de Ropp's time in Lisbon and London would also have given him time to reflect on what lay ahead. He knew that the Night of the Long Knives had been a watershed event for several reasons. The Reichswehr had won its battle against the SA as to which group would provide the military muscle for the Nazis' ambitions. But simultaneously Himmler's SS had won its own struggle against the much larger SA about who would control state security. The Nazis were no longer just a boisterous and noisy political party but a lethal ideology melded with the resources of the German nation state.

This must have been the moment that Bill asked the MI6 doctor in London for some suicide pills. 'He gave me two sinister-looking white capsules, one for me and one for my wife. "One quick bite will be sufficient," he added cheerfully.'[336] Bill de Ropp had special pockets sewn into all his waistcoats where he could hide his cyanide pill.

On his return to Berlin Bill de Ropp would need to watch out for three specific threats to his safety. The first came from the Abwehr (Military Intelligence) which had existed since 1920 and was still small but would soon grow and would make Great Britain one of its primary targets. In 1936 a naval captain, Wilhelm Canaris, would be made its chief. Although he would later be associated with anti-Nazi sentiments and would develop an arm's length relationship with MI6 (*see* Chapter 24), Canaris was a German patriot and a serious threat.

The second would be from the Gestapo, which in 1934 was transferred from Göring's command to that of Himmler. Under its new leadership it would become more formidable and its powers would increase exponentially. One of its jobs was to uncover foreign spies.

And the third would be from the SD (the Sicherheitsdienst), which had been created as the security arm of the SS in 1931 under the ambitious and ruthless Reinhard Heydrich. In 1935 a new name would become associated with the SD, Walter Schellenberg, one of Heydrich's most effective and dangerous assistants.

As so often happens with intelligence and security services the three entities not only competed (which can sometimes enhance effectiveness) but they also detested each other and rarely cooperated. The mutual dislike and distrust between Canaris and his one-time naval subordinate Heydrich were indicative of the wider relationship.*

By 1934 Bill de Ropp would probably have already come to the attention of all three services for his contacts with Röhm, Berthold, von Reichenau and Lüdecke but he would have been well down their priority list. There were several much bigger threats to the regime to worry about first. Furthermore it would be a brave (and foolish) official who would take too much hostile interest in a friend of Rosenberg. Although weakened by his 1933 trip to London Rosenberg was still a big beast in the party and would, to the surprise of almost everyone, remain so until the very end.

* In 1939 Himmler would bring the SD and Gestapo under one umbrella, the RSHA (Reich Main Security Office), and the Abwehr would be added in 1942. However, for most of this story they were three separate and distinct organisations.

Mixing business with pleasure. Shortly before Winterbotham's epic visit to Berlin in 1934, four members of the MI6 station were involved in this evening of amateur dramatics on the Kurfürstendamm. Some signed the poster in their own names but most in the identities of their characters. Frank Foley's signature is at the bottom and there are photos of Kay Foley (his wife) and Cecil Insall, among others. (*Lynn Insall*)

16

THE NAZIS ARE 'INTENSELY SINCERE'

1934–1936: The minds of the British people and the royal family

Nothing reflects the ambiguity of Bill de Ropp's position better than the two British delegations which he accompanied around Germany in 1934 and 1936. They also indicate the gradual evolution of MI6's approach towards Germany. In 1934 Admiral Sinclair still saw Germany as a potential ally in the more important battle against Bolshevik Russia. By 1936 there was a (perhaps still grudging) realisation that Nazi Germany itself represented a future threat. Even in 1936 the intelligence effort seems half-hearted. As we saw from 'What Should We Do?' (*see* Chapter 2), MI6 and much of Whitehall only became deadly serious about Nazism in 1938.

On 11 July 1934 Rosenberg noted in his diary, 'The Fight for England continues unswervingly. Obermüller is back from London.' Obermüller had floated the idea of a delegation to visit Germany finishing with the highlight of each Nazi Year, the annual *Parteitag* at Nuremberg, the party convention better known nowadays as the Nuremberg Rally.

Rosenberg's foreign policy unit, the APA, had just been set up and was still in its original quarters in an annex of the Adlon Hotel. It fell to Horst Obermüller, as Head of the Western European department, to choose and then issue invitations to the British guests. Obermüller was a war hero. He had commanded three U-boats and sunk ten ships with a total weight of over 42,000 tons and had won the Iron Cross both first and second class.[337] In 1925 he had worked for the Abwehr for a short period.[338]

Rosenberg explained that he particularly sought British visitors and was pleased to get sixteen acceptances in spite of the summer holidays. He complained that the German Embassy in London had been unhelpful, first advising against inviting guests and then insisting they were 'unreachable'.[339]

From contemporary newspaper reports we can recreate the delegation list.

> Captain (later Major) Hubert Fitzroy Fyers, of the Rifle Brigade, had been equerry (later Comptroller) to Field Marshal the Duke of Connaught since 1929. (He rejoined the Rifle Brigade and served during the Siege of Malta during the Second World War.)

> Captain Guy Hardy MacCaw came from a very wealthy Calcutta-based family. He had served in the 3rd Hussars and won the MC. He was staff officer to General Hanbury-Williams, Chief of the British Military Mission at St Petersburg.[340] He spoke fluent Russian. He was a member of the Anglo-Ukraine Committee from 1931 to 1934.[341] (His son Derek would die flying an RAF Hurricane over France in 1940.)

> The Earl of Brecknock was the eldest son of the Marquess Camden. He served in the Scots Guards after the war until 1927. He and his wife were society figures and close to the Prince of Wales (the future King Edward VIII). (He rejoined the Scots Guards in the Second World War.)

Colonel Lord William Percy was educated at Eton and Oxford and served in the Grenadier Guards in the war. He won a DSO when severely wounded at Neuve Chapelle. Thereafter he was best known as an ornithologist in Norfolk.[342]

Roger Chetwode of Martin's Bank was the only son of Field Marshal Sir Philip Chetwode. He was educated at Eton and Oxford. He trained as a banker with JP Morgan in New York. He was only twenty-eight when he visited Germany in 1934. (He would die in 1940 aged thirty-four.)

Lieutenant Colonel James Viner Delahaye was educated at Haileybury and the Royal Military Academy. He served in the Royal Field Artillery throughout the war and was awarded a DSO and MC. In 1919 he was in North Russia and the Baltic States before a long stint at the War Office until 1928. Afterwards he became a Labour politician, failing to win Exeter in 1931, Camberwell in 1935 and North Bucks in 1937.[343] He was a strong opponent of capitalism and a supporter of a Popular Front against fascism. From 1928 he was a member of the Savile.

Lieutenant Colonel W. A. Greenley, CMG, DSO, had served in the Army Service Corps during the war. He was a former member of Bromley Town Council and a partner in J. F. Adair, the pepper traders, which was bankrupted in 1935. (In the Second World War he rejoined the RASC but left due to ill health in 1943.)

The Rev. Harold Victor Hodson was educated at Cheltenham College and Oxford. He won a Military Cross in the war as an army chaplain. He was a Bush Brother in Queensland 1913–16 and Vicar of Northleach, Gloucestershire in 1934.

Philip Farrer was appointed Secretary to the Earl of Salisbury in 1924. He mixed in far-right circles in the 1930s and as late as

1939 attended a dinner with the Mosleys attended by Admiral Barry Domville, who was later imprisoned for Nazi sympathies.

G. E. O. Knight. After the war (during which he was a prisoner) he became a journalist, an explorer and a publisher. He led a 1922 expedition to Tibet before becoming interested in natural cures for nervous diseases. He wrote a pro-German pamphlet in 1934 and was Chairman of the Anglo-German Group. He was strongly opposed to war.

Eustace Robb was one of founders of BBC Television from 1932 to 1936 and the company's first Producer. His father had been a general in Kitchener's army. Eustace himself had served in the Coldstream Guards.[344]

Rosenberg was uncharitable about the German Embassy's help in enticing one of the more important guests:

An overjoyed Otto Bismarck [the Counsellor at the Embassy] reported in March 1934 that he had caught a big English fish: 'a close acquaintance of mine, the adjutant of the Duke of Connaught, Captain Fitzroy Fyers, has told me that he would like to travel to Germany to meet prominent representatives of the new Germany.'

A few weeks later Bismarck was more precise:

Fyers wants to be brought into contact with several members of the [German] government and the NSDAP to inform the Duke of Connaught about Germany from the best sources. The Duke is very interested in Germany and because of his influence within the royal family it is important to inform him correctly.

Fyers wants to know about: 1. Our fight against unemployment. If possible he would like to visit an *Arbeitslager* [forced labour camp] near Berlin. 2. The current situation regarding the Jewish question. 3. The conflict within the Evangelische Kirche [Protestant Church].[345]

We have the Reverend Hodson to thank for one of the best accounts of the trip, provided in a report in the *Gloucestershire Echo*.

> I had over an hour's conversation with Dr Rosenberg when I stated quite frankly what I thought of the anti-Jewish campaign and told him the whole of the Christian civilised world was aghast at the treatment of Jews in Germany. Dr Rosenberg tried to defend the attitude by saying how Germany had suffered from Jews in the past.

Like most people Hodson was deceived by Hitler.

> [I] was introduced to Hitler and stood by him for four, five and six hours at a time. He did not seem a brutal hard man but one who, while not handsome, was not of unattractive appearance and had at times a merry twinkle in his eyes.

However, Hodson was puzzled by the invitation.

> What object the Germans had in asking them over [reported the *Gloucestershire Echo*], he did not know, but they showed them the labour camps which might be described as rather like unemployment centres in England. He presumed they showed those in order to make them believe they were recovering from the depression and were out to pay the debts they owed . . . Mr Hodson described as most impressive the march past of the troops, which took four hours . . . Germany had recently got . . . a new spirit of hope.[346]

One of the most fascinating and rapid transformations can be seen in the case of Knight. In 1934 he wrote a pamphlet 'In Defence of Germany' which can only be described as trenchant.[347] In his foreword he asked:

> How often must it be repeated that there is no alternative to the Hitler regime in Germany but Communism. Once Communism gets control there it will speedily spread its evil influence to every country in Europe. I can scarcely believe there is a responsible Englishman who wishes to see the German Reich fall into the hands of Communists. Every article that appears in the London and Provincial Press to-day against Germany and its Government is a direct incitement to the Communists.

Of the Jews he claimed:

> Before the revolution of March 1933, the Jews in the Reich overran many Government Departments, and enjoyed the highest privileges in every profession and calling. They were the principal organisers of the German Communist Party and became identified with every one of the warring political sects in the country. In every way they proved themselves eminently capable businessmen and politicians. Many had grown very wealthy. Nearly every German war profiteer was a Jew.

And he even had some thoughts on espionage:

> The British Foreign Office is well aware that not a few men attached to newspapers in foreign countries are employed for purposes of espionage. In the course of my wanderings round the European capitals I have met newspaper men who openly boasted of having been employed in this and that country's secret service, who have accepted the hospitality of people whom they later on wantonly betrayed.

It is an intemperate paper and one which he would have cause to regret. In *The Scotsman* exactly one year later he announced that one hundred members of his 'Anglo-German Group' had resigned over the treatment of the Jews in Germany before adding that he was in full sympathy with them.[348] The speed of Knight's Damascene conversion is much to his credit and compares starkly with the dilatory behaviour of much of the political class.

It is intriguing to speculate whether Knight was thinking of Bill de Ropp as one of the journalist spies. Bill was sometimes described as a correspondent of *The Times*. His views on communism certainly matched those of Knight and it is quite probable that it was Bill who arranged for Baroness von der Goltz (wife of the General who fought the Baltic campaign in 1919) to write the appreciation that appeared at the front of his pamphlet.

Rosenberg was very pleased with the results. He wrote in his diary:

> The gentlemen flew to East Prussia and Schleswig Holstein to convince themselves first of the serious work and then came to Nuremberg where they were wide-eyed at the genuine public feeling and the exemplary displays of marching. They were deeply impressed . . . Of interest was the conversation with Reverend Hodson, a friend of the Bishop of Gloucester. He had suspected me of being a gruff anti-Christian and a violent madman but to his amazement found me to be a person like everyone else. The long very candid talk made a good impression on him. In a public meeting in Gloucester he voiced this impression as well, out of decency.[349]

It is interesting that it had not occurred to Hodson that he had been invited because of his proximity to the Bishop of Gloucester, whose pro-Nazi statements would continue right up until 1938. In August 1938 the Bishop (Arthur Headlam) criticised the Labour

Party for 'the insulting language used about Hitler. It is no business of ours if Germany prefers . . . a government which is not democratic.'[350] It is also disturbing that Rosenberg could still not understand his own fatal dichotomy between being quite a thoughtful, soft-spoken person in conversation whilst also espousing a doctrine that incited hatred and (eventually) mass murder.

Rosenberg was particularly pleased with Colonel MacCaw, a 'private citizen'. McCaw claimed to be the political adviser of the British War Office. He allegedly told Rosenberg that 'the Treaty of Versailles had been a crime. [President Woodrow] Wilson an imbecile, Lloyd George an ignoramus. In the foreseeable future one must get together to effect a new order.'[351]

During the war MacCaw had been Kitchener's aide. He had waited for him at St Petersburg when Kitchener made his fatal voyage and died aboard HMS *Hampshire* in June 1916 when it hit a mine en route to Russia. MacCaw thought that Kitchener's death had done great harm to peace: 'He would have prevented all the lunacy of Versailles.'[352] Finally Rosenberg noted that 'Captain Fyers . . . as the aide-de-camp of the Duke of Connaught . . . has reported on Nuremberg to the Royal Family.'

In his diary entry on 21 January 1935 Rosenberg observed:

> A few days ago Baron de Ropp dropped in again. Secretive: only for me and the Führer. His Majesty the King of England has expressed to his political adviser his utmost astonishment that England was so poorly informed about the true situation in the Saar. In particular he said the 'serious press' fell short in this case. This displeasure has produced considerable commotion. The adviser in question turned to the British Air Ministry which had reported correctly (through me) and requested further briefing on the situation in Germany. Whereupon Major Winterbotham phones de Ropp and requests that he travel to London. Ropp will meet the King's

> adviser in a club and tell him what he needs to know about the entire movement. He set off yesterday.

This was skilfully handled by Winterbotham. Fyers's report to the Duke of Connaught had sparked the interest of the Palace. Fyers must have consulted the Air Ministry, which had alerted Winterbotham who spotted a golden opportunity to burnish Bill de Ropp's credentials with both Rosenberg and Hitler. It was lucky that this happened in early 1935 when pro-German sentiments were commonplace. Had it happened later, either when Edward VIII was King or as the chances of another world war approached, it would have posed a major quandary for MI6. Should Bill de Ropp give a pro-German account to the royal family or should he break cover and give an honest view and thereby risk his position in Berlin?[353]

Rosenberg noted in his diary for 2 February 1935:

> Ropp back from London. He was with the Duke of Kent. This was the person mysteriously represented as 'adviser to the King'. Introduction at a ball, then conversation in private until 3am. The son of the King repeated His Majesty's displeasure at the reporting in England about Germany. They have resigned themselves to German rearmament, he said, but it is important to have precise knowledge of the mentality of the leading figures. Whether they are aggressive or want to work with the structures of an organic strategy. What is Hitler like? Hess? Rosenberg? Whereupon Ropp described his many years of acquaintance. I briefed the Führer on this.[354]

Prince George, Duke of Kent, was the fourth son of George V and had caused his parents a great deal of worry, first over his drug-taking and later due to his affair with Kiki Preston, the American socialite and member of the Kenyan Happy Valley set. In 1934 the Prince had begun to 'settle down' having met and married Princess Marina of

Greece. He lived at Fort Belvedere on the edge of Windsor Great Park.[355] Like his brother, the future King Edward VIII, he had pro-Nazi leanings in 1935 in common (as we have seen) with much of the British upper and middle classes.

The second delegation to Germany in 1936 was very different. On the surface it looked remarkably similar to the first: a group of influential figures with outstanding war records and apparent sympathies for Germany. The origins of this visit, however, were different. This time the delegates were all selected by Whitehall and all had held government roles and could be trusted to accept an intelligence brief.

Bill de Ropp later gave an outline of the trip.

> I had a most amusing time in 1937 [in fact 1936] when Rosenberg conceived the idea of inviting a dozen prominent Englishmen to tour Germany as guests of the Government ending with a visit to the Nuremberg Rally. I was asked to supply a list of suitable guests. I had great difficulty in arranging this but I got together a fully-fledged peer, a courtesy Lord, two Generals, an Admiral, a journalist and a sporting parson.* They were all flown over in Hitler's beautiful [Junkers 52] plane and I met them in Berlin. The whole junket was laid on with German thoroughness, lasted 14 days and cost the government £4,000.

Fortunately we know that Bill de Ropp had more than a little help in arranging the visit. One of the guests, General Karslake, received a handwritten letter from Stewart Menzies:

> Dear General. I am writing in an unofficial capacity. I have been asked to secure the names of one or two distinguished soldiers

---

* For the 'sporting parson' de Ropp must have been thinking of Hodson and the 1934 visit.

> who might care to attend the grand party rally at Nuremberg, as the guests of the German government from about 4th to 12th September. The trip which would be by air would mean a visit to Berlin, possibly Kiel, 3 days at Nuremberg and back by the Rhineland. Several MPs have accepted and one or two business people as well as an admiral. The party would comprise about eight and I know those who went on a previous trip enjoyed it greatly.

The letter written on 24 July was signed S. G. Menzies MI1c (here being used as the War Office cover name for MI6). Karslake accepted and attended a lunchtime briefing by Fred Winterbotham at the Cavalry and Guards Club. Karslake had originally wanted to take his son too and Menzies had argued the case on his behalf 'that it is as important to educate the next generation upon the virtues of Nazism!!'[356] The double exclamation marks make it clear that Menzies was being ironic; so the days of uncritical admiration of Nazism were definitively over.

The delegation comprised:

> Lord Apsley who had met Rosenberg during his 1931 visit to London as the guest of Fred Winterbotham. He had been Conservative MP for Southampton and then Bristol Central. In 1936 he was Parliamentary Private Secretary to the Minister of Defence Co-ordination, Sir Thomas Inskip. He was a keen aviator.
>
> Admiral Sir Rudolf Miles Burmester was a Royal Navy officer who had served off Gallipoli during the war and commanded the battleship HMS *Warspite* in the mid-1920s. In 1929 he was appointed Commander-in-Chief Africa Station until 1931.
>
> Captain Randolf Gresham Nicholson had just returned to Britain from Malaya where he had been ADC to the Governor. In 1936 he was appointed captain of the cruiser HMS *Curacoa*.

Major-General Ernest Swinton had served in the Boer War but is most famous as one of the instigators behind the invention of the tank. In 1916 he was involved in training the first tank crews.

Major-General Sir Henry Karslake served in the Royal Artillery and later as a Staff Officer during the war. In 1936 he had just returned to London after commanding in Baluchistan, a province then of British India, now in Pakistan. He acted decisively in declaring martial law after the massive Quetta earthquake of 1935 (which killed over 30,000 people), for which he was knighted.[357]

Major Eric Dutton was Secretary to the Governor of Rhodesia. He was the man whom Bill de Ropp met in Nairobi. He was a fellow member of the Savile Club, and in 1936 married the daughter of General Sir Hubert Gough who had led the British Mission in the Baltic States in 1919. He was a man of great courage but was widely disliked for his boorishness.[358]

Squadron-Leader Fred Winterbotham also travelled with the delegation. For some curious reason he gives the impression in his memoirs that he was the only guest.[359] However, it is clear from Menzies's letters that he coordinated the trip and was responsible for the collection of intelligence from the other invitees.

Bill de Ropp described the trip:

First they were worked to a standstill visiting schools, hospitals, camps, drainage schemes and so on. Then I joined them for a tour of East Prussia where Gauleiter Koch looked after them superbly. He arranged for them to visit Trakehnen Stud Farm, the world-famous centre of producing highly bred riding horses. Here the stallions lived luxuriously in individual thatched

> stables with one room to each horse. The Peer and the Generals were vastly impressed.
>
> Then we stayed on the large estate of an old Teutonic Count with Nazi sympathies (naturally) where there was a wonderful stud of thoroughbred Arabs. The sporting parson had never seen anything like it. Finally a beautiful Countess threw a huge party for us to meet all the local aristocracy.[360] The Admiral enjoyed himself hugely.

The first half of the trip owed everything to Bill de Ropp's burgeoning relationship with Erich Koch who was a close friend of Rosenberg's.* Koch ran East Prussia more as a socialist than a National Socialist and some of his social projects were certain to impress visitors. Winterbotham, however, was keen on the East Prussia visit for intelligence reasons.

He claims to have asked the pilot of the Junkers 52 to fly over several airfields, which enabled him to confirm intelligence received from other sources. However, he felt he had to turn down an invitation to visit the important U-boat training base at Pilau (now Baltysk in Kaliningrad). 'I noticed that Bill had been watching me rather anxiously and no doubt that he too thought it too risky to accept.'[361]

Winterbotham noted that amber resin was being used to provide insulation at extremely high temperatures. The most important intelligence to emerge was when Koch told Winterbotham that he expected 'Generals' from Berlin to come and concrete over his quiet province in preparation for what Winterbotham suggested was the expected invasion of Russia. [362]

Bill de Ropp continued:

> Then on to the Nuremberg Rally to see the various Party organisations and have a private audience with Hitler and Hess.

* Rosenberg and Koch would become mortal enemies after Hitler's invasion of Russia in 1941.

> Hitler was all tact, love and friendship that day. The polished diplomat, the courteous host, the statesman who lived only to serve his country. It was clear that my 'prominent party' was greatly impressed. They had seen Nazi Germany through rose-tinted spectacles and were about to return to Britain suitably indoctrinated. I was in an odd spot. I dared not comment adversely on anything for what I said would certainly be passed on and eventually come home to roost.
>
> Then I hit upon the idea of taking them to hear Hitler's main speech. There on the platform they saw a completely different Hitler, one they scarcely recognised as the man they had met. He raged and shouted. They could understand little but the English morning papers contained long reports of his tirade against the Jews. 'Remarkable creature' shuddered the Peer. 'What an anti-climax' commented the General. They were intelligent enough to see what a snake Hitler was.[363]

Sadly Bill de Ropp's assessment contained more than a little self-delusion. He speaks as if the Hitler speech was an optional extra, whereas it was the highlight to which all the guests were invited. And at least one of the guests was thoroughly impressed by the whole experience.

General Karslake wrote copious notes on the visit, some on plain paper and some on headed paper which he had retained upon leaving 'Headquarters House, Quetta, Baluchistan'. Few of the points are worth repeating because they represent a simplistic acceptance of the Nazi Party line, but his limp agreement with Nazi views on Jews is arresting.

> [I] accepted the invitation with some other gentlemen to attend a *Reichparteitag* at Nuremberg in 1936. Before the rally started we were taken for an information tour to Hamburg and East Prussia and were shown various social schemes for the benefit of

> the working classes. During the whole period we had the honour of meeting several of the leading members of the Nazi Party, including the leader Herr Hitler. There were never any limitations to answer all our questions however tactless they appeared to be.
>
> Herr Hitler was firmly convinced that communism was and is the greatest danger in the world today. Most Jews are potential communists; therefore to moderate communism the Jews had either to leave Germany or be treated in such a way that they would be regarded as suspect and not allowed to be recognised as Germans. German citizenship was to be exclusively German and no Jew would be allowed to be a German citizen with all that implies. They pointed out . . . that it was impossible to discriminate between good and bad Jews.[364]

Karslake returned to Nuremberg for the 1937 Rally. On the notepaper of the Grand Hotel (in 1936 he had stayed at the Park Hotel) he wrote a draft letter to one of Britain's ten field marshals (possibly the Duke of Connaught). There were three points of particular note.

'The question of colonies is still a very sore point and they are not going to let it drop. Even if they expand eastwards they will still demand colonies.' He was intrigued by a Canadian idea of getting Britain, France and Belgium to give the Cameroons and part of the Congo to Germany.

'The question of loyalty of the army to National Socialism was raised. But there are senior officers who are very much against some of the measures. On the other hand the bulk of the rank and file has been trained under National Socialism and even if the officers wanted to do anything it is very doubtful if the rank and file would back them e.g. it was said that Gen von Fritsch does not see eye to eye always with von Blomberg.'

'On my second visit to the *Reichparteitag* I have a feeling that the German nation is beginning to lose all hope of securing any friendly feeling of the British nation. What is the matter? Why do we still apparently maintain the attitude of suspicion and mistrust? In my humble opinion formed from perfectly frank talks with members of the Nazi Party from top to bottom I have no doubt that they are intensely sincere.'[365]

Hopefully Swinton, Nicholson and Burmester were more discerning than Karslake but it is hardly surprising that, in his diary entry for 17 September 1936, Rosenberg was purring. He had just been awarded the Führer's prize and Hitler had described both his speeches as 'outstanding'. He had also told another senior Nazi that 'Rosenberg is our best mind. I don't need to look over his speeches at all, they are all so crystal clear that not a word has to be changed.' Rosenberg was so starved of compliments from his hero Adolf Hitler that he confided to his diary, 'Those brave men who would like to see the Rosenberg era brought to an end have now, at least for a time, changed their colours again.'

He then added:

> I had to take care of about 60 guests, some of them quite prominent. Among others, a number of important British guests whom I brought to the Führer who talked to them about the colonial demands . . . The Führer emphasised that the colonial question is not one of prestige but rather one of purely economic matter. Dutton came to see me later and we talked for two hours about possibilities.[366]

Dutton's inclusion in the MI6-selected delegation could only have been to discuss colonies. This was an area where it was still felt in Whitehall that concessions could be made to Germany (although it is noteworthy that Britain seemed more interested in offering colonies administered by other countries than its own).

On his arrival back in Britain Lord Apsley gave an address in Cirencester.

> I am afraid that Germany is almost bound to make war [with Russia] because of natural circumstances. Hitler himself is a constructive not a destructive man as I found when I talked to him. He has an intense dislike of war and will do anything to keep Germany out of it. I am afraid that they will be driven to it by economic circumstances alone, one of the chief circumstances being that they have no gold.[367]

A few months after the second visit Bill de Ropp took a break in London.

> After one or two incidents which made me feel that I was under suspicion we went to London tired and frayed, feeling we must get away for a while from the explosive atmosphere of Germany. It was only a few days before the coronation of George VI [Wednesday, 12 May 1937]. I wanted to see something of the procession but it was far too late to attempt to get seats. However, an influential friend of mine managed to get me two, for my wife and myself, right on the corner of Whitehall with a view of the Abbey.
>
> The coronation fascinated Hitler so much that he was full of it when I next saw him. General von Blomberg, later disgraced for marrying a known prostitute, had represented him and been most impressed. 'Blomberg told me that the condensed impression of the might of the British Empire was something to marvel at,' Hitler told me. What he had also not failed to notice and report to his Führer was the genuine affection of the entire nation towards the new monarch. This surprised Hitler. He had expected half the population to want the Duke of Windsor on the throne. He never could get the Windsor story into true perspective.[368]

Hitler's inability to understand the Windsor story led to the ill-advised visit of the Duke and Duchess to Berlin in October 1937, which concluded with a visit to Berchtesgaden to meet Hitler[369] but, by then, according to Rosenberg, Hitler had given up any idea of an alliance with Great Britain.

If the MI6 aim of the second visit was to change British or German minds it clearly failed. More likely is that Winterbotham and Menzies hoped that the likes of Karslake and Nicholson would have conversations with German generals and admirals as revealing as his own remarkable lunch with von Reichenau. However most of the guests on both delegations were too easily duped by the Nazis, and Bill de Ropp could not afford to point out the flaws and fallacies to the guests. His survival depended on sticking to his cover and appearing to be sympathetic to some of the Nazi policies.

One defining aspect of this chapter is that almost everybody, except Rosenberg himself, had served in the Great War. It is easy to underestimate the trauma which many had experienced and sometimes still relived at night. To have friends blown up by artillery shells, to wipe their brains and excrement from your face, to live in the cold, wet mud with the constant concussion of bursting shells – the idea of another war was unthinkable. Even Winterbotham flying his Nieuport Scout and Bill de Ropp in his kite balloon had seen enough horror and experienced enough fear for one lifetime. Their brand of appeasement is surely beyond criticism; at least until the evidence of Nazi crimes became too apparent to ignore.

17

'YOUR WONDERFUL FÜHRER'

1930–1938: Diplomats, journalists and spies in London and Berlin

Everybody's views evolved during the 1930s. In 1930 Hitler was convinced that Britain was his natural ally. By 1937 he had abandoned the idea. Most British people began the 1930s as appeasers and gradually came to see Nazi Germany as a threat; Vansittart made the transition very early and Chamberlain very late.

Bill de Ropp's views also evolved. In late 1938 he had dinner at the Savile Club with his son, Bob, and explained his feelings with his usual fluency assisted by several glasses of Vermouth.[370]

> 'In the beginning . . . [Hitler] had a programme that made sense. *Drang Nach Osten.** Hold Europe against the great grey mass of the Slavs. Push them back. Hold the Ukraine,† the breadbasket of Europe. It was the original dream of the Teutonic Knights,

* Literally 'Push to the East'. The theory encourages the idea of German migration towards Eastern Europe.

† Since 1991 use of the definite article before 'Ukraine' is seen as offensive, but it was the norm in English in the 1930s.

our forebears. It makes sense. If the Russian avalanche ever gets moving it could overwhelm us all.'

He continued that it had been Germany's great opportunity. All the nations of northeastern Europe – Poles, Finns, Lithuanians, Latvians, Estonians and Ukrainians would flock to the German banner and embark on a holy war to crush the Bolshevik menace. The Germans can do it now. It's their great opportunity. They could become masters of Europe. They could drive back the Slavs and hold a line east of Ukraine. They could impose a Pax Germanica. But I think they will miss their chance.

'Something is working against us.' It was a force that worked in the soul of Adolf Hitler that compelled him to deviate more and more from his original programme. 'He trusts all the wrong people. He has surrounded himself with the scum of the earth. Himmler, Bormann, Heydrich, Streicher! Monsters absolute monsters! He has alienated the aristocracy and the responsible elements in the Wehrmacht. They are only waiting for an opportunity to bring him down. But you know the Germans. Sheep. Obedient to authority. Even the aristocracy . . . It's incredible. Loss of nerve, total loss of nerve. No-one dare lift a finger and to think that, in the early days, I could have put an end to little Adolf myself. One well-placed bullet . . . It might have changed the history of Europe.

'The French are shaking in their shoes and the British are as bad. All we have is an elderly ostrich with an umbrella who knows nothing, absolutely nothing, about the situation in Germany. Neville Chamberlain! Ugh! . . . Here we are in the twentieth century, the age of science, totally at the mercy of the Dark Force. If I were a religious man I suppose I'd call it the Devil.'

Spies are real people and they have their own views and motivations. MI6 would have known Bill de Ropp's views and Woollcombe would have understood the need to aim off for some of his instinctive prejudices. Furthermore what Bill de Ropp saw with such complete clarity seemed to the likes of Chamberlain, Horace Wilson, Halifax and even Cadogan as a fog of confusion.

Both London and Berlin were teeming with intrigue in the 1930s and the domestic counter-intelligence agencies were desperately trying to make sense of what they were seeing. To reach a clear view of the quality of Bill de Ropp's reporting it is important to look at his rivals and competitors on both the German and British sides. How well or badly were they representing what they heard and saw back to their capitals?

In retrospect both German and British intelligence made very little headway against each other before 1939. The French and Czechs each provided some impressive military reporting on Germany although it is worth noting that they were walk-ins (or write-ins). Just like MI6 they did not seem actively to target and cultivate individuals who might be ripe for an approach.

The Germans had had a major success against the MI6 station in the Hague but did not perform particularly well in London. After the Second World War MI5 were able to interrogate many of the people they had monitored in London during the 1930s and found that they had all been working for different organisations with little or no coordination let alone cooperation. Most of them were not even professional or trained spies and made no attempt to hide their Nazi credentials.

First, there was the German Embassy at No. 8 Carlton House Terrace. The ambassador, Leopold von Hoesch, presided until he died in 1936. He was widely respected in Whitehall but distrusted by the Nazis. Hitler replaced the aristocrat with the middle-class former champagne salesman Joachim von Ribbentrop* who tried to inject Nazi ideology into both the embassy and its diplomacy.

* The von was an invention.

He was loathed in almost equal measure by the British government and his own diplomats. The hatred which he developed for Great Britain would have serious consequences as would his crucial misjudgement that the Chamberlain government would never declare war over the invasion of Poland.

Following Ribbentrop's departure the Counsellor at the embassy, Theo von Kordt, developed a close relationship with the FO and gave every impression of being out of sympathy with his own government. The press attaché, Fritz Hesse, retained a link to Ribbentrop after the latter's return to Berlin and established a direct channel to No. 10 through George Steward (Chief Press Officer in HM Treasury with an office in 10 Downing Street) to Sir Horace Wilson.[371] This channel made both the FO and MI5 uncomfortable.

MI5 had a ringside view of the German Embassy thanks to Klop Ustinov, who was Hesse's predecessor as press attaché. Klop (whose son, Peter, would become a famous actor, director, and comic) had been recruited by MI5 and was known as U35. He was run by Jack Curry and then Dick White,[372] and Klop in turn handled the German diplomat Wolfgang zu Putlitz who arrived in London in 1934 and spied against Nazi Germany until he departed in 1938.[373]

Dick White was one of the few MI5 officers with direct experience of Germany, having served a nine-month internship with MI5 there in 1936.[374] The U35 and zu Putlitz cases were an excellent intelligence operation only marred by the fact that the London embassy was so distrusted by Hitler that it rarely possessed secrets from his inner circle.

MI5 began to circulate U35's reports directly to Vansittart and Cadogan and this caused some tension with Sinclair. The FO got round this problem by asking Sinclair to comment on MI5's reports, which he did with commendable balance, doubtless thanks to Woollcombe's expertise and diplomatic skills. In August 1938 a senior Wehrmacht officer, from Berlin, called on Ustinov at his flat and urged the British government to 'stand firm' on the Czechoslovak issue.[375] This was one of a number of signals sent by German military sources which Whitehall chose to ignore.

Also situated at the German embassy were the attachés of the armed services: Ralph Wenninger – who had attended the lunch at Horcher's in Berlin – became Germany's first air attaché in London from 1935 until war was declared in September 1939. Baron Geyr von Schweppenburg, who became a major-general in 1935 (and full general in 1937), was military attaché from 1933 to 1937. He and Wenninger had a difficult relationship. The former reported through the Defence Ministry to General Blomberg while the latter's chain of command was through the German Air Ministry to Göring. The lack of clarity about roles (and particularly who was responsible for reporting on British anti-aircraft capability) created yet another fault line in the German system.[376]

There were also some unofficial German offices operating in London. Even when he was ambassador in London and later Foreign Minister Ribbentrop maintained his own *Dienststelle* or Büro separate from the AA. It was based in Rudolf Hess's building at 64 Wilhelmstrasse.

It was led in Britain by Theodor Böttiger, a career journalist, who remained in London from 1936 to 1939. He was captured and interrogated after the war and explained how, in 1935, he was obliged to join the SS. His role was to report the news, act as Ribbentrop's personal press adviser and to seize every opportunity to highlight Ribbentrop's successes. In 1938 he became London correspondent for *VB*.

Alfred Rosenberg maintained his APA which he had set up in 1934. At the end of the war the interrogation of Hans von Chappuis, the head of the APA's English section, provided a good retrospective insight into the work of this department. Arno Schickedanz was the Chief of Staff, Captain Horst Obermüller was head of the Western department, von Chappuis himself was head of the English section,

Karl Bömer*[377] for the USA and Press, and Hans Thost as the *VB* correspondent in London followed by Dr Theodor Seibert.

The APA was ineffectual, only achieving influence in rare cases, two being Norway and Romania. Von Chappuis, who had English relatives, including a member of the FO, Berkeley Gage,[378] would later comment to his interrogators:

> Rosenberg's knowledge covered Russia, the Baltic States and his field of interest was, of course, concerned from the beginning with the fight against Bolshevism, freemasons and Jews. His knowledge of Western European countries was negligible . . . Rosenberg was a man of theories, he was continually outmanoeuvred by other members of the regime, and he lacked appreciation of practical things and of the value of personal contact . . . Rosenberg not only lacked initiative but failed to issue briefs and coordinate the work of his APA.[379]

One of the regular visitors from Germany who MI5 tried to assess was Bill de Ropp's brother, Friedrich. This was a very different man from the dangerous intriguer of the Great War and the early 1920s. Friedrich was now both a German citizen and a Protestant zealot who hoped for an understanding between the Church and National Socialism. In his memoir he wrote, 'My unofficial assignment at the Foreign Office ended shortly before Hitler came to power. I only maintained personal contact with individual gentlemen who remained in office and was occasionally supported by them.'[380]

One of the latter was Freiherr Albert Dufour von Féronce who had served in the German Embassy in London. MI5 finally decided that Friedrich himself was relatively harmless. This was certainly U35's view.[381] But Friedrich still retained his old ability to unsettle MI5. Why did he stay in Bristol with the brother of Sir Thomas

* Winterbotham went to great lengths to cultivate Bömer.

Inskip (Minister for Coordination of Defence) and what was he doing having dinner with Lord Dawson of Penn (the physician to the royal family)? Above all why was he trying to invite Colonel Arthur Smith of the Coldstream Guards to a Christian meeting at his estate at Grünheide?[382]

The vehicle for Friedrich's new venture was the Anglo-German Brotherhood (not to be confused with the more important Anglo-German Fellowship) founded in 1935. Significantly its Treasurer was none other than Dufour von Féronce. As before, Friedrich was remarkably energetic. In February 1937 he was in Edinburgh lecturing to the Rotary Club and insisting that Germany was turning away from atheism.[383] In March he addressed the Coventry Rotary Club. 'The Baron declared that all sensible Germans . . . realised that another war in Europe would mean an end to this civilisation and would leave the yellow and black races in possession of the world.'[384]

In an article for the Civil Service Prayer and Christian Unions in January 1937,[385] Friedrich wrote that 'Hitler hoped for and expected the support of the churches, being ready to support them in return.' He was wrong. The Nazis were not in favour of the established religions and were not sure about Friedrich either. In late July 1937 Dufour von Féronce wrote to the Brotherhood to inform them that 'Ropp is having certain difficulties with his work here. Some people say it is all nonsense and others that he has no connections in England worth having.' He urged influential people to write to him to testify to the importance of Friedrich's work. Two months later the Brotherhood announced that Friedrich was 'seriously ill with pneumonia and nearly died'.[386] Although he recovered the Brotherhood never got back to its former level of activity.

This therefore was the chaotic scene that MI5 was trying to monitor. Dr Bömer of the APA once told a visiting ambassador that Hitler had a deliberate policy of 'using several forces at once to achieve certain goals'.[387] The sheer waste of time and effort in having warring subordinates and expensive and overmanned departments was extraordinary and shows Nazi Germany in a far less efficient light than usually portrayed.

The British effort in reporting from Berlin was not a lot better. Sir Horace Rumbold was a top-class ambassador and between 1928 and 1933 he provided some early warning about the Nazi regime. This allowed Vansittart to send a paper marked Secret: 'The Future of Germany' through Sir John Simon (Foreign Secretary) to the Cabinet which stated (in Vansittart's usual pugnacious style) that 'One thing admits no query. The proclaimed ends of Nazi Germany can only be realised as the result of great sacrifices of, or on the part of, other Powers including ourselves . . . There is probably no immediate danger. We have time, though not too much time to make defensive preparations.'[388] This was in 1934, four full years before Munich.

The ambassadorship of Sir Eric Phipps broadly continued Rumbold's assessment of the Nazis, his clarity of message assisted by the horror of the Night of the Long Knives. When he left on a posting to Paris in 1937 he adopted, to Vansittart's irritation, a more conciliatory line towards Berlin.

His successor Sir Nevile Henderson seems to have believed that his mission was to prevent a war rather than reporting accurately to London on the Nazis' aims and intentions. In his book *Failure of a Mission*, rushed out in the three months after Hitler's invasion of Poland, he wrote, 'For two years I hoped against hope that the Nazi revolution, having run its course, would revert to a normal and civilised conduct of internal and international life.'[389] Given what had gone before – the murder and the mayhem – this was an extraordinary hope.

Vansittart wrote a sulphurous letter to Lord Halifax in March 1939. Describing Henderson's reporting as 'rubbish' and him as a 'nitwit' he concluded, 'Sir Nevile Henderson is a national danger in Berlin.'[390] Alex Cadogan would not have been so intemperate but he too realised that Henderson's reporting was providing false reassurance to the likes of Lord Halifax, Sir Horace Wilson and Neville Chamberlain who were prone to grasp at any straw of optimism.

The British military attachés in Germany made some valuable interventions. Colonel Frederick Elliot Hotblack was military attaché in Berlin between 1935 and 1937. He accompanied General Sir Cyril Deverell, the Chief of the Imperial General Staff (CIGS), to the German army manoeuvres in 1937. Deverell endorsed his report which included some trenchant observations.

> The army is devoted to Hitler who has done everything for them. It is in course of a vast expansion . . . They have no sympathy with weakness and might is right in their minds. They would like us to be friends with them for reasons to their own advantage and it would be a mistake to imagine that they would care so much for our friendship were we so weak and disarmed as to be unable to interfere with their aims.
>
> [The report continues:] I feel that the German General Staff have no desire to embark upon a great war whilst their expansion is proceeding – they are not ready for any such war [for] . . . two years at the earliest, I should say.

Possibly thinking of the state of the British army he concluded, 'It is remarkable to note the spirit of comradeship now existing between officers and men of the German army; generals conversed with the soldier in a friendly way and showed appreciation of the good work done or explanation given.'

The patchy record of diplomatic reporting from Berlin was mirrored in the press. There were some capable British correspondents in Berlin. One of the best was Ian Colvin of the *News Chronicle* who had good German military sources and was well known to Foley, not least because Colvin's wife worked for Foley at Tiergartenstrasse.[391] Norman Ebbutt of *The Times* was well-informed and frequently infuriated the Nazis;[392] Frederick Voigt of the *Manchester Guardian* broke the story of German-Russian military cooperation.

However, George Ward Price of the *Daily Mail* was an apologist for the Nazi regime. His 1937 book *I Know These Dictators* was pure appeasement. 'If the leading power in the world can devise some means of conceding peacefully to Germany . . . Europe may be able to settle down to another period of security.'[393] (After 1945 Ward Price tried to massage the record with a dubious 1957 memoir, *Extra-Special Correspondent*, in which he cast himself as an anti-fascist.)

The Passport Control Office (PCO) in Berlin, which provided cover for the MI6 station, also produced a separate line of reporting – about the Jews. On 7 May 1935 Frank Foley sent an eight-page minute with ten pages of appendices from the PCO office at 17 Tiergartenstrasse to Chancery (the Political Section) in the main Embassy building at 70 Wilhelmstrasse.

'Since the beginning of 1935 a recrudescence of antisemitism has become evident and it is becoming increasingly apparent that the Party has not departed from its original intentions and that its ultimate aim remains the disappearance of Jews from Germany'. This unsolicited intervention from the PCO office may have caused irritation in Chancery but Phipps duly sent a dispatch to Whitehall in which he (unusually) credited Foley by name but spoilt the effect in his final paragraph by drawing a distinction between 'patriotic, decent, and industrious' Jews and the rest. [394]

Apart from the MI6 reporting, the most voluminous and regular contributions to Whitehall came from Group Captain Grahame Christie reporting directly to Vansittart. It is true that Vansittart had some contacts of his own in Germany but most were Christie's. Unlike the MI6 archives, which have been drastically weeded, Christie's papers and Vansittart's still exist in the archives at Churchill College, Cambridge.

Christie had retired from the RAF and from the post of air attaché in Berlin in 1930. During the war he had joined the RFC and commanded a squadron in France and even went into combat as a young Wing Commander. From 1922 to 1926 he was Air Attaché in Washington before being moved to Berlin in 1927. He spoke fluent German having taken an engineering degree in Aachen before the war. He was also a workaholic to such an extent that his health was fragile.[395]

Following retirement, and based in his house on the German-Dutch border, he decided to dedicate himself to understanding the rebuilding of the German air force and German politics. Most of his work seems to have been self-funded although Vansittart drew on FO resources from time to time. Christie was an unsung hero but his output was decidedly mixed.

In the nine years before the outbreak of war Christie's papers suggest he worked with at least twenty-three sources. They broadly fall into four categories. There were major regime figures who would grant Christie the occasional interview. Prime amongst these were Hermann Göring and Erhard Milch, State Secretary for Aviation. Some of these meetings provided fascinating insights.

Next was a category of critics of the regime, including Dr Carl Goerdeler (the Mayor of Leipzig), Dr Hermann Rauschning (President of the Danzig Senate), Robert Bosch (the industrialist) and Otto Strasser (former Nazi and brother of Gregor who was murdered in the Night of the Long Knives).

The third category comprised people who reported back on Christie's activities. Max von Hohenlohe was one of these, Karl Abetz (Ribbentrop's Chief of Staff) another and a third was Konrad Henlein (the leader of the Sudeten Germans).

This left a fourth category of genuinely secret sources. Hans Ritter was one, although it is hard to see how he could have remained unidentified given Christie's amateurish methodology. Ritter, who Christie called Knight (the English translation of Ritter) was formerly of the Junkers aircraft company and attached to the German Embassy in Paris.[396] There was a second secret source who Christie denoted as X. As we shall see in Chapter 19 he reported on the Luftwaffe. It is noteworthy that MI6 was extremely reluctant to take on Ritter as an agent in 1939 and 1940 in spite of pressure from Vansittart, who commented testily, 'the whole Service is too bad and blinkered'.[397]

Christie's feeble attempts to conceal identities can be demonstrated by reference to one of his 'sources' the (deeply untrustworthy) Max von Hohenlohe-Langenburg. MI5 could have warned Christie if he had asked. His file reads 'Hohenlohe is a Bohemian of Lichtenstein nationality whose sole political interest centres on the preservation of his Czech estates.'[398] He was very close to Ribbentrop and was also used by the Abwehr Chief Admiral Canaris as one of his 'gentleman agents' to penetrate diplomatic and social circles abroad.[399] Christie refers to him variously as Max, MH, Mary Herbert, Holy, and Langenburg. None of this – Rauschning was described as Rausch and Goerdeler as Gord – was going to fool anyone, least of all the Gestapo.

The danger of using semi-clandestine techniques across all four categories of contacts is that it endangers the few genuinely secret ones. Christie's methodology would often involve booking a hotel room, sometimes the Kaiserhof in Berlin or hotels in the main Swiss resorts like Lausanne and Gstaad, and then asking his contacts to meet him there. Routine police work would easily list all the visitors from his usual two- to four-day stays. The SD Chief Walter Schellenberg wrote that the SD monitored Christie's contacts with Henlein and wrongly assumed that Christie was working for 'the British Secret Service'.[400]

The various German agencies would have known the identities of his contacts and, in some cases, the contents of the discussions. This does not mean that all his reporting was worthless. In fact there is some excellent material in his papers. What it does mean, however, is that Christie needed a team like Woollcombe's in Broadway to sift through the material and reach individual judgements about its reliability.

Instead Vansittart used Christie's material routinely, only filtering it to ensure that it supported his world view. This was not always easy because (like most people) Christie began as an appeaser and only became more sceptical in the mid to late 1930s. Vansittart made this same transition but much earlier than most and he was anti-German from the start. He always described 'his' sources as reliable, leaving nobody any leeway to doubt or challenge him.

On 9 August 1938 Vansittart wrote a letter marked 'Secret' to the Foreign Secretary, Lord Halifax, while Cadogan was on leave in France:

> I have at various times in the past reported that Germany intends to realise her ambitions by force . . . I produced information on several occasions in May of the preparations actually made by the German government for the purposes of invading Czechoslovakia. Our Embassy in Berlin denied these preparations . . . Our Secret Service and my own sources were at one about this . . . It is therefore the more significant that they are always in accord with the reports of the Secret Service; and it should now further be noted how they are borne out by the information that has come into Colonel Christie's possession.[401]

The former Prime Minister David Lloyd-George went to see Hitler at Berchtesgaden in 1936. The official record of their meeting still has the capacity to shock. 'One realised that the great war leader of the British Empire and the great Leader who had restored Germany to her present position were meeting on common ground. One seemed to be witnessing a symbolic act of reconciliation between two peoples.'[402] Lloyd George later thanked Ribbentrop for the visit (during which he met Friedrich von der Ropp in Heidelberg): 'You know well that before I ever went on this tour I had the greatest admiration for your wonderful Führer . . . that admiration has been deepened and intensified . . . He is the greatest piece of luck that has come to your country since Bismarck . . .'[403]

Tom Jones, who had been with Lloyd-George during his Downing Street years as Deputy Cabinet Secretary, accompanied him to Berchtesgaden. Jones was an arch-appeaser but his Damascene conversion happened suddenly in September 1938 when he swung 180 degrees to become an advocate of preparation for war. He began to correspond with oppositionists in Germany and future propagandists in London like John Beresford, Hilda Matheson of the BBC, and the 'Secret Service'. One of his draft papers was tellingly entitled 'Six years of lies'.[404] These were the very lies for which Jones himself had fallen.

The problem was not just the quality of reporting from diplomats, journalists, travellers and spies or the capacity to assess their product but the fact that the recipients, in both governments and publics, were predisposed to accept only what they wanted to believe. In Germany's case they became convinced that Britain was weak and had lost the moral fibre to stand up for itself and its empire. And in Britain there was a determination to avoid war at any cost and to think well of the Nazis until the evidence to the contrary became overwhelming. In many cases that change only happened in late 1938 or early 1939.

This was a world in which there was a dearth of information; very different from today's overload. One intriguing aspect is that Bill de Ropp knew almost everyone cited above: Ribbentrop, Hesse, Ebbutt, Colvin, Voigt, Phipps, Christie, Wenninger, von Schweppenburg, Hotblack, etc. He was ideally placed in Berlin and in daily contact with the Nazi regime. He also had the innate ability not just to report intelligence but also to provide assessment.

How well he performed must be judged, not just against his peers but by reference to the quality of the material he provided to the government in the years before the Second World War. Some of this was included in 'What Should We Do?' In Chapter 21 we shall look at some of his other reports on the eve of the Second World War.

18

'MADMEN'S DREAMS'

1932–1939: Nazi plans for the Soviet Union

The invasion of the Soviet Union in 1941 was the undoing of Adolf Hitler and his Nazi regime. In one of Bill de Ropp's early meetings with Hitler his host brought up the subject of Russia. Bill recalled the conversation twenty-five years later.

> One of my most astonishing interviews with Hitler took place at the end of 1932. He was then assuring the world that, while he would demand the return of Germany's lost land, he had no interest whatever in any non-German territory. His main cry was for the return for Saargebiet* and Sudetenland and Anschluss with Austria. We were discussing Russia in the course of a general conversation. Rosenberg as usual was present.
>
> 'Russia,' said Hitler, 'is a mere geographical conceit. It is inhabited by a heterogeneous conglomeration of peoples differing in languages and characteristics. The Russians are the biggest and strongest tribe of barbarians ruling other barbarian

* The Saar Basin, which was occupied by France and Britain under a League of Nations mandate from 1922 to 1935.

tribes. It is against the rules of history that such a state of affairs should be allowed to continue especially now when Bolshevism is poisoning the whole world.'

It so happened that I had with me a little pocket atlas. I took it out and looked at Russia. 'Give it to me,' said Rosenberg, 'I'll show you what we mean.' He sketched roughly Hitler's and his own plan on this map which I still have. Across an area comprising southern Russia, Ukraine and the Caucasus, he placed the letters OF representing East (Ost) Federation. This was where he proposed to set up vassal states under German domination. He then set aside a wide strip of territory in Eastern Russia as a British sphere of influence and solemnly told me that Hitler would be quite happy to let the United States and Japan share Siberia.

The grotesque unreality of this meeting suddenly struck me. Here were we, a crazy German politician, a rather muddle-headed philosopher and an ordinary British subject of no political significance whatever, reshaping the world. Yet madmen's dreams can come true in a mad world and within ten years Hitler had occupied a greater part of the OF territory.[405]

One wonders whether Woollcombe produced a CX report from this material. He probably decided against it. Whitehall would have dismissed the report as the crazed ravings of a lunatic who would almost certainly never attain power in Germany.

One problem for Bill de Ropp was that he and Rosenberg, both being Balts, were more interested in Eastern questions – Russia, Ukraine, the Baltic States, Poland, etc. – than most politicians and officials in Whitehall. Both men harboured a visceral hatred for Bolshevism and the Soviet Union. In fact Rosenberg became, by default, the Nazi Party's expert on the East. This is why his career suddenly experienced a renaissance in 1941 when Hitler decided to invade the Soviet Union. To the horror of Goebbels, Himmler and Heydrich,

Rosenberg was appointed Reich Minister for the Occupied Eastern Territories. The result was the greatest catastrophe in human history.

Even in 1934 when General Reichenau had told Winterbotham about the invasion plans for Russia the prospect of an actual invasion was still several years away. Winterbotham claims to have calculated that 1941 was the earliest date that the German army and air force would be ready.

As always, Rosenberg was Bill de Ropp's main source on Eastern questions along with the APA deputy Arno Schickedanz. Another productive source was Erich Koch, the Gauleiter for East Prussia. Rosenberg had sent Bill to Königsberg (now Kaliningrad) in May 1934 with an introduction to Koch. Two years later Bill would take Fred Winterbotham to East Prussia to meet his new friend.

Winterbotham wrote:

> Erich turned out to be a veritable cock-sparrow of a man; he had been born and brought up in the Ruhr, a railway worker by trade, and he was a passionate Socialist. He had, however, seen no future in trades unionism under the Nazis, so had wisely decided to achieve his ambitions by joining the Party in 1925 [in fact 1922].
>
> A natural organiser, whose stocky 5 foot 6 inch frame exuded energy. He survived the infighting in the Party and managed, when Hitler came to power, to be given the job of Gauleiter of East Prussia, an area cut off from the rest of Germany by the Polish Corridor. Here he hoped to carry out his Socialist plans with little interference from Berlin. I liked this enthusiastic man as soon as I met him, for he had none of the arrogance of the jumped-up Nazi yet was close enough to the hierarchy to know a great deal.[406]

This final point tells us something interesting about intelligence officers and spies. The friendships they develop with their main sources are usually real and often deep. It begins out of professional necessity; the intelligence officer has a job to do and if that means befriending an extremist or even a terrorist then so be it. Thereafter the shared interests (and the danger of discovery) bring them closer together.

Only in rare cases does an intelligence officer genuinely dislike the source whose reporting brings him or her satisfaction and career success. It is difficult to conceal dislike or disdain. One could argue that these are cynical friendships based on mutual exploitation, but they are real nonetheless. From listening to Winterbotham's twenty-five hours of oral testimony at the Imperial War Museum he seems to have liked both Koch and Rosenberg. That both men later committed terrible crimes only adds to the paradox.

Of course Koch did not wittingly provide secrets to MI6. In speaking frankly to Bill de Ropp he thought he was confiding in a supporter of Germany and a not-uncritical sympathiser of the Nazis. None of Bill de Ropp's CX reports from Koch appears to have survived. We know, however, that the principal subjects discussed were Memel, Danzig and its Corridor, Poland, Ukraine and the eventual invasion of the Soviet Union.

Memel (now Klapeida) is the only major port on the Lithuanian coast. It had been a German possession from 1422 until 1920 when, under the provisions of the Treaty of Versailles, German troops departed and the Allied Powers took over administration. The French governed the territory until January 1923* when the Lithuanians seized it in a brilliant *coup de main* and the allies limply acquiesced to the fait accompli. In 1924 an Organic Statute of Memel was agreed which gave Memel independent status within Lithuania. It was a controversial document which was intended to guarantee rights to the German majority but Lithuania increasingly behaved as if Memel was just part of Lithuania.

In 1927 German newspapers were suppressed. Lithuania used its

* Areas of Klapeida still have a distinctly French atmosphere in spite of only four years of occupation.

new control of Memel as leverage against Poland for the return of Vilnius, which was still in Polish hands. From 1930 Germany started to protest and in 1935 the Memellanders of German descent began to agitate. Lithuania claimed that the German Nazis were behind the movement and were planning a revolt.[407] In 1932 following an election which saw the German parties increase their majority in Memel the Lithuanians banned the two local Nazi parties.

All of this was of some passing interest in Whitehall because 'the British Empire' was one of the guarantor powers along with France and Italy. When Foreign Secretary Sir John Simon visited Berlin in March 1935 Hitler demanded that Britain fulfil her duties as guarantor to protect the Germans in Memel, 126 of whom were standing trial in Kovno (Kaunas) for planning a coup.[408]

Bill de Ropp was in an unusual position because one of his relatives, Hanno von der Ropp, was one of those under trial for conspiracy. Hanno's unpublished memoir is an astonishing document. As a Balt with Russian nationality he joined the Prussian army in 1914 and fought against the Russians. After being wounded near Vilnius he joined the German air force as an observer and fought in the Balkans where he survived being shot down four times by British aircraft. After the war he returned to farm his land in Lithuania and qualified as a judge in Memel. He takes up the story.

> During this time I began to take part in the public life of the Memelland and became a . . . City Councillor. [In 1933] I was accused of having the intention of tearing Memel area away from Lithuania with a group of German-minded Memellanders and reincorporating it into the German Empire. Although I had received Lithuanian nationality when I was appointed as the Memelland Public Prosecutor, I was sentenced to a longer prison sentence with another large group of 120 defendants after I was arrested one night in the Memel area by the Greater Lithuanian secret police.

> The allegations were completely unjustified. After the collapse of the German Empire [in 1918], I made myself available as a volunteer to the Excellency Eberhard's volunteer army corps and, as a German officer, I went into action with the first Lithuanian volunteers against the communist troops that had penetrated far into Lithuania. I have always proven through my personal commitment that there were good relations between the Lithuanian people and Germany ... The political confusion then led to the above-mentioned proceedings before the Kovno court martial, which seriously tarnished the previously good German-Lithuanian relations. This was not among the ideas that I have always represented.

The treason trial of the 126 'Nazis' was published in British newspapers in December 1934. 'Among the accused are Dr Ernest Neumann the leader of the Nazi Party in Memel, Pastor Theodor von Sass and Baron von Ropp, the heads of the rival Nazi party.'[409] In March 1935 the court handed down five death penalties but Hanno received a sentence of 12 years in prison.[410] A report in *The Times* spoke of the trial being conducted with 'tolerable fairness', agreed that the Memellanders had been guilty of 'indiscretion' and 'semi-military marching practised by the Nazis in Germany' but noted 'the paucity of arms discovered . . . suggests the indictment exaggerated the immediate danger of an armed rising.'[411]

This *Times* report is so kind to the Memellanders that one wonders if Bill de Ropp (still often described as a journalist on *The Times*) was the author. But it also leads to another question: the degree to which Bill de Ropp drew upon the wider von der Ropp family in his espionage work. Many secret agents refuse to involve their families and friends in their activities but others feel less constrained.

The von der Ropps were more of a clan than a family. There was Edward, who was Bishop of Mogilev (now in Belarus) and Vilnius (then still in Poland), who was a famous Polish patriot who had been expelled by the Tsarist authorities but was still alive at the time. The Bishop's nephew, Professor Stefan de Ropp, settled in Poznan and would later escape to the United States after the Nazi invasion. In fact there were von der Ropps throughout the Baltic States, Poland and Germany. Most scandalous was the beautiful Dorothea von der Ropp who allegedly had an affair with King Zog of Albania before she committed suicide on a beach near Athens in 1934. She was the daughter of the Baron serving in Manchuria who had known Vernon Kell and who died at the siege of Port Arthur (*see* Chapter 5).[412]

One von der Ropp relative insisted in 2023 that the family would never have assisted a 'traitor'.[413] One can debate whether Bill de Ropp was ever a traitor because, after 1910, he never claimed to be anything other than British and he was never German. However, in 1934 he was ostensibly working for Rosenberg. Perhaps after the outbreak of the Second World War he could be seen by Germans as a traitor who had misled them over his apparent German sympathies.

Another issue was Danzig. Danzig (now Gdansk) featured as one of Woodrow Wilson's Fourteen Points. Like Memel it is a port on the Baltic Sea. Wilson believed that Poland's independence should be restored and that it should also have access to the sea. That decision involved drawing a corridor from Poland to Danzig which cut off Germany from its own province of East Prussia. Because of its large German population Danzig was to become a 'Free City' overseen by a Commissioner appointed by the League of Nations.

In 1933 the Nazis in Danzig increasingly dominated the local government and the Commissioner from 1937, a Swiss diplomat, Carl Burckhardt, adopted a generally pro-German stance. From 1938 onwards Germany demanded the return of Danzig.

Whereas Whitehall had only taken a remote interest in Memel there was a clear recognition that Danzig was a tinder box. France had a bilateral agreement with Poland so a German move against Danzig would lead to war between France and Germany. The French knew full well that they could not fight Germany without British assistance.

As it happened it was the German invasion of Poland which started the Second World War.

In the MI6 paper submitted to Whitehall 'Germany. Factors, Aims, Methods etc.' (*see* Chapter 21) Bill de Ropp's reporting assessed the situation correctly. 'Danzig, already completely Nazified, can be formally incorporated in the Reich whenever it suits Herr Hitler . . . Memel is but incidental . . . and present indications are that, unless the Germans allow Memellanders to enjoy complete autonomy for a time, its return to the Reich, with the grant of facilities to Lithuania, will be shortly arranged.' In the event, Memel was ceded to Germany by Lithuania on 22 March 1939 following a German ultimatum.

The report continued: 'Poland is now regarded as an obstacle . . . and this, if the Rosenberg school of thought has its way, as seems likely, will be part of the process of reducing Poland to her natural frontiers . . . The Poles know what is in the wind.' Two options were being discussed – 'One radical element is for making a clean sweep of Poland by attacking her in or before the summer of 1939 thereby settling finally the Danzig and Corridor etc questions and clearing a free passage to south Russia. Another school of thought advocates more insidious methods, on atomisation lines.'[414]

The third area of Bill de Ropp's involvement in the East was Ukraine. The German government and Rosenberg were attracted to the idea of Ukrainian independence from the Soviet Union. Anything which weakened the Soviet Union was desirable and there was the added motivation of Ukraine's massive natural resources, an area in which Germany was seriously deficient. The lure of the oil in the Caucasus region was a particular attraction.

One possible candidate to lead any new state was Pavlo Skoropadsky, the former Hetman (Commander) who had been a brigadier in the Tsarist army. There had been a brief Ukrainian Republic from January 1918 to December 1920 during which time it had to fight off challenges both from Russia and Poland. It was an

Adolf Hitler, whom Bill de Ropp met periodically between 1931 and 1939. Hitler used him as a sounding board on policy towards Great Britain.

(Das Jaar im Bild 1935)

Bill de Ropp, from a passport photograph probably issued in Montreux during the 1940s.

(© James de Ropp)

Erich Koch, the Gauleiter for East Prussia who was befriended by Bill de Ropp. Koch migrated from being a leftist social reformer to become a major war criminal.

(© German Federal Archives)

Erhard Milch, the field marshal of Jewish extraction who was tasked with the development and expansion of the Luftwaffe. He arranged for de Ropp and Fedden to tour German aviation factories in 1937 and 1938.

(© State Treasury of Poland)

General Franz Ritter von Epp, the Bavarian hardcore Nazi and Wagner enthusiast who became Bill de Ropp's main source on German colonial aspirations.

(© Kaiserreich Wiki)

General (later Field Marshal) Walter von Reichenau, who outlined his ideas for the invasion of the Soviet Union to de Ropp and Winterbotham in 1934. Bill de Ropp reported that he committed suicide in 1942.

(© German Federal Archives)

Above: Alfred Rosenberg (right), Bill de Ropp, an SS officer named Riemer and a member of Rosenberg's staff clowning for the camera during their trip to Austria in 1938. *(© James de Ropp)*

Below: Bill de Ropp interviews a secret Nazi printer in Austria in 1938 as Rosenberg (second from left) and two SS officers look on. *(© James de Ropp)*

Above: Alfred Rosenberg relaxes in his official Mercedes Tourenwagen during his tour of Austria with Bill de Ropp in 1938. *(© James de Ropp)*

Below: Bill de Ropp in Austria in 1938. The original German caption reads 'Contemplative view of Graz'. *(© James de Ropp)*

Top left: Roy Fedden, the brilliant but exigent aero engineer who accompanied Bill de Ropp on three tours of German aircraft factories in 1937 and 1938. *(© National Portrait Gallery [NPG])*

Top right: Fred Winterbotham and Bill de Ropp during a visit to the Baltic coast of East Prussia in 1936. This is a rare, albeit blurred, image of an agent with his MI6 case officer. *(© Sally Maitland)*

Bottom: The assembly hall for He-111s at the Heinkel factory at Oranienburg outside Berlin, which produced valuable intelligence for Fedden and de Ropp in 1938. *(© Associated Press/Alamy Stock Photo)*

Top left: Hugh Whittall, the British Honorary Vice Consul in Montreux who maintained clandestine contact with Bill de Ropp throughout the Second World War. This drawing is by Maurice Gruiffenhagen. *(© Colonel Philip Horwood)*

Top right: Claude Dansey, Assistant Chief of MI6 during the Second World War, who set up the service's large wartime station in Switzerland. He had little time for Bill de Ropp. *(© NPG)*

Bottom: The Hôtel des Alpes at Glion, above Montreux, where the de Ropps spent the early years of the war. The funicular railway runs directly below the hotel *(© Chapallaz fils postcard)*

Right: Friedrich von der Ropp in later life. He complained that this photo made him look too benign.
(© Fritz Böttcher)

Below: An elderly Bill de Ropp takes a walk with his daughter Ruth near Peterchurch in Herefordshire, south west England, in 1967.
(© Sue Huntsman)

unhappy three years with several groups battling for power in Kiev including Bolsheviks and White Russians.

Skoropadsky's conservative Hetmanate movement was supported by Germany and was dominant from April 1918 until Germany's defeat in November. One month after the Armistice Skoropadsky abdicated and took up residence in a villa at Wannsee just outside Berlin. In March 1921 the Peace of Riga divided Ukraine between Poland, Romania, Czechoslovakia and the Soviet Union. Ukraine retained a fig-leaf entity as the Ukraine Soviet Socialist Republic.

After the defeat of the White Russians Whitehall paid little interest to Ukraine until the early 1930s. Skoropadsky's MI5 file shows that there were occasional CX reports about his activities and his German connections. In the early 1930s interest began to increase. In 1932 Vivian assured MI5 that MI6 had good coverage of Skoropadsky's dealings with General Kurt von Schleicher who was German Defence Minister (shortly afterwards to become Chancellor).[415]

In November 1932 an MI6 note recorded a discussion with a member of the Anglo-Ukraine Committee which suggested a plan was afoot involving Skoropadsky and Sir Henri Deterding, the Chairman of Royal Dutch Shell, which involved starting a guerrilla uprising in Ukraine.[416] The writer (wisely) dismissed the idea as incredible but it is certainly true that the loss of his Caucasian oilfields after the Russian Revolution still rankled with Deterding who remained in touch with Rosenberg and eventually moved to Germany in 1936.[417]

A CX report has survived on MI5 files dating from December 1933 that provides a more mature perspective.[418] It draws on a number of sources to provide a 'Periodical Report on the Ukrainian Emigre movement'. Parts of it were clearly contributed by Bill de Ropp, particularly where the focus was on Germany and Rosenberg.

> Rosenberg's Eastern schemes have not been abandoned. It is realised, however, that these schemes cannot come within the realm of practical politics for some time to come, in view of the

existence of questions of more immediate importance, such as that of German economic and military rehabilitation, relations with France etc. The Eastern schemes have been put, therefore, more or less into cold storage.

In the meantime there is good information to show that the Nazi contact with Skoropadsky and his organisation is being maintained in spite of denials by [Vladimir] Korostovetz, Skoropadsky's agent in London, and that Skoropadsky is in receipt of a small subsidy from the Nazis. As regards [Yevhen] Konavalets [the former Hetmanate military commander who now ran a rival organisation] there are indications that this individual, whose organisation has hitherto been used by the Reichswehrministerium (the German Defence Ministry. It was renamed the War Ministry in 1935) for carrying out anti-Polish activities in Galicia has recently been ordered by the Germans to cease these activities. Konovalets is reported, however, to still be in the pay of the Germans.[419]

Some more of Bill de Ropp's reports are to be found on the MI5 file on one Jacob Makohin (variously spelt, including Mohonin, Makolin and even MacOwen), an American-Ukrainian with Canadian connections who had served in the United States Marine Corps during the war. Makohin first came to MI5 attention when the Poles arrested him in Lemberg (now Lviv). Makohin was opposed to Skoropadsky and, as a Galician, he was particularly focused on reuniting Galicia with Ukraine. MI5 and the Royal Canadian Mounted Police struggled to work out whether he was a Bolshevik agent or a genuine nationalist.

He was a wealthy man and based his Ukraine Bureau at 40 (later 27) Grosvenor Place in central London. He improbably claimed to be a descendant of a former Hetman (of the Razumovski family) and he employed a Labour MP, who had just lost his seat at the 1931 General Election, as his local representative. Lt-Colonel Cecil

L'Estrange Malone had briefly been Britain's first Communist MP before he joined the Labour Party.

Bill de Ropp was able to purloin an APA report on Makohin, which was translated in Berlin or Broadway and sent out to Whitehall customers, including MI5. This four-page document is the first evidence we have that Bill de Ropp would, when he deemed it safe, remove documents and pass them on to MI6. The APA report is surprisingly impressive (given what von Chappuis told MI5 about the department's dysfunctionality) and is based on five separate sources. It fails fully to establish who Makohin was working for but it does nail one of his falsehoods. 'The two brothers, the Counts Razumovski, the Hetman's descendants who are settled on an estate in Czechoslovakia stated . . . that, apart from themselves, no other Counts Razumovskis are in existence.'[420]

In May 1934 Bill de Ropp obtained another important snippet from Arno Schickedanz, the Near Eastern expert in Rosenberg's Foreign Political Department [APA]. 'Korostovetz had reported on various occasions most unfavourably on Makohin to Skoropadsky. Schickedanz had seen these reports, in which Makohin was described as a probable agent of the Soviets and in which it was stated that he appeared to be in contact with the Secret Service of several nations including the British.'[421] Vivian describes Bill de Ropp as 'a most reliable source'.

A separate report by Rosenberg's APA on Soviet policy in Ukraine which Bill de Ropp copied to London in May 1934 mentions attempts to obtain British support for Skoropadsky and the 'Ukraine Bureau'.[422] One of those targeted was William Allen, a former Northern Ireland politician, known German sympathiser, and friend of Oswald Mosley and the Duke of Kent.

Bill de Ropp's next CX report on the Makonin file was entitled 'Japanese activity in Berlin etc.' and dated February 1935. He had obtained it from someone at the APA, most likely Arno Schickedanz. 'Colonel Tanaka had visited Berlin in the Spring of 1934 and had propagated an ambitious scheme whereby, in the event of a war between the USSR and Japan, the Poles and Germans should profit by Soviet disintegration . . . to establish zones of influence in the Ukraine and Caucasus'. Although this plan had gone quiet recently 'there had been a noticeable revival of Japanese activity in the past week or so and this activity had so far been chiefly directed at Herr Rosenberg and his department. This was probably because the Japanese realised that Herr Rosenberg was the most determined opponent to the understanding with the USSR in Herr Hitler's immediate entourage.'[423]

Woollcombe warned his Whitehall customers that 'This source, however, is in a delicate position and has to be careful over putting questions that might arouse suspicion.'

The best-known Ukrainian in London was not Makohin but Vladimir Korostovetz, who was Skoropadsky's London representative from 1928. He had been a member of the Tsarist Foreign Service but fled to Poland after the 1917 Revolution. In the mid-1920s he joined Skoropadsky in Berlin.[424] He was unwise or unlucky enough to get involved with one of the period's great fraudsters.

Maundy Gregory had been a private in the Irish Guards but after the war developed a business in the sale of honours, including knighthoods and peerages. Some of the money was paid into the coffers of David Lloyd-George's Liberal Party. In 1927 this practice was stopped by the incoming Conservative government and in 1933 he was convicted, briefly imprisoned and declared bankrupt. Before his downfall he had an office at 38 Parliament Street, was the proprietor of the *Whitehall Gazette* and owned the Ambassadors' Club in Conduit Street.

This was the man who set up the Anglo-Ukrainian Committee in November 1931 ostensibly to provide financial support to Skoropadsky's Ukrainian nationalist movement. Gregory always claimed to have been in touch with both MI5 and MI6. It is true that he tried unsuccessfully to join MI5 in 1917. On his MI5 file there is a letter which might suggest an MI6 interest. Vivian sent a handwritten note in red ink to Captain Miller in MI5: 'DM [Desmond Morton] has asked me [to inform you] that CSS [Sinclair] keeps a private file on the MG [Maundy Gregory] contacts.'[425] Gregory did maintain (a sometimes surreptitious) contact with Sir Basil Thomson, formerly Director of Intelligence at the Home Office. MI5 wrote to Hankey in 1926 about Gregory (with commendable frankness): 'We don't like him and don't trust him.'

Korostovetz had first met Gregory in 1928 and fell under his spell, even believing him, at one point, to be the Head of the British Secret Service. In 1931 he asked Gregory to help him raise funds and 'was a little surprised by the enthusiasm with which the suggestion was received'.[426] The Committee had a smattering of Lords on its Council plus another fraudster, Louis Tufnell. Gradually it dawned on Korostovetz that Ukraine's interests were getting confused with cash-for-honours. Thus Sir Henri Deterding was allegedly willing to provide £40,000 to Ukraine from the £75,000 offered for a peerage.[427] Finally, Korostovetz warned Skoropadsky of the need to extricate himself from the Committee.

This mess is redolent of the whole Ukrainian opposition effort. Indeed it is hard to escape the conclusion that German policy towards the East – whether Memel, Danzig, Poland, Ukraine and indeed Russia itself – had not really progressed since the meeting between Bill de Ropp and Hitler in 1932. Given Hitler's hatred of the Soviet Union this seems extraordinary but it was a function of his management style; allowing Rosenberg, Ribbentrop, Himmler, Goebbels and Göring each to have their own policy preferences with no attempt to impose or even encourage any synthesis. This made the job for MI6 extraordinarily difficult, especially as their insight was almost exclusively from the Rosenberg viewpoint.

For a full assessment of Bill de Ropp's work on the Eastern questions the destruction of so much of his CX output obliges us to look back at the three strategic reports mentioned in Chapters 2 and

21 and retained by the FO. They show that even as late as 1938 Hitler thought he had a number of options available.

'What Should We Do?' identifies one of Germany's aims as 'The downfall of the Soviet regime'. It then adds:

> German aims as regards the USSR fluctuate. It has latterly been maintained that a German empire cannot be built up in Russia and the idea has been that, after the disintegration of the Soviet system, autonomous states would emerge some or most of which Germany would exploit on the 'vassal state' basis. A solution of the Czech issue may however bring more concrete ideas.[428]

'Germany: Factors, Aims, Methods etc.' begins with identifying Hitler's 'incalculability'.[429] 'He has always been incalculable, even to his intimates, uncommunicative in a high degree, often keeping them guessing until the last moment, and then acting on sudden intuition.' As examples it gives the Night of the Long Knives, the remilitarisation of the Rhineland and the occupation of Austria.

Turning to the East the report talks of:

> Bringing, through the disintegration of the Soviet regime, of a large part of south Russia within Germany's political and economic orbit – an independent Ukraine embracing both Russian and Polish territory, to be established under Germany's auspices. . .
>
> It is primarily in the direction of the Ukraine, and even further east in Russia, that the Nazis have been and are looking for the satisfaction of their desire for *Lebensraum* – colonisation apparently being the present aim – and adequate supplies of raw materials and agricultural produce.

And finally the paper looks at Ukraine itself.

> The project for creating an independent Ukraine, to embrace the whole of Soviet Ukraine, Polish eastern Galicia and Carpatho-Russia (Ruthenia) has been given quick and practical impulse. The main idea – and there may be other ideas – is that the new state following on the collapse of the Soviet regime, should be part of a Russian federal system and should be allied to Germany . . . It would be virtually a German protectorate. Indeed the Nazis are already talking of acquisition of the riches of the Ukraine being vital for Germany's progress to World Power.
>
> Already the following are among the practical steps being taken under the principal direction of Dr Rosenberg. Hust, the capital of Carpatho-Russia [now Khust in Ukraine], is being made, in various ways, the centre of German agitation. Sections of Dr Rosenberg's office, the APA, are being established at Hust. Emigrant Ukrainians are being assembled and a Ukrainian militia is being formed with headquarters there.

Bill de Ropp was reporting what he heard and saw. He could not help the fact that, in spite of seven years to work out the detail, the Nazi policies towards the East were just a series of vague options without any meticulous planning behind them. Little wonder that things went so disastrously wrong after the 1941 invasion.

There could hardly be a better example of Hitler's 'incalculability' than the Nazi-Soviet Pact signed on 23 August 1939. Nobody was more appalled by the Molotov-Ribbentrop Pact than Rosenberg. His diary entries on 22 August read like a tug of war between his loyalty to Hitler, his distaste for Ribbentrop's diplomatic coup and his personal aversion to the agreement.

> The Führer's change of direction probably was a necessity, in light of the given situation and because it is a 180-degree turnaround, very far-reaching consequences will be drawn from

> it as well . . .[and the] trip of our Minister to Moscow. A moral lessening of respect, given our struggle of now twenty years, given our Parteitag, given Spain . . . The Soviets are said to have already marked down names of a delegation to the Nuremberg Parteitag.[430]

Three days later he felt less constrained about committing his genuine thoughts to his diary:

> I feel as though this Moscow pact will eventually exact revenge from National Socialism . . . It was not a voluntary move but rather an action taken in a tight spot, a petition made by one revolution to the head of another revolution, the destruction of which has been held up as the ideal of a twenty-year struggle. How can we still speak of the salvation and shaping of Europe when we are forced to ask the destroyer of Europe for help?
>
> If in addition we must abandon the territory of the Polish Ukraine to the Soviet Union, then that is, after the Carpatho-Ukraine, the second blow dealt by us to the strongest anti-Moscow force. It may not yet have repercussions now but surely in future times . . . and again one wonders was this situation bound to come about? Did the Polish question have to be solved now and in this way?[431]

Most humiliating of all was that Hitler had never let him into the secret.

Cadogan wrote in his diary on the 24th: 'A black day. Terms of the German-Soviet Pact out.' Only ten days later the Second World War would begin.

19

'THE KNOCK-OUT BLOW'

1934–1938: The race against the Luftwaffe

There was no single issue as important to British intelligence as understanding the size, capabilities and intentions of the German air force, the Luftwaffe. Bill de Ropp had been active on the aviation target in the 1920s when his main concern had been covert German-Russian cooperation. When, in March 1934, he arranged for Fred Winterbotham to call on Adolf Hitler at the Reich Chancellery so began a new four-year involvement which would produce vital intelligence.

Alfred Rosenberg's account of Winterbotham's meeting with Hitler reads:

> The Führer said that the truly knightly weapon of the Great War had been the air force. Besides, he said, the English had been a dangerous enemy as Germany had been forced to concentrate two thirds of her aircraft on the English front. Moving on to current issues, the Führer expressed his conviction that although the French air fleet is numerically far superior to the British he

> regards the latter as stronger in terms of value. As for the rest, he said, he is very much in favour of a broad strengthening of the English air arm.[432]

Winterbotham recalled this first conversation with Hitler rather differently.

> We talked about the First World War and the fact that I had been shot down by Göring's bunch but [that I] was in no way bitter about my eighteen months as a prisoner of war pleased him . . . He was a perfectly ordinary relaxed human being chatting about old times and being skilfully led on by Bill to talk of the present. Yes, he too believed in the strange comradeship of the air and he hoped I would find the lads of his new air force as good as the old ones.
>
> Oh yes, the German air force was coming along nicely. The young men could now abandon their gliding exercises and get down to real flying training. He went on to tell me the latest figures of aircraft which no doubt included those both in the flying training schools and in the squadrons. He was well briefed and proud of it and obviously enjoyed talking quite freely . . . But now Hitler turned towards me and looked me straight in the eye and informed me that his Luftwaffe would have some 500 operational aircraft by the end of 1934 or early 1935.[433]

Rosenberg's diary entry was almost contemporaneous whereas Winterbotham was trying to remember a conversation forty-four years earlier. Nonetheless it was clear that Hitler was building up the Luftwaffe. In October 1933 Germany withdrew from the Disarmament Conference and only a few months after this discussion Britain decided to double the size of the RAF from 42 to 84 squadrons under Expansion Scheme A.

In March 1935 Hitler told Foreign Secretary Sir John Simon and

Anthony Eden during their visit to Berlin that Germany had reached air parity with Britain. So within a year Scheme A was superseded by Scheme C with the objective of 123 squadrons comprising 1,512 front-line aircraft by March 1937. In 1936 it was yet again upgraded, this time to Scheme F for 1,736 aircraft by March 1939.*

So began one of the most formidable arms races in history. In 1932 the RAF had only 42 squadrons of which only 13 comprised fighters. All the aircraft were biplanes and many still had open cockpits. The cloth-covered Handley Page Heyford bomber could only manage a stately 108 mph. It remained in front-line service until 1937. The main fighter was the Bristol Bulldog with a top speed of 174 mph and guns which fired through the propellers just like its First World War predecessors. It remained in service until 1936. The Hawker Hart entered service in 1930 but with only a marginally greater top speed of 184 mph.[434] The Gloster Gladiator started to be delivered in 1937. It had an enclosed cockpit and could manage 257 mph but it was still a biplane.

Even as late as May 1938 there was only one production Spitfire flying in Britain.[435] The story of the desperate struggle to build a fleet of fighters to protect the British homeland has often been told. It is usually told as a success but there were moments of utter despair as British industry failed again and again to meet production deadlines and as the Air Ministry clung to outmoded methods and thinking.

There was the parallel battle to understand the requirement and the threat posed by the sudden expansion of the Luftwaffe. This story is usually told as one of failure and it is true that the effort to penetrate the Luftwaffe's secrets was slow and painful, full of inter-departmental feuding and posturing. But Britain got to the right answers in the end, enabling the correct decisions to be taken: to focus first on building fighters and then four-engine bombers.

Two myths had grown up after the Great War, which would

* Winterbotham mistakenly dates this visit as being before his own meeting with Hitler in 1934.

persist until at least 1940. The first was that 'the bomber will always get through'. It was included in a statement by Stanley Baldwin to Parliament in November 1932 that 'I think it is well also for the man in the street to realise that there is no power on earth that can protect him from being bombed. Whatever people may tell him, the bomber will always get through. The only defence is in offence, which means that you have to kill more women and children more quickly than the enemy if you want to save yourselves.'[436]

The second linked myth was the 'knock-out blow' whereby an enemy bomber force would deliver a killer blow to your capital city, population and industries, thereby winning a war outright. In the pre-atomic age this too turned out to be mistaken.

Winterbotham knew that he needed to develop reliable sources on the German air force and the aviation industry. A breakthrough on this question was his prime function as head of Section IV (Air) in MI6 headquarters in Broadway. He was assiduous in chasing down all possible sources.

Rudolf Wenninger, now promoted to General, was Germany's air attaché in London and he became a useful contact for the Air Ministry and MI6. Bill de Ropp would meet him for lunch during Wenninger's visits to Berlin. Frank Foley had a productive relationship with a Luftwaffe colonel who worked in the German Air Ministry in Berlin whom he met fortnightly.[437] Winterbotham himself had a slice of luck when a presumed official at the German Air Ministry started sending secret papers to him through the air attaché at the British Embassy in Berlin.

Another successful approach was to use MI6's longstanding connection to the Bristol Aeroplane Company at Filton. Winterbotham narrates how,

> I went down to the Bristol Aero Engine factory to have lunch with Ken Bartlett [the Continental Sales Manager]. I'd known him for some time and found him most useful in briefing me on

> the output, construction and performance of the Bristol engines which powered so many of our aircraft in the early thirties. It would be a sprat to catch a mackerel but if we could get Ken Bartlett in among the German aero engine engineers some useful information might be obtained.

Captain Ken Bartlett had served in the Royal Army Service Corps during the war and had joined the Bristol sales team in 1927. With his fluent French and German he was soon Continental Sales Manager and selling and licensing Bristol engines all over Europe for installation in Fokker (Dutch), Savoia Marchetti (Italian), Letov (Czechoslovak), and Anbo (Lithuanian) aircraft. He also sold the Bristol Bulldog fighter. Not only did the RAF operate thirteen squadrons of Bulldogs in 1933 but the Latvians, Danes, Finns, Estonians and Swedes also bought the aircraft.[438] In Germany the Jupiter was still being built under licence by Siemens.

Winterbotham obtained permission for Bartlett to show the Germans details of 'an engine which was still on the secret list but which was not our latest model'. This was presumably the Perseus, Bristol's first single sleeve-valve engine. Sleeve-valves were designed as an improvement on the old poppet valves but had proved difficult to perfect in aero engines.

Germany had built the Jupiter under licence for some years and Winterbotham was confident that Germany had already decided against using radial engines for fighter aircraft. He explains:

> By 1934 we had learned from our successes with seaplanes in the Schneider Trophy races against the Italians that, as speeds of aircraft were increased, so was the necessity to streamline the aeroplane itself, and the great areas of the air-cooled Bristol radial engine caused far too much resistance at these increased speeds to make them a suitable proposition for future fighters.[439]

Rosenberg noted in his diary in early 1934:

> Captain Bartlett from the Bristol Aeroplane Company in London was in [Berlin] with a letter of introduction from the [British] Air Ministry Squadron Leader Winterbotham. He wants to sell the new still secret engine here. He emphasised that this is the first time the Ministry itself has given him a letter of introduction to take with him.
>
> I arranged a breakfast for him through Obermüller in which the chief design engineers of the [German] Army, the Navy and the Air Ministry will take part. Hence one and a half years of work are crowned with success because the British Air Staff has thus officially given its permission for the build-up of German air defences.[440]

Here we encounter a real danger when an espionage ploy affects real-life policy. What Winterbotham saw as a sprat to catch a mackerel was interpreted in Berlin as official endorsement of Hitler's plan to enlarge the Luftwaffe. Furthermore, Winterbotham was mistaken in his belief that Germany would not employ radial engines on fighters. The BMW factory was developing its 801 radial engine which it would use on the Focke-Wulf 190 aircraft. BMW largely overcame the problem of drag caused by the large surface area of the radial engine and the FW190 became one of Germany's most effective fighters. The engineer at BMW who masterminded this success was Helmuth Sachse whom we shall encounter shortly.

Winterbotham's risky ploy did bring one advantage. The involvement of Bristol provided an additional role for Bill de Ropp. As Bristol's agent in Germany (a position that seems to have been formalised in 1934 although it began in the late 1920s), he would be responsible for arranging Bartlett's visits and using his Nazi sources to obtain the necessary permissions. Another advantage for MI6 was that this initiative allowed Rosenberg to retain a foot in the aviation field because of his notional link to the British Air Ministry, unaware that Winterbotham actually worked for MI6. Göring had no time for Rosenberg but for as long as Hitler took him seriously Göring had to play along; he, however, left the detail to Erhard Milch.

Milch was an interesting character. The son of a Jewish father from Wilhelmshaven he had served in the air force during the Great War before starting his own small airline in Danzig. Göring appointed him State Secretary for Aviation with the task of developing the Luftwaffe. By most accounts he was a personable man and Bill de Ropp focused his considerable charm on him.

But even Milch was suspicious. Rosenberg notes, 'Our Reich Air Ministry, however, has got slightly cold feet and wants this support promised on official British letterhead. Somewhat naïve! In the near future I will present to the gentlemen the official letterhead of the British Air Ministry that I received. More one cannot ask, the question is only whether the Bristol engines are as good as Bartlett claims. That is something our experts must decide.'[441]

This was a dangerous moment for Bill de Ropp. Milch did not suspect him but he clearly wondered whether the permitted access to a Bristol secret engine was a legitimate government-to-government initiative or some sort of stratagem. Presumably Milch's doubts were allayed but such doubts tend to stick in the back of the mind only to resurface later.

Meanwhile Rosenberg had sent Obermüller of the APA to England. He returned with the idea that 'the young generation in the British Air Force . . . requests us to deal only directly with its General Staff without the FO, and without the German Embassy in London. That's the only right thing and thus the problem has been tackled in the right way so as to stymie, bit by bit, the side loyal to France.'[442] By 'the side loyal to France' Rosenberg meant Vansittart.

So began a theme which would later have important consequences. It was true that there were significant tensions between the Air Ministry and the FO and that the Nazis, rightly or wrongly, believed them to represent a major fault-line in British politics. This even led General Erhard Milch to suggest setting up a channel between the two air ministries whereby they could warn each other of emerging political problems without escalating to ambassadors.[443]

Bill de Ropp played on such impressions of division to leverage an enhanced role for himself. As we shall see, this narrative of division would be partially responsible for Hitler's conviction that Britain would not go to war for Poland; and in 1941 it would influence Rudolf Hess to make his fateful flight to Scotland.

The whole question of the expansion of the Luftwaffe became one of the most complicated issues for Whitehall to grasp. Figures from different sources rarely seemed to match. Comparing like with like was a constant problem. Above all, the degree to which the Nazis might be talking up their numbers to achieve a deterrent effect or playing them down to lull the allies into apathy was anything but clear.

There was also tension within the German system. In August 1935 Geyr von Schweppenburg, the military attaché in London, wrote to Berlin warning about the expansion of the RAF which he felt was due to Germany's 'reckless air rearmament'.[444] He claimed in his post-war memoir to have told Berlin that Britain would first develop its fighter capability to defend 'the mother country' before focusing on dominating the air over Germany in order 'to destroy German war industries'.[445]

Wenninger was initially less anxious than von Schweppenburg. Soon after his arrival in London he suggested sharing details of experimental aircraft and proposed an exchange of officers between the British and German air forces. Wing Commander Charles Medhurst (Deputy Director of Intelligence) was wary of the latter point, feeling that the German officers would learn too much and the RAF in Germany would be shown too little.

In December 1936 Medhurst bumped into Wenninger and Colonel Rulof Lucht at the Paris Air Show. Wenninger stressed the importance of dive-bombing to destroy particular targets like bridges. Lucht, who was an engineer, bemoaned that Germany did not have the equivalent of the Merlin engine. Otherwise the design of the new Messerschmitt and Heinkel fighters was as good as, 'if not superior to the Spitfire and Hurricane'. Referring to the Daimler-Benz DB 600 engine and the Junkers Jumo 205, Lucht concluded that the Daimler-Benz was nearly as good as the Merlin and the Jumo was effective up to 4,000 metres' altitude but 'after that height the power curve fell off badly'.[446]

The number of German aircraft continued to increase rapidly. In September 1936 the Committee on Imperial Defence produced a paper, 'The present strength of the German air force', which concluded that British and German estimates were reassuringly similar. Germany claimed to have 88 squadrons whereas the British estimate was 90.[447] That feeling of comfort did not last long.

Only seven months later the CID circulated another paper; marked 'Most Secret' on 'The future of German air rearmament'. It quoted General Wenninger's concerns about the size of Russia's air force. Taken together with recent German public statements the paper speculated that Germany was seeking parity with Russia. The Germans put the Russian air force at 4,500 whereas the British Air Ministry thought the figure closer to 3,500.[448] The report concludes by noting a new increase in aircraft production in Germany and her continuing inability 'to produce an engine which is satisfactory at high-altitude work'.*

Group Captain Christie entered the fray with some good material from his new source described as X. He passed the reports to Vansittart who used them to chide the Air Ministry, which reacted with churlish scepticism. Much of the discussion was over the fundamental question of whether a German squadron comprised 9, 12 or 15 aircraft.

---

* It is interesting to see that Lucht's comment on the Jumo had found its way into the CID paper.

One clear failing in the whole debate was the fixation on aircraft numbers whereas the snippet obtained by Medhurst from Lucht on the performance of aircraft engines at higher altitudes was arguably of equal significance. From this emerged the idea of sending a British technical expert to Germany. The obvious person was Bristol's legendary engineer, Roy (later Sir Roy) Fedden, the man responsible for Bristol's successful family of radial engines including the Jupiter, Mercury, Pegasus, Perseus, Hercules and Taurus.

The job of arranging this visit was given to Bill de Ropp. This was a dangerous moment for him. It was true that Germany used such visits for deterrent purposes. The classic example was Charles Lindbergh, the great American aviator, who was so impressed by his four separate visits to the German aviation factories that he argued that the United States must never go to war with Germany.

The Germans had similarly impressed various British visitors who could not help comparing the gleaming new German plants with Supermarine's antiquated wooden sheds in Southampton, and Germany's keen young technicians with Britain's discontented and unionised workforce. The visits were carefully orchestrated to give an appearance of superiority.

However, Fedden was an altogether different prospect. He would notice small technical details which might enable the British Air Ministry to extrapolate some strategic conclusions. On the other hand, Fedden was known to have solved the intractable problem of sleeve-valves on radial engines. A few incautious revelations from Fedden to Helmuth Sachse could be worth their weight in gold to the Germans.

We do not know which arguments Bill de Ropp deployed to get Fedden's visit approved but they worked. Bill's championing of Fedden's visit may have raised suspicions about his motives. He was Bristol's agent in Germany but there was no commercial benefit for Bristol from the visit. So what was Bill de Ropp's game? Whose side was he really on? As the prospect of war with Britain became ever greater these questions would be asked more and more.

Bill de Ropp's case was helped by the fact that the two men most responsible for German aircraft production, Erhard Milch and Ernst Udet, had recently paid a visit to Britain and been shown various aircraft plants and had visited Bristol where they had been introduced to Fedden. Bristol management had been puzzled that Milch's delegation had shown no interest in the prototype Bristol Blenheim aircraft and rather a lot in Fedden himself.[449]

Although we tend to think of Bill de Ropp primarily as a spy and an astute political observer it is worth recalling that he was an engineering graduate, albeit with a specialisation in electrics, who had worked as an engineer in both Rugby and London. In the war he had wanted a role involving aircraft engines before he was summarily posted to balloons. He too would be an intelligent observer during these factory visits and would also seek to befriend any new contacts. His biographical notes to Broadway on the key figures in Heinkel, Junkers, BMW and Krupps would be valuable indeed. So too would be the whereabouts of the shadow factories. Already the Air Ministry was assembling details of potential future bombing targets.

Roy Fedden was a larger-than-life figure. His biographer describes him as a Titan.

> He was one of the greatest intuitive engineers in history and between the World Wars was the highest paid engineer in Britain and probably in Europe; yet he never formally qualified as an engineer. He was possessed of great charm and magnetism and went out of his way to avoid causing the slightest offence; yet he made many bitter enemies. He sought to get the very best out of those who worked for him, yet he drove them close to the limits of their endurance, and some beyond it. He was gifted with remarkable strategic vision, which he was constantly using; yet he often failed to see that he was on a tactical collision course. He was unbelievably meticulous about the wording of reports and memoranda.[450]

In other words he was a talented but difficult man.

The first Fedden visit was in June 1937 and included the Henschel, Mercedes-Benz, Junkers and Siemens factories.[451] Fedden, Bartlett and Bill de Ropp not only met Milch and Udet but also Helmuth Sachse, now the Director-General of Engine Development at the German Air Ministry, who accompanied them on all the factory visits. Sachse had the dubious privilege of having a BMW factory at Kempten named after him working on his 801 engine. It was an offshoot of Dachau concentration camp employing slave labour.

Roy Fedden described his first evening.

> By the courtesy of Baron de Ropp, the Bristol agent in Germany, we had the good fortune to meet Alfred Rosenberg, and spent four very interesting hours discussing every kind of social, political and religious problem connected with the new Germany . . . I was deeply impressed by Mr Rosenberg, his ability, his earnestness and single purposeness [*sic*] of mind.

So much for Fedden's political acumen.

Technically, the visit provided some useful insights. Fedden's reports were all marked up to Sir Thomas Inskip, the Minister for Coordination of Defence, with various extracts highlighted in red ink. At the Mercedes-Benz factory Fedden was shown the latest 34-litre inverted-V liquid-cooled engine which he thought was superbly made. This was the DB 600. He reckoned that the 27-litre Merlin developed far more power at 4,000 metres altitude. By contrast he believed that the Dornier 17 with a top speed of 305 mph and a bomb load of 2205 lbs and a range of 1500 miles outperformed the Wellington bomber.

Fedden repeatedly commented on the superb quality of German engineering and the equipment available to them. 'I saw equipment which I have wanted in our factory [at Filton] for years.' He was impressed that the Germans regulated the number of aircraft to be developed; one single-engine fighter, one twin-engine fighter, one medium twin-engine bomber, one dive bomber etc. He contrasted this with the multiplicity of British variants. He made the same point about engines and listed the seven engines under development.

He noted that there were no night shifts or overtime being worked in any of the factories he visited and that therefore the Germans' 'emergency expansion possibilities are vastly greater than ours'. All engines of similar type are 'entirely interchangeable, for example the Mercedes Benz 34 litre engine is interchangeable with the Junkers 36 litre as regards mounting, control etc.' Fedden gleaned the impression that 'for the next 4 or 5 years' four-engine bombers like the Junkers 90 would be a focus for manufacture.

He reserved his biggest criticism for British aircraft factories, which are 'hopelessly inadequate and amateurish compared with corresponding German plant'. He signed off, 'I cannot over-estimate how profoundly concerned I feel about the whole position.'

The second visit was in September and included the IG plant and BMW factory as well as a number of shadow facilities. After two days attending the Nazi Party Rally at Nuremberg the group finished the tour with visits to Rautenbach and Krupps at Essen. Again Herr Sachse accompanied Fedden throughout.[452]

On this visit Fedden was accompanied by Colonel Wallace Devereux, Managing Director of High Duty Alloys. He noted that the invitations 'had been negotiated for us through the efforts of Baron de Ropp . . . The main object of my visit was to concentrate on the supply of raw materials for aero engines, especially magnesium . . . I also wished to glean some information on the Shadow Industry organisation for aero engines and raw material operating in Germany.' Devereux was Britain's leading authority on light alloy castings.

These clear objectives for the second visit suggest that Fedden's first report had found its way to Desmond Morton's Industrial Intelligence Centre (IIC). Morton, the former MI6 officer, who had played a role in the Zinoviev Letter scandal and had shared an office in Broadway with Winterbotham, was now heading up his own unit in the Department of Overseas Trade. His reports on German industrial developments were informed by a wide range of reporting from diplomats and industrialists but he was also an enthusiastic if demanding recipient of MI6 CX reports. These IIC papers introduced a genuinely new insight into Germany's economic predicament.

As Morton's biographer has observed, 'Germany was indeed expanding her industrial capacity at a furious rate and producing aircraft and engines with increasing efficiency but she was doing so, in [Morton's] view, at considerable economic cost to herself.'[453]

The IIC report of May 1939 concluded that Germany could not yet have made herself 'indefinitely self-sufficient in all raw materials and foodstuffs'. It identified a large number of 'deficiency commodities' including timber, rubber, jute, sisal, aluminium, asbestos, chrome, copper, iron, lead, manganese, nickel and petroleum. The report concluded that Germany had probably the equivalent of one year's peace time requirement and that she might be able to maintain her industrial activity without contraction for fifteen to eighteen months of war. This report did not, however, take into account Hitler's idea that he would seize key resources during his attack on the Soviet Union or, as later transpired, by reaching an agreement with the Soviet Union.[454]

In the light of Morton's work many of Fedden's own observations could be turned around and viewed from a more discerning angle. Whereas Fedden marvelled at the quality of the Daimler Benz aero engine with its four-inch-diameter crankpins, the question perhaps should have been asked whether the engine lent itself to mass production. Similarly Fedden's comment that all the factories he visited were working one shift with no overtime might have led him to wonder at the reason.

However, Fedden's notes on the Jumo 207 engine which have survived in the Imperial War Museum show the value of these visits. He made meticulous graphs to calculate the performance of the Jumo 207 (the Jumo 205 but with superchargers) which demonstrate how meticulously he observed everything he saw. There are graphs for 'engine blower discharge pressure', 'Turbine RPM' and 'Boost pressure'.[455]

At Nuremberg Fedden and Devereux were accommodated at the Grand Hotel (where Bill de Ropp also stayed) and sat on the rostrum during the rally at the Zeppelin Stadium just behind the Führer himself. Afterwards Rosenberg hosted a dinner and Fedden was critical of some British visitors who 'caused adverse criticism and personally made me feel rather ashamed of my own countrymen'. On political matters Fedden was a complete innocent.

On returning to England he engaged in an increasingly tetchy correspondence with Sir Thomas Inskip and he produced in November 1937 a rather imprudent report, 'Draft notes on a suggested scheme of reorganisation for the supply of Royal Air Force equipment', which proposed the creation of an Aircraft Controller with dictatorial powers, 'to cut out, once and for all, the soul destroying procrastination and pin pricking delays with which the present organisation is at present hidebound'. One wonders who he imagined as the Aircraft Controller.

Whatever the mixed feelings in Adastral House when Fedden and Devereux were invited back to Germany in October 1938, the intelligence requirement was now of the utmost importance. After the Munich crisis Whitehall knew there was a strong likelihood of war. Any insights would be worth the weight in gold. Bill de Ropp accompanied the British team throughout.

A menu has survived from the official dinner hosted by BMW.[456] Either Fedden, Devereux, or more likely Bill de Ropp, had the idea of getting the guests to sign the menu. Someone wrote: 'Please put your addresses' in pencil at the top. Baron Igor Heyking, Helmuth Sachse and Kurt Loehner included only their job titles but Dr Seidel, Bruno Bruckman and Peter Groebe obliged with their private addresses. Bruckmann would later become Chief Engineer of BMW's advanced jet and rocket programme during the war.[457]

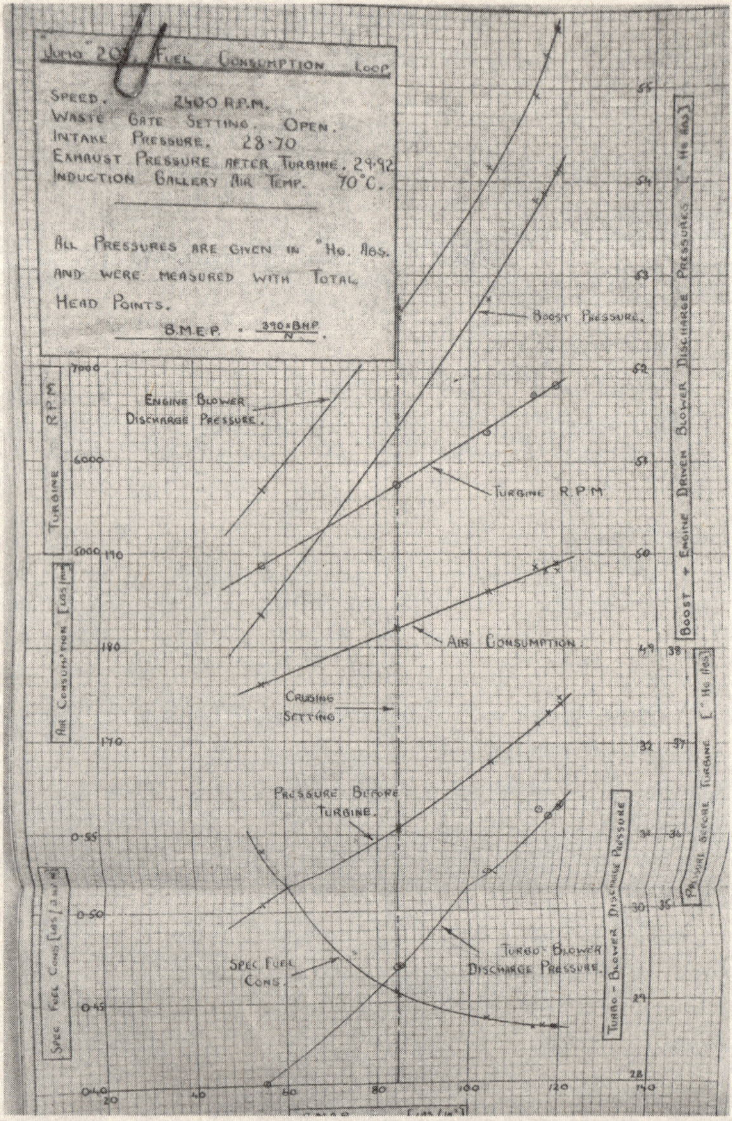

Roy Fedden's calculations for the Junkers Jumo 207 aero engine, September 1937. (© *The Trustees of the Imperial War Museum*)

The dinner menu for Fedden's visit to BMW in October 1938 annotated with guests' names and addresses. (© *The Trustees of the Imperial War Museum*)

The highlight was the visit to the Heinkel factory at Oranienburg near Berlin. Fedden believed 'we were the first Englishmen to see this plant' where the focus was on the twin-engine Heinkel He 111 bomber. Fedden was mesmerised by the scale and the modernity of the operation. He estimated that they were producing eighteen bombers per week but were working one single shift per day. An official noted in the margin '900 per year'. These were the very bombers which would attack Britain in 1940 and so these insights were truly priceless.

At the Mercedes-Benz factory they saw the various changes made to its aero engine, now with a Bosch direct fuel injection pump fitted as standard and providing more power at high altitude. These modifications developed an additional 190 horsepower providing a total of 1150hp at 15,000 feet with no increase in engine weight and a reduction of fuel consumption of 5 per cent. The fitting of fuel injection upgraded the old DB600, which Fedden had seen in June 1937, to the DB601 which would be installed in both the Messerschmitt 109 and 110 fighters that would be in combat within two years against the Spitfire and Hurricane. These details would allow British engineers to estimate the improved performance of the modified engine. So again this was intelligence of enormous importance.[458]

Fedden noted that on the Friday evening, 'As on a previous visit, through his friendship with Baron de Ropp, I had the opportunity to go to the house of Alfred Rosenberg and had a long talk with him on the political situation.'

Fedden concluded that Germany was winning the arms race because 'of the selfless devotion of the whole country to one aim' and Britain could only hope to compete 'by a complete overhaul of our political and economic system'.[459] This time Devereux submitted his own separate report, possibly not wishing to be associated with Fedden's outspoken criticisms. He also seemed to be answering a series of pre-agreed and numbered questions probably provided by Morton's IIC on subjects such as organisation, capital, labour, the views of industrialists, worker conditions, food shortages and lack of gold.

Professor Hinsley in his iconic *British Intelligence in the Second World War* states that 'it is significant the visits by British observers to German factories, the first by an Air Ministry mission in May 1936 and the second by Mr Roy Fedden in the summer of 1937, are recorded as a major source of intelligence used in correcting estimates based on other material.'[460]

It is unfortunate that none of Bill de Ropp's independent reports on the aviation target seem to have survived, but it is quite clear that he facilitated the Rosenberg-Winterbotham relationship, the Wenninger-Air Ministry connection and the three Fedden visits.

It may have been messy and acrimonious at times but collectively the Air Ministry, the FO, MI6, the Deuxième Bureau, the IIC, and the CID got there in the end. Disaster was averted by the slenderest of margins. Had it not been for the extra year of peace negotiated (or surrendered) at Munich and the subsequent Phoney War the RAF would not have been ready for the Battle of Britain.

Bill de Ropp's cover as a spy had been gradually eroding over the years and only the protection of Rosenberg and Hitler had prevented him from being investigated. After the October 1938 visit to Nazi Germany's most secret sites he became nervous and returned to London. The mood in Broadway was unsympathetic. On the brink of another world war Bill de Ropp was needed in Berlin more than ever.

20

'A RED LIGHT OF PERSONAL WARNING'

1938–1939: Sex and suspicion on the eve of war

> Hitler had scarcely arrived in Vienna to celebrate the Anschluss before Rosenberg was on the phone inviting me to join him. It was March 1938. I reached Vienna in time to hear Hitler make his big speech and to note that the relatives of the murderers of Dollfuss had been honoured with front row seats. Then I was taken to meet Hitler at his hotel. He was stalking about like a dog with two tails. I had never seen him so excited 'Na, Baron' he exulted 'At last I have my Austria.'[461]

Bill de Ropp was then rewarded with a journey around Austria with Alfred Rosenberg in his big open-top Grosser Mercedes W150 Tourenwagen. When Bill died in 1973 one of his only possessions was the small photograph album of the trip presented to him by Rosenberg's staff with a covering note pasted inside the front cover: 'Baron de Ropp, the true friend of Germany, in memory of our shared experience'. It is signed by Gotthard Urban, Rosenberg's adjutant.[462] (Urban would be killed in September 1941 on the Russian front.)

There are photos of Graz, the monastery at Melk and of Carinthia. Some of the captions are light-hearted. Others are propagandistic. Bill was taken to an illegal printing press which had been producing pro-Nazi material before the Anschluss. One picture bears the caption: 'over there is Yugoslavia, that too was German territory'. One has a profile view of Dr Siegfried Uiberreither, the SA Chief in Styria, 'The Man of the Hour'. He would later become Gauleiter of Styria where he pursued a ruthless programme of Germanisation, and implemented Aktion T4, the Nazis' enforced euthanasia policy.

The album conveys two clear impressions. The first is how relaxed Rosenberg was in Bill's company. Everyone else describes Rosenberg as stiff, dull, morose, turgid and insipid, but in this album he is smiling, laughing, even clowning. The other is Bill de Ropp's concentration and charm; for example as directed at one of the illegal printers. Here is Bill de Ropp the dangerous spy, combining a bland exterior, middle-aged, greying, medium height, in a heavy brown overcoat and homburg hat – an altogether forgettable man in a crowd – and yet with a formidable intelligence and an ability to direct his charm with a laser focus.

In the photographs – one of which shows Bill apparently wearing a monocle – there are no signs of the suspicions that would begin to accumulate. Quite the contrary. There are smiling SS officers (with the Totenkopf – death's-head – badge clearly visible on their caps) in the background, watching as Bill de Ropp quizzes the illegal printer.

De Ropp had encountered a few scares during his eight years in Germany. One was when Heydrich sat next to him at a Nuremberg dinner (*see* p. 171). There had also been occasions when Rosenberg, Koch and Schickedanz had been warned against him by German officials in London – which warnings had all been dismissed.

Bill de Ropp mentioned a third incident:

> I had another bad fright at about this time. Rosenberg had suggested that it might be a good idea to invite a knowledgeable

Englishman over to Berlin to lecture to leading Nazis. I found a university professor* who was willing and Rosenberg made all the arrangements which included £50 for the professor and a cocktail party with Hitler's inner circle. Hitler at that time had a weekly luncheon at the Chancellery with those who had meant most to him in the very early party days.

Among the men who attended fairly regularly was Putzi Hanfstaengl. He held no rank in the party and was regarded as a bit of a fool but he had hidden Hitler after the aborted 1923 Munich putsch so he was always welcome. Putzi was at the professor's cocktail party and went out of his way to discuss me with the professor, questioning him closely about my English connections. Later the professor told me 'Do you know he actually told me he thought you were a British spy?'[463]

By 1938 the mutual suspicions between Britain and Germany were increasing. When Winterbotham made a trip to Berlin that August and September he found a changed Rosenberg. There was the usual dinner for him and Bill de Ropp at Rosenberg's house. Winterbotham wrote:

> By this time it had become obvious from his conversation that he was trying to warn me in some way. I sensed too from the whole set-up that this was probably the last time Bill and I would see him alone on the old basis of friendship.
>
> Somewhere in the back of my head a red warning light of personal danger lit up. How much did he know? . . . The meal was over but Rosenberg had a final message to deliver . . . The Germans and Italians had become very close indeed; so close

* This may have been Arnold Toynbee, who visited Germany in 1936. He was Director of Studies at Chatham House which had close links to British government. During the war he had worked for the Political Intelligence Department of the Foreign Office and would have had close relations with MI6.

> in fact that they were exchanging intelligence information. Under the circumstances he felt it might be better if, after the Nuremberg Rally, I were not to come back to Germany.[464]

Fred Winterbotham had noticed in August 1936 that he had been followed during a visit to Rome and had wondered how the Italians might have discovered his MI6 role. He speculated that his close relationships with both the French and Czechoslovak intelligence agencies might have been the source of the leak. Both those services had maintained liaison with the Italians.

There was a second, and more convincing, reason. MI6 had been penetrated by the Germans. As he admitted many years later, Dick Ellis,* an Australian MI6 officer working on Dunderdale's Paris station, was recruited by the Germans at about this time. He was married to a White Russian woman and had serious financial problems. He would certainly have known Winterbotham's true MI6 role but Bill de Ropp may, almost miraculously, have escaped his attention.[465] Ellis was an officer on Foley's station in Berlin from 1923 until 1926, when he was posted briefly to Vienna, and in 1927 to Geneva to cover the League of Nations.[466]

In the summer of 1939 the Abwehr managed to recruit Folkert van Koutrik, an assistant to a head agent at the MI6 station at The Hague. This was the main base for spying on Germany. In theory MI6 stations were not permitted by the FO to spy on their host nation; so operations were supposed to be mounted from a neighbouring country. The Bill de Ropp case was a rare exception. Koutrik betrayed a number of agents being run against Germany. However, if restrictive security operated correctly, van Koutrik should not have been aware of Bill de Ropp.

By the late summer of 1938 there was no indication that Rosenberg's suspicions extended to Bill de Ropp. Still, Bill was understandably

* His full name was Charles Howard Ellis but he was known as Dick.

anxious. His tradecraft in Berlin had always been meticulous. In his *Daily Mail* articles in 1957 he explained how . . .

> The job also involved getting to know as many as possible of the top-ranking Nazis. It meant living a lie for eight long years. After the Nazis came to power it was a highly dangerous lie. If I had been found out I should have vanished into a Gestapo dungeon.
>
> In consultation with my wife I developed a reasonable, safe technique for dealing with information. Immediately after a chat with Hitler or anyone else of importance I would run through the contents with my wife. Together we would pick out the salient points then we would both memorise them. I seldom committed anything to paper.[467]

Keith Jeffery's authorised *MI6: The History of the Secret Intelligence Service* agrees.

> De Ropp was mainly briefed and debriefed by Woollcombe during visits to London but he also reported discreetly in Berlin, met by Foley or a colleague from the Berlin Station. This though became increasingly hazardous. There exists on file a copy of some extremely detailed security instructions laid down by Sinclair personally to Foley in October 1933 for meeting de Ropp and handling his reports so as to avoid the slightest risk to compromise.
>
> No papers relating to the agent were to be kept in Foley's office or typed there; no meetings held in apartments or in the PCO's office; de Ropp's reports were to be written on the day fixed for a meeting and at the last minute before the meeting 'so that he walks straight out to the meeting with them and they are in his possession or in his flat for as short a time as possible; meetings to take place on the last day before bag day (when

> the diplomatic bag was sent to London) 'according to a pre-arranged roster of varying rendezvous. This in order to avoid telephone messages about meetings.' These instructions are a clear indication of the importance attached to the case and of Sinclair's close attention to detail.[468]

In retrospect it is curious that Bill de Ropp was not equipped with Secret Writing equipment. He could then have written his notes at home, then have added some bland text on top in normal ink (perhaps a shopping list or a letter) and finally carried them to a meeting with his Case Officer without risk of discovery. When Malcolm Muggeridge was recruited by MI6 at the start of the Second World War he was instructed in SW techniques. In an emergency agents could even use bird shit (known as BS).[469] Semen was another effective emergency measure when an agent's inks had run out.

We are fortunate that Cecil Insall, who worked under Foley at the MI6 station in Berlin, wrote a private memoir. As the eighth officer on Berlin station, his designation was 12800 (the code for Germany being 12000) and he was thus Bill de Ropp's designated case officer.

> My next contact lasted much longer, in fact right up to a day or two before the outbreak of war. He was a former Baltic Baron who had served in the British Forces during the First War as a kite balloonist. He had been granted British nationality and, strangely enough, had been an instructor at the kite balloon training centre in Richmond where I had received my training. We had not actually met there. He was, of course, a fluent German linguist and had a number of influential friends in the Nazi Party and attended most of the big gatherings. I suppose his main acquaintance was Rosenberg, then a sort of Cultural Minister and a close friend of Hitler.
>
> My contact's name was Baron William (or Bill) de Ropp

and he had a young English wife. I never discovered from which Baltic State he came. He made much of the fact that he and I were old 'war comrades', which gave us a very good excuse for meeting frequently, some of which meetings were business when matter passed from one to the other, the others acted as a smokescreen and were social meetings over a glass of beer.

There was one occasion when a business meeting fell through. We had selected a certain bier-halle for our next meeting place with a second meeting place an hour or two later should things go awry. I got to the rendezvous first and sat down at an empty table and ordered a beer then a very inebriated German came in and staggered over to my table, sat down and started talking to me . . . Out of the corner of my eye I saw my friend come in, he saw me and thinking that perhaps something was amiss, turned and went away.

On another occasion when I met de Ropp he suggested that we should try a new place he had heard of and his wife, Jimmy de Ropp, came along too. We had to walk some way down the Kurfürstendamm, the popular promenade with restaurant tables set on the pavement where one could sit and watch the passing crowds. It was an autumn day, I remember, because Jimmy was wearing a fur coat and large fur gauntlets. She was a little person but very easy on the eye. She suddenly pulled off one of her gauntlets and held it out to me saying, 'Here Cecil, try this and see how beautifully warm it is.' Unsuspectingly I put my hand in, as far as it would go, my hand being some sizes larger than hers. Inside was an envelope.

After some contortions I managed, single handed, to work the envelope round to my palm where I was able to grip it tightly and withdrew my hand and its load and get it into my side pocket. I should have to wait for a better occasion to transfer it to a safer resting place when we sat down ourselves to have

> a drink of beer. The only consolation I had was that I felt that anybody looking at us would be sure to have his eyes fixed on Jimmy rather than on her male companion.[470]

Cecil Insall was spending more and more of his time issuing visas to Jews trying to escape Nazi Germany. It was either he or Foley who managed to obtain a visa for Bill de Ropp's physician, a Dr Perlmann, who twice had to intervene in 1934 to treat Jimmy for a suspected heart condition. Berlin street directories show a Dr Georg Perlmann in Meraner Strasse in the Schöneberg district of Berlin just two miles from Bill and Jimmy de Ropp's apartment.[471] Bill de Ropp claimed many years later to have hidden Perlmann and his family in the rafters above their Berlin apartment* 'for several weeks'.[472]

Kristallnacht (the Night of Broken Glass) in November 1938 saw 30,000 Jews rounded up and taken to concentration camps. This would have been no surprise for Bill de Ropp who understood Nazi psychology. Bill and Jimmy would have known about and possibly even witnessed one of the first examples of such brutality on the Kurfürstendamm (where Bill and Jimmy had their apartment) back in September 1931 when a large group of SA members ran amok attacking anyone they thought might be Jewish.

Goebbels expressed a particular disgust for the popular K'damm, which he called 'the abscess' of Berlin. 'The bells on the streetcars ring, buses clatter by honking their horns, stuffed full with people and more people; taxis and fancy private automobiles hum over the glassy asphalt. The fragrance of heavy perfume floats by. Harlots smile from the artful pastels of fashionable women's faces; so-called men stroll to and fro, monocles glinting: fake and precious stones sparkle.'[473]

Fred Winterbotham, who in his books comes across as somewhat libidinous, described Bill's wife as 'a brunette, slim and with deep

* We know from Winterbotham that it was a top-floor apartment, which lends some credibility to this story.

brown eyes [who] was almost aggressively British and amused the Nazis by wearing a large Union Jack brooch on all possible occasions! Jimmy, as she was called, was the envy of the not-so-slim Berlinese of the thirties.'[474]

Bill de Ropp was quick to give full credit to Jimmy.

> She is one of those remarkable cool-headed Englishwomen who take everything in their stride. The fact that her marriage to a respectable Baltic baron had turned out to be life with a spy appeared to worry her not at all. She shared all my worries and often advised me what to ask [Hitler]. Occasionally, relying on instinct rather than judgement, she would say, 'I wouldn't do that, Bill.' She was always right. She kept me sane all those turbulent years. If I had not had her with me my nerves would not have stood the strain.[475]

Winterbotham added another angle.[476] 'His wife was a great favourite of the foreign diplomats in Berlin and she did a lot of good work between the sheets with them which all helped Bill's knowledge of the politics.'[477]

Many years later when she lived in England Jimmy would enjoy telling shocked villagers that she had slept with 'Goebbels and Göring'.[478] So the idea that she slept around may not just have been a figment of Winterbotham's imagination. It is also true that Goebbels had numerous affairs and that the atmosphere in 1930s Berlin was sexually permissive.

Winterbotham also suggests a sexual liaison with an Italian connection. 'Billy de Ropp's wife . . . was asked to pay a visit to Italy to go down there with Graziani who had been up in Berlin. So she went and stayed with Graziani in Rome for some time and he told her everything we wanted to know and it was an extraordinarily valuable source at the time.'[479]

The key to understanding a putative connection between Jimmy de

Ropp and General (later Field Marshal) Rodolfo Graziani is Marchese Francesco Antinori who was the Press Attaché at the Italian Embassy in Berlin from 1925 to 1940. He came from a famous aristocratic family with large wine-growing estates near Florence.

Bill de Ropp knew him well and in June 1935 proposed him as a temporary member of the Savile Club. Antinori had been in England to ask G. K. Chesterton to appear at the Florence Music Festival[480] and Bill was in London too. This was unlikely to have been a coincidence. We also know that Antinori was deeply anti-Nazi. In her book *The Europe I Saw* the journalist and academic Elizabeth Wiskemann wrote that Antinori 'was notorious for his detestation of Hitler and the Nazis'.[481]

Writing to his editor from Paris in 1937, Frederick Voigt of the Manchester *Guardian* described Antinori as a liberal, Roman Catholic, and Italian patriot, appalled by the atmosphere of Berlin: 'When he arrived in Paris he felt that he had come out of prison. When he had to go back again there were tears in his eyes.' According to Voigt, 'Already before the war Antinori was passing information to the British.' Being in Berlin his access to secrets was excellent – in 1940, for instance, Antinori attended both the meetings between Hitler and Mussolini.[482]

Antinori was one of Bill de Ropp's sub-sources and was able to produce CX on German-Italian relations, a major intelligence requirement throughout the 1930s. The British hope, almost up to the declaration of war, was that Mussolini could be peeled away from Hitler and remain neutral in any war. In January 1939 Neville Chamberlain visited Rome to meet Mussolini and as late as 31 August 1939 the British Ambassador in Rome was convinced that Italy would not join Germany in a war.[483]

Jimmy de Ropp's intelligence coup was probably short-lived. Graziani can only have visited Berlin in 1934 because beforehand and afterwards he was almost permanently in Africa. He came from a modest background and trained for the priesthood before becoming a soldier and then was badly gassed in the war; from 1921 to 1934 he served in Libya.

Said to possess the looks of a Greek god, he was guilty of appalling crimes throughout his career. In February 1935 he set off on the conquest of Abyssinia (Ethiopia). The invasion of 1935 became a major British foreign policy preoccupation and eventually led to the fall of the British Foreign Secretary (and former MI6 officer) Sir Samuel Hoare. Mussolini sacked Graziani in November 1937 and later contemptuously advised him to go and grow bananas.[484]

When he met Rosenberg on 16 August 1939 Bill de Ropp had just returned from the South of France and Corsica.[485] This visit may well have been connected with the requirement for intelligence on Italian intentions. Mussolini had long been hinting to Hitler that he would require a revision of the frontier with France near Nice and the transfer of Corsica by France to Italy in the event of a successful war.* Italy also wanted Tunis and Djibouti from the French.[486]

In 1938 and 1939 there was increased Gestapo surveillance of foreigners. In July 1939 MI6's long-standing agent providing intelligence on the German Navy, Dr Karl Krüger (known inside the service as 33016), was finally arrested, betrayed by van Koutrik (*see* p. 268) and confessed. Krüger committed suicide in September. He was one of MI6's all-time greatest spies and his betrayal was a huge blow to the service. He was run using very similar tradecraft to Bill de Ropp with no written notes permitted until the day of meeting his Case Officer. Sinclair may have based his instructions for Bill de Ropp on the Krüger case.

Three years earlier four men accused of working for the British had been beheaded, one of them being Gustav Hoffman who was caught taking illicit photographs in Magdeburg. He confessed to having been recruited by the British station in The Hague.[487]

---

* Both these stipulations were included in Hitler and Mussolini's discussions at the Brenner Pass in October 1940. In November 1942 Italy would occupy Corsica before the island was liberated a mere eleven months later.

In August 1938 the MI6 Head of Station in Vienna, Thomas Kendrick, was arrested by the Gestapo. The following day Nevile Henderson delivered a formal protest to the German government (which now controlled Austria) and four days later Kendrick was released and quickly removed from Austria via Budapest back to England. Head Office was concerned that the Germans appeared to know a lot about Vienna Station's operations.[488]

There was something of an MI6 hysteria developing in Germany. Walter Schellenberg, the young and brilliant deputy to Heydrich in the SD, wrote that Hitler thought that 'the cunning and perfidy of the British Secret Service was known to the world but it would avail them little unless Germans themselves were ready to betray Germany.'[489]

Goebbels had a similar view. Schellenberg wondered why . . .

> . . . in his propaganda Goebbels singled out the British Secret Service as one of the main targets for his spiteful attacks. He represented this excellent and efficient service as an organisation of criminals and murderers and continually hammered this impression into the minds of the German people. Goebbels and the Party leaders entirely forgot that the British Secret Service had a very long tradition and could count many of the ablest and most intelligent of British people amongst its collaborators . . . If the peculiarly insular character of the British with their maritime and global thinking had done so much to further the importance of their Secret Service then we must catch up with them.[490]

Himmler opined that 'Our achievements in this special sector still could not compare with those of the British Secret Service.'[491] Ribbentrop took these opinions in the direction of paranoia. 'He,' wrote Schellenberg, 'had quite a phobia about British espionage and maintained that every single Englishman who travelled or lived abroad was given assignments by the Secret Service. His deep hatred of all things English was noticeable in everything he said.'[492]

Most of these views comprised an exaggerated view of MI6's competence. Many of MI6's inter-war staff and operations were second-rate. Bill de Ropp was fortunate that he had only met the better performers: Menzies, Woollcombe, Sinclair, Morton, Winterbotham, and Foley, and some others who were perfectly competent like Darwin, Vivian, Farina and Insall.

It is hardly surprising that, in August 1938, Bill de Ropp began to get edgy and asked to be moved away from Germany, but Sinclair did not approve. 'If de Ropp is to be of any use,' he wrote, 'he must work between here and Germany.'[493] Sinclair was right, of course. This was not the first time (nor will it be the last) when an MI6 Chief has had to put the national interest before the safety of an individual agent, however loyal and deserving. There was still serious work to be done.

21

'I SUGGEST YOU LEAVE GERMANY'

1938–1939: Countdown to world war

In Chapter 2 we saw how Alex Cadogan's request to Admiral Sinclair to contribute his thoughts on future policy towards Germany resulted in the paper 'What Should We Do?' Not only was it a fine albeit grimly pragmatic piece of work which influenced the Chamberlain government to sell out Czechoslovakia to buy time for rearmament, but it also put MI6 on the map, for the first time in its history, as a trusted supplier of foreign policy advice based upon its political reporting on Germany. Seventy per cent of that reporting came from a single source in Berlin: Bill de Ropp.

Two other similar MI6 strategic papers have survived in the National Archives. They were retained by departments for future reference. They were either commissioned by Cadogan or submitted by Sinclair speculatively. This, of course, was exactly what FO diehards would have feared. Give Sinclair an inch and he will take a mile. Nonetheless both CX-based assessments are of high quality and both bear the distinctive hallmark of Bill de Ropp's contribution.

The first was dated 15 November 1938 and the existing copy in the National Archives was sent to Major General Hastings (Pug) Ismay (Hankey's successor as Secretary to the Committee of Imperial Defence) having been prepared at the request of the FO. Its title was as utilitarian as its predecessor 'The Crisis and Aftermath: Tendencies and Reactions'.[494] It looks back at the Munich crisis and draws conclusions.

'Not even Herr Hitler, or his intimates, according to one of them, knew for certain if he would risk a world war.' MI6 only had one agent who was close to one of Hitler's intimates (Alfred Rosenberg) and that was de Ropp. Whilst noting the public opposition to war over the Sudetenland the report is very cautious in assessing the extent of German opposition to Hitler. Nonetheless it clearly identified the German Chief of Staff General Ludwig Beck as an anti-Nazi,* but doubted that there was any general willing to lead a coup against Hitler.

This was an important and controversial judgement. Since the war a near-consensus has developed among historians that the generals would have rebelled against Hitler if only Britain had stood firm at Munich instead of conceding the Sudetenland to Germany. The American journalist, William Shirer, wrote that General Franz Halder, the Chief of the General Staff, was in close touch with Colonel Hans Oster of the Abwehr and General Erwin von Witzleben who commanded the Berlin Military District. Hjalmar Schacht, who was a member of Hitler's Cabinet, was also aware of the coup plan as was Hitler's interpreter, Paul Schmidt, and Erich Kordt of the AA.

The plan was to mount the coup on 14 or 15 September upon Hitler's return from Nuremberg. However, Hitler travelled to Munich and to Berchtesgaden to meet Chamberlain. Kordt's brother, Theo, an official at the German Embassy in London, warned the plotters that Chamberlain seemed likely to make more concessions

* Beck was later executed after the failed 20 July 1944 bomb plot.

(as 'What Should We Do?' had recommended). Hitler returned to Berlin on 24 September. As Shirer asked, 'What were the conspirators waiting for? All the conditions they themselves had set had now been fulfilled.' There was talk of a coup on the 28th or 29th but Hitler's more moderate tone towards Chamberlain caused the plotters to stand down.[495]

As we saw in Chapter 17 Bill de Ropp himself was critical of Britain's stance. He told his son Bob, 'the only solution was for the Wehrmacht to overthrow Hitler but Britain and France first needed to stand up to him and show some backbone. Only then would the German officer corps take action.'

The one sensible comment which General Karslake brought home from his two visits to Nuremberg was to doubt whether a coup could be successful.

> The question of loyalty of the army to National Socialism was raised. But there are senior officers who are very much against some of the measures. On the other hand the bulk of the rank and file has been trained under National Socialism and even if the officers wanted to do anything it is very doubtful if the rank and file would back them.

It would be helpful to see the background thinking in Whitehall on the likelihood of a coup. It is not clear whether there was any formal review and, if there had been, it is doubtful that the intelligence would have been load-bearing. Cadogan and Vansittart would have been aware of the general (sometimes thought to be von Schweppenburg) who had called on Ustinov (U35) at his London flat. Some of Christie's reporting would have been relevant. However, in the final analysis, no government can make its policies dependent on whether a coup will or will not take place in another country. Most coup plots come to nothing and many of them fail.

'The Crisis and Aftermath: Tendencies and Reactions' continues with an analysis of the leading members of the regime, with Ribbentrop and Propaganda Minister Joseph Goebbels in the ascendency, with Hermann Göring, the chief of the German air force, seen as a moderate (except on Jewish questions), and Himmler focused on 'internal stability'. The report was not sure about General Franz Ritter von Epp's current state of mind (because Bill de Ropp had not been able to see von Epp, his regular sub-source, since leaving Berlin in October after the Fedden visit). It recorded a disagreement between Rosenberg's APA and Epp's Colonial Office about whether priority should be given to Eastern Europe or to the 'recovery' of colonies. Both organisations were key areas of de Ropp's access in Berlin.

The paper stresses that Germany still wants close relations with Great Britain but that Ribbentrop and Goebbels are 'the mainsprings' of anti-British influence on Hitler. One active measure against Britain was the encouragement of anti-British sentiment amongst Arabs due to Jewish migration to Palestine, which London administered under a League of Nations mandate. Berlin sought to add to these tensions by increasing emigration from Germany. Meanwhile German-Italian relations were stronger as a result of the Munich Conference.

Political and economic hegemony in south-east Europe 'was the primary objective of Herr Hitler'. There is a fascinating paragraph on German thinking about atomisation of nationalities with 'each powerless and probably unwilling to resist German political and economic domination'. This too smacks of Rosenberg's thinking for the future of Eastern Europe including the 'permeation' of Poland and the Baltic States. Bill's absence from Berlin is again reflected in the comment on Baltic policy: 'More definite information is being sought.' Naturally enough, Woollcombe wanted Bill both in Berlin, producing new intelligence from his sub-sources, and in London, helping him draft these strategic reports.

The final two pages packed a heavy punch. 'The general Nazi aim seems to be the disintegration of the USSR.' However, it was still unclear whether Germany intended to take action in Ukraine or Poland first. The paragraph concluded with a snippet 'that there might be an improvement in Soviet-German relations'. This important observation was made nine months before the Molotov-Ribbentrop Pact was concluded in August 1939.

The conclusion sums up the preceding points concisely and then adds two additional observations from previous reports. The first repeats 'the Ribbentrop thesis' that 'England is determined not to tolerate the emergence of a world power on the continent' and the second quotes another of Bill's sub-sources, Ernst Bohle (mistyped Bohlo in the report), the Bradford-born Nazi, that plans were afoot to foment trouble in the British Empire.

The third MI6 strategic report was dated 20 December 1938 and bore the even more prosaic title 'Germany: Factors, Aims, Methods'.[496] It catches the attention immediately with the words: 'The following is based on inside information in the proper sense of the word'. It then goes on to claim that it was 'obtained through a number of independent channels of proven reliability'. This was true to an extent. It doubtless includes French and Czech intelligence which was being shared with MI6, but much of the British material can be identified as coming from Bill de Ropp. MI6 was not in the habit of incorporating a lot of Signals Intelligence into such reports. What we now call SIGINT was collected by the Government Code and Cypher School (GC&CS), which was co-located with MI6 at Broadway and submitted its reports (known as BJs) separately.

Its fifteen pages begin with a warning about 'Hitler's incalculability'. He keeps his intimates guessing and then acts at the last moment with 'sudden intuition'. This was why events like the Night of the Long Knives, the remilitarisation of the Rhineland and the occupation of Austria were not reported in advance. One can imagine some FO readers observing that this was a convenient excuse for MI6's failure to warn of all three events. However, as the world would discover later, it was also demonstrably true.

The report goes on, 'In the eyes of his disciples and increasingly in his own "The Führer is always right".' Despite disagreements and even opposition within Germany the country would follow Hitler into a war and Hitler would 'dispose summarily of those who did not obey'. 'Eastern expansion has always been Hitler's first and true love' – and the paper points again to German intentions for Ukraine and the 'disintegration of the Soviet regime'. These pages clearly come from de Ropp's frequent late-night discussions with Rosenberg, and occasionally with Hitler himself, as does the chilling section on 'The Cult of Strength and Force' with a particular focus on 'the blood and iron principle' to inculcate German youth with a blind faith in Germany's supremacy.

Bill de Ropp's reporting is also responsible for the paragraph on Hitler's frustration that his desire for a natural alliance with Britain had not borne fruit, 'revealing all the symptoms of unrequited love'. After a short extract, which pondered the seeming popular opposition in Germany to a war over the Sudetenland, the paper restates the ascendancy of the 'extremists' Ribbentrop and Goebbels, to whom Woollcombe adds Rosenberg (de Ropp's primary source) as 'the arch exponent of eastern expansion'. Page 8 is almost entirely about Rosenberg's plans in the East. 'There is an accumulation of corroborative evidence pointing to the "eastward drive" being the primary objective.' It was likely to begin with 'fomenting of internal disorders within the USSR' to be followed by a coordinated attack by Germany and Japan.

Crucially, it then added that 'Germany may make certain ostensible conciliatory approaches to the USSR.' Quoting Rosenberg again, Poland is to be reduced 'to her natural frontiers'. Danzig will be incorporated into the Reich 'whenever it suits Herr Hitler'. Germany will be satisfied with nothing less than a pro-Nazi regime in Romania. The page on 'Colonies' comes directly from von Epp to Bill de Ropp. Nearer to home Germany intends to widen the divisions between Britain and France and to support Italian ambitions in France.

The core of the report, however, is on page 13, where (unlike 'What Should We Do?') it clearly identifies Britain as 'Enemy No. 1'. Woollcombe provides several reasons why Hitler had altered his long-term view that Britain and Germany were natural allies against the Bolshevik threat to Europe. He was angered by Munich and by the popularity that it gave Neville Chamberlain in Germany. He resented German naval inferiority and London's moves towards rearmament. He disliked the Anglo-French alliance and London's diplomatic efforts with Italy.

In particular, Hitler was 'angered by Britain's attitude over the anti-Jewish measures in Germany', and finally he hated 'and always has, Britain's smug superiority'. Hitler had persuaded himself that Britain had been employing 'consistent and arbitrary attempts to block Germany's progress'. Meanwhile, Ribbentrop and Goebbels had instilled in Hitler the idea that 'Britain is decadent, incapable of fighting and that the British Empire is on the verge of disintegration'.

Hitler's change in attitude towards Britain was a crucial alteration of emphasis between the September and December 1938 reports. In fact Hitler's disillusionment with what he had viewed as a fellow Germanic power had been developing over a longer period. Bill de Ropp had been monitoring the change of mood since 1937.

Taken together, these two MI6 strategic reports provided the government with much of what it needed to know about Germany and its intentions, albeit relying on a thin base of source material. They provided a crispness and clarity which was notably lacking in diplomatic reporting, in particular when compared to the craven performance of Sir Nevile Henderson, the ambassador in Berlin. All that was needed now was the when, where and how Nazi aggression would happen.

This was all too much for one senior FO official. Early in March 1939 George Mounsey, the Assistant Under Secretary (AUS), put pen to paper twice to his boss's private secretary, Gladwyn Jebb. His ten pages of manuscript reveal his frustration. While stressing that he did not wish to belittle 'our secret agents' he suggested that they were sent abroad to find threats to Britain and therefore had an incentive to find them. He added, rather uncharitably, that he 'would back foreign agents at this sort of game against our own'. After making some valid observations about how secrecy can give false importance to reports, he concluded by saying that 'I am heretic enough to embrace all reports of a secret nature in my general dislike of the article.'

Jebb replied to Mounsey with a stalwart defence of MI6 and its system for validating reporting. He gently mocked Mounsey's insinuation that British agents were 'hired assassins'. He went on to deliver a remarkable compliment to Woollcombe. 'The head coordinator at this end is a man of really remarkable intelligence and discretion.' He then listed a string of senior FO officials who would regard a suggestion that [MI6 reports] should be suppressed 'with frank dismay'.

At the end of March 1939 Cadogan made his own comments on Mounsey's minutes. 'I cannot ignore the fact that they [MI6] did warn us of the September crisis and they did not give any colour to the ridiculous optimism that prevailed up to the rape of Czechoslovakia,* of which our [FO] official reports did not give us notice'.

Bill de Ropp's occasional sessions with Hitler continued.

> I talked with [Hitler] several times between the Anschluss with Austria and the outbreak of war. He told me enough to make me realise he would not be satisfied with Austria, or with Sudetenland, or Czechoslovakia or Poland. His mind was set on the conquest of Russia and the colonisation of the Ukraine and of the Caucasus.
>
> I told him that Britain would go to war if he attacked Poland. I told him that their people would be behind their government and that the Commonwealth would support England. 'I think

* Czechoslovakia was occupied by the Nazis on 15 March 1939.

> you must be misinformed, Baron,' he said at our last interview. 'Ribbentrop tells me the British won't fight. They couldn't get the backing of Australia, Canada or South Africa and their youth is too decadent and pacifist.'[497]

This point about the Commonwealth is important and gets all too little attention. The files in the National Archives testify to the Commonwealth's reluctance to be drawn into another European war. The memoirs of Sir Samuel Hoare paint the problem starkly:

> The fact remains the Commonwealth Governments were unwilling to go to war on the issue of Czechoslovakia. Dominion opinion was at the time overwhelmingly against a world war. This opposition was continually in our minds . . . As early as March 18th 1938 we had been told that South Africa and Canada would not join us in a war to prevent certain Germans from rejoining their Fatherland.[498]

A 'circular telegram' marked 'Most Secret' sent by the FO to the Dominions of Australia, Canada, New Zealand, South Africa and Eire in January 1939 demonstrates the considerable care employed by Whitehall in communicating with them.[499] It was one of a series of such messages. There is no sign of taking the Dominions' support for granted. Instead the aim was to highlight the considerable political risks expected later that year, the measures that Britain was taking in preparation, while also suggesting future arbitration measures. It draws on intelligence material and very noticeably does not use any of Nevile Henderson's reporting from Berlin, which was widely distrusted.

'Reports indicate that Hitler is considering an attack on the western powers as a preliminary to subsequent action in the east.' Probably thinking of Vansittart and Christie's sources as well as Theo Kordt, MI5's von Putlitz and Bill de Ropp the telegram continues:

'Some of these reports emanate from highly placed Germans of undoubted sincerity who are anxious to prevent this crime; others come from foreigners, hitherto Germanophile, who are in close touch with leading German personalities.'

It goes on to speak of Hitler's uncertainties about his army's reliability, 'his insensate rage at Great Britain' and his 'megalomania'. Britain had consulted experts who concurred that the Germans would carry out Hitler's instructions 'and that no revolt can be anticipated'. In response London 'have decided to accelerate . . . defensive and counter-offensive measures.'

This is a fascinating example of intelligence and diplomatic material being used to help bring onside a group of countries whose support (except for neutral Eire) was going to be crucial to Britain's survival, let alone eventually winning a war. It was telegrams like this, as well as the clear evidence that Chamberlain had explored every avenue for peace, which finally brought the Dominions around, proving Ribbentrop and Hitler wrong.

Back in London Bill de Ropp found MI6 increasingly on a war footing. In Broadway there was hectic activity. The MI6 'War Station' at Bletchley Park was now up and running. New people were being hired and retired officers were being brought back.

One of these was John Darwin, who had been exporting aircraft for the Bristol Aeroplane Company in Europe and the Far East. In 1936 he had become Managing Director of Saunders-Roe on the Isle of Wight but had not been a success in the role and left after little more than a year. In February 1938 he was summoned back into MI6 by Sinclair to assist Winterbotham on the aviation target. Soon afterwards he volunteered to help Brigadier Richard Gambier-Parry install wireless sets to provide MI6 stations and some agents with a means of communication in wartime.[500]

This was an urgent and largely successful task involving visits all over Europe. When Gambier-Parry visited Berlin Darwin noted in his diary for 14 August, 'Parry returned from Berlin.

[Illegible] installed and everything OK. Nevile Henderson optimistic. But no great love shown to Parry who was "trailed all the time" he was there. General feeling: anti British.'

A week later, 'Russo-German Pact everything very alarming* - Parliament to meet Thursday. etc. CSS [Sinclair] on warpath in view of possibility that we have been accused of letting FO down. The usual chase after a scapegoat that can't defend itself. I think this one can.'[501]

From the few reports that have survived it seems that Bill de Ropp had a mixed record in the last few months before the war. On 13 March Sinclair sent Cadogan a CX report quoting the German ambassador in London. Von Dirksen (who was on friendly terms with Bill de Ropp) had just returned from a visit to Berlin He claimed not to have seen Ribbentrop and painted a picture of confusion in Berlin with the AA out of the loop on the foreign policy thinking of the 'Berchtesgaden clique', the economy in crisis and Göring seemingly absent. Cadogan marked the report up to both Halifax and the Prime Minister.[502]

Historians have since claimed that von Dirksen did see Ribbentrop during his visit and was told of Germany's intention to seize the remainder of Czechoslovakia.[503] If true, this highlights a weakness in having an agent like de Ropp reporting discussions with a contact who, for whatever reason, might not be willing to tell the whole truth.

In June 1939 Menzies sent Vansittart a paper on propaganda from 'a very highly qualified and objective source in Germany'.[504] The paper bears all the usual hallmarks of Bill de Ropp's work. He identifies three German characteristics which could be crucial in the coming war.

The first is the fear of encirclement. Bill identifies three interpretations of encirclement – geographical, intellectual and commercial ostracism – and a blockade. The first two are not necessarily

* It is a myth that some form of Russo-German rapprochement came as a complete surprise. See, for example, the MI6 letter to FO dated 10th May 1939 at TNA FO 1093/87 Folios 56 to 58.

a problem for most Germans. 'The chief difficulty when trying to dispel this fear of encirclement is the vivid recollection ... of the post-war blockade [and] the inhumanity of which Englishmen, Frenchmen and Americans are capable.'

The second is the 'idea ... that England and France are bluffing and that neither would fight unless attacked. Military quarters in Germany suffer least from [this] illusion.' In this context he pointed to Wenninger's reporting back to Göring as important.

And the third is the myth of victimhood. Germans like to accuse President Wilson and his Fourteen Points as a betrayal, yet they 'forget that Germany became the Godmother of Bolshevism when she sent Lenin and his collaborators into Russia'.

De Ropp was back in Berlin in mid-August 1939. He was well-placed to dispense some useful advice. Ewan Butler was the deputy head of *The Times* office in Berlin and was married to Lucy the sister of Robert Byron, the travel writer and member of the Savile. In his biography of Byron, James Knox wrote: '[Byron's] thoughts turned to Lucy who had remained resolutely in Berlin with her young daughter throughout August, not leaving until the 25th, after a friend, a baron from one of the Baltic states, urged her to get out. Ewan timed his departure even more finely. He escaped to Denmark only twenty-four hours before Hitler launched his "blitzkrieg" against Poland.'[505]

On 16 August 1939 Bill de Ropp called on Rosenberg who noted in his diary:

> '... in the last few days [de Ropp] had spoken to the officers of the British Air Staff and Air Ministry who he knew. The views in these quarters were exactly the same as before. It was absurd for Germany and Britain to engage in a life and death combat on account of the Poles. As things were, the result could only be the destruction of each other's air forces and, at the end of such a war, the destruction of the whole of European civilisation leaving Russia with her forces intact as the only beneficiary.

> . . . He said he was telling me this in confidence on account of a long acquaintance because he was firmly convinced that everything must be done to prevent war. But judging from the present situation he believed that, in the event of a war-like conflict between Germany and Poland, France and Britain would automatically be brought in. Even in this event . . . the possibility of not letting it develop into a war of extermination for both sides must still be kept in mind.[506]

'The British Empire and Germany could not stake their whole existence for a state which would then have practically ceased to exist in its previous form.' In France: hatred of Italy had greatly increased; Corsica [which de Ropp had recently visited] was filled to over-flowing with troops and there was no doubt that the Corsicans themselves felt they were French . . . In the event of a general conflict there were battles between the French and Italian air forces that would automatically lead to general warfare between Germany and Britain.

De Ropp emphasised that he trusted that 'if after establishing herself in the East, which his friends particularly advocated because in this they saw for Britain's future not only no harm but an advantage – Germany [would not have] subsequent designs on the British Empire'.[507]

Rosenberg added, 'I consider it my duty to inform the Führer of these statements emanating from the British Air Ministry and of the views of those in the highest levels of the British Air staff, especially as these views coincide with what they have so far publicly stated in the newspapers.'[508]

We must pause here and consider what Bill de Ropp was saying and where it came from. Chamberlain had guaranteed that Britain would go to war for Poland. However, there were several politicians in London who thought the Polish guarantee had been a serious mistake. Kingsley Wood of the Air Ministry was one as was R. A. Butler at the FO. The idea of going to war for Poland (and yet not even saving

Poland from conquest) seemed unwise. So Bill de Ropp's comment that a war over Poland would be 'absurd' was not an uncommon view. Nevertheless he did make clear to Rosenberg that an invasion of Poland would lead to war with Britain and France.

Instead Bill de Ropp suggested another course of action whereby Britain would declare war against Germany following the invasion of Poland but the conflict would be conducted 'on both sides as a defensive war' without 'aerial bombardment of open cities' leaving open the possibility of the war ending soon after Germany had defeated Poland.

His suggestion that Britain might almost welcome Germany 'establishing herself in the East' is odd. We know it was de Ropp's personal view that Germany should work with the Finns, Poles and Baltic states and establish control of the Ukraine. But this was never British government policy unless it was devised in London as a last-ditch ploy to stop an invasion of Poland.

All these ideas, although smacking of desperation, were in keeping with MI6's paper 'What Should We Do?' The aim was still to delay war until the RAF had enough Spitfires and Hurricanes to mount a credible defence against the Luftwaffe. Professor Donald Cameron Watt, writes, 'De Ropp's line of patter . . .was calculated to raise every Soviet hackle.' He speculates that Sinclair and Menzies 'shared Winterbotham's critical attitude towards the guarantee of Poland and the approach to the Soviet Union'.[509] This may be so, but it is unlikely that MI6 would have promoted these ideas without the approval of Cadogan at the FO.

Cadogan's diary for August 1939 shows a man at the end of his tether in what he calls 'the War of Nerves'. He saw a great deal of Sinclair over this period but does not refer to the concept of (what was essentially) a fake war with Germany followed by a quick peace after the Nazi defeat of Poland. Indeed one message to the Germans spoke of the 'dangerous illusion to think that once war starts it will come to an early end'.[510] Nevertheless there were lots of drastic ideas flying around the corridors of Whitehall. One was an MI6 plan to bring Göring to secret talks in London. Another was Henderson's suggestion of a Non-Aggression Pact with Germany.[511]

Fred Winterbotham wrote in his 1968 book *Secret and Personal*, 'Now as I look back over the past thirty years, I allow myself perchance to dream of a world in which the two major forces for evil in modern times, the Nazis and the Communists, had been allowed to fight each other to a standstill of destruction . . . What a chance for a Britain not ruined by a second world war.'[512]

On 21 August 1939 Bill de Ropp called again on Rosenberg and said he was now flying to London.* Rosenberg asked him to inform 'the circles of which he was speaking' that Britain's guarantee to Poland should not cover 'her attempts to wipe out her minorities [which] was destroying the principles which had led to the recognition of the Polish state'. He also believed that the Dominions 'had every reason to draw Britain away from her present policy'. De Ropp told Rosenberg that he would be moving to Geneva and would use the name George in future communications.[513]

Later the same day Bill and Jimmy de Ropp must have flown from Berlin's Tempelhof to Heston Aerodrome just outside London. Two days later they took a flight to Switzerland and booked into the Hôtel du Mont-Fleuri above Montreux. The purpose was to meet their new case officer, Hugh Whittall, to discuss safe arrangements for future contact in Switzerland, before the couple hurriedly returned to Berlin via Heston. Doubtless the full day in London enabled Head Office staff (probably Woollcombe or his deputy David Footman) to debrief Bill on his 21 August meeting with Rosenberg and to prepare him for any subsequent sessions with senior Nazis.*

On 25 August Frank Foley left Berlin, ending his posting in Germany after nearly twenty years. He drove to Copenhagen and thence

* John Darwin's diary testifies to all the frantic flights being taken around Europe as MI6 prepared for war, all a far cry from Percy Sykes's insistence on economical rail travel.

travelled to Oslo to take up his next assignment. The rest of the MI6 station closed up the PCO on Tiergartenstrasse and took the train to the Hook of Holland and the ferry to Harwich.

Cecil Insall stayed on for a few more days. 'I had a last meeting with my contact de Ropp a few days before war was declared, this time over a drink at the Adlon Hotel. He was on his way to Switzerland and I never saw him again, although, some years later, I read an article published by him on his life in Berlin.'[514]

Bill de Ropp concluded that very article: Three days before the Germans walked into Poland Rosenberg asked me to call. "Things are beginning to look really black, Baron," he said. "I suggest that you leave Germany for the time being." So on that day . . . I went home with a heavy heart.'[515]

Recalling the events of March 1939 Cadogan wrote, 'We were daily inundated by all sorts of reports. It just happened that these were correct; we had no means of evaluating their reliability at the time of their receipt. (Nor was there much that we could do about it.)[516]

An attempted solution to all this random and unassessed information from diplomats, journalists, spies and travellers was the Situation Report Centre, with a representative of the FO and the three Service Directors of Intelligence, which was set up in April 1939 to bring together the material received from abroad, and issue a report each day.

An earlier measure was the Joint Intelligence Committee (JIC) established in 1936, though the early JIC was a purely military body, to collate and assess military reporting. 'It was not established to consider the kind of subjects that the FO would have been involved with.'[517] The FO and MI6 attended their first meeting of the JIC in November 1938. Menzies commented that 'our own constantly recurring experience of being called upon for ad hoc notes on various aspects is our strongest proof that such machinery is badly needed.'[518]

It was all too little, too late. The world stood on the brink of another catastrophic war.

22

'HEAVY NEW SNOW'

1939–1940: Bill de Ropp's peace efforts from Switzerland

Bill and Jimmy de Ropp left Berlin on 29 August 1939, just three days before the Nazi tanks rolled into Poland. They took a train from Berlin's Anhalter station to Basel via Hanover and Mannheim. The arrival at Basel was a tense experience for anyone leaving the Third Reich. The Basel Badischer Bahnhof was a German station on Swiss territory operated by the Deutsche Reichsbahn. Papers were scrutinised by the German authorities.

Bill de Ropp may have had a *laissez passer* signed by Reinhard Heydrich. The five British journalists in Berlin had persuaded Heydrich to issue the document by pointing out that there were nearly a hundred German correspondents in England who might otherwise be detained.[519] The last British reporters left for Denmark on the 30th.

Bill and Jimmy caught the shuttle to the Basel Central station operated by SBB, Swiss railways. They transferred to a Swiss connecting service via Olten to Vitznau on Lake Lucerne. After eleven years in Berlin this must have been a long, tense and depressing day.

They did not spend the night in Basel. Far better to put some distance between them and the German frontier. Bill would have remembered the case of Georg Bell, the associate of Röhm, Rosenberg and Deterding, who in 1933 thought he had reached safety in Austria only to be pursued and killed there by stormtroopers.[520] Bill was right to be cautious. Around the time that he and Jimmy crossed into Switzerland, Grahame Christie, tipped off by Göring, fled from his Berlin flat only fifteen minutes before the Gestapo arrived to arrest him.[521]

Bill de Ropp knew Switzerland well because when he was a child his father and mother had brought the whole family for long summer holidays at the lakes, and in 1911 Bill and his first wife had spent some weeks at the Hotel Berthod at Château d'Oex. Those were the early days of winter sports in Switzerland when English tourists arrived in droves. The Berthod was famous for its annual fancy dress ball.[522]

After some well-deserved rest at Vitznau Bill and Jimmy moved to Montreux on Lake Geneva. Montreux had been well chosen by MI6. The main reason was the presence of Bill's new case officer Hugh Whittall, who had lived in Montreux for several years and was currently working at the British Consulate in nearby Lausanne. (He would become Honorary Vice Consul in Montreux itself in 1940.) It was also well placed for access to the three main MI6 stations in Berne, Zurich and Geneva and for coverage of visitors from Italy, France and the German Reich.

Back in London the whole service was in transition. In 1936 the Head of Station in Rome, Claude Dansey, had been summoned home to London by Sinclair and given instructions to implement his own idea of setting up a parallel service known as the Z Organisation. Dansey himself was given the designation of Z. The plan was truly radical. The myth was circulated that Dansey had been sacked and was in disgrace. This was intended to ensure that MI6 and Z were kept totally separate with only a few people aware that Z was a secret offshoot of MI6.[523]

Dansey was a man of strong and intemperate opinions. He had long been impatient with the existing MI6, which he saw as slow, complacent and unprofessional. In particular, he wished to free up his officers from the endless grind of PCO work. He was also keen to create a clean organisation unsullied by the sort of German penetration that the Hague station had suffered.

The Z Organisation was based in Bush House on the Strand and Dansey recruited officers at breakneck speed. One of his earliest recruits was Frederick van den Heuvel (known as Fanny) who was a director of Eno's Salts and later of Beecham's Pharmaceutical Company. He would become Z1, Dansey's representative in Switzerland.[524] The other officer to play a role in the de Ropp story was Hugh Whittall, He was a mining engineer from the famous Constantinople family, who had worked with Cecil Rhodes in Africa and had served in MI6 during the Great War in Salonika and Lausanne. After mining in Smyrna (Izmir in modern-day Turkey) and farming in Devon, he had moved to Montreux in 1930 in the hope that his younger son's tuberculosis might respond to the healthy climate. There he was Bill de Ropp's closest MI6 contact.[525]

Some of Dansey's newly recruited agents also had linkages to the Bill de Ropp story. We have encountered Henri Deterding of Royal Dutch Shell before as a contact of Rosenberg's who was keen to wrest back the Baku oilfields from the Soviets. He had given Horst Obermüller a job at Shell whilst he remained a member of Rosenberg's APA. Deterding had also been caught up in the Maundy Gregory scandal. In 1936 he moved to Germany although he kept a house at St Moritz. Unfortunately for Dansey he died in February 1939 before he could be much use, and it remains an open question as to where Deterding's true loyalties lay.[526]

Dansey also recruited the Los Angeles-based aircraft manufacturer James Howard Kindelberger, of German extraction himself, who had once employed Erhard Milch and Ernst Udet between the wars as he built up his 'North American' aircraft company.[527] Another recruit was Frederick Voigt of the *Manchester Guardian* who was now back in London, from where he delivered fortnightly talks on foreign affairs for the BBC.[528]

These recruitments demonstrate how liberating it must have been for the Z Organisation to operate without the leaden burden of PCO work and FO oversight. The tragedy is that Z had so little time to flourish. When war was declared the fateful, but probably inevitable, decision was taken to merge the two organisations into one. Z officers found themselves in the dreaded PCO roles which Dansey had so wished to avoid.

At the outbreak of war the MI6 order of battle in Switzerland was one of the most elaborate in any country. There were stations in Berne, Geneva, Zurich, Basel and Lugano. Dansey himself helped set up his Swiss empire before returning to London on the news of Admiral Sinclair's death.

John Darwin noted in his diary on 4 November: 'Life has been made even more bloody with the death of our beloved CSS. He died at 4.30 pm. He is quite definitely irreplaceable. There never will be anyone like him.'[529]

Sinclair had been ill for a long time and Alex Cadogan had been aware. In March he wrote to Sinclair who had just discharged himself from a cancer clinic: 'Congratulations to you on having walked out of the home like the man you are.' His obituary in *The Times* makes no mention of MI6. It merely says that Sinclair retired from the Royal Navy in 1926 but was promoted to Admiral in 1930. That must have puzzled some readers.

To lose the Chief of MI6 in the second month of a world war was far from ideal and the race was on to find a successor. For many the obvious choice was Admiral John Godfrey, the Director of Naval Intelligence. The two previous Chiefs had been naval officers and Godfrey had the backing of Winston Churchill. However, Sinclair had clearly specified that his choice was his deputy, Stewart Menzies.

Menzies was a safe choice, a man with a truly extraordinary record for avoiding death in wartime whilst being in the thick of the fighting, but he was not widely liked in MI6. He was seen as too careful and calculating. Some, including Dansey, saw him as a social butterfly. Winterbotham did not trust him to have his back as Sinclair had done so often.*

Patrick Reilly was seconded from the FO to work as Menzies's Staff Officer and became devoted to him. He conceded that his boss had no intellectual pretensions and that he failed to assert himself over his warring deputies but he was fundamentally honest and possessed a considerable flair for intelligence.[530] Bill de Ropp would have thought it excellent news that his first case officer and long-time supporter was now C. However, the new Chief would have very little time to protect his protégé in faraway Switzerland from the vituperative Dansey.

Menzies's immediate problem was the Hankey Review, which had been commissioned to look into MI6's performance. On the positive side Maurice Hankey was a long-time securocrat and could be relied upon to be both objective and sympathetic to the trials of a service which had been under financial pressure for most of the 1920s and 1930s. On the other hand, nobody commissions an enquiry into its Secret Service in wartime if everything is going well.

The three armed services and the Air Ministry were dissatisfied with the quality of intelligence received. Desmond Morton was also scathing of MI6's production of Economic Intelligence. However, on political reporting MI6 received plaudits from the FO. 'There is general agreement that the service of information of a general and political character is very satisfactory. The Foreign Office and the Ministry of Economic Warfare are well content with the supply of political intelligence.'[531] This was a definite feather in Woollcombe's cap and indirectly Bill de Ropp's too.

The first crisis to hit Menzies was the Venlo Incident. For some

* Hugh Trevor-Roper is savage about Menzies, but on the basis of very little personal knowledge.

time MI6 had believed that they were in contact with a disgruntled group of Wehrmacht officers. This was not particularly improbable; after all, there had been approaches to London from General Ludwig Beck and there had been the message passed to Ustinov before Munich that the British government should stand firm. At the time it was suggested that the Wehrmacht was ready to arrest Hitler in September 1938.

But MI6 had fallen into a snare laid by the youthful Walter Schellenberg, who was the most talented of Heydrich's deputies in the SD. The Germans finally sprung the trap by kidnapping the Head of Station in The Hague, Richard Stevens, and the head of the Z organisation in Holland, Sigismund Payne Best, at the Café Backus near Venlo, barely a hundred yards from the border crossing. In the process a young Dutch officer was shot dead.

Stevens and Best spent the whole war in German prison camps. It was alleged that they had divulged a great deal about MI6, its organisation, officers and agents. After the war, however, Best insisted that the SD already had the information. The probability is that the true culprit was Dick Ellis. Chapman Pincher, the veteran intelligence writer, recorded that in 1965, 'under further questioning [Ellis] admitted handing over detailed charts of the organisation of British Intelligence before the war, knowing that they would go both to Germany and Russia. This had been the source of much of the information that the Abwehr used during its interrogations following the Venlo kidnappings.'[532]

There were several strands of peace feelers in the months before and after the declaration of war. The most promising was from Carl Goerdeler, the Mayor of Leipzig, who made several trips to London at some personal risk to himself, but Vansittart described Goerdeler as 'a stalking horse for Germany's military expansion'.[533] Goerdeler was later executed for his role in the July 1944 bomb plot so his sincerity was proved post-facto.

There was also the approach by the brothers Theo and Erich

Kordt, the former a member of the German Embassy in London and the other in the AA. They began their discussions with Cadogan in September 1938.[534] Less convincing was Birger Dahlerus, a Swedish businessman and friend of Göring, who called on Cadogan in August.[535] In October Vansittart had messages from K [Hans Ritter] and Max Hohenlohe which were said to be similar to the ideas of Dahlerus and the Generals.[536]

This does not pretend to be a comprehensive analysis of the various peace efforts. The intention is to show both the variety of channels being used and the lack of consistency in the evaluation of the validity and worth of each approach. This should allow us to judge whether Bill de Ropp's own peace attempts, which so alarmed Peter Lawrence in 1954 (*see* Chapter 3), were in keeping with the general intentions of the British government. Even this is hard to judge because there appears to have been no agreed script or 'line to take' in any discussions with either the enemy or intermediaries. The amateurishness of MI6 in the 1930s was matched by a lack of rigour in the FO.

On the other hand, as we have observed before, a country cannot devise a foreign policy based on vague promises that there will be a coup against the enemy leader. Even in 1944, with Germany's cities lying in ruins, and its forces defeated in the east and under intense pressure in the west, a coup against Hitler failed, not just because he escaped death but because the majority of the armed forces remained loyal to the Führer.

Bill de Ropp sent his first message to Rosenberg only a month after arriving in Switzerland. He suggested someone from Berlin should be sent to meet him in Montreux 'for a private exchange of views' to include the German opinion of Britain and France and, in return, the thoughts of the [British] Air Ministry which had now 'become of extreme importance as a result of the war situation'.

Upon receipt of Bill's message, Rosenberg sent the idea to Hitler with a note reminding him that 'the personalities who are especially close to Chamberlain are fellow club members of Baron de Ropp'.

He also mentioned a note he had sent him in mid-August that Baron de Ropp was to become adviser on German issues to the British Air Ministry with the rank of Squadron Leader and that he wished to discuss continued contacts between Britain and Germany following the likely fall of Poland.[537]

Thanks to Rosenberg's diaries we know that he discussed this message with Hitler at the end of September.

> Today the Führer called me to the Reich Chancellery at 4 o'clock to discuss de Ropp's proposal . . . As regards de Ropp's suggestion: he grants him safe conduct and will receive him! He should ask his government whether it will permit him to make the trip. Also the Führer will now propose a large peace conference; to this end, ceasefire, demobilisation, settlement of all questions on a basis of reason and equity . . . If the English do not want peace he will attack and destroy them with all available means . . . Afterwards I immediately sent a card to Ropp in Montreux to let him know that 'the excursion will take place'. Am sending Harder there to get R[opp] to Berlin. Whether he can mobilise the forces in the British Air Ministry against Churchill's forces will be shown later.[538]

Hermann Freiherr von Harder was a member of Rosenberg's foreign affairs bureau, the APA. He was a good choice to send to Bill de Ropp. Harder was an aristocrat who had served in the Prussian Cavalry during the Great War. Before joining the Nazi party he had been a Hamburg businessman. Harder was a convinced Nazi who had joined the party in 1933, but he was a reasonably thoughtful one.

Rosenberg's diaries include an entry for 5 October: 'Harder is back from Switzerland today. Ropp has inquired in London whether he should come here. Reply from his Ministry: chauvinism is running so high in England that at the moment there is no opportunity for exerting any influence. Ropp added in explanation: the British air force cannot fight to the last because England would then be at the mercy [of Germany].'

There followed a long note of the rather unstructured conversation between de Ropp and Harder. One has to aim off for it being Harder's version of the conversation in which he would have wished his arguments to prevail.

De Ropp 'took the position that the outbreak of war between England and Germany was inevitable because of the chauvinistic attitude of the English people'. Harder replied that 'the German nation was determined to accept the fight forced upon it by England . . . They were of the opinion that attempts to reach an understanding with England had finally come to an end after six years of interminable effort.' However Christian [Harder's bizarre pseudonym for Rosenberg] wanted to make one more attempt 'to save the British Empire'.[539]

Harder said de Ropp's concern about 'the Bolshevisation of Europe was entirely unfounded . . . Just as Poland had fallen much more rapidly than I had expected so the British Empire would also collapse very much more rapidly than the world considered possible today because of our new weapons with which England would very soon become acquainted . . . The Vistula-San Line was actually predestined to create an even stronger eastern wall than our present west wall.' (The Pissa-Narew-Vistula-San Line was the partition line in Poland agreed between Russia and Germany.)

De Ropp thought the 'political swing in German policy towards Russia could not be made comprehensible to the German people'.[540] Only at the 1938 Nuremberg Rally the Nazis had called Russia 'the seat of infection that had to be eradicated'. Harder (surprisingly) replied that Hitler had only been elected by a minority of the German people. Stalin was now ousting the Jews from all posts. And the German people had always had great sympathy for the Russian people. He implied that Rosenberg's was a minority view.

Harder insisted that Britain and France were wrong to think that Germany could not cope without raw materials. He added that they now had access to coal from Poland and lumber from Finland. By contrast England had to import nearly 70 per cent of its raw materials.[541]

De Ropp then made the following 'statement'.

> The British Air Ministry . . . by no means wished to be a party to the present policy of England of waging the war to the finish . . . The Air Ministry believed that it would constantly gain in political power at home. It was convinced that the war would be decided by the Luftwaffe . . . But it was necessary first to await the first clash and the resulting losses. He hoped that in the interests of the Aryan race Germany's Luftwaffe would be so victorious as to create this basis . . . Daniels was of the same opinion, even if he did not say so officially . . . He also advised that German propaganda should hit England in her weakest spot 'that the destruction of Germany would lead to Bolshevism'.[542]

The reference to Daniels was to Bill's old friend from the Savile Club and *The Times*, Harold Griffith Daniels. He had been one of Bill's sponsors when he joined the club in 1917 and had been the Berlin correspondent of *The Times* when Archibald Church visited Berlin in 1925 (*see* Chapter 10). He was now press attaché at the British Embassy in Berne.[543]

At the beginning of November Rosenberg reported to Hitler another message from de Ropp sent from Switzerland 'saying that the forces of peace were eclipsed in London by the Churchills so that a visit to Berlin simply does not promise success'.[544] Hitler replied that he still considered 'a German-English rapprochement' to be the right long-term solution. Rosenberg concluded by telling Hitler that he would have someone write to de Ropp to say that 'talk would have meaning if <u>deep snow</u> really has fallen and one can undertake <u>skiing trips safely</u>'.*

---

* The underlinings are in the original documents.

The document that would later arouse Peter Lawrence's greatest suspicions (*see* p. 26) was undated* and described de Ropp's second meeting in Switzerland in early November with von Harder.[545] Two days later Rosenberg wrote, 'Von Harder was back from Switzerland yesterday. The second talk with de Ropp was more serious. The "English Party" has an influx from the City . . . under the leadership of Sir [Ralph] Glyn.'[546]

De Ropp had alleged that there was a circle in England (known as the 'English Party') that wanted peace with Germany. Once this party was strong enough to gain power over 'the warmongers', de Ropp saw value in the idea of his visiting Berlin. The 'English Party' did not just consist of the Air Ministry but also the City of London, which feared for the value of sterling.

Quite why Glyn's name cropped up in this context is puzzling. In May 1940 he would be one of the Conservative MPs who voted against Chamberlain's handling of the Norwegian campaign. He was also one of Dansey's recruits for the Z Organisation.† A more obvious example of an appeaser in the City was none other than the Governor of the Bank of England, Montagu Norman, who was firmly against war with Germany. Norman was said to 'prefer the industriousness of the Germans to the fickle selfishness of the French'.[547] His biographer describes him 'as the last of the sleepwalkers to stir'.[548]

Von Harder made it clear that he could not engage in another long discussion as before. Little wonder! He had probably received a sharp rebuke from Rosenberg for some of his comments at the previous meeting. So Bill de Ropp confined himself to two concerns. He claimed that the British government was worried by the withdrawal of the Baltic Germans (which was one of the stipulations of the

* The editors of Volume VIII of *Documents on German Foreign Policy* estimated that this meeting took place at the end of October but Rosenberg's diaries show that it probably happened on 9 November.

† S*ee* Read, *Colonel Z*, p. 175..

Ribbentrop-Molotov Pact); and, secondly, the question of what would become of Poland.

Harder explained that the withdrawal of the Baltic Germans was not a retreat but a strengthening of the East through abandoning lost posts and eliminating all points of friction.[549] Harder replied that he would not submit either question to his government because they were none of Britain's business.

Von Harder concluded, 'I left him little hope for the possibility of continuing the talks. But he insistently begged me to underline the importance of remaining in touch . . . When the time arrived for concrete preliminaries to appease only Christian [Rosenberg] and not the Foreign Minister [Ribbentrop] would be able to conduct negotiations successfully.'[550] De Ropp proposed a complex arrangement for a future Berlin visit by which he would travel 'officially' from London via Holland, having been invited to inspect housing arrangements for displaced Baltic Germans on behalf of the Red Cross.

What can we make of these exchanges?

De Ropp still had the ability to seize Rosenberg's attention and Hitler too continued to take him seriously enough to be willing to allocate him time for a meeting. Neither Rosenberg nor Hitler seemed to regard him as a traitor nor did they view him as their German agent, but as a well-connected British contact who wanted to stop hostilities between Germany and Great Britain.

Rosenberg was still fooled by the notion that Bill de Ropp's membership of the Savile Club gave him access to the Chamberlain government. The Savile had many influential members, although it was better known for its links to the arts than politics. Rosenberg (even with the APA at his disposal) was woefully ignorant of British society and politics.

The key question, however, is whether Bill de Ropp was making up his own arguments or was faithfully communicating points prepared for him by Broadway. It is very hard to see that Whitehall would have approved a message that 'British air force cannot fight to the last because England would then be at the mercy [of Germany]'.

The talk of 'An English Party' consisting of the Air Ministry, the City and others battling against Churchill's war party (albeit not named as such) was partly true but it is hardly ideal to give a hostile government the impression of deep division. Furthermore Churchill was already seen by many as a likely successor to Chamberlain.

It is true, however, that the Air Ministry had often been a centre of appeasement. This dated from Samuel Hoare's term of office in the 1920s and continued under Lord Londonderry in the 1930s. Londonderry's book *Ourselves and Germany* was written after he left the Ministry but clearly reflected his views. His pro-German opinions were taken to extraordinary lengths and he even sought to understand the anti-Semitic nature of the regime given that 'the Jews had absorbed a great number of positions far in excess'[551] of their proportion of the German population.

He believed that British rearmament had been stimulated by a false assessment of the size of the Luftwaffe. Londonderry's successor at the Air Ministry, Philip Cunliffe-Lister,* was also an appeaser, as was Kinglsey Wood. He even shelved the plan to build a shadow factory for Vickers at Castle Bromwich which would have increased the output of Spitfires.[552]

Anthony Eden pulled no punches in his memoirs about the Foreign Office's long-running dispute with the Air Ministry over the threat posed by the expanding German air force. He not only criticised Londonderry and his Air Chief Marshal Edward Ellington over five detailed pages[553] but also devoted almost twenty more to the new Minister of Coordination of Defence Sir Thomas Inskip who 'was too inclined to take a rosy view'.[554] He quoted Kingsley Wood in 1937 as muttering, 'It is time the Foreign Office thought less about France and tried to get on terms with Germany.'[555]

* Later Lord Swinton. Of the four ministers mentioned he did the most to enhance the RAF's numbers and capabilities.

Another factor was the RAF's reluctance to use its fighter aircraft in combat at a time when Supermarine were still finding it hard to produce the Spitfires in bulk. During October 1939 only about 25 were built. One year later that figure would be nearer 150.[556] Each month that passed was increasing the chance of winning the future Battle of Britain.

At first sight Bill de Ropp's 'official statement' on 10 October seems almost to border on treason. As a former RAF officer, it is improbable that Bill de Ropp would have said that he wanted the Luftwaffe to win the battle in the air,* even as a tactical argument to prevent war with Germany. Again one is left to wonder whether Winterbotham alone or Broadway collectively were behind the statement and whether they had official government sanction. Or was this a case of Bill de Ropp, perhaps lacking clear instructions from his case officer, indulging some of his own political views?

Bill de Ropp's peace feelers do not seem quite so bizarre when one compares them to Grahame Christie's frantic efforts on behalf of Vansittart after the declaration of war. His handwritten notes, now kept at Churchill College, Cambridge, demonstrate the desperation of the times.[557]

Much of the focus centred on the suggestion that Göring did not want war and was prepared to replace Hitler. Christie's most frequent interlocutor was Max von Hohenlohe, still using unconvincing aliases like Mary Herbert and Pimpinela Langenburg. Christie met Hohenlohe in Switzerland in late October and some of the themes were strikingly reminiscent of Bill de Ropp's discussions with von Harder, particularly 'the danger of Bolshevisation of Germany'.

Hohenlohe claimed that the Gestapo, being loyal to Göring, 'could be swung over to us and against Hitler'. The RAF should keep up pressure by bombing German targets such as chemical factories around Cologne. Britain 'should support the various anti-Nazi movements in

* De Ropp cannot have been referring to the Polish air force because Poland had been finally defeated by 6 October; four days before this meeting took place.

Germany secretly'. 'Göring is now the most popular leader because he is for peace.'

Christie then reported to Vansittart that Hohenlohe 'has gone back to Germany and will tell of his meeting with two English friends (unnamed) in Lausanne and of how he sounded them for their opinions.' Hohenlohe asked Christie to confirm that he would be able to travel to England 'to see and sound a wider circle of his influential friends'.

The truth is that, whatever Göring's views might have been, Hitler was calling the shots following his victory in Poland. Hohenlohe may or may not have reflected Göring's genuine views but he also reported to Ribbentrop. So any channel involving Hohenlohe was compromised from the outset.

Also note the circularity of the various discussions. The theme of 'Bolshevisation' was Bill de Ropp's great concern (the British government had far more immediate worries) and Bill de Ropp knew Hohenlohe. Indeed 'the two English friends in Lausanne' must have been a reference to Bill de Ropp and H. G. Daniels.[558]

Thanks to the diaries of John Colville, an official working in the British Prime Minister's office, we know that Christie's efforts were being relayed to No. 10 Downing Street and that Hohenlohe was believed to be a genuine opponent of Hitler. 'Poor wretch,' writes Colville, 'if Hitler should hear of his machinations.' This channel was still being taken seriously as late as 29 December 1939.[559]

Rosenberg's diaries suggest that his exchanges with Bill de Ropp came to an end on 3 March 1940. Rosenberg told Hitler of yet another card he had just received from de Ropp in Switzerland reporting 'heavy <u>new</u> snow' and requesting a visit. Rosenberg had replied that von Harder 'could make a trip [to Switzerland] only if the new snow is expected to <u>last</u>.'[560]

23

'INFLUENCED BY AGENTS OF THE BRITISH SECRET SERVICE'

May 1941: The Hess mission to Scotland

The Deputy Führer Rudolf Hess took off from the Messerschmitt works at Augsberg just before 6 p.m. on Saturday 10 May 1941 in an ME110 twin-engined aircraft. He flew to the Dutch coast near Harlingen and thence over the North Sea west towards Great Britain. He crossed the Northumberland coast soon after sunset and was picked up by British radar stations. He continued at low level and crossed the Scottish border. Having missed his intended destination, Dungavel House, he bailed out over moorland about ten miles south of Glasgow.[561]

Some historians have tried to suggest that MI6 deliberately lured Hess out of Germany to undermine the Nazi regime. However the evidence simply does not stack up. Churchill was embarrassed and annoyed by Hess's arrival in Scotland. He worried that it would provide ammunition for the appeasers to seek an early peace with Nazi Germany.

The German secret agencies, on the other hand, were convinced there was a secret British hand in the affair. They believed that Hess had been influenced by British agents. Amongst their list of prime suspects would have been Kurt Jahnke, Albrecht Haushofer, Ulrich von Hassell, Federico Stallforth, Carl Burckhardt and Bill de Ropp. All of them had had complicated and covert relations with London but only one of them was formally an MI6 agent. Bill de Ropp's role in the Hess affair can only be identified in short glimpses.

Hess was an unusual Nazi in having an international outlook. It was something which he and Rosenberg shared although, in both cases, there was little depth in their experience: Hess as a boy in Egypt and Rosenberg as a student in Russia. The two men got along well. Both were introverts and doubtless felt at a disadvantage in the face of the bombastic Göring, the insidious Himmler, the efficient Bormann and the manipulative Goebbels. Both also shared Hitler's belief that Britain should be Germany's natural ally.

In the early days after the Nazis assumed power Hess had a considerable task in administering the party from his offices at 64 Wilhelmstrasse. In common with many other senior Nazis he set up his own intelligence office led by two powerful and unscrupulous men.

The first was Franz Pfeffer (Pan) von Salomon. After a distinguished service in a Westphalian Regiment during the war he was the first leader of the SA. When Hitler forced him to resign and summoned Röhm from Bolivia to replace him, he duly joined Hess's staff and set up the Abteilung (Department) Pfeffer.

The second was Kurt Jahnke, a Pomeranian landlord, who had been a saboteur in the United States in the Great War and whose political loyalties were opaque. He formed the Büro Jahnke, which was theoretically under Pfeffer's overall supervision. But Jahnke was not a man willing to take orders from anybody. At various times he was suspected of being a Russian, American and British agent, of being a communist and an anarchist.[562]

No. 64 Wilhelmstrasse was also the home of von Ribbentrop's own Büro, the Dienststelle (office) Ribbentrop. This was originally intended as an act of kindness by Hess towards a new arrival at the top of the party but the arrangement became less and less comfortable as Ribbentrop became more powerful in the party and as his extreme anti-Britishness conflicted with Hess's own views. In 1940 Himmler took over Hess's operations and obliged Jahnke to join Heydrich's SD under Walter Schellenberg. This was the first of several humiliations for Hess.

There were two other big influences on Hess. The first was Karl Haushofer, a German general who devised *Geopolitik,* the study of the role of geography in foreign policy. He was a professor at Munich University. Haushofer befriended the young Hitler and Hess in the early days of the Nazi Party in Munich in the 1920s. One of his ideas which the Nazis adopted was the concept of *Lebensraum*. As one historian has observed *Geopolitik* gave an 'intellectual smokescreen' to some of the Nazis' wilder ideas.[563]

The other was Karl's son Albrecht who became an adviser on British affairs for Hess's Büro and then Ribbentrop's Dienststelle. He never joined the Nazi party but was supported by Hess because of the quality of his understanding of Britain. Hess granted the family protection for Albrecht's mother who was a Jew.

In June 1938 Albrecht wrote a paper for Hess:

> Britain has still not abandoned her search for chances of a settlement with Germany . . . The Chamberlain-Halifax government sees its own future strongly tied to the achievement of a true settlement with Rome and Berlin ... But the belief in the possibility of an understanding between Britain and Germany is dwindling fast . . . A German attempt to solve the Bohemian-Moravian question by military attack would . . . under present circumstances . . . [represent] a *casus belli* . . . in such a war the British government would have the whole nation behind it.[564]

This line contradicted everything that Ribbentrop had been telling Hitler. Ribbentrop was furious and passed it on to Hitler with the comment 'Secret Service Propaganda' (doubtless meaning the British Secret Service). Hitler was not inclined to listen. According to Fritz Hesse, 'Hitler told Haushofer, "This fellow Chamberlain shook with fear when I uttered the word war. Don't tell me he is dangerous!"'[565]

After the outbreak of war Hitler made two offers of peace to Britain. The first was in early October 1939 after the Nazi victory in Poland. It was a speech full of triumphalism and bile and nobody could blame Whitehall for failing to identify it as a peace offer. In words which chime closely with Bill de Ropp's conversation with von Harder he implied that a small clique of British warmongers was keeping the war alive. 'Mr Churchill ought perhaps for once believe me when I prophesy a great empire will be destroyed, an empire which it was never my intention to destroy or even harm.'[566]

In mid-July 1940 Hitler made another peace offer to the British Empire. This time he had just conquered France and there was the same tone of bombast. He reminded Britain of his previous peace offer and reckoned that London was clinging onto the hope of a split in the Nazi-Soviet alliance.

Hitler continued:

> I saw it proper to enter into straightforward discussions with Russia in order to define clearly, once and for all, what Germany believes she must regard as the sphere of interests vital to her future and which Russia on the other hand considered essential for her existence. This clear definition of their several spheres of interest was followed by a new basis of German-Russian relations. All hope that the completion of this might give rise to fresh tension between Germany and Russia is futile.[567]

Hitler was lying. At the end of July General Franz Halder (Chief of Staff of the Army High Command-OKH) noted that Russia's destruction would begin in spring 1941. Rudolf Hess knew about the plan and was frequently briefed on its evolution.

He knew about it long before Hitler issued his order for Operation Barbarossa on 18 December 1940.[568]

This awakened in Hess the old fear of fighting on two fronts. In *Mein Kampf* in 1923 Hitler had written, 'If European soil was wanted . . . it could be had only at the expense of Russia . . . Only with England covering our rear could we have begun a new Germanic migration.'[569] Both Hess and Rosenberg were anxious that Hitler might launch his attack against Russia without first sealing a peace with Britain.

Alfred Rosenberg was the last senior Nazi to visit Hess before his flight to Scotland. He wrote in his diary, 'Because I was the last one who spoke with Hess it may be of historical and psychological interest some day to put this visit with him down in writing.' Evidently Rosenberg knew that his trip to see Hess would put him in the crosshairs of any investigation and he wanted to get a defensible version onto paper.

> I wanted to brief Hess privately on the assignment from the Führer concerning the eastern question . . . The visit with him on Saturday May 10th at 6pm had been agreed for that purpose. On the evening of the 9th Hess's adjutant phoned Dr [Werner] Koeppen [Rosenberg's adjutant]. It is urgent that Hess leave around midday on Saturday, will I be so kind as to come in the morning. Because it was too late for the train, Hess sent his plane to Berlin for me and it got me to Munich around 11am.
>
> Hess walked quickly toward me in the garden, he looked pale and ill which was not a cause for concern since it had been a chronic condition for years.

They then discussed Rosenberg's new responsibilities in the East: 'When I then tried to raise a few other questions Hess requested that I cover only the most important matters because a thought was occupying him to such an extent that he had to refrain from discussing less essential things. This was stated with simple passion and yet I could not even guess what he was intending to do.'[570]

None of this makes any sense. If Hess was so preoccupied why did he send his plane to collect Rosenberg from Berlin and then listen to his plans for the East? Hess knew perfectly well that Rosenberg's plans were insignificant when compared to those of the OKH and the SS.

The strong probability is that they discussed Hess's intention to make peace with Great Britain (if not his intention to fly there that evening) and that Rosenberg's input to the conversation was coloured by the advice of Bill de Ropp; either old advice from 1939–40 or from more recent contacts through von Harder (which de Ropp alleged continued until 1944). His usual refrain was to appeal to the 'English Party' (or Peace Party) and to the Air Ministry.

Rosenberg then tried to explain away the actions of his friend. 'I thought it likely that Hess had suffered from serious bouts of depression, had had little to do in practical terms, the Party's leadership had slipped from his control and he felt that he was not measuring up to the post.'[571]

It is true that Hess was gradually declining in importance because of the rise of Himmler, Ribbentrop and Bormann. He was not seen as an efficient or competent administrator as more and more work was undertaken by the meticulous Bormann. Hanfstaengl wrote, 'Hess gradually became a nobody, a flag without a pole.'[572]

Walter Schellenberg later recalled that 'After the flight of Rudolph Hess to Scotland . . . Hitler was momentarily filled with such consternation that he was hardly capable of any reaction. It was now that Martin Bormann . . . invented the theory that Hess had become insane.'[573] Schellenberg continued:

> I received the order to complete a report which I was preparing for Hitler. In it I said that our secret information showed that for some years Hess had been influenced by agents of the

> British Secret Service and their German collaborators and that they had played a large part in bringing about his decision to fly to Scotland . . .[574]
>
> Following Hitler's original conceptions and his attitude towards England he had considered it his messianic task to reconcile the two peoples . . . Hess kept repeating to his intimate circle that the English were a brother people and the bonds of race made it obligatory to preserve them. One must not forget that, as a German born abroad, Hess had been subjected to British influences during his youth and education.[575]

In Scotland Hess (calling himself Alfred Horn) was initially watched over by the Home Guard. A member of the Polish Consulate in Glasgow asked him some questions. Hess wanted to see the Duke of Hamilton and had a message for him. When asked about the message he replied that it was in the highest interests of the British Air Force.[576] This was an odd remark to make and again reminiscent of Bill de Ropp's constant theme that the Air Ministry and Air Force had different views from the government.

The Duke of Hamilton interviewed Hess on 11 May. Hess introduced himself: 'I do not know if you recognise me but I am Rudolf Hess.' In fact neither man ever claimed to have met the other before although they had both attended a dinner in honour of Vansittart in the margins of the 1936 Berlin Olympic Games.[577]

Hess went on to say that he was on a mission of humanity and that the Führer did not want to defeat England and wished to stop fighting. His friend Albrecht Haushofer had told him that 'I [Hamilton] was an Englishman* who, he thought, would understand his [Hess's] point of view. He had consequently tried to arrange a meeting with me in Lisbon.'[578]

It was true that Hamilton had been sent a message by Albrecht

* He was, of course, a Scot.

Haushofer, agreed by Hess, written in September 1940 through a Mrs Violet Roberts[579] in Lisbon. Although only signed AH it would be very clear to Hamilton who the missive was from. However Hamilton did not receive the letter for several months. It had been opened by the censor and a copy sent to MI5 to discover the identity of AH.

Hess's choice of Hamilton was interesting, especially in view of his comment that his message was 'in the highest interests of the British Air Force'. Hamilton was a Wing-Commander in the RAF. Back in 1939 he (then the Marquis of Clydesdale) had also been one of the believers in a 'Statement of British War Aims' and wrote a letter to *The Times*. 'I believe that the moment the menace of aggression and bad faith has been removed, war against Germany becomes wrong and meaningless.' This letter was quoted on German news on 6 October 1939,[580] and was widely viewed as a tactic of appeasers to limit the extent of the war.

Ivone Kirkpatrick was the next person to interview Hess. He had, until recently, been the No 2 at the Berlin Embassy. Hess spoke of a settlement whereby Germany should have a free hand in Europe and the British Empire should be left intact save for the return of the former German colonies.

Almost a month later Lord Simon (previously Sir John Simon) met Hess. Simon recorded that Hess . . .

> arrived under the impression that the prospects for his mission were much greater than he now realises they are. He imagined there was a strong peace party in this country . . . At first he asked constantly to see leaders of opposition . . . He constantly asked to have a further meeting with the Duke of Hamilton under the delusion that [he] . . . would be the means of getting him contact with people with a different view from the clique who are holding Hess prisoner i.e. the Churchill government.[581]

Meanwhile the British government propaganda department was producing some thoughts as to how to extract the most value from what could be portrayed as a defection, but Churchill was having none of it. For him the danger was that appeasers would use Hess's story to argue for new negotiations with Germany. There was substance behind this concern. MI5 reported to No. 10 that Lord Noel-Buxton was planning to write suggesting 'negotiations with the enemy for an immediate peace'.[582]

The Prime Minister sent a firm note to Cadogan that 'Hess must be kept in strictest seclusion.' The only contact with him was to be for intelligence purposes.[583] Hess was duly handed over to MI6 for supervision at Camp Z at Mychett Place in Surrey.

Back in Berlin Schellenberg consoled himself with two firm conclusions: 'I can say definitely that it is quite impossible that Hitler ordered Hess to fly to Britain to make a last offer of peace',[584] and 'I was convinced . . . that because of his fanatical devotion Hess would never betray the details of our strategic plan to the enemy, though certainly he was in a position to do so . . . As far as the imminent Russian campaign was concerned . . . it seemed to me very doubtful whether the English would be prepared to send a specific warning to the Russian leaders as a result of the first interrogation of Hess.'[585]

Hitler was not only worried that Hess could leak the details of Operation Barbarossa. He was also concerned that Britain would use Hess's flight to convince the Italians and Japanese that Germany was trying to negotiate a separate deal, leaving his two allies out in the cold. Little did he know the frustrations of British propagandists like Sefton Delmer and Richard Crossman who wanted to do exactly that.

Schellenberg alleged in his memoirs that he never got to the bottom of what negotiations had been taking place prior to Hess's flight, but those memoirs need to be taken with more than a pinch of salt. He would have been well aware of all the main players and he was already considering some of them to provide Himmler with his own backchannel to London.[586]

Apart from Albrecht Haushofer the two main players were Carl Burckhardt of the International Committee of the Red Cross (ICRC) in Geneva, and Ulrich von Hassell, the former German ambassador to Italy. All three men were well known to the British government. Haushofer had been a frequent traveller to Britain and had several close British friends including the late Patrick Roberts (Violet's son) of the FO and Lord Clydesdale.

Burckhardt, as the former commissioner for Danzig, had been a regular visitor to Whitehall. He was from an aristocratic Swiss family with close links to Germany and shared Bill de Ropp's conservatism and deep distrust of Russia and communism.

Lord Halifax himself had facilitated a British man, James Lonsdale-Bryans, to have two secret meetings with von Hassell in February and April 1940,[587] but the FO had shut down the channel, possibly because Lonsdale-Bryans had far-right leanings and was seen as unreliable but also because of the changed politics in London with the arrival of Churchill as Prime Minister in May 1940.[588]

Following the failure of the letter to Hamilton via Mrs Roberts, Haushofer met Hess again in April 1941 and suggested Burckhardt as a suitable intermediary with Britain. At the outbreak of war Burckhardt had been expelled from Danzig and made his escape via Lithuania. Back in Geneva he resumed his career as a professor at the Graduate Institute of International Studies in Geneva in addition to his ICRC role.

In December 1941 Menzies sent Peter Loxley (Cadogan's new Private Secretary) some observations made by Burckhardt at a recent meeting with 'quite* a reliable source who has known B for a long time'. This was evidently Bill de Ropp and he was quoting Burckhardt on one of Bill de Ropp's favourite themes, as the German advance into Russia stalled in the face of winter.

Burckhardt 'spoke much of the Russian Bolshevik danger to

* 'Quite' in this context was probably used to mean 'totally or completely' rather than 'moderately'.

Western Europe and civilisation, the fear which it inspired in all Continentals, the Germans first and foremost. The revenge of the Czechs, Poles and Russians would be terrible . . . The English, he found, could not and did not understand this fear . . . England would win this war by her Navy and by her character but others won her wars on land for her, in the last war the French, in this the Russians.'[589]

A few months earlier Menzies had written to Cadogan with a request from Burckhardt. He had just returned from Berlin where he had met Ernst von Weizsäcker, the Head of the AA, the Duke of Coburg,* General Alexander von Falkenhausen, the military governor of Belgium, and others from the War Ministry. 'Burckhardt has refused to divulge the details "to my informant" [Bill de Ropp] but would do so if he could have a personal interview with the Prime Minister.' De Ropp insisted that this should not be handled through the British Embassy in Berne. Eden noted on the letter, 'We surely could not agree to his seeing PM . . . B[urckhardt] is able and ambitious but I have little confidence in him.' Cadogan disagreed and noted, 'I should be rather in favour of his coming.'[590]

The sudden interest in German military circles about negotiating with Britain had been stimulated by the setbacks in the Russian campaign. We have already seen that von Reichenau's plan in 1934 had been to start the invasion at the melting of the snows; more likely early April rather than the eventual date of 22 June.

Burckhardt had been having important discussions before Hess's flight. While in Geneva in January 1941 he had approached von Hassell and told him that some people in London were ready for a negotiated peace. Burckhardt believed the British would be willing to talk although he thought Anthony Eden would be a hindrance.

At the end of April Haushofer travelled to meet Burckhardt in Geneva. Albrecht asked Burckhardt to get in touch with his British contacts but Burckhardt replied that Britain wanted peace on a

* Charles Edward, Duke of Saxe Coburg and Gotha, was a grandson of Queen Victoria and a long-time Nazi supporter.

rational basis but not with the Nazi regime.[591] Burckhardt was correct. Churchill was getting annoyed by unauthorised peace discussions. He issued an instruction in February 1941 that 'all such enquiries and suggestions should be [met with] absolute silence.'[592]

The refusal of Churchill to talk peace must have spurred Hess's decision to fly to Britain and consult with the notional opposition. Hess's flight to Scotland was a disaster for the Haushofers. They had lost Frau Haushofer's protector and the Nazi leadership would doubtless suspect their involvement in Hess's hare-brained scheme. On 12 May Albrecht Haushofer was arrested in Berlin and taken to Hitler at Berchtesgaden where he was given pen and paper and told to write down his version of events.

In his paper Haushofer admitted meeting Burckhardt in Switzerland in April. Burckhardt had allegedly told him that 'A person well known and respected in London, who was close to the leading Conservative and City circles, had called on him in Geneva. This person whose name he could not give,* though he could vouch for his earnestness, had, in a rather long conversation expressed the wish of important circles for an examination of the possibilities for peace.'

Haushofer had replied that he could return to Geneva to meet this person. Burckhardt agreed that he would communicate to England 'through an entirely safe channel that there was a prospect for a trusted representative from London . . . to meet in Geneva a German also well-known in England who was in a position to bring such communications as there might be to the attention of the competent German authorities.'[593]

Meanwhile Hassell was also in touch with the Mexican-born German-American Federico Stallforth who was known to operate in significant American financial and political circles. Stallforth met Hassell in April 1941. What Hassell did not know was that Stallforth

* This could have been Professor Carl Borenius, the Finnish art historian and diplomat (who is mentioned in von Hassell's diaries).

had been a German agent in the Great War and was in regular touch with Kurt Jahnke.

In July 1941 MI5 compiled a file note on everything they knew about Jahnke. This listed Jahnke's suspected agents. When it came to Stallforth the note mentioned some financial claims due to damage by German acts of sabotage in the USA during the First World War. With the advent of the Nazis, Stallforth reckoned he could short-circuit the process by dealing directly with Pfeffer von Salomon. He travelled to Europe in 1936 and got Pfeffer to sign off on the claim on behalf of the German government.

Shortly afterwards Pfeffer's signature was repudiated and it became apparent that Stallforth was caught between 'two rival factions in the Nazi hierarchy, each out for self-enrichment. On the one side were Pfeffer, von Reichenau, Hess and [Karl] Markau [President of the German Chamber of Commerce in London], on the other were Ribbentrop, Dieckhoff and the [AA] set.' At a much later date in 1939 or 1940 it was reported that Stallforth was still visiting Germany escorted by Hans Daufeldt, a Gestapo man.[594]

The key question here is where Jahnke's loyalties lay at this particular moment in history (the view in MI5 post-war was that Jahnke had been a Soviet agent).[595] Was he reporting to Schellenberg in the hope of sabotaging all discussions and betraying Hassell as the anti-Nazi conspirator that he was becoming? Was he just trying to make money? Or was he still loyal to Hess and trying to construct a channel for a secret discussion with London either directly or through Washington? A future Chief of MI6 – Sir Maurice Oldfield, who was C from 1973 to 1978 – was convinced that Jahnke played a significant part in Hess's decision.[596] Oldfield's conviction would have been informed by the fact that MI6 recruited Jahnke's assistant Carl Marcus, codename Dictionary, in late 1944/early 1945.[597] Adolf Hitler believed that Jahnke was a 'British agent in disguise and . . . partly responsible for the flight of Hess'.[598]

It was probably the failure of these twin tracks of diplomatic feelers on his behalf which finally persuaded Hess to make his flight in the belief that, by one dramatic intervention, he could establish contact with an opposition that existed only in his mind and that of Rosenberg, thanks to repeated briefings from Bill de Ropp. In one bound he would also restore his reputation with Hitler and within the Nazi party.*

Schellenberg's memoirs suggest that he, later, had his concerns about Jahnke's loyalties. 'While Jahnke was in Switzerland I received a shattering secret report. It was 30 pages long and was a painstakingly exact compilation of evidence proving that Jahnke was a top-level British agent. The real purpose of his trip to Switzerland was to receive new directives. I at once gave orders for the most careful surveillance of Jahnke and for a close watch to be kept on his movements in Switzerland.'[599]

No Hess story would be complete without a final puzzle. In 1944 the United States Counter Intelligence Corps based at 20 Grosvenor Square, London asked MI5 for information on Bill de Ropp. John Balderston, who had been Bill de Ropp's employer when he was writing for *Outlook*, had been in London in 1942 and had seen de Ropp. He gathered that he was employed by American censorship in London. Two years later he got in touch with American intelligence in the US and told them that, in his opinion, de Ropp was pro-German. In replying to the Americans, MI5 (with MI6 approval) said that 'the London Club of which he is a member [the Savile] indicate that he is enrolled in a category of membership which means that he is no longer in this country and almost certainly has not been since the outbreak of war.'[600]

Some authors have suggested that Bill de Ropp interviewed Hess. That might explain Balderston spotting Bill in London in 1942. The idea would doubtless have occurred to Frank Foley who spent months

* Although Hess would later claim to have made three previous attempts at the flight it seems more likely that these were trial runs to check his navigational equipment, etc. in his ME-110. (Padfield, *Hess, Hitler and Churchill*, pp.152-153.)

trying in vain to extract some value out of the former Deputy Führer. Hess and de Ropp had always got along well in the 1930s. It would have been risky for de Ropp to leave Montreux and travel across Vichy France to neutral Spain and Portugal from where he could fly to London. The return journey would have compounded the risk and MI6 would have worried that he had twenty-three years of knowledge about the service in his head. However, so long as he travelled before 10 November 1942, when the Germans occupied Vichy France, and with his linguistic aptitude it would have been possible.

In summary the Hess affair combines two strands. One was Hess using his various colleagues and contacts to discuss methods to achieve an agreement with Great Britain. By April and May 1941 all their efforts were running into the barrier of the refusal of Churchill and Eden to contemplate a deal with Germany. The second was the mercurial Hess looking for one miraculous coup that would solve the problem of a war on two fronts and restore his ebbing career.

None of this was an official MI6 plan but Bill de Ropp's shadow can be discerned behind several of the participants and their actions. Fred Winterbotham was convinced that Bill de Ropp had played a part in the Hess affair. He drafted a letter to *The Times* on the subject but decided not to send it.[601] In 1987 he corresponded with the journalist Robin MacWhirter, mentioning Bill de Ropp's role and arguing that a peace with Germany in 1941 might have been possible thereby preventing a great deal of British bloodshed.[602] His contention was that Britain had wittingly refused to consider repeated peace feelers including from those who wished to remove Hitler.

24

TWILIGHT OF A MASTER SPY

1939–1945: Bill de Ropp in wartime Switzerland

The Second World War was a difficult time for Bill de Ropp. Separated from his best German sources by the war he was no longer the Swiss stations' star performer as he had been in Berlin. He was still well-paid and that fact placed considerable expectations on him. Few of the new recruits staffing MI6's stations in Switzerland* cared about Bill's glory days. To them he seemed to be overpaid, underproductive and rather liable to rest on his laurels.

There was another, more insidious factor. Bill de Ropp was Menzies's great case. Menzies would sometimes highlight this to customers, citing a 'source who has worked for me for many years'. By closely associating himself with Bill de Ropp Menzies made his star agent a target for the vicious Dansey. Now that war had been declared Dansey could ridicule Bill de Ropp's record. Had he predicted the occupation of the Rhineland? Had he warned of the

* In MI6 Switzerland was known as 42-land or 42000, just as Germany had been 12-land or 12000.

invasion of Czechoslovakia? Had he provided prior notice of the Mototov-Ribbentrop Pact? The answer to all three questions was: Not sufficiently.

Dansey was a great believer in detailed military reporting and was not impressed by political commentary. However, there had been a clear requirement for the latter in the 1930s, as Lord Hankey's 1939 review of the intelligence service had confirmed. Now that Britain was at war there was less need for reports on the relative influence of Göring and Goebbels and much more on exact dates for attacks, and the detailed composition of enemy forces.

The most damaging of Dansey's insinuations was that de Ropp had merely provided German propaganda. In reporting Rosenberg's, von Epp's or Koch's views there was an inevitable risk of doing exactly that, except that those views were not always known at the time. Furthermore, during the years of appeasement which stretched right up to 1939, Britain eagerly sought Nazi wishes and intentions and often sought to placate them.

This is what is behind Keth Jeffery's paragraph in the official history of MI6: 'The agent [Bill de Ropp] however relocated to Switzerland that August and although he continued to report for the next seven years his work was increasingly discounted at Head Office. By July 1944 Claude Dansey, then Vice Chief of the service, decided that all de Ropp represented now was "a vehicle for Nazi propaganda".'[603] This was Dansey's view but certainly not that of Menzies and Woollcombe. By this stage Winterbotham, Bill de Ropp's third great supporter, had moved on to his new role involving the presentation and security of Ultra material to senior customers.

Patrick Reilly, who was seconded to work for Menzies from the FO wrote, 'Dansey's influence with Menzies was too strong. Dansey is one of the very few people I have met who seems to me to have been truly wicked: an extraordinary man, impossible to understand. He seems to be consumed by hate, of everything and everybody. I do not know how he came to hold such a dominating position in SIS: for he was old, sixty-six in 1942, and his career had been mediocre.'[604]

Switzerland was, not for the first time nor the last, the espionage centre of Europe. One of the lures of Switzerland is its neutrality but the greater attraction is its banking system, which in the 1940s still offered total discretion. It served as a magnet for people with questionable business transactions, profits and secrets to hide. It was also surrounded by enemy countries: Germany, Austria, Italy and Vichy France. So it was an ideal place for MI6 to have its largest and most active stations. The only problem was that it was very difficult to get personnel and intelligence in and out. All the borders were closed to British passport holders and the Swiss imposed strict limits on radio traffic.

By leaving Germany at the outbreak of war some of his contacts reckoned Bill de Ropp had chosen to side with Britain. He seems to have told some of them that he was to be an adviser to the British Air Ministry. This must be why Claus von Stralendorff described him as a traitor.

Most of the von der Ropp clan sided firmly with Germany. The old Baltic loyalties to Russia were long forgotten. Dietrich von der Ropp was the commander of the third U-boat to be sunk in the war, on 8 October 1939. His body was washed up on the French coast; the U-12 had probably hit a mine in the English Channel. Georg von der Ropp was the chief training officer for the contingent of Soviet troops under General Andrei Vlasov who had defected to Germany.[605] Christoph von der Ropp was a war journalist who also wrote for the Nazi Party's *Der Führer*.

This perception of betrayal (and the logistics of cross-border contact in wartime) may also have made it difficult to remain in touch with people like General von Epp and Erich Koch. On the other hand Rosenberg had wanted him to stay in contact. In his diary he wrote: 'So he [de Ropp] has kept his word and a thread – albeit a thin one – to London still holds.'[606]

MI6 in Switzerland started the war with a major setback. Jeffery records that 'An SIS agent arrested in Switzerland in October 1939, while under interrogation, had already blown Dansey's cover as Z. So concerned was Dansey to secure this agent's release that in late November 1939 he . . . asked the Treasury to sanction a trade deal with the Swiss to secure his release.'[607]

This arrested agent may have known about Bill de Ropp's role but another arrest in Paris must have finally convinced the Germans that Bill de Ropp had, all along, worked for MI6. Maundy Gregory, the fraudster who had sold knighthoods and had lured Skoropadsky into his Ukraine Committee, was captured by the Germans in France in November 1940 and may have divulged his dealings with MI6 under interrogation. He spent nearly ten months in the dreadful Drancy Camp (primarily but not solely an internment camp for Jews) near Paris before he died. He would have known of Bill de Ropp's close dealings with the Ukrainian opposition in London on behalf of Sinclair.

Bill de Ropp was also named in the Sonderfahndungsliste G.B. or Nazi Black Book of British people to be taken into detention upon the successful German invasion of Great Britain.[608] This was compiled by Schellenberg's section of the RSHA. Most of the names were submitted by Amt IV E4, the Gestapo section for Britain and Scandinavia. Some of them, however, were allegedly contributed by Hans Thost who had been Rosenberg's man in London and who had begun to harbour suspicions about Bill de Ropp.[609] His entry reads:

'103. Rope, William Sylvester, 7.12.86 Dresden, brit. N.-Agent, London W. 1, 69 Brookstreet, Savile Club, RSHÀ IV E 4.'

Apart from the misspelling of his name it is interesting that in 1940 he is listed as a British agent and that he is wanted by Amt IV (the Gestapo) not VI (SD Foreign Intelligence).

Intriguingly Bill's brother, Friedrich, was also included (even though he spent all of the Second World War in Germany). He was never a member of the Savile.

'104. van [*sic*] der Ropp, Freddy, London W. 1, 60 Brook-Str., RSHA IV E 4.'

We saw in the previous two chapters that Bill de Ropp maintained his contact with Rosenberg and the emissary von Harder into 1940. Harder's own account of their meetings provides an illuminating view of Bill de Ropp.

> My special assignment during the war involved several trips to Switzerland between the end of September 1939 and the beginning of 1940 . . . I was to meet secretly on neutral ground in Montreux on Lake Geneva with a representative of the British Admiralty,* Baron de Ropp, because the Führer was determined to make peace with England . . . I then received a special pass from Reich Minister Lammers personally from the Reich Chancellery [Hans Lammers was Chief of the Reich Chancellery from 1933 to 1945] and travelled on his behalf. The pass included the instruction that foreigners I named could cross the German borders under my protection and incognito without being checked in order to be received by the Führer in Berlin.
>
> In Montreux I then met the envoy of the British Navy; he gave me the impression of a staunchly loyal Englishman who only thought about his fatherland as I thought about mine; he declared that England would again defeat Germany as completely as in 1918 but was also just as convinced that the British Empire would not survive a Second World War. In other words, the British Admiralty's fatherland and thus the preservation of the British Empire were primary and the destruction of Adolf Hitler secondary, as long as a mutually honourable peace was still possible and the prestige of Great Britain remained untouched.[610]

* Writing fifteen years after the war, Harder seems to have confused the Air Ministry with the Admiralty.

As we saw in Chapter 22 the loquacious von Harder also provided some useful intelligence on thinking in Berlin. Given that we know Bill de Ropp and Harder talked for three days one can assume that Harder provided a lot more useful insights than he included in his six-page report, which alone must have provided material for at least five CX reports (Harder's own account of his conversation with Bill de Ropp on 10 October 1939 suggests that he did most of the talking):[611]

German attitudes towards the Soviet Union including the remarkable claim that Stalin had removed Jews from positions of influence, presumably to please Hitler. This reflected an alleged wider sympathy for the Russians among the German people.

How Germany thought that the Vistula-San line across Poland had actually increased the security of the Reich in spite of the loss of the Baltic states as part of the Ribbentrop-Molotov deal.

The easing of Germany's raw materials shortages thanks to access to Polish and Moravian territory and also its new ability to import from the Soviet Union. Germany could now resume exports of manufactured goods and was now able to feed itself. A new Four-Year plan was being produced to reflect this new reality.

How Germany thought that Britain was 'superannuated' and that its foreign policy was similarly sclerotic. The British Empire would collapse rapidly and Britain's collapse would be quickly followed by France. Britian had to import 70 per cent of her commodities and her currency was no longer backed by gold. In such circumstances it was crazy to fight a war over a now-defeated Poland.

Harder's enigmatic reference to 'our new weapons with which England would soon become acquainted'. This report was extremely thin on detail but would have sparked particular interest in London. Shortly after its arrival in Broadway a young scientist in MI6 was examining a suspicious package. 'Fred Winterbotham came into my room and dumped a small parcel on my desk.'[612] The contents would come to be known as the 'Oslo Report' and it contained a treasure trove of intelligence on German weapons technology.

According to the official records (*Documents on German Foreign Policy*), Harder made three trips to see de Ropp in late 1939 and early 1940. Bill de Ropp claimed that they met six times and that contact continued well beyond 1940 and that Harder provided a useful insight into the mood in senior Nazi circles. He also spoke of 'secret new weapons that would utterly destroy England'.[613]

We cannot be certain whose memory is correct. Bill de Ropp was writing in 1957 and von Harder in 1960. Both men were, to some degree, massaging their reputations. Von Harder's extraordinary 1,000-page typed memoir did not include much regret about his involvement in Nazism or his role in Rosenberg's Reich Ministry for the Occupied Eastern territories. Even his thoughts on the 'gassing of the Jews' were heavily qualified. His admiration for Rosenberg was undimmed even fifteen years after his boss's execution. His only regret was that Rosenberg did not resign when he saw that his wishes for the occupied lands were being ignored by Hitler, Bormann, Himmler and Koch.

Fortunately another of Bill de Ropp's CX reports was retained in FO departmental files and has thus, mercifully, survived. It could have come from one of his other sources but the probability is that it was from von Harder, who was now working for Rosenberg's new ministry and therefore had access to the military situation in Russia.

On 25 September 1941 Menzies sent the report to Cadogan: 'furnished by a source who has worked for me for a long period and has been absolutely reliable in the past. His information is derived from the German General Staff but I have now asked him precisely how this information came to his knowledge.'[614] Cadogan read it on the 26th and marked it up to the Foreign Secretary Anthony Eden, who saw it the following day. Eden asked for it to be returned to him on Monday probably so that he could brief the Prime Minister. Copies were sent to the three armed services and extracts delivered to General Mason-MacFarlane, Head of the British Military Mission in Moscow.

> German troops operating against USSR are commencing to tire and army commanders are demanding rest. Ministry of War has therefore decided to cease offensive operations on November 1st 1941 and to take up suitable defensive positions and give troops rest until spring 1942. C-in-C has ordered the following line to be occupied by November 1st 1941: Murmansk-railway-Lodehoe Pole-Kalinin-Moscow-Kolomna-Ryazan-Vorenezh-River Don to Sea of Azov. In spring 1942 a new advance will commence to final line. Germans hope for revolution in USSR during winter, failing this war with USSR cannot be terminated in 1942.
>
> Invasion British Isles has been finally abandoned. In summer 1942 it is proposed commence intense aerial warfare against civilian population United Kingdom with object forcing public opinion to favour a compromise peace and of convincing the people of futility of continuing war. A revolution in the United Kingdom is hoped for.

Menzies spotted immediately that this was not a typical de Ropp report; more military in character than political. He sent it to Cadogan before being sure of the full sourcing chain. He retained the question mark before 'finally abandoned', which itself raised questions. And he left the report in its terse telegraphese style without adding the missing words. Perhaps this was an indication of the busier wartime environment but Menzies clearly thought the report important enough for Cadogan to see it promptly.

How good was the report? It was pretty accurate about where the front line would be by November. It ran from Leningrad via Demyansk and Kalinin but never quite reached Moscow or Kolumna or Voronezh before ending at the Sea of Azov just short of Rostov. The failure to take Moscow would, of course, assume huge significance. If there was a decision to take up defensive positions on 1 November it was overtaken by events. The attempt to take Moscow was not suspended until 6 December.

The main significance of the report was the remarkably early news that Operation Barbarossa was running into serious trouble. Woollcombe would probably have received it on 24 September from the MI6 station in Berne following a meeting between de Ropp and his case officer, Hugh Whittall. However, Bill de Ropp's source (whether Harder or someone else) would have had to travel from Germany to Switzerland. The underlying facts of the report must have been a week old.

That Operation Barbarossa was running into serious trouble did not become more widely apparent until at least a month later when the October rains turned the ground into a quagmire and as it became clear that the fierce Soviet resistance and the various deviations from the original plan made it unlikely that Moscow would fall that year. On 16 October six inches of snow was reported and on 12 November the temperature reached minus 12 degrees C.[615] An American journalist in Berlin, Howard Smith, detected trouble because of a new Nazi sensitivity about war news in October and November and a ban being imposed on listening to foreign broadcasts.[616]

Another fascinating element was the view that, without a revolution in Russia, the war would not finish in 1942. This revealed an unexpected German military pessimism which ran counter to the mood prevalent among the Nazi leadership. To have real impact in Whitehall, however, these observations needed some better sourcing –

for example, to someone of seniority such as General Franz Halder, the Chief of Staff of OKH, or a specific colonel on the General Staff. Halder was one of the first Germans to realise that Barbarossa was failing. By mid-August he recognised that he had underestimated the strength and determination of the Soviet forces.

Even with the inclusion of the question mark the observations about the invasion of Great Britain were important. The invasion (Operation Sealion) had been suspended a year earlier, on 17 September 1940, but planning had resumed in May 1941 until an order to cease all further preparations on 23 September 1941. So Bill de Ropp's report contained some predictive news from a source who must have known of the intention to cease all planning before the ink was dry on the order. This prompted one or more of de Ropp, Whittall, Woollcombe or Menzies to insert a question mark into the text. It would have been better if Woollcombe had replaced the mark with a note explaining that the source had heard that Sealion planning was to be suspended but that the order had not yet been signed by Hitler.

The idea that Germany would mount 'intense aerial warfare' against Great Britain in 1942 is the one aspect of the report that is more puzzling. Göring's Luftwaffe was already over-extended in trying to support Barbarossa. In mid-November Bill de Ropp's former contact Ernst Udet committed suicide partly due to the failures of the Luftwaffe. The extent of that failure in Russia would not, however, become fully apparent until 1942.

Sometimes a CX report can be too far ahead of the received wisdom to have the impact it deserves. In September 1941 most people in Whitehall thought the German advance was unstoppable. Cadogan makes no mention of the report in his diary. As usual he was in a depressed mood. On 21 September he wrote: 'The Russian news is bad – Kiev is gone and the Germans are driving straight for the Caucasus.'[617] And yet on 22 October he noted: 'Rather a good report on Russia, from a good source.'[618] However, it was not until he visited

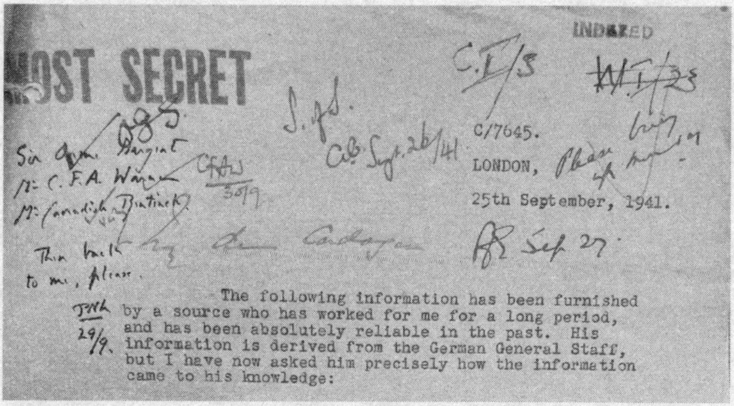

MOST SECRET

C/7645.

LONDON,

25th September, 1941.

The following information has been furnished by a source who has worked for me for a long period, and has been absolutely reliable in the past. His information is derived from the German General Staff, but I have now asked him precisely how the information came to his knowledge:

Menzies's covering letter for Bill de Ropp's 1941 report on the Nazi invasion of Russia, marked up to Anthony Eden. (*TNA*)

Moscow in December that Cadogan began to believe that German military morale had been severely damaged.

If the report did come from von Harder, as seems probable, that opens the intriguing idea that he may have continued to act as the secret go-between to Rosenberg throughout 1941, including that period when Rosenberg and Hess were discussing the latter's peace moves. Harder's memoir makes no reference to Hess's flight.

Some months later Bill de Ropp was told by one of his sources (possibly von Harder, given the context) that Field Marshal von Reichenau whose plans for Blitzkrieg against Russia had so excited Fred Winterbotham at Horcher's in 1934, had committed suicide. The CX report has not survived but Winterbotham mentions it in one his books.[619] This provoked the eminent historian Stephen Roskill to send an intemperate letter insisting that official and authoritative sources confirmed that Reichenau died of a stroke.[620]

There is more than one version of von Reichenau's death. The official account relates that he had a suspected stroke while on an early-morning run in freezing conditions at Poltava in January 1942. He was put on an aircraft to Leipzig but the plane made a forced landing at Lemberg (modern Lviv) on the way. The pilot lost control and von Reichenau received serious head injuries before dying of a second stroke. This explanation seems somewhat over-elaborate; so it is worth looking at the Field Marshal's last few weeks.[621]

During Barbarossa von Reichenau commanded the Sixth Army which was part of Army Group South. He made good progress across Ukraine despite encountering increasingly strong Soviet resistance. In October he issued his notorious order which spoke of 'necessary executions of criminal, Bolshevik and mostly Jewish elements'. In late November he replaced von Rundstedt as Commander of Army Group South following the German retreat from Rostov, the strategic city which provided access to the Caucasus. Reichenau was ordered personally by Hitler to halt the retreat but after what Antony Beevor calls 'a shamelessly short time', he replied that the withdrawal was inevitable. This was said to be the Germans' first retreat of the Second World War.[622]

It seems altogether more likely that the Field Marshal, a committed Nazi, who had been one of the designers of the whole Russian campaign, could not bear the ignominious failure that he knew it was becoming. Although Barbarossa had been implemented several weeks too late and was constantly altered by Hitler, the fact is that the plan was over-ambitious. The Germans did not have the capabilities (particularly the aviation support) to deliver the plan against robust opposition. That the Nazis would wish to cover up the suicide of their favourite soldier and had the means to do so is surely beyond doubt.

Fortunately Bill de Ropp was not totally dependent on Harder's occasional visits to Switzerland. In the German legation at Berne was Colonel Helmuth Gripp who Bill knew well from his regular meetings with Erhard Milch before the war. Furthermore Gripp was Hermann Göring's man in Switzerland and was used to manage money transfers between Berlin and Zurich.

A Swiss memorandum of March 1945 observed that 'The centre of all Nazi money transfers in Switzerland is Colonel Helmuth Gripp (air attaché of the German legation in Berne). His representative Herbert Mack, aviation staff engineer, also at the German legation in Berne, is Gripp's right-hand man in Nazi money transfers. So to speak, all Nazi money is to be brought from Germany to Switzerland with the help of Kadgien* and secured by Gripp/Mack in Switzerland.'[623]

The Gripp connection must have given Bill de Ropp some access to high-level Luftwaffe intelligence in Germany. It also gave Bill opportunities to provide reports to support the local MI6 stations. In June 1942 two Messerschmitt 109 fighter-bombers (a variant of the famous fighter) were due to be flown from the Channel Ports where they had been operating against British shipping to North Africa. They were to be ferried to their new location by student pilots who, through navigational errors, ended up in Swiss airspace and landed at Berne-Belmopos where they were impounded due to Swiss neutrality for six months while a diplomatic tug-of-war ensued.[624]

More important, at the end of April 1944 a Messerschmitt ME110 night-fighter aircraft equipped with new top-secret night detection equipment made an emergency landing at a Swiss airfield. The Nazis were concerned that the British Intelligence Service would get a close look at it. At one point Otto Skorzeny, the Waffen SS officer who had rescued Mussolini from allied captivity, planned a raid to blow up the aircraft.[625] In the end the Swiss agreed to destroy the night-fighter and received six Messerschmitt ME109s at a reduced price in return.[626]

As MI6 Head of Station Fanny van den Heuvel had to manage his relationship with the Swiss carefully. In the first days of the war the Swiss had feistily protected their neutrality. Switzerland had purchased German fighter aircraft just before the war and used them effectively to prevent German incursions into Swiss air space. During the so-called Battle of Switzerland between May and June 1940, several Luftwaffe aircraft were shot down. Hitler was irritated and threatened retaliation, and the Swiss backed down.

---

* Friedrich Kadgien was Minister Counsellor at the German legation in Berne.

From that moment the Swiss feared a German invasion and sought means of appeasing the Nazis. The head of the Swiss Military Intelligence Service, Colonel Roger Masson, was reputed to have had good relations with Dansey. However, with Germany clearly winning the war from 1939 until at least December 1941, Masson saw his main role as preventing a German invasion. Switzerland therefore leant towards the Axis Powers for the first half of the war and then towards the Allies in the second half. This policy can be described simultaneously as breathtakingly cynical and eminently sensible.

The copious evidence in the Swiss Federal Archives demonstrates the meticulous and sustained Swiss coverage of the telephones of the MI6 station in Geneva. When suspicious activity was identified it was followed up with physical surveillance. This is not the activity of a country merely going through the motions of protecting its neutrality. Much the same happened in Zurich and periodically there were in-depth reviews of MI6 activity like the 30-page report dated 17 May 1941,[627] which provided details of the MI6 officers and of their contacts with additional comments of their use of cars, aliases and the telephone.

Surprisingly there is no mention in the Swiss Federal Archives of Bill de Ropp. A major reason was the inspired choice of Hugh Whittall as his case officer. Whittall was sixty-three when the war broke out and was retired, living at the spacious Chalet Kariya at Chernex above Montreux, financed by his shareholdings in the family shipping firm Gilchrist Walker.

Even though the author Compton Mackenzie had blown Whittall's MI6 role during the Great War in his book, *First Athenian Memories*,[628] published in 1931, it clearly never occurred to the Swiss that an elderly honorary vice consul would be engaged in clandestine activity.

Whittall was ten years older than Bill de Ropp and with a similarly cosmopolitan outlook. He recruited a fiercely loyal Swiss secretary, Marianne Coigny, to assist him at the vice consular office at 8 Avenue

Nestlé and he kept a secret refuge in the hills above the town. Bill and Jimmy de Ropp lived for much of the war at the Hôtel des Alpes at Glion above Montreux next to the funicular railway which snakes up to Rochers-de-Naye. This line would have been ideal in enabling Whittall and de Ropp to travel separately to the refuge without being seen together.*

Whittall's unenviable task was to act as a shock-absorber between Bill de Ropp and the intemperate Claude Dansey and his acolyte Van den Heuvel. Keeping abreast of Bill de Ropp's numerous contacts and the policy implications of his activities (or those of which he was made aware) must have been taxing.

In November 1942 Allen Dulles arrived in Berne as the representative of the OSS, the United States' new Office of Strategic Services (forerunner of the Central Intelligence Agency or CIA). One has to aim off for Dulles's gift for self-promotion but he proved to be a natural operator, much to the annoyance of Dansey.

Bill Casey (who, like Dulles, would later become Director of the CIA) was posted to London. He wrote that 'Sir Claude Dansey, for one, viewed any other clandestine activity on the Continent, whether foreign or British, as a mortal threat to the security of his own networks . . . MI6 held us at arm's length. We suspected that one reason for Dansey's reluctance was his embarrassment over the paucity of MI6's direct information from Europe in general and Germany in particular.'

At the end of 1942 another of Bill de Ropp's former sources arrived in Switzerland from Madrid. This was Francesco Antinori, who was posted to the Italian Legation in Berne and was thus able to provide intelligence of German–Italian relations which became increasingly important as Mussolini's regime began to collapse.

Bill de Ropp had to manage some unexpected complications. In Berne Antinori began a romantic relationship with Elizabeth

* Whittall also kept a yacht with black sails, which was useful for clandestine missions over to the French side of Lake Geneva.

Wiskemann,* an assistant to the British press attaché, H. G. Daniels. Wiskemann did not like Daniels and she may have felt uneasy that Jimmy de Ropp had been Antinori's lover in Berlin. Furthermore Wiskemann was notably left-wing, in stark contrast to de Ropp's conservatism and entrenched anti-communism.

Wiskemann was a talented networker (albeit not a professional intelligence officer) and her real role in Berne was to provide economic reporting for the Political Warfare Executive (PWE) based at Woburn Abbey outside London. She had dozens of contacts (including Carl Burckhardt)[629] and she extracted some useful material from some of them, although PWE was not always appreciative.

Switzerland was a hive of spying activity during the war. There is a mass of literature about the many great cases, including the Rote Kapelle, Hans Bernd Gisevius, Fritz Kolbe, Lucy, Madame Szymanska and her connection to Admiral Canaris. But from early 1941 it was also a centre for peace feelers as some Nazi leaders sought to make contacts which could eventually help in any future negotiations. This had begun before Rudolf Hess's fateful flight to Scotland, with people like Carl Burckhardt, Albrecht Haushofer, Ulrich von Hassell, Kurt Jahnke and Federico Stallforth.

Such activity was anathema to Claude Dansey. He was conscious that Churchill did not want to talk to the Germans; he wanted to defeat them. MI6 was still traumatised by its one venture into negotiations, the Venlo disaster. So Bill de Ropp's involvement in this domain was bound to attract further criticism. By contrast, Dulles loved all the politicking and the backchannels and, in so doing, he became more aware of the fissures developing inside Germany and the plotting against Hitler which led to the 20 July 1944 bomb attack.[630]

At no stage was Bill de Ropp 'declared' to the Americans as a British agent. We saw in the previous chapter how an American enquiry about Bill de Ropp in London was brushed off with reference to the

* She registered Antinori as her contact Q6. (Field, *Elizabeth Wiskemann: Scholar, Journalist, Secret Agent*, p.313.)

Savile Club saying he was out of the country. The Americans were not even told he was in Switzerland, let alone Montreux. However, it is possible, even likely, that some of his anonymised reporting (which always conceals the identity of the source) was shared with the OSS in London and/or in Berne.

Bill gained a privileged insight into Germany's increasingly desperate search for a deal with London and Washington. This quest was driven by the ambitious and capable SD officer Walter Schellenberg, the same man who had played a key role at Venlo. Against Hitler's wishes and with Himmler's timorous semi-support he made numerous attempts to establish contacts with the Western allies from as early as mid-1942.

One of his chosen routes was through Max Hohenlohe, who Bill de Ropp had met in Lausanne early in the war. Hohenlohe was now tasked by Schellenberg to make contact with Sir Samuel Hoare, the British ambassador in Madrid and his military attaché, Brigadier William Torr, with the assistance of Karl Lindemann, the Chairman of the Norddeutscher Lloyd shipping line.[631]

Later in the war Schellenberg entered into discussions with Carl Burckhardt about releasing political prisoners and Jews to prepare the way for potential talks. Burckhardt then got involved with Schellenberg's boss, Ernst Kaltenbrunner, and his madcap scheme to set up an independent Austrian regime following the collapse of Nazi Germany. Kaltenbrunner asked Burckhardt to facilitate contact with Dulles.

It was a third source who gave Bill de Ropp his best insights into Schellenberg's plans. Hans Eggen was the son of a farmer. He joined the Nazi Party in 1933 and the SS in the same year. At the outbreak of war he was transferred to the Waffen SS and worked with Schellenberg in Amt VI of the SD.

Eggen's initial purpose for visiting Switzerland was to set up the liaison relationship with Colonel Masson for Schellenberg. In November 1941 Masson held his first meeting with Schellenberg who used the threat of invasion to cement a relationship of dependency with Masson.[632] As Germany's situation became ever more precarious Eggen asked Masson to put him and Schellenberg in touch with Dulles. Eggen also had an intelligence brief. He maintained a liaison with Brigadier Kiyatomi Okamoto[633] who was the Japanese military attaché in Berne and believed to be the head of Japanese intelligence in Europe.[634]

Meanwhile one of Schellenberg's own staff in Berne, Major Alois Auersperg (an Austrian prince whose family dates back to the Holy Roman Empire), whose cover role was as Gripp's deputy in the air attaché's office, was himself involved in the opposition to Hitler. After the July 1944 bomb plot Auersperg thought it wiser to leave German-speaking Switzerland for the safer French-speaking area around Geneva. He made contact with Dulles and was given the codename Picasso and the number 502.[635]

Thus all roads seemed to lead to Dulles. Through Dansey's lack of flair and creativity, MI6 with its well-staffed stations in Switzerland lost out on a wealth of good intelligence and some attractive recruitment prospects. Furthermore Dulles was wise enough to stall the various peace feelers. He knew that Washington and London had no wish to do a deal behind the backs of the Soviet Union or to have anything to do with Hitler or his murderous regime.

Some of the other leads that Schellenberg followed suggest an element of desperation. He funded Erna, the older sister of Putzi Hanfstaengl, who claimed that she could make contact with Churchill's son, Randolph. He employed a Dr Hitter, a psychologist from the Charité Hospital in Berlin, who thought he could get in touch with the Archbishop of Canterbury, William Temple. There was an attempt by the SD office in Stuttgart to open talks with Eric Grant, the British Consul-General in Zurich.[636]

During his lengthy interrogation in London after the war Schellenberg mentioned another case. 'A certain Brettschneider, a Hamburg industrialist, [told him] that one Garrit (or Guerrit) a

British subject believed to be correspondent of "The Times" in Berne had quite unofficially and entirely on his own initiative put forward the suggestion that some German plenipotentiary should open peace conversations with an equally accredited British representative.'[637] Schellenberg reported the case to Himmler who passed the report to Ribbentrop.*

Eggen's links to the Swiss hierarchy led to an altogether more remarkable effort by a former President of the Swiss Confederation, Jean-Marie Musy, to obtain the release of Jews from concentration camps. Musy had several meetings with Schellenberg and secured the freedom of a trainload of 1,200 Jews from Theresienstadt. Schellenberg's problem was that Himmler was always too fearful of countermanding Hitler's orders and on this rock all the Swiss strands of negotiation foundered.[638]

We don't know if Eggen ever told Bill de Ropp about another SD officer, who had worked in Schellenberg's British section and had spent time in London before the war. Hans Daufeldt arrived in Lausanne in June 1942 with three female wireless operators.[639] He had impressed Ulrich von Hassell with his (probably feigned) scepticism about the Nazis as early as September 1941.[640] From Lausanne he managed a number of operations. He sent six German agents in two U-boats to the United States, the first of which disappeared with all its occupants, possibly having hit a mine. He managed the communications between an SD agent, Waldemar von Petrov,[641] and Kaltenbrunner. He provided the link between Jahnke in Germany and Stallforth.[642] He was also supposed to maintain contact with the two Swiss Nazi parties.

During his interrogations by the Americans and British after the war, Daufeldt was reluctant to discuss what he had been doing in

---

* This story might appear to have some tenuous resonance with Bill de Ropp or even H. G. Daniels. There was no *Times* journalist with a similar name in Switzerland. However, there was a Giro von Gaevernitz working for Dulles who is mentioned by Gisevius in *To the Bitter End* (p. 589).

Switzerland.[643] However, in 1950 he wrote to Stallforth claiming to have been working for peace with 'England and America'.[644] Among the list of contacts he included 'the Englishman Carr' a probable reference to the MI6 Head of Station in Helsinki, Harry Carr,[645] who had been working from Stockholm since 1941.[646] In 1962 he told the CIA that he had also been trying to establish a channel to the Soviet Union.[647]

What is clear is that Bill de Ropp was swimming in a pool of contacts, some of whom had knowledge of the growing opposition to Hitler and to the increasingly frantic efforts by senior Nazis to establish communication channels to the Allies. However, he worked for an MI6 station in Switzerland which was under Dansey's firm orders to ignore such matters and focus entirely on Churchill's aim of military victory. Bill de Ropp's knowledge of such plotting infuriated Dansey but also frustrated de Ropp who felt it was important.

Menzies was in no position to help his old agent. Increasingly, as the war progressed, he had been drawn into the day-to-day management of Ultra signals intelligence for the Prime Minister.* John Colville commented that Menzies used to deliver it in buff-coloured boxes bearing the initials V.R.I. (Victoria Regina et Imperatrix), for which Churchill himself held the key. Menzies never established an easy relationship with Churchill and had to work hard to ensure that he was fully briefed both on the intelligence itself but also on its implications for the war effort.

* To the very few people in Whitehall who knew about this material, it was better known as Boniface. How Ultra material was handled between Bletchley Park, Broadway and No. 10 Downing Street is best described in Lewin's *Ultra Goes to War*, pp. 185–6.

25

DOWNFALL

1945–1946: The defeat of Nazi Germany

None of the Swiss channels of negotiations worked and eventually Schellenberg identified the Swedish Count Folke Bernadotte as his preferred channel for Himmler's ill-fated negotiations in Berlin and Stockholm in the final weeks of the war.[648]

Friedrich von der Ropp was also considered for the same purpose. He had spent most of the war at his wife's house, Grünheide,* a few miles outside Berlin. After his attempt to blend his brand of evangelical Protestantism with National Socialism he had become increasingly disillusioned. His daughter Birute (Buti) had married a Wehrmacht officer in 1939 and the wedding photo shows a phalanx of military uniforms. The young man was killed just outside Kiev during the first months of Barbarossa.

Woldemar Hartmann was the half-brother of Friedrich's wife, Elisabeth (Lili), the woman whose quick thinking had saved her husband from execution as a spy in 1917 and who had so charmed

* Now overshadowed by a Tesla factory.

Archibald Church in 1925. 'In the summer of 1942 we visited the Ropps in their pretty villa in Grünheide [near] Berlin . . . almost everyone believed in German victory, except for the Ropps, who knew both England and North America well and did not adhere to the ban on listening to foreign broadcasts.'[649]

Friedrich observed:

> My family lived in Grünheide in the country and we felt secure, although we heard a lot and we suffered with some friends without being able to help them. The certainty of impending doom weighed heavily on us all but we were powerless. Our house was soon filled with refugees. I had the potato cellar converted into a small shelter, and we followed the terrible attacks on Berlin every midday and every night.
>
> When the wind blew from the west, the smoke came in dark, yellow-black clouds, and the sun lost its shine. How much merciless misery and pain went over this gigantic city cannot be described by any pen. We saw the complete destruction of our neighbouring town of Erkner, which housed a ball-bearing factory . . . We ourselves were spared. Two bombs fell close to our house. All the windows burst.[650]

The Hartmanns returned to Grünheide in early 1945. This time the visit was not for pleasure. His family had owned land in Estonia but they had been forced to move to Poznan in Poland under the terms of the Molotov-Ribbentrop Pact. As Soviet forces advanced the family went to stay with Friedrich.

Hartmann explains:

> At the end of February [1945] something strange happened. Friedel [the diminutive of Friedrich, used by his family and friends] was known as a fairly black sheep. We were all the more astonished when a senior SS officer appeared one evening

> and told Friedel he needed to talk to him. Not very pleased, Friedel went into the study with the man, where they talked for almost an hour. When he had left, Friedel said that Himmler had wanted to inquire whether Friedel, who had good relations with the English, would be willing to represent the German government with permission to negotiate an agreement or armistice immediately with the Western powers.
>
> He, Friedel, at first thought that a trap was being set, but then he was informed that it was a really serious matter. Friedel finally rejected it because he emphasised that it was too late and that the main thing now was to turn the Western powers against [the Soviets]. Himmler intended to outsmart the Soviets. We were very glad that Friedel had not got involved in this rather fantastic affair, as tempting as it was for him because he had always had a penchant for big politics.[651]

This refusal to help may have been responsible for the Nazis confiscating Grünheide and expelling the family. Friedrich asked the Hartmanns to stay and protect the house and their possessions.

> As he knew from the London and North American broadcasts, the Soviet Russians weren't so bad any more. He asked me to stay in the villa as his representative and to protect it from looting and destruction. The Ropps had a lot of nice things, which of course they had to leave in Grünheide: the souvenirs of his travels in Africa, good pictures, etc. Since I thought I could judge the Bolsheviks better and more accurately than Friedel, I declined.[652]

So this was the von der Ropp brothers' last hurrah. After thirty years of politicking and intrigue both brothers were identified by the Nazis as potential channels for a futile and vain last-minute peace attempt to prevent a total Soviet victory in Germany.

Hermann von Harder found himself involved in the final battle for Berlin. He was disappointed that his mentor and idol, Alfred Rosenberg, left Berlin without informing him. So, as a former soldier, von Harder volunteered to fight under General Erich Bärenfänger's command to defend the German capital. He was given the role of finding ammunition for his unit. It was a nightmare scenario as they fought in the ruins of Berlin as the Russians advanced street by street. He later wrote in wonderment at the dedication of the civilian population and young members of the Hitler youth. Finally he persuaded a civilian to give him some clothing and with his greying hair and a broken heel which obliged him to limp he managed to make his escape from the doomed city posing as an old man.[653]

While in his cell at Nuremberg Rosenberg wrote his memoir.[654] It describes the end of the Third Reich in compelling terms. The RAF bombing of Berlin on the night of 21 March 1945 destroyed Rosenberg's house in Dahlem in the Berlin suburbs.

> The air pressure was so strong that our own roof caved in and we had to move to the cellar. My daughter Irene, who had been looking forward to a small birthday party on March 22nd had to spend the day amidst dirt and rubble . . . I still see her before me: tall, young with blonde hair falling down over her shoulders, dressed in long slacks and a grey fur coat, carrying a handbag with long straps. I often stood on the balcony, our Ingo beside me, his paws on the railing both of us watching Irene . . . Early in April I became bed-ridden. On a walk in Dahlem I sprained my ankle thus bringing about an inflammation and a haemorrhage . . .
>
> [On 13 April] I tried to reach the Führer to try to find out what his intentions were but was referred to Bormann . . . Two days later I learned that my boyhood friend, Arno Schickedanz, had killed his wife, his eight-year-old daughter and himself. He was a clear-headed politician, the only one with whom I had

> been able to discuss frankly the dangerous turn of events . . . I had managed to get hold of a sufficient quantity of cyanide for it went without saying that neither I nor my family would voluntarily fall into the hands of the Soviets.

On the night of the 20th there came a call from the Reich office – all Ministers were to meet at Eutin. This was a small town to the north of Lübeck. It was a risky trip with refugees flooding the roads and the occasional aerial attack. From there the family travelled to Mürwick near Flensburg where Rosenberg was found a bed aboard the steamship *Patria*. Mürwick was and is the site of Admiral Dönitz's impressive Gothic red-stone Naval Headquarters, and neighbouring Flensburg was the official capital of Germany for the three weeks until the arrest of Dönitz and his ministers by British troops on 23 May.

It was at Mürwick that Rosenberg heard the news of Hitler's death and reality began to dawn. None of the inhabitants of the town wished to provide accommodation for his wife, Hedwig, and daughter, Irene. Hedwig told one person, 'Let's be frank. You want to get rid of us because I am the wife of Alfred Rosenberg.' He caught a glimpse of Himmler but refused to speak a word to the man he blamed for the downfall of the Reich.

It was typical of Rosenberg's hauteur that, on 12 May, he wrote a letter to Field Marshal Montgomery informing him that he was at the naval hospital at Mürwik having sprained his ankle. Rosenberg doubtless imagined a knightly scene in which he and Montgomery would salute each other and Rosenberg would hand over his sword.[655] When the arrest happened at Flensburg Hospital a week later it was very different.[656]

On 18 May British Military Police arrived. The sergeant knew nothing about his letter to Montgomery. Rosenberg was handcuffed and taken to Kiel and put aboard an aircraft: 'Then below us I see Düsseldorf and Cologne or rather what had once been Cologne. As if trampled down by gigantic beasts. Cologne's rubble lies heaped round the skeleton of the Cathedral. Blown up bridges in the river. A desert giving evidence of the terrible fate of people and Reich.' They arrived at Luxembourg and were taken to the Palace Hotel at Mondorf. This is where they were detained until the material could be assembled for their prosecution at the Nuremberg War Crimes tribunal.

Rosenberg had dictated his will and political testament to his secretary Hildegarde Elze on 5 May at Mürwik on board the *Patria*. Since then the loyal woman had hidden both documents. In the court's quest for evidence Elze was tracked down and obliged to write a statement about the testament which she insisted 'showed [Rosenberg's] attitude and criticism of the politics of the National Socialist State'. He was particularly critical, she said, of Himmler and Goebbels. She added that Rosenberg had a 'big fight' to carry out his ideas on Ost (eastern) Politics. 'The hardest fight Rosenberg had was against Gauleiter Koch who was then Governor of the Ukraine who acted arbitrarily on basic issues and often overruled Rosenberg, his superior.'[657]

In spite of Frau Elze's stoical efforts the British finally managed to find the hidden Political Testament. It was a sickening piece of self-justification and yet, unlike some colleagues, Rosenberg did not resile from his warped philosophies. 'It is the fate of great ideas that they cannot always perfect execution at the time of their possible realisation.'[658]

He pinned much of the blame on Bormann's refusal to grant him more access to Hitler: 'In the course of bad experiences the Führer had with some personalities, the circle of his cooperators narrowed down more and more so that finally many of his oldest Reichsleiter and Gauleiter were unable to bring their worries and suggestions to him.'

On foreign policy he continued to insist that the big mistake had been in the management of the relationship with Britain. Here he was clearly thinking of Ribbentrop.

> In the basic trend of foreign policy I followed Adolf Hitler with deepest and innermost conviction. A pact with England and with the Germanic states of the north against the Bolshevist peril in the east was to be desired. The fact that this peril was not recognised and that Germany remained alone is a great tragedy of the German people . . . In 1931 I went to London with the Führer's knowledge. In May 1933 I once more went to London to canvass cooperation with the new Reich. In later years I invited many influential Englishmen to the Reich's Party Festival in Nuremberg.

As for Nazi policy in the East, 'With regards to the policy adopted in the formerly occupied eastern territories . . . apart from the catastrophic failure of the Luftwaffe . . . the blame lies with the deliberate ignoring of a sensible German Eastern policy based on the respective nations' qualities.' Of all his statements this one, above all others, completely fails to understand the sheer scale and gravity of the catastrophe.

His final thought was probably why Frau Elze wanted to prevent the document falling into the hands of the prosecutors. It was guaranteed not to endear him to the court. 'I know that the coming generation will cast away much in these troubled times and it will be once again able to create a proud German Reich.' Doubtless Rosenberg did not have in mind the Germany of Konrad Adenauer, Willy Brandt, Helmut Kohl and Angela Merkel.

At the London Conference throughout July 1945 the four victorious powers mapped out the Nuremberg process. This was a remarkable achievement given that this was breaking entirely new judicial ground. On 29 August the list of defendants was agreed. Simultaneously there was an urgent and massive search for evidence. The trial itself began on 20 November.

Rosenberg was charged on all four indictments by the court. These were crimes against peace, crimes against humanity, war crimes and conspiracy to commit the previous three. An abridged list of judgements read that:

> As head of the APA, Rosenberg was in charge of an organization whose agents were active in Nazi intrigue in all parts of the world. His own reports, for example, claim that the APA was largely responsible for Romania's joining the Axis. As head of the APA, he played an important role in the preparation and planning of the attack on Norway.
>
> Rosenberg was responsible for a system of organized plunder of both public and private property throughout the invaded countries of Europe.
>
> With his appointment as Reich Minister for the Occupied Eastern Territories on 17th July 1941, Rosenberg became the supreme authority for those areas. He helped to formulate the policies of Germanization, exploitation, forced labour, extermination of Jews and opponents of Nazi rule, and he set up the administration which carried them out.
>
> Upon occasion Rosenberg objected to the excesses and atrocities committed by his subordinates, notably in the case of Koch, but these excesses continued and he stayed in office until the end.

This final paragraph says a lot about Rosenberg. He was one of those extreme idealogues who shrank from the implications of their own philosophy. This is reminiscent of his discussion with the Reverend Hodson back in 1934. Rosenberg was pleased that Hodson had assumed he was a monster only to find out he was actually a reasonable person. But when push came to shove Rosenberg never had the courage to say no to the man whose approval he constantly sought, Adolf Hitler.

His biographer, Robert Cecil, summed up Rosenberg perfectly,

'Rosenberg's real offence was not that he acted like a weak man but that he had written and spoken like a strong man.'[659]

Bill de Ropp must have felt all these ironies as he followed the trial in the Swiss newspapers and on the wireless on the BBC Overseas Service*. He had once described Rosenberg as a 'muddle-headed philosopher', but he had spent a lot of time with him over a period of eight years, from late 1930 to late 1939. Although de Ropp had an ulterior motive – to extract intelligence from Rosenberg – he could not help but feel some affection even for a man whose personality flaws were so evident. Furthermore, the two men genuinely enjoyed each other's company, as can be seen so clearly in the photograph album which was one of Bill de Ropp's few treasured mementoes.

As described in Chapter 1, Broadway managed to keep Winterbotham and de Ropp from testifying. One can just imagine the anxiety in Menzies's office when Thoma's application was submitted and the urgent discussions with Cadogan and government legal advisers. How was it that Lord Halifax, Beaverbrook, Vansittart and Cadogan himself were due to appear at the tribunal but Winterbotham and de Ropp could not? The answer was simple. The Allied governments decided who would appear and there was no mechanism for appeal.

There were a couple of other scares for Broadway, one minor and one major. The prosecution found a paper in which Bill de Ropp had sought a meeting with Hitler. This was clearly another example of Bill de Ropp maximising his access as a spy. Rosenberg had written, 'Right after the death of Count Gravina, Schickedanz proposed to Baron de Ropp to have one of his military friends appointed as League of Nations Commissar for Danzig . . . The Baron conferred with London . . . and informed him yesterday that he would like to report the Führer's approval to the plan . . . therefore he would like to have a conference with the Führer.'[660]

* It was the BBC Empire Service from 1932 to 1939 when it became the BBC Overseas Service. In 1965 it was renamed the BBC World Service.

The Italian Count Manfredi Gravina had died in office in September 1932 having been High Commissioner for just over three years. Britain had provided no fewer than four of the first seven High Commissioners and so Gravina was replaced temporarily by a Dane, Helmer Rosting, and then an Irishman, Sean Lester, until Burckhardt took over in 1937.[661]

The bigger alarm came on 10 January 1946 when the British Embassy in Washington sent the FO a *New York Times* article by Tania Long which referred to 'Successful contacts' with the British Air Staff, with the Duke of Windsor (then King Edward VIII), the Duke of Kent and Viscount Templewood, while a 'feeling of cordiality' was maintained with the Prime Minister's (Mr Ramsay MacDonald) Private Secretary 'a Mr Barlow'. 'A firmer bond has also been established between Rosenberg's British division and Sir Henry Deterding, the oil magnate and his associates.'

This press report caused alarm in London, which complained to the Americans that this was due to their careless handling of a Nuremberg document.[662] In fact the British press had also picked up on the story. *The Scotsman* on the same day had three headlines:

ROSENBERG AND THE LATE DUKE OF KENT
Story of an interview in London
'FRIENDS IN BRITISH AIR STAFF'

The article began 'Nuremberg, Wednesday – allegations that staunch support for German National Socialism was given by the British air staff before the war and that "every detail pertaining to National Socialism" was explained to the late Duke of Kent in a three-hour interview in London were made by Alfred Rosenberg.' It continued:

> He alleged that, as a sequel to his visit to London in 1931, contact was made with a member of the British air staff [Winterbotham]

> who was firmly of the opinion that Germany and England must stand together in defence against the Bolshevik danger. This officer visited Germany and saw Hitler in 1934 and cordial relations were established with other members of the British air staff . . . This staunch group, namely the air staff, which was run by younger officers, had proved itself to be a solid and constant support in all changing situations.

Rosenberg's report said that a person to whom it referred as W [Winterbotham] was instrumental in introducing him to a representative [Bartlett] of a firm making aircraft engines [Bristol Aeroplane Company] for the RAF and that he met this representative later in Berlin.

'One day we received a request from London to make it possible for our English agent [Bill de Ropp] to take a trip to London in order to orientate the Duke of Kent in every detail pertaining to National Socialism in order to convey this information to the King.' Rosenberg's report said that a person whom he identified only by the initial R [Ropp] went with him* to London 'and had a three hour talk with the Duke of Kent'. Rosenberg also claimed that Captain MacCaw, semi-official counsel to the British Ministry of War showed a favourable attitude towards Germany.

The articles also made reference to the British periodical *The Aeroplane*, a magazine that Rosenberg described as 'printed under the guidance of the Air General Staff'. *The Scotsman* pointed out that this comment was erroneous. The editor of *The Aeroplane* Charles Grey undoubtedly had fascist sympathies. 'Germany was the first line of defence against Eastern barbarism'[663] was a view with which Winterbotham and de Ropp would have agreed. He was also an anti-

---

* This is almost certainly a mistake by Rosenberg or in the recording of his testimony. There is no evidence that he accompanied de Ropp to London on this occasion. Note too that several newspapers assumed that R stood for Ribbentrop. See Chapter 16 for de Ropp's meeting with the Duke of Kent and Captain Guy MacCaw's visit to Germany in 1934.

Semite. He was obliged to resign as editor in 1939 but there is no evidence that his editorial policy was influenced by the Air Ministry. Nonetheless it might have suited Bill de Ropp's purposes to suggest that *The Aeroplane*'s editorial policy reflected his own influence or a wider British opinion.[664]

The document that the prosecution had managed to obtain was 'A short report on the activity of the APA' submitted to Hitler by Rosenberg.[665] It was undated but was probably written in 1935. Rosenberg's intention was to tell Hitler how well he was doing on foreign affairs as part of his campaign against Göring, Goebbels and Ribbentrop whom he saw as his detractors. Much of it was about his supposed achievements in Scandinavia, Austria, Hungary and Romania and in the fields of foreign trade and the press. However, the *New York Times, Scotsman* and numerous other newspapers were right to identify the core of the document as being about Britain.

By far the biggest embarrassment concerned the royal family and the allegations about the late Duke of Kent and the Duke of Connaught. It was the suggestion that they had Nazi sympathies which had provoked the Washington Embassy to alert the FO and prompted the subsequent protest to the Americans. MI6 must have been relieved that Winterbotham was not named as one of its officers. Some of the items not picked up by the press were also damning:

'The Air General Staff always inquired of us what they could state to refute the anti-German elements in London in a manner favourable to us.'

'The ex-Minister of Air, Samuel Hoare. who till this day still keeps up his personal contacts with the Air Ministry . . . request[ed] a memorandum on the spiritual foundation of national socialism.'

'The Chief of our England Division (Kapitänleutnant Obermüller, reserve) took two representatives of the German Air Ministry to London and himself undertook several trips to London. He was the first German to receive an invitation from the Air Vice-Marshal to view the British Air Force and British air strength.'

Alfred Rosenberg finally got his three days in court on 15, 16 and 17 April 1946. Alfred Thoma, for the defence, gave him a relatively easy time, as one would expect. The British were doubtless pleased that the document which had so excited the *New York Times* was not mentioned except in passing. There was a brief mention of the 1931 trip to London: 'I tried to find a way to an understanding by personal contacts I had made. Frequently, I had conversations with British Air Force officers of the British Air Forces General Staff. On their invitation I visited London in 1931, and at that time had purely informal conversations with a number of British personalities.'[666]

There was a similarly brief mention of the 1933 visit:

> In May 1933 I was again in London, this time by Hitler's personal order; and I visited several British ministers, whose names are not relevant here, and tried again to promote understanding for the sudden and strange development in Germany. My reception was rather reserved, and a number of incidents occurred which showed that the sentiment was very repellent. But that did not prevent me from keeping up these personal contacts and from inviting a great number of British personalities to come to Germany later.

On the following day Thoma gave Rosenberg an opportunity to attack Erich Koch and Bormann for the brutality in Ukraine: 'I was afraid that Koch, due to his temperament and being so far removed from the Reich, might not follow my directives. To be sure, while making the protest I could not have known that Koch later on, in disobeying my directives, would go as far as he did and – I shall add – upon special instigation by the head of the Party Chancellery [Martin Bormann].'[667]

Rosenberg's fate was sealed on the third day, Wednesday 17 April. The prosecutors got to work. It was not so much the breathless, almost rabid, questioning of the Soviet Prosecutor Roman Rudenko –

whose style sometimes annoyed the President, Sir Geoffrey Lawrence – that undermined Rosenberg's case but the subtler and more forensic questions of the US Prosecutor Thomas Dodd.

> I think [probed Dodd] you will agree that in the Ukraine your man Koch was doing all kinds of terrible things, and now I don't understand that you dispute that Lohse and Kube were helping to eliminate or liquidate the Jews, and that Brautigam, an important member of your staff, and that Leibbrandt, another important member of your staff, were informed of the program.* So that five people at least under your administration were engaged in this kind of conduct, and not small people at that.

Rosenberg was obliged to concur although he tried to add several caveats.[668]

Dodd cuttingly observed that when Rosenberg threatened to resign, on 12 October 1944, 'the German Army was practically out of Russia. It was on the retreat, isn't that so?'[669]

Rudenko extracted a fascinating observation on Rosenberg's policy on the Baltics: 'The aim of a Reich Commissioner for Estonia, Latvia, Lithuania, and Bielorussia [Belarus] must be to strive for the creation of a German protectorate, with a view to transforming these regions later into a part of Greater Germany by the Germanisation of racially admissible elements, the colonisation of Germanic peoples, and the resettlement of undesirable elements.'[670]

There was a second telling description of Eastern policy: 'The task of the Ukraine is to provide Germany and Europe with foodstuffs and the continent with raw materials. The task in the Caucasus is, above all, of a political nature and represents the decisive extension of continental Europe, under German direction, from the Caucasian

* These were Heinrich Lohse, Wilhelm Kube, Otto Brautigam, Georg Leibbrandt.

isthmus to the Near East.'[671] Slightly earlier he was quoted as writing: 'From the economic point of view the German Reich must take control of the total oil supply. The necessary participation in the riches could be discussed in the future.' Rudenko accused Rosenberg of 'the aggressive and plundering character of Germany's war against the Soviet Union and your personal responsibility for the planning and carrying out of this aggression?'[672]

The seventeenth of April was the day that Rosenberg's goose was well and truly cooked. He was one of the few Nazis convicted on all four counts. The sentence was handed down on 1 October 1946.[673] 'Defendant Alfred Rosenberg, on the Counts of the Indictment on which you have been convicted, the Tribunal sentences you to death by hanging.'

Bill de Ropp, following the trial from his Chalet Tzi-No at Glion, above Montreux, must have guessed the inevitable outcome. One can only imagine his thoughts when he heard that the death sentence had been carried out.

At the end of the war in Europe MI6 did not waste any time in retiring Bill de Ropp. He was granted a final gratuity of £500. Bill must have felt bruised by the disrespect shown to him by Dansey and his acolyte van den Heuvel. His mild revenge may have been in not telling his MI6 handlers everything he was doing; particularly when it came to peace negotiations.

Agents were being laid off everywhere and case officers returned to their previous professions. There were no gold watches or farewell parties at St Ermin's Hotel. All he had was the Letts diary with Rosenberg's sketch of what a future Nazi Russia would look like, and the little cloth-bound album of his travels in Austria with the Reichsleiter Alfred Rosenberg.

26

'ON THE KNEES OF THE OLYMPIAN GODS'

1945–1973: The players depart

On 8 May 1944 (his fifty-third birthday), just a month before D-Day, Malcolm Woollcombe walked out of 54 Broadway and took his familiar route to Victoria Station where he boarded an evening train to Hove. On arrival it was only a few hundred yards to his house at 52 Palmeira Avenue just near the Sussex County cricket ground. He walked upstairs and lay motionless on his bed for hours on end to the distress of his wife, Eileen.

On many weekdays during the war he had been obliged to work late and stay overnight in the office on a camp-bed. The pressure of work was relentless and Broadway was a miserable place to work. It was dark, dingy and cold.* Its only redeeming feature was its staff canteen which provided excellent cheap meals.[674] With his long experience of warfare Woollcombe was a reassuring figure at Broadway. Evelyn Sinclair, the former Chief's sister, long remembered how he had calmed her nerves during early days of the Blitz.[675]

* According to Patrick Reilly the heating only came on from 31 October (Reilly papers p.287).

This evening something was different. Woollcombe knew that he could never go back to Broadway. He spoke of his insomnia and of 'a black cloud'. Nowadays we would recognise that he was having a nervous breakdown. Some understood better than others. Woolly's deputy, David Footman, stepped up into his role as head of the Political Section and performed admirably but, according to Harold Gibson, 'lacks your vast experience and understanding of our work'.[676]

Gibson, the man who had evacuated the leadership of the Czech Intelligence Service from Prague in 1939, with just hours to spare, wrote, 'I feel we can ill spare men of your experience these days and hope it will not be long before you can return to your task.' Cadogan waited until August after Woollcombe had tendered his resignation. 'I hope with rest and country air you will soon be well on the road to recovery,' adding, 'We can never adequately express our gratitude to you.'

Woollcombe died in 1968. He spent much of his retirement compiling anthologies of the works of George Eliot and Anthony Trollope. He was a member of Hove Special Constabulary. To most of the neighbours in Hove he was a retired civil servant who had had a rather dull job in Passport Control. He retained his love of France and especially of Arras where he had served in the first war and where he cherished the wayside obelisks which proclaimed: 'Here the invader was repulsed'. Menzies wrote to Eileen, 'I always remembered the devotion to duty and for my part I am grateful how much he did to work for the cause which he ennobled by his wisdom.'[677]

Fred Winterbotham's close association with Bill de Ropp ended when he was appointed the key MI6 officer responsible for the distribution and security of Ultra material to military commanders in the field. With his self-confidence and determination he was the perfect person for the job. He set up the Special Liaison Units (SLUs) which all top British and American commanders had attached to their HQs to handle the vital intelligence. At the end of the war he knew that peacetime MI6 work would be comparatively dull and he resigned to take up a position at BOAC (British Overseas Airways Corporation) and later at the Colonial Development Corporation (CDC) before returning to farming in Devon.

In 1969 he published *Secret and Personal*, which included descriptions of his activities in Germany in the 1930s with Bill de Ropp, Alfred Rosenberg and Erich Koch. He doubtless felt justified in writing about de Ropp because Bill himself had written a series of five articles in the *Daily Mail* in 1957. Later Winterbotham wrote two more books, often using the same verbatim material, *The Nazi Connection* (1978) and *The Ultra Spy* (1989). In all his books he wrote from memory and there are small errors of fact although the general narrative was broadly correct.

However, it was the publication in 1974 of *The Ultra Secret*, just twenty-nine years after the end of the war that caused great controversy and made him a lot of money. This was the first clear revelation of the spectacular successes at Bletchley Park and the book became a bestseller. At the same time many of the tens of thousands of people who had kept the secret secure were outraged at his indiscretion, especially coming from the man responsible for its security. Contrary to popular belief, Winterbotham did seek and obtain government clearance,[678] but the Foreign Secretary had to issue guidance to vetted staff about their continuing obligations of secrecy.[679]

Following *The Ultra Secret* Professor Harry Hinsley was commissioned to write his epic *History of British Intelligence in the Second World War*. This drew on very little MI6 intelligence partly because MI6 has to protect its sources but also because the MI6 archive had been so drastically culled. Much of this could be dated to the period when Dick Ellis was (incredibly) put in charge of weeding the archive in 1963 as a post-retirement job in London while he was under investigation for being both a German and Soviet spy.[680]

Fred Winterbotham lived to the age of ninety-two. His injection of energy and ambition into MI6 before the war and his willingness to tread new ground by meeting Hitler paved the way for the service's successes during the war, much of it based on SIGINT. As he acknowledged in his books it was Bill de Ropp who made his early success possible.

No. 54 Broadway still stands opposite St James's Park Underground station. Its exterior has not changed although the modern executive offices inside have nothing in common with the dark and dingy rabbit-warren of the 1930s with its famously unreliable lift. The corridor which Menzies used to access the Chief's flat at 21 Queen Anne's Gate no longer exists. St Ermin's Hotel is physically unchanged albeit a lot smarter than in the days when it was used as the MI6's all-purpose meeting place and watering hole. The tube station itself has been preserved as it was, with its wooden benches and magazine stalls. This part of London is almost a time capsule, the only new buildings being the Justice Ministry and the Guards Chapel. When the V1 flying bomb smashed into the chapel during the Sunday service on 18 June 1944 killing 121 worshippers it must have literally shaken Broadway and the service which had done so much to expose the development of Hitler's Vergeltungswaffen (Vengeance weapons).

Having refused to help Himmler reach a deal with the allies, Friedrich von der Ropp was expelled from Grünheide in March 1945. For a while he practised as a Protestant pastor in Thuringia. The Americans arrived in April but Thuringia was then handed over the Russians. He and Lili managed to procure a farm wagon and moved their possessions to Einbeck in Hanover. With British permission, he was allowed to preach Christianity at a camp full of captured SS men. His son Christoph was released from US captivity and his widowed daughter (Birute, known as Buti, who had so delighted Archibald Church in 1925) brought up her two children (Fritz and Christoph) and remarried in 1949.

The British offered Friedrich the use of the confiscated estate of one of the top Nazi leaders, Robert Ley, who had committed suicide just before the Nuremberg trial. This was the Gut Rottland estate at Waldbröl near Cologne. The main house had been burned down on Ley's orders to avoid it falling into American hands but the imposing front gate remained complete with a large statue of an SA stormtrooper. Here, beginning in January 1947, the irrepressible Friedrich started a training establishment for young men, using the remaining half-timbered stable blocks and outbuildings.

In 1951 Friedrich moved to the outskirts of Bonn and worked on his memoirs which were published in 1961 in German under the title *Zwischen Gestern und Morgen*. He used to tell his family that he did not like the photograph of him in the book because it made him look too benign. He died aged eighty-five, in 1964, at Bad-Godesberg near Bonn. By any standards his life was extraordinary; he packed more into one life than most people would manage in five – and yet he must have felt strangely unfulfilled. His dream of Dauzogir had gone for ever and Grünheide was behind the Iron Curtain. His Anglophilia had failed to prevent a catastrophic war and his sudden dedication to evangelical Christianity had coincided with the most bestial period in world history.

Benno von Wildemann and his family had emigrated to Southern Africa in 1928; not long after arriving there, however, Benno was killed by a leopard while on a hunting trip to Angola. The family had sold up in Germany and had no option other than to remain in South Africa.

The von Stralendorffs' life at Gamehl was curtailed by the arrival of the Soviet army in 1945. Their son, Claus, had been asked to join the July plot against Hitler by his friend and neighbour Fritzi von Schulenberg but felt that he could not break his oath of allegiance to Hitler. His friendship with his regimental colleague, the son of Field Marshal Keitel, was also a factor. He was captured by the Russians (ironically) in Courland, and would not emerge from captivity until

1954, a broken man; he died just a few years later having worked as a translator in Brussels for the European Economic Community.

After five years of being trapped in Switzerland it is hardly surprising that Bill and Jimmy de Ropp moved to Bordighera in Italy in 1946, doubtless as the guests of Francesco Antinori whose family owned properties and vineyards producing some of the finest Chianti in the region. When they returned to Switzerland they moved south from Montreux to the Canton de Valais, where they lived in small chalets in Sion, Salvan and Grimisuat. They had retained a liking for winter resorts and Valais provided easy access to Italy. Jimmy's future travels abroad would mostly be from the port of Genoa.

Bill made a living using his languages for private tuition and translations. However, it was a dull life after a career in espionage and Jimmy was getting itchy feet. She trained as a milkmaid, learning how to milk Swiss cows. But her love of animals was matched by her addiction to travel. Twelve years younger than Bill and still attractive, she wanted to see more of the world. She set off for Australia in 1951 aboard the SS *Surriento* travelling first-class from Genoa to Brisbane. She arrived in September.

In October and November there were some anxious advertisements in leading Australian newspapers: 'Marie Winifred de Ropp recently arrived from Switzerland on MV Surriento or anyone knowing present address please write Taylor, Glossodia NSW.' This may have been placed by Mabel Sprent who had married Norman Taylor, the ICI manager in Australia and New Zealand in 1944–1947.[681] Jimmy seems to have made a similar trip to Australia in 1954 and again in 1956 plus a visit to New York and one to Illinois in 1962.

With an itinerant wife operating to a carefree schedule Bill de Ropp decided in 1952 to return to England and live with his daughter, Ruth. Ruth had been in Liverpool as a nurse during the war. She passed her nursing exams and registered with Herefordshire General Hospital in 1944 and, three years later, as a midwife. She practised as a midwife in Birmingham before returning to the Hereford area to become a District Nurse for the Golden Valley, renting a room at Lower Park (farm) at Vowchurch. This was the moment she agreed to let her father come and live with her.

Father and daughter lived very happily together for twenty years. In December 1953 Ruth bought a tiny one-bedroom house outside Peterchurch with an extra bed placed on the upstairs landing. It cost £850 which Ruth managed with a £500 mortgage. The Baron had to get used to sharing the house with two large German Shepherd dogs who accompanied her everywhere in the back of her Morris Traveller car. Ruth became something of a legend in the community and was credited with having assisted at the birth of generations of children. She was so delightful that the villagers forgave the dog hairs which covered both her uniform and their homes.

The local paper, the *Golden Valley News*, always reserved the first inside page for 'Nurse's Notes', in which Ruth updated villagers on the health of the village and of her work for Guide Dogs for the Blind.

Apart from his two brief brushes with notoriety – in 1954 with Peter Lawrence's two articles in the *News Chronicle*, and then his own five pieces in the *Daily Mail* in 1957, Bill de Ropp kept a low profile. Eva Morgan, as a schoolgirl, remembers that they both took the 7.30 bus each weekday morning to Hereford where the Baron gave language classes at 'the Tech', Hereford College of Further Education. He always wore his homburg hat and a heavy brown coat.[682]

Bill kept clear of the ex-Indian Army brigadier who 'ruled the village'.[683] He never attended St Peter's Church. He did not mix with the four Poles who had stayed on in the village after the war and he avoided the three pubs, the Boughton Arms, the Nag's Head and the Plough. He occasionally walked to the village shop and would politely touch his hat to any passers-by.

Bill was never reconciled with his son, Bob, who became a well-known author, academic and cult-figure in 1960s United States. Bob firmly turned down a request from Bill to go and live with him in

California and also the suggestion that he should write his father's biography. The scars from Dauzogir and Australia never healed. Bob's life story is told in his disturbing autobiography *Warrior's Way*.

Bob's children did, though, get to know their grandfather. Jim was a soldier serving with the US Army in Germany and he travelled to Peterchurch in 1963, later returning with his sister Sue and later still with his wife Diane.

One cross the Baron had to bear was Ruth's devout Roman Catholicism. After suffering from his mother's conversion to Missouri Lutheranism, Gertrud's conversion to the Orthodox Church and then Friedrich's evangelical Protestantism, Bill had had his fill of religion and specified in his will that he did not want a funeral. Ruth went each Sunday to Mass at Belmont Abbey and to a convent in Sidmouth for her holiday retreats.

Jimmy would visit England from Switzerland where she was living at Le Bioley near Salvan. In 1961 she spent some months near Leamington Spa helping out at a boarding kennels. She gave an interview to the local newspaper giving the false impression that she was a wealthy aristocrat 'with a chalet in the Swiss mountains, a farmhouse in the West of England and various other residences dotted around Europe.'[684]

She increasingly gravitated towards Peterchurch where Ruth did not welcome her presence but she moved in regardless after Bill's death. Villagers remember 'the Baroness' as small, tanned, well turned-out with bright red lipstick and her hair tightly coiled. She would chat to a neighbour's children and once told them she had been a spy and had visited the Eagle's Nest.* Young Jim de Ropp, visiting from Germany, recalls her in knee-length leather boots, holding a gardening hook (she had been cutting the hedge) and her man-eating expression. He found her terrifying.

---

* She doubtless meant Hitler's retreat of the Berghof at the Obersalzburg near Berchtesgaden in Bavaria. The Eagle's Nest, now a mountain-top café, was part of the complex.

Jimmy chain-smoked and Ruth worried about her cottage burning down. In addition, Jimmy would be gratuitously rude about Ruth to neighbours. Eventually Ruth's tolerance was stretched too far and she moved Jimmy into a retirement home at Holmer, just to the north of Hereford, where Jimmy died in 1986.

Bill de Ropp's letters from his final years demonstrate his charm and humour. Complaining about the winter of 1967 he wrote to his granddaughter, 'I don't expect to warm up until my incineration,' and a couple of months later, 'As you may notice from this epistle, I am still more or less alive, sitting on the very edge of the knees of the Olympian Gods, a rather slippery and knobbly affair.'[685] In January 1970 Ruth wrote to Sue, 'Your grandfather is now very frail and nearly blind. The dogs are his only amusement.' In 1973 she wrote to Jim, 'Father was in a home where he goes now and again to give me a break.'[686]

Bill de Ropp, MI6's spy of the 1920s and 1930s, died on 3 October 1973 at Kingswood Hall, a care home at Kington near Peterchurch, aged eighty-seven. He left his whole estate of £964 to Jimmy. There was no funeral and there were no letters from the MI6 officers who had known him so well. There are strict rules preventing contact between retired officers and their agents. Frank Foley had died in 1958, Woollcombe in 1968, Menzies just three months after Woollcombe. Only Fred Winterbotham survived from the old team. One would like to think that, on hearing the news, he would have raised a glass to the Baron who had brought him so much success.

27

THE VERDICT

How important was the Bill de Ropp case?

It would obviously have been better if MI6 had had an agent closer to Hitler's secret intentions; someone with privileged access to Himmler, Goebbels or Göring. But such agents are vanishingly rare. Imagine in 2025 how difficult it would be to recruit an agent with access to Valdimir Putin's private thinking on Ukraine or Xi Jinping's innermost thoughts on Taiwan. Managing any such source and processing the intelligence would require a whole team of experts.

In that context it is remarkable that a financially and intellectually impoverished service like MI6 between the two world wars could have run an agent so close to Hitler's inner circle. It is easy enough to identify the various failings but MI6 had never had to deal with a case of such complexity before.

Human intelligence is an intensely complicated science because it involves human beings. Misjudging human beings is what we all do most of the time. If we could get better at assessing each other and our motives there would be less discord and conflict.

By any standards the Bill de Ropp case was complex because there were so many variables and because he fulfilled so many roles. The variables included:

A British government that was unclear about how it intended to deal with a resurgent Germany right up to the very last moment. There was no clear policy beyond an appeasement about which most (but not all) protagonists felt increasingly uncomfortable.

An intelligence service that was used to low-level tactical reporting but not yet accustomed to strategic nation-state espionage. In truth it had not yet developed the skills to run a case of the complexity of Bill de Ropp.

Case officers with strong political views of their own who may have unduly influenced the agent. There seems to have been no system for checking what Bill de Ropp should say to Rosenberg on key issues. Nor is it clear that an agreed formula would ever have emerged from a putative committee comprising the FO, MI6 and the Air Ministry.

Bill de Ropp was a man with intense loyalty to Britain but he had other motives too: notably a hatred of Soviet Russia, a degree of sympathy with the old German aristocracy, and a hankering for the old order in the Baltic States.

His most important source (Rosenberg) was an oddball who had access to the top of the regime but was widely ridiculed and ignored. This had advantages (notably ease of access to a man who was not as busy as Himmler or Goebbels) but also disadvantages (in that he was not kept abreast of Hitler's innermost thoughts).

At the same time that Bill de Ropp was Britain's secret agent against the Nazi political target he was also Rosenberg's 'English adviser'. In many ways this helped reinforce his access and his cover but there needed to be a system for approving what he would tell Rosenberg and others on return from each of his visits to London.

He never had one dedicated case officer. Foley and Insall were constrained by the hostile environment in Berlin to receiving his latest reports and relaying them to London. Woollcombe was the officer who met him most and prepared his material for distribution in Whitehall. Winterbotham was the closest approximation to a Case Officer but was mostly engaged with the Air Force aspects of the case. On the back of the photograph of him and de Ropp on the Baltic Coast he has written: 'In Germany 1936 with Baron Bill de Ropp, my agent and confidant of Hitler'. The person who regarded him most as his Joe (the MI6 terminology of the time) was Menzies but he became too senior to be closely involved.

If those were the variables then it was very fortunate that MI6 had an officer of the calibre of Malcolm Woollcombe to try to make sense of the reporting which emerged from this multiplicity of factors. When we add Bill de Ropp's plethora of roles the picture becomes even more demanding:

Bill de Ropp's prime role was to produce political and military intelligence on Nazi Germany, such as the regime's plans for Eastern Europe and von Reichenau's early exposition of Blitzkrieg in 1934.

As a side-effect of his cover-role as the local representative of Bristol Aeroplane Company, he developed an important ability to report on German aircraft production and technical developments, primarily through arranging visits by Bartlett and Fedden.

With Woollcombe he also became MI6's main analyst on Nazi Germany. The three big surviving strategic reports on Germany were full of his analysis and many of the judgements were based on his (and some other) prior reporting.

By default he became an agent of influence. His long discussions with Rosenberg and von Harder in 1939 and 1940 raise fundamental questions about what he was being asked to say. A secret agent cannot convey British government policy without burning himself. On the other hand, it can be very damaging for an agent with influence over a significant, albeit flawed, personality like Rosenberg to espouse ideas which are at odds with the national interest.

As we saw from his report from the Kaiserhof Hotel in Berlin he provided low-level personality reporting in support of MI5's counter-intelligence requirements.

He had a liaison role with Ukrainian opposition movements simultaneously for both MI6 and for Rosenberg. He also tracked the Danzig and Memel issues for both countries.

He organised and accompanied trips of influential Britons to Nazi Germany both for Rosenberg and for Menzies and Winterbotham. He attended every Nuremberg Rally between 1933 and 1938.

With those extensive roles it is little wonder that Bill and Jimmy occasionally needed to travel to London for rest and recuperation. Just simple spying can be exhausting, but to have so many parts to play, each with its own implications for cover and purpose, must have constantly required reassessment and recalibration. He was lucky to have Jimmy with whom to discuss these issues. She seems both to have relished the challenge and to have been a reassuring influence.

Claude Dansey's simplistic view of the Bill de Ropp case failed to understand any of this complexity. He was a man in a hurry with a major job to do; to turn the service from a small under-performing organisation into one which could help win a world war. For him all the pre-war nuance was just a distraction. It was unfortunate for de Ropp that he was marooned in Dansey's area of operations in Switzerland for nearly six years.

Even Dansey never alleged that de Ropp was a German agent but we should nevertheless examine the idea. Keith Jeffery questions which side got the most value from de Ropp but one suspects that he would not have asked the question if more of de Ropp's CX had survived in the National Archives and MI6 files.

In nine years in Berlin (1930–39) Bill de Ropp must have produced hundreds of CX reports. In the National Archives there are probably no more than two dozen, of which three are the big compilations discussed in Chapters 2 and 21. We know the quality of his reporting was good because of the Hankey Review. One of the papers which Woollcombe took home with him was from Vansittart when he was still PUS: 'I want to thank you most warmly . . . for the summary of Germany dated November 30th 1936. It is a most thorough and valuable record. Indeed I would say that your work as a whole is invaluable to me in this Office.'[687] With Bill de Ropp providing 70 per cent of Woollcombe's German XP (political reporting) the encomium equally attached to him.

If Bill de Ropp had been a German agent he would have been handled either by Heydrich's SD or by Canaris's Abwehr. Wenninger and Obermüller went on to join the Abwehr in the war and could theoretically have been Abwehr officers under cover while notionally working for Rosenberg. In theory Daufeldt could have been sent to Lausanne to maintain contact with de Ropp on behalf of Schellenberg.

However MI5 made sure that all the main Nazi intelligence officers were interrogated after the war. Some were more helpful than others but most knew that there was a chance of re-employment by the Allies against the Soviet Union if they could produce important intelligence. Nobody made the slightest suggestion that Bill de Ropp had worked for the Germans as an agent against Britain.

Among those interrogated were Nazis who had a particular knowledge of Britain, such as Walter Schellenberg,[688] Carl Marcus, Wilhelm Höttl and Hans Daufeldt of the SD, Richard Protze and Hermann Giskes of the Abwehr, Horst Kopkow of the Gestapo, Hans von Chappuis and Hans Thost of the APA, and Fritz Hesse. There are eighteen volumes of Schellenberg interrogation files alone. Not everyone was forthcoming but a large number of secrets emerged. In addition vast quantities of German intelligence records were captured after the war, none of which even mentioned Bill de Ropp, let alone questioned his loyalties.[689]

It is curious how few people who knew Bill de Ropp made any mention of him in their memoirs or diaries. There are plenty of references to him in Rosenberg's diaries. However, even though Bill de Ropp knew the journalistic community well, he receives not a single mention in William Shirer's books. Kurt Lüdecke does not allude to him by name although he may be 'the Englishman' with whom he celebrated the 4th of July over dinner outside Berlin, Lüdecke's last day of freedom in Germany.[690] A. L. Kennedy of *The Times* refers to him once and Ewan Butler just describes him once as a Baltic Baron. Elizabeth Wiskemann's biographer refers to dozens of her contacts but not to Bill de Ropp. Archibald Church mentions him only a few times, Harder devotes just two paragraphs to him, and Carl Burckhardt's papers mention him not at all.

One reason may be that Bill de Ropp deliberately kept a low profile. His relationship with Hitler was unknown except to very few. He did not advertise his connections to any of the senior Nazis – Rosenberg, von Epp, von Reichenau, Röhm, and Koch. He met his more junior sources like Schickedanz, Obermüller and Wenninger over dinner at one of the many good restaurants on the Kurfürstendamm.

It is also notable how few of the British visitors in 1934 and 1936 mentioned their guide, Bill de Ropp. Karslake makes no reference to him, neither does G. E. O. Knight nor the Reverend Hodson. Bill de Ropp was one of those people who may be seen as helpful and friendly but makes no lasting impression. Such people can make excellent spies because they seem so unthreatening.

There is another factor. Diarists often avoid mentioning people who they think might be involved in secret or nefarious activities, partly for fear of later complications and occasionally out of loyalty. The British Conservative Member of Parliament, Sir Page Croft, who was very friendly with Friedrich de Ropp (so much so that they sent their daughters to the same school in Bournemouth) makes no reference to him in his autobiography *My Life of Strife*. He may have suspected that Friedrich had been, and might still be, a German agent and that this would not reflect well on him if ever exposed.

Bill de Ropp's low profile helped him survive the Zinoviev Letter scandal without ever being mentioned in the dozens of books about the affair. That also kept him out of the crosshairs of Soviet Intelligence (from the OGPU to the KGB). Berlin in the 1920s and even the early 1930s was teeming with Soviet intelligence officers and agents. Bill de Ropp's involvement with Ukraine, the Baltics, Danzig and Memel would have brought him to their attention but in such a target-rich environment they presumably left him alone. The Soviets also had multiple penetrations of the German services and might well have considered an approach to de Ropp after the war but, by then, he had retired and lost his access.

The final question is whether the conviction that Winterbotham and Bill de Ropp shared that Nazi Germany and Soviet Russia should fight out their differences with Britain watching from the sidelines had any effect on real-world politics? And was it, as Bill de Ropp repeatedly claimed, a philosophy which was widely shared within the British Air Ministry and beyond? It was, after all, much the same ambition that Hitler, Hess and Rosenberg had espoused since the early 1920s.

Since the war there have been revisionist historians who have argued exactly that. John Charmley's *Churchill: The End of Glory* contended that Britain should not only have kept out of the war but should also have accepted Hitler's two peace offers in 1940 and explored the Hess offer in 1941.[691] Hitler could then have attacked the Soviet Union and the two malign powers could have destroyed each other. The debate was livened up by Alan Clark (a minister in the Thatcher government) supporting the argument.[692] Niall Ferguson later revisited the idea in his book *Virtual History*.

For our purposes, however, the more important point is whether such a lobby existed in Whitehall in the late 1930s. In 1942 John Moore-Brabazon was removed as Minister for Aircraft Production. The *Daily Herald* on 3 September 1941 quoted Jack Tanner of the Amalgamated Engineering Union: 'There are people in high places who declare that they hope the Russian and German armies will exterminate each other and while this is taking place we, the British Commonwealth, will so develop our air force and other armed forces that if Russia and Germany do destroy each other we shall have the dominating power in Europe.' The *Daily Herald* revealed that the speaker had been Brabazon. But that was in 1941 after the Nazi invasion of the Soviet Union and when the Soviets were important allies against Germany.

So who espoused such views in the 1930s? The idea of the Nazis fighting the Soviets attracted lots of Conservatives, many of whom would have avoided saying so too loudly in public. John Colville mentioned in his dairy in October 1939 that Arthur Rucker, Chamberlain's Principal Private Secretary, thought Soviet Russia was a bigger threat than Nazi Germany and that Britain 'must not destroy the possibility of uniting, if necessary, with a new German government against the common danger'.[693] Colville also remarked in 1941 that Moore-Brabazon's sentiments were 'widely felt'.[694]

Sir William Seeds, the British Ambassador in Moscow, is quoted by Colville as believing that 'all neutral states consider Russia more dangerous than Germany and would welcome our changing our present state of undeclared war against Moscow into a real one.'[695]

At an official level, there was a clear view that Britain should not get involved in Eastern Europe, including Poland. Austen Chamberlain (a former Foreign Secretary and Neville's half-brother) had 'famously informed Lord Crewe that no British Government ever will or ever can risk the bones of a British grenadier for the Polish corridor'.[696] Lord Simon, a former Foreign Secretary and the leading Liberal Party coalition member in the cabinet, advised after the assassination of Dollfuss: 'Our own policy is quite clear. We must keep out of trouble in Central Europe at all costs.'[697]

So Bill de Ropp could be forgiven for seeing the British guarantee to Poland as something of an outlier from mainstream British foreign policy thinking, because it was. The guarantee was issued hurriedly, without sufficient thought and consultation, and in a spirit of frustration.

Friedrich Gauss, the Head of the Legal Department of the German Foreign Ministry, quoted Ribbentrop in August 1939 during the talks which led to the Molotov-Ribbentrop Pact. Ribbentrop 'stated . . . that England had always been trying and was still trying to disrupt the good relations between Germany and the Soviet Union. England was weak and wanted to let others fight for its presumptuous claim to world domination.'[698] Who was Ribbentrop thinking of? Certainly not Neville Chamberlain, Horace Wilson or Lord Halifax. Perhaps he had Vansittart or Hankey in mind?

Even late in the day there were British establishment figures who were unpicking the deterrent effect of the Polish guarantee. When he visited Berlin to attend Hitler's fiftieth birthday Lord Brocket[699] told the head of Ribbentrop Bureau's English Section that Britain would not move if Germany seized Danzig, and the Duke of Buccleuch was reported to have confirmed this opinion. Even as late as August 1939 Rab Butler, one of Halifax's Foreign Office ministers, was still trying to weaken the Polish guarantee by suggesting Poland should make concessions to Germany and by urging Chamberlain and Wilson (who were still prepared to listen to such appeasement even at the eleventh hour) to offer colonies to Hitler in lieu of his invasion of Poland.[700]

It would therefore be absurd to claim that Bill de Ropp's statement to Rosenberg that Britain should not go to war over Poland caused the Führer to send his Panzers across the border a few days later, not least because Bill de Ropp (unlike Ribbentrop) insisted that Britain and France would fight.

However, the fiction of an opposition to Churchill in 1941 may have tipped Hess's calculation, following the failure of Haushofer's and Jahnke's diplomacy, to put on his flying jacket and strap into his ME-110.

By any standards Bill de Ropp was a major agent, certainly one of the most significant in MI6's history. That he also played a key role in the Zinoviev Letter, the Baltic States in 1919 and in Berlin in the late 1920s makes him one of the most long-lasting secret agents in history. That he lived to an old age and died peacefully in his bed is testament to his skill and resilience and to MI6's enhanced security arrangements. A veteran MI6 officer has said that 'I became aware that there were at least two "CSS only" [meaning the Chief (C or CSS) controlled the file] cases in the 1920s and that they had a Baltic provenance . . . but never got anywhere near identifying them.' That is testament to the secrecy accorded to the Bill de Ropp case.[701]

If he had been employed by a government with a clearer idea of its objectives and a service with more experience in running agents of strategic importance he might have achieved even more. Bill de Ropp helped put MI6 on the map. Without him 'What Should We Do?' could not have been written and MI6 might have remained a source of low-level tactical information rather than the global geopolitical service that it is today.

POSTSCRIPT

In January 2026 I stumbled across a document in the National Archives at Kew which reinforces most of the judgements made between Chapters 22 and 27. It is a note from Stewart Menzies to Henry Hopkinson (Cadogan's Private Secretary) dated 16th June 1941. It is reproduced overleaf. What does it show?

It demonstrates that Bill de Ropp was indeed sending to London the details of various messages from Rosenberg. As we know most or all of these were routed through Harder acting as Rosenberg's emissary.

However there were also messages being sent by General von Epp and even by someone in Goebbels' 'entourage'. Other than Jimmy's claim to have slept with Goebbels this is the first indication that Bill de Ropp had any connection with the propaganda minister.

From the tone of the messages one can see that Bill de Ropp, after he had moved to Switzerland at the outbreak of war, was viewed by the Nazis as a backchannel to London. It also confirms why Claude Dansey began to see de Ropp as a mouthpiece for German ideas (and unacceptable ones to boot) despite the valuable CX which he produced from the long discussions with Harder.

Crucially, if we are to believe the final paragraph, MI6 gave Bill de Ropp no material with which to respond to the German messages. He was left to fend for himself and, in so doing, was obliged to improvise. This led to the danger of Germany interpreting his thoughts as British government policy.

Finally Menzies was still concerned to protect the agent he recruited back in 1919; thus the request to Hopkinson to delete references to Rosenberg and von Epp from any wider distribution.

Note: Yōsuke Matsuoka was the pro-German Japanese Foreign Minister. He visited Berlin in March 1941 when Ribbentrop encouraged the Japanese to attack the strategic British base of Singapore. Presumably Berlin thought that London would prefer to sign a peace deal with Germany than risk losing a crucial outpost of her empire. At the time, however, Singapore was believed by the British to be impregnable.

MOST SECRET

Mr. Grey's excellent and comprehensive survey can be made more complete by including the following from the same source who reported Goebbels's message of the 4th March. If, however, there was any likelihood of this survey being given publicity, it would be preferable not to mention the names of Rosenberg and von Epp, but simply to refer to them as close associates of Hitler, or as members of the Nazi hierarchy.

17. Miscellaneous approaches through Switzerland.

(1) On the 13th June, 1940, a message was received in Switzerland from Rosenberg and von Epp expressing the hope that after the fall of Paris the British would make a peace initiative.

(2) Towards the end of June, 1940, a further message was received from these same Reichsleiter, expressing disappointment that Britain had not made use of the French collapse to secure the best terms for herself by making a peace initiative. Hitler, it was stated, would now be compelled to proceed with his plans against England. and the rising Bolshevik danger would force him to act with the least possible delay.

(3) On the 18th July, 1940, a message was received from Rosenberg, stating that now was the last moment for England to come to an understanding, otherwise her destruction was inevitable.

(4) On the 15th January, 1941, a message was received in Switzerland from another Nazi Reichsleiter. This was to the effect that the Italian setback would facilitate a compromise peace move by England, which would leave the Empire practically intact; but a British initiative was ~~practically~~ essential, as Hitler was unwilling to risk another snub. Recognition of the New Order and the return of Germany's colonies would be essential; otherwise the destruction of the British Empire was a certainty. This message hinted that the Gestapo and influential forces within the Nazi Party would support a British peace move.

(5) On the 18th March, 1941, a message was received from a member of Goebbels's entourage stating that the British would be well advised to find means of entering into conversations with the Germans. Matsuoka's visit to Germany, it was stated, might provide the last breathing space which could be utilised by the British to avoid final destruction.

(6) Towards the end of April, 1941, a further message was received from this member of Goebbels's entourage, stating that it was believed in Berlin that important changes in the British Government would follow on the collapse of the British in Greece, which would offer a possibility of peace negotiations before the final attack on England took place. The message added that a continuation of the severe air raids on Berlin would be likely to jeopardise peace chances, as they had infuriated Hitler.

(7) No replies were returned to any of these approaches.

16th June, 1941.

Extract from the note from Menzies to Hopkinson (TNA)

ACKNOWLEDGEMENTS

Secret agents tend to leave few traces and relatives are often reluctant to talk. Bill de Ropp was no exception. However, a few hours on the internet put me in touch with Eva Morgan in Peterchurch, a small village in Herefordshire's Golden Valley. She remembered the old Baron and recalled that he had a grandson and granddaughter in the United States.

My very first message – on LinkedIn to a de Ropp in South Carolina – scored a bullseye. Valerie put me in touch with her father, Jim, in Tennessee. He is Bill de Ropp's grandson and when, a few weeks later, I arrived from London there was a table piled high with family papers and photographs.

I should first thank Jim de Ropp who has followed my progress with great enthusiasm and made several important introductions. Also to Diane his wife who made me so welcome for nearly a week in their home, and to Sue Huntsman, Jeff de Ropp and Ryan de Ropp in the United States.

After many dozens of hours in the British National Archives at Kew it was time to go over to Germany and Lithuania. There followed an epic journey to Cologne, Munich, Nuremberg, Berlin, Rostock and finally Vilnius, Klapeida (formerly Memel) and Dauzogir. Wherever we went we were met with extraordinary hospitality and disturbing stories of wartime hardship. Attics and cellars were scoured for letters and photographs.

In Germany, my appreciation goes to Christoph and Hildegarde Böttcher, Fritz and Renata Böttcher, Dagmar von Stralendorff von Wallis, Jutta von Eichhorn, Babu de Ropp, Gundula Konold née von Wildemann, and Dietgard von Busse née von Schnurbein. Ulf and Godela von Samson-Himmelstjerna explained the complex story of the German Balts. In Lithuania we were assisted in finding Dauzogir, Eichenpomusch and Blaupomusch by Zivile Valousaityte.

In the UK, Robert Harding (former Chairman of the Savile Club) provided extensive access to the club records. Mike Adlem was very generous with his own research. Sally Maitland (nee Winterbotham) in Devon spoke about her father. Tamsyn Woollcombe and her sister Sara Stannus discussed their grandfather, Malcolm. Colonel Philip Horwood, John and Michael Whittall recalled their grandfather Hugh.

For insights into the Sprent family, I am grateful to Ross Smith, Ian and Tony Sprent in Australia and Catherine Sprent in London. For the Woodman connection Philip Hunter took a lot of tracking down but it was worth it in the end. David Ewart let me look at the lovely Court Hill House at Potterne and dug out some records.

Historians and academics Christopher Andrew, Mike Goodman, Huw Dylan, Michael Smith, Richard Langworth, Andrew (Lord) Roberts, Tony Blishen, Major-General Mungo Melvin, Colin Cohen, Clovis Meath-Baker and Tony Insall were generous with their time and knowledge. Lynn Insall kindly allowed me to quote from her father-in-law's memoir. Ngairi and Lecia Mettam provided German-language expertise.

Neil (Lord) Kinnock, Des (Lord) Browne and Gill Bennett helped considerably with the endlessly complicated Zinoviev Letter.

In Peterchurch, Eva Morgan proved to be an enthusiastic and active supporter with a phenomenal memory and knowledge of the area. She helped put me in touch with her son Glyn, Royston Parry, Carol Bowyer, Claire Rouse and others who provided insights into the Baron, Ruth de Ropp and the elusive Jimmy.

My wife, Ali, has been a tireless supporter of this project, which has taken us from the Golden Valley and the Zeppelin Field in Nuremberg to the shores of the Baltic and finally to the ruins of Dauzogir.

Thanks are also due to my literary agent, Tom Cull, and my editor at Bonnier Books, Toby Buchan.

Finally, my appreciation goes to the staff at the National Archives, the Imperial War Museum, the National Maritime Museum, the British Library, National Library of Wales, the Bodleian Special Collections, Cambridge University Library, Churchill College Cambridge, the Liddell Hart Archives at King's College London, Bishopsgate Institute, Warwick University, Herefordshire Archives and Aerospace Bristol. My thanks also to the researchers who scoured German and American archives for me, and to the Swiss Federal Archives, ETH Zurich, the Archives Cantonales de Vaud and du Valais and the Archives de Montreux.

SOURCES AND BIBLIOGRAPHY

The following are the main sources used. Additional sources, including all files viewed at the National Archives, fuller archival details and newspapers consulted, will be found in the Notes.

Primary sources that mention Bill de Ropp

Air Ministry files AIR series at the National Archives

Ancestry and Findmypast websites/genealogical and travel data

Army Lists 1914–1920 Liddell Hart Library and Imperial War Museum

Australian newspapers National Library of Australia, Trove website

Board of Trade files BT series at the National Archives

British newspapers British Newspaper Archive website

Cabinet Office files CAB series at the National Archives

Church, Archibald papers at Cambridge University Library

Demm, Eberhard *Friedrich von der Ropp and the Lithuanian Question 1916–1919*, Marburg, 1984

Documents on German Foreign Policy, Series C, Vol 3, London: HMSO, 1957

Documents on German Foreign Policy, Series D, Vol 7, London: HMSO, 1956

Documents on German Foreign Policy, Series D, Vol 8, London: HMSO, 1954

Fedden, Roy Reports on three visits to Germany in 1937 and 1938. National Archives and Warwick University

Foreign Office files FO series at the National Archives

Harder, Hermann von *Memories, Vols* 5 and 6. Archiv für Zeitgeschichte der Eidgenössischen Technischen Hochschule, Zurich, 1959–60

Insall, Cecil memoirs (privately held)

International Military Tribunal for Germany The Avalon Project, Yale Law School

Jeffery, Keith *MI6: The History of the Secret Intelligence Service 1909–1949*, London, 2010

Kennedy, A. L. *The Times and Appeasement: The Journals of AL Kennedy 1932–1939*, ed. Gordon Martel, Cambridge, 2000

Matthäus, Jürgen et al. *The Political Diary of Alfred Rosenberg and the onset of the Holocaust*, Lanham, MD, 2015

MI5 files KV series at the National Archives

Ropp, Friedrich von der MI5 Files. KV2/2830 and 2831, National Archives.

Ropp, Friedrich von der *Zwischen Gestern und Morgen*, Stuttgart, 1961

Ropp, Friedrich von der two letters sent to the German Foreign Ministry 1930 and 1931 (privately held)

Ropp, Robert de *Warrior's Way: A Twentieth Century Odyssey,* Nevada City, CA, 2002

Ropp, William de article in *The English Review*, 1932

Ropp, William de articles in *Outlook* Magazine, 1926-1927

Ropp, William de 'I spied on Hitler', *Daily Mail*, October 1957 (five articles)

Ropp, William de papers and photographs (privately held)

Savile Club Bulletins XI (September 2020), XIV (December 2020), XVII (April 2021)

Savile Club membership registers and bedroom books

Schlözer, Leopold von *Maria: Briefe einer Baltin aus verklungener Zeit* ('Maria: Letters from a Baltic Lady'), Dresden, 1940

Sonderfahndungsliste G.B. ('Special Search List Great Britain', known as The Black Book) Hoover Institution (https://digitalcollections.hoover.org/objects/55425/die-sonderfahndungsliste-gb) Hoover ID: DA585 .A1 G37 (V)

Swiss Newspaper Archive e-Newspaper Archives, CH website

Vaughan Williams, Ursula *R. V. W.: A Biography of Ralph Vaughan Williams*, Oxford and London, 1964

War Office papers WO series at the National Archives

Wildemann, Marina von 'Chronicles of the Wildemanns' (privately held)

Winterbotham, F. W. *Secret and Personal*, London, 1969

Winterbotham, F. W. *The Nazi Connection*. New York, 1978

Winterbotham, F. W. *The Ultra Spy: An Autobiography*, London, 1989

Winterbotham, F. W. Imperial War Museum Oral History, 7462, 36 reels, 1984

Secondary sources that mention Bill de Ropp

Cecil, Robert *The Myth of the Master Race: Alfred Rosenberg and Nazi Ideology*, London, 1972

Farago, Ladislas *The Game of the Foxes*, London,1971

Hastings, Max *The Secret War*, London, 2015

Heins, Nigel '*Flashback II*', *Hereford Times*, 2000

Howard, R. T. *Spying on the Reich: The Cold War against Hitler*, Oxford, 2023

Pool, James et al. *Who Financed Hitler: The Secret Funding of Hitler's Rise to Power, 1919–1933*, New York, 1978

Watt, Donald Cameron *How War Came*, London, 1989

Wittman, Robert et al. *The Devil's Diary: Alfred Rosenberg and the Stolen Secrets of the Third Reich*, London, 2016

Additional sources of reference

Berlin street, telephone and postal directories 1927–1941

Bristol Review, Aircraft Issue, Vols 1 and 2, Bristol Aeroplane Company, 1931 and 1937

Bristol Review, Engine Issue, Vols 1 to 15, Bristol Aeroplane Company 1930–1939

Cash Book No 9. 1936–1940, Bristol Aeroplane Company, Aerospace Bristol, Filton.

Conference of Governors of the British East African Dependencies *International Labour Review,* Vol. 15, No. 3, (March 1927), Geneva

Documents on British Foreign Policy 1919–1939, London, HMSO, 1949

Dodis: Diplomatic Documents of Switzerland, website

Foreign Office List and Diplomatic and Consular Yearbook, London, 1919–1945

German newspapers: *Deutsches Zeitungsportal*, website

Report of the East Africa Commission, London: HMSO, 1925

Unpublished papers

Balderston, John L. papers at New York Public Library

Berrington, Major J. S. D. papers and photographs at the Imperial War Museum

Christie, Gp Capt M. G. papers at Churchill College, Cambridge

Darwin, Sqn Ldr C. J. W. papers at the Imperial War Museum

Dawson, Geoffrey papers at the Bodleian Library Oxford

Dutton, E. A. J. papers at Bodleian Library Oxford

Fedden, Sir Roy papers at the Imperial War Museum

Jones, Tom papers at the National Library of Wales

Karslake, Lt Gen Sir Henry papers at the Imperial War Museum

Reilly, Sir Patrick papers at the Bodleian Library, Oxford

Ropp, Friedrich von der papers (held by his family)

Ropp, Hanno von der memoir (held by his family)

Sinclair, Admiral Sir Hugh papers at the National Maritime Museum

Stralendorff, Margarethe von Memories of 1945 (held by her family)

Stralendorff, Margarethe von childhood memories (held by her family)

Vansittart, Robert (Lord) papers at Churchill College, Cambridge

Winterbotham, F. W. papers at the Imperial War Museum

Winterbotham, F. W. papers held by his family

Woollcombe, M. papers held by his family

Books

Andrew, Christopher *Her Majesty's Secret Service*, London, 1987

Andrew, Christopher *The Defence of the Realm: The Authorized History of MI5*, London, 2009

Avon, the Earl of *The Eden Memoirs: Facing the Dictators*, London, 1962

Barker, Ralph *The Royal Flying Corps in World War I*, London, 2002

SOURCES AND BIBLIOGRAPHY

Bayles, William D. *Postmarked Berlin*, London,1942

Beevor, Antony *Stalingrad*, London, 1998

Bennett, Gill *Churchill's Man of Mystery: Desmond Morton and the World of Intelligence*, Abingdon, 2007

Bennett, Gill *The Zinoviev Letter: The Conspiracy that Never Dies*, Oxford, 2018

Bennett, Gill *'A Most Extraordinary and Mysterious Business': The Zinoviev Letter of 1924* (History Notes), London, 1999

Bollmus, Reinhard *Das Amt Rosenberg und seine Gegner: Studien zum Machtkampf im nationalsozialistischen Herrschaftssystem* ('The Rosenberg Office and its opponents: Studies on the power struggle in the National Socialist system of rule'), Stuttgart, 1970

Bower, Tom *The Perfect English Spy,* London, 1995

Boyle, Andrew *Montagu Norman*, London, 1967

Braunschweig, Pierre-Th. *Secret Channel to Berlin: The Masson-Schellenberg Connection and Swiss Intelligence in World War II*, Havertown, 2004

Brook-Shepherd, Gordon *The Storm Petrels: The First Soviet Defectors, 1928–1938*, London, 1977

Brook-Shepherd, Gordon *The Iron Maze: The Western Secret Services and the Bolsheviks*, London, 1998

Casey, William *The Secret War Against Hitler*, Washington, 1988

Cave Brown, Anthony *'C': The Secret Life of Sir Stewart Graham Menzies, Spymaster to Winston Churchill*, London and New York, 1987

Channon, Henry *Chips. The Diaries 1938-43* (ed. Robert Rhodes James), London, 1967

Chester, Lewis et al. *The Zinoviev Letter*, London, 1967

Colville, John *The Fringes of Power: Downing Street Diaries*, Vol. 1, London, 1985

Colvin, Ian *Admiral Canaris - Chief of Intelligence*, London, 1951

Colvin, Ian *The Chamberlain Cabinet*, London, 1971

Conwell-Evans, T. P. *None So Blind: A Study of the Crisis Years 1930–1939*, London, 1947

Croft, Brigadier General Lord *My Life of Strife*, London, 1948

Cross, J .A. *Lord Swinton*, Oxford, 1982

Dewar, Hugo *Assassins at Large: being a fully documented and hitherto unpublished account of the executions outside Russia ordered by the GPU*, London, 1951

Dilks, David (ed.) *The Diaries of Sir Alexander Cadogan 1938–1945*, London, 1971

Dodd, William (ed.) *Ambassador Dodd's Diary*, New York and London, 1941 and 1942

Douglas-Hamilton, James *The Truth about Rudolf Hess*, Barnsley, 2016

Edelman, Maurice *The Mirror: A Political History*, London, 1966

Erlacher, Trevor *Ukrainian Nationalism in the Age of Extremes*, Harvard, 2021

Ferris, John *Intelligence and Strategy: Selected Essays*, London, 2005

Field, Geoffrey *Elizabeth Wiskemann: Scholar, Journalist, Secret Agent*, Oxford, 2023

Fink, Jesse *The Eagle in the Mirror: In Search of War Hero, Master Spy and Alleged Traitor Charles Howard 'Dick' Ellis*, Sydney, 2023

Fisher, H.A. L. *An Unfinished Autobiography*, London, 1940

Fritzsche, Hans *The Sword in the Scales*, London, 1953

Gannon, Franklin Reid *The British Press and Germany, 1936–1939*, Oxford, 1971

Garleff, Michel *Deutschbalten, Weimarer Republik und Drittes Reich* ('German Baltics, Weimar Republic and Third Reich'), Vienna, 2008

Garnett, David *The Secret History of PWE: The Political Warfare Executive 1939–1945*, London, 2002

Gilbert, Martin *Prophet of Truth: Winston S. Churchill 1922–1939* (Vol. 5), London, 1976

Gilbert, Martin *Finest Hour: Winston S. Churchill 1939-1941* (Vol. 6), London, 1983

Godfrey, Major E. G. *The History of the Duke of Cornwall's Light Infantry 1939-1945*, Aldershot, 1966

Goodman, Michael S. *The Official History of the Joint Intelligence Committee*, London, 2015

Grose, Peter *Gentleman Spy: The Life of Allen Dulles*, New York, 1994

Gunston, Bill *Fedden – The Life of Sir Roy Fedden*, Derby, 1998

Hanfstaengl, Ernst *The Unknown Hitler: Notes from the Young Nazi Party 1921–1936*, London, 2004

Hartmann, Woldemar *Erinnerungen 1874–1962* ('Memories 1874–1962'), Norderstedt, 2004

Haslam, Jonathan *The Spectre of War: International Communism and the Origins of World War II*, Princeton, 2021

Hassell, Agostino von et al. *Alliance of Enemies*, New York, 2006

Hassell, Ulrich von *The Von Hassell Diaries 1938–1944: The Story of the Forces against Hitler inside Germany*, Boulder, 1994

Heiden, Konrad *Der Fuehrer: Hitler's Rise to Power*, London, 1944

Heineman, John L. *Hitler's First Foreign Minister: Constantin Freiherr Von Neurath*, Berkeley, 1980

Henderson, Nevile *Failure of a Mission: Berlin 1937–1939*, London, 1940

Hesse, Fritz *Hitler and the English*, London, 1954

Hiden, John *Defender of Minorities: Paul Schiemann 1876–1944*, London, 2004

Hinsley, F. H. et al. *British Intelligence in the Second World War*, Vol. 1, London, 1979

Hoffmann, Peter *The History of the German Resistance, 1933–1945*, Harvard, 1988

Hooton, E. R. *Phoenix Triumphant: The Rise and Rise of the Luftwaffe*, London, 1994

Jones, R. V. *Most Secret War: British Scientific Intelligence 1939–1945*, London, 1978

Jones, Thomas *A Diary with Letters 1931–1950*, Oxford and London, 1954

Kahn, David *Hitler's Spies. German Military Intelligence in World War II*, London, 1978

Kelly, David *The Ruling Few, or The Human Background to Diplomacy*, London, 1952

Kempka, Erich *I was Hitler's Chauffeur: The Memoirs of Erich Kempka*, Barnsley, 2010

Kennedy, Aubrey *The Times and Appeasement: The Journals of A. L. Kennedy, 1932–1939* (ed. Gordon Martel), Cambridge, 2001

Kershaw, Ian *Making Friends with Hitler: Lord Londonderry and Britain's Road to War*, London, 2004

Knight, G. E. O. *In Defence of Germany*, London, 1934

Landau, Henry *All's Fair: The Story of the British Secret Service Behind the German Lines*, New York, 1934

Larson, Erik *In the Garden of Beasts*, London, 2011

Lewin, Ronald *Ultra Goes to War*, London, 1978

Lochner, Louis (ed.) *The Goebbels Diaries*, London, 1948

Londonderry, the Marquess of *Ourselves and Germany*, London, 1938

Longerich, Peter *Goebbels*, London, 2015

Lüdecke, Kurt G. W. *I Knew Hitler: The Story of a Nazi Who Escaped The Blood Purge*, New York, 1937

Moravec, Frantisek *Master of Spies: The Memoirs of General Frantisek Moravec*, London, 1975

Michie, Lindsay *Portrait of an Appeaser: Robert Hadow, First Secretary in the British Foreign Office, 1931–39*, Westport, 1996

Nayler, J. L. et al. *Flight To-day*, London, 1937

Neave, Airey *Nuremberg*, London, 1978

Nicolson, Nigel *Alex: The Life of Field Marshal Earl Alexander of Tunis*, London, 1973

Northcliffe, Lord *At the War*, London, 1941

Pearson, Michael *The Sealed Train: Journey to Revolution. Lenin – 1917*, London, 1975

Petkunas, Darius *Lithuanian Lutheran Church during World War Two*, University of Klapeida, 2014

Philby, Kim *My Silent War: The Autobiography of a Spy*, London, 1968

Phillips, Robert Foster *British Policy in the Baltic Region*, PhD thesis, Oregon, 1957

Pincher, Chapman *Their Trade is Treachery: The Full, Unexpurgated Truth about the Russian Penetration of the World's Secret Defences*, London, 1981

Read, Anthony et al. *Colonel Z: The Secret Life of a Master of Spies*, London, 1984

Roberts, Glyn *The Most Powerful Man in the World: The Life of Sir Henri Deterding*, London, 2018

Roskill, Stephen *Hankey: Man of Secrets*, Vol. 3, London, 1974

Schacht, Hjalmar *My First Seventy-Six Years*, London, 1955

Schellenberg, Walter *The Schellenberg Memoirs: A Record of the Nazi Secret Service*, London, 1956

Schweppenburg, Geyr von *The Critical Years*, London, 1952

Shirer, William *Berlin Diary 1934–1941*, London, 1942

Shirer, William *The Rise and Fall of the Third Reich: A History of Nazi Germany*, New York, 1960

Sisman, Adam *Hugh Trevor-Roper: The Biography*, London, 2010

Smith, Michael *Foley: The Spy Who Saved 10,000 Jews*, London, 1999

Smith, Michael *Six: A History of Britain's Secret Intelligence Service*, London, 2010

Smith, Howard K. *Last Train from Berlin*, London, 1942

Speer, Albert *Spandau: The Secret Diaries*, London, 1976

Spicer, Charles *Coffee with Hitler: The British Amateurs Who Tried to Civilise the Nazis*, London, 2022

Sprent, James *For Women: Advice from a Medical Practitioner*, Hobart, 1926

Stevenson, William *Intrepid's Last Case*, London, 1984

Sudoplatov, Pavel *Special Tasks: The Memoirs of an Unwanted Witness – A Soviet Spymaster*, London, 1994

Taylor, Frederick *Dresden: Tuesday, February 13, 1945*, London, 2004

Taylor, Telford *Munich: The Price of Peace*, New York, 1979

Templewood, Viscount *Nine Troubled Years*, London, 1954

Tobias, Fritz *The Reichstag Fire: Legend and Truth*, London, 1962

Ustinov, Peter *Dear Me*, London, 1977

Vansittart, Lord *The Mist Procession*, London, 1958

Ward Price, George *I Know These Dictators*, London, 1938

Weitz, John *Hitler's Diplomat: Joaquim von Ribbentrop*, London, 1992

West, Nigel *MI6: British Secret Service Intelligence Operations 1909–45*, London, 1983

West, Nigel and Tsarev, Oleg *The Crown Jewels. The British Secrets Exposed by the KGB Archives*, London, 1998

Whitwell, John *British Agent*, London, 1966

Wrench, John *Geoffrey Dawson and Our Times*, London, 1955

Wright, Peter *Spy Catcher*, Richmond (NSW), 1987

Young, A. P. *The 'X' Documents: The Secret History of Foreign Office Contacts with the German Resistance 1937–1939*, London, 1974

Young, Kenneth (ed.) *The Diaries of Sir Robert Bruce Lockhart*, Vol. I, *1915–1938*, London, 1973

Articles

Andrew, Christopher 'The British Secret Service and Anglo-Soviet Relations in the 1920s Part I', *The Historical Journal*, September 1977

Andrew, Christopher 'More on the Zinoviev Letter', *The Historical Journal*, 22, 1 (1979), pp. 211–4

Anon 'That Confounded Zinoviev Letter', *New Statesman*, 10 March 1928, pp. 684 –5

Carr, E. H. 'Communications: The Zinoviev Letter,' *The Historical Journal*, 22, 1 (1979), pp. 209–10

Crowe, Sybil ' The Zinoviev Letter: A Reappraisal', *Journal of Contemporary History*, July 1975

Demm, Eberhard 'Propaganda and Caricature in the First World War', *Journal of Contemporary History*, January 1993

Dongen, Luc van 'Le refuge des vaincus', *Annales valaisannes: Bulletin trimestriel de la Société d'histoire du Valais romand*, 2005, pp.141 –59

Goldstein, Eric 'Neville Chamberlain, the British Official Mind and the Munich Crisis', *Diplomacy & Statecraft*, 1999

Grant, Natalie 'The Zinoviev Letter Case', *Soviet Studies*, 1967

Kalijarvi, Thorsten 'The Problem of Memel', *American Journal of International Law*, Vol. 30, Issue 2, April 1936, pp. 204–15

Kangeris, Kārlis 'The Repatriation of the Baltic Germans after the signing of the Pacts', 2004

McDonough, Frank 'Norman Ebbutt and the Nazis, 1927–37', *Journal of Contemporary History*, July 1992

Senn, Alfre d'Garlawa: A Study in Émigré Intrigue, 1915-1917', *The Slavonic and East European Review*, Vol. 45, No. 105, July 1967, pp. 411–24

Thompson, Lee '"To Tell the People of America the Truth": Lord Northcliffe in the USA, Unofficial British Propaganda June–November 1917', *Journal of Contemporary History*, Vol. 34, No. 2, April 1999, pp. 243–62

Wark, Wesley 'British Intelligence on the German Air Force and Aircraft Industry 1933-1939', *The Historical Journal*, September 1982

Wolf, John 'Memelland: A Focal Point in Contemporary Diplomacy', *World Affairs*, December 1935

NOTES

1 Cecil, Robert, *Myth of the Master Race*, p. 2. Cecil had worked at MI6. Bill de Ropp was by far the most accessible of Rosenberg's close associates still alive when Cecil was writing his book.
2 Neave, *Nuremberg*, p. 109
3 Ibid., p. 110
4 Ibid., pp. 112–3
5 TNA FO 1019/40A
6 Kingsbury Smith, 'The Execution of Nazi War Criminals', UMKC Law School website (accessed 23 March 2024)
7 He would be knighted in 1939 as a KCMG
8 Andrew, *Her Majesty's Secret Service*, p. 350
9 Foreign Office List, 1939, p. A3
10 I have based this paragraph on several conversations with senior FO and MI6 officers in the early 1980s. Most of them had started their careers in the 1940s.
11 Dilks, *Cadogan Diaries*, pp. 43, 44
12 Andrew, pp. 344–5
13 Discussion with the Woollcombe family 22 February 2024
14 TNA FO 371/21659
15 In MI6 an intelligence officer is a salaried member of MI6 staff and thus a British government employee. By contrast, an agent will usually have his or her own job (or other position) with access to secrets on overseas threats to the United Kingdom.
16 Jeffery, *MI6*, pp. 297
17 For a full analysis of 821's sub-sources see Chapters 14 and 15
18 Letter held by the Woollcombe family
19 Plaudits held among the Woollcombe family papers
20 See Lewin, *Ultra*, 1978

21 See Masterman, *The Double Cross System*, Yale, 1972

22 *The Daily News* was part of the *News Chronicle* owned by the Cadbury family, following its merger with the *Daily Chronicle* in 1930

23 Malcolm Woollcombe's eldest son, Robert, a young officer in the 6th Battalion of the King's Own Scottish Borderers (KOSB), had embarked at the same port only six days earlier (D+9). The previous day he had waved goodbye to his anxious father outside the family home in Hove.

24 Peter Lawrence, *News Chronicle* journalist and editor of CBI News, *Press Gazette* 11 March 2004

25 *Documents on German Foreign Policy*, Series D Vol. VIII, p. 713, dated 27 January 1940

26 Ibid., p. 785 dated 19 February 1940

27 Ibid., p. 134 dated 25 September 1939

28 Ibid., pp. 363–8, undated

29 Baltic Germans (mostly landlords of German descent living in Latvia and Estonia plus a few from Lithuania) had been displaced by the Molotov-Ribbentrop Pact and were eventually rehoused, mostly in the Poznan (Posen) region of Poland.

30 Consulted at the Hereford Archives and Record Centre.

31 Wittman et al., *The Devil's Diary*, pp. 1, 2, 59–60

32 *Documents on German Foreign Policy*, Series D Vol. VII

33 *Daily Mail*, 12 February 1957, p .6

34 'I Spied on Hitler', *Daily Mail*, 28, 29, 30, 31 October and 1 November1957

35 Stephen Dorril, '"Russia accuses Fleet Street": Journalists and MI6 during the Cold War', *The International Journal of Press/Politics*, Vol. 20, issue 2, March 2015

36 F. von der Ropp, *Zwischen Gestern und Morgen*, 1961

37 Many of these works of art are still kept at Göttingen University. See Georg-August-Universität Göttingen website (accessed 4 November 2023).

38 F. von der Ropp. *Zwischen Gestern und Morgen*

39 Chronicles of the Wildemanns by Marina von Wildeman

40 See for example the *Middlesex Gazette*, 7 September 1895

41 Darius Staliunas. 'Antisemitic tension during the 1905 revolution in Lithuania', on the Lithuanstika website (accessed 2 November 2023)

42 *Daily Mail*, 28 October 1957, p. 4

43 *Daily Post* (Hobart), 7 August 1909, p. 10

44 Family of Albert Bulteel Fisher and Edith Jacob. From woodlloydfamilyhistory.com (accessed 3 November 2023)

45 *Her Love's Apprentice* (London, 1913); involves a flirtatious woman and a visit to Dresden

46 *Bath Chronicle and Weekly Gazette*,14 April 1910

47 *Sydney Morning Herald*, 5 January 1910

48 *Encounter* would later be transferred to the Royal Australian Navy. See Wikipedia page for HMAS *Encounter* (1902) (accessed 3 November 2023)

49 The *Hobart Daily Post*, 16 July 1910, p. 9

50 The *Coolgardie Miner*, 20 October 1910, p. 2, with a longer list printed in the *New South Wales Police Gazette* of 19 October: a pearl brooch with flower and leaves in pearls; an uncut turquoise pendant; two enamel pendants; a pearl and amethyst pendant, amethyst surrounded with pearls; a pendant with hanging stones, pink tourmalines, gold and enamel; a gold neck-chain; a gold bracelet, links set with amethysts and pearls; a blue enamel watch; a paste pendant, with heart set with a blue stone; a paste brooch; an old paste buckle; a gold safety pin brooch with green stone; two pairs of earrings and a number of small brooches.

NOTES

51 *Adelaide Advertiser*, 11 October 1910, p. 10
52 Amethyst is found in many places but Lithuania is a significant exporter of the mineral
53 *The Mercury*, 23 December 1910, p. 8
54 *Melbourne Leader*, 11 February 1911, p. 46
55 *The Australasian*, 4 March 1911, p. 49
56 See Potterne on the Great English Churches website (accessed 3 November 2023)
57 *The Times*, 16 January 1912, p. 4
58 From 'Willans and Robinson to GEC and Alstom' by Judith Court, 31 October 2003. Originally written for the *Coventry Evening Telegraph*. Available on the Free Library website (accessed 3 November 2023)
59 My thanks to Blundells School for these details
60 TNA HO 144 1402
61 Ray Westlake, *British Regiments at Gallipoli*, London, 1996
62 Nayler et al., *Flight Today*, 1942 ed. pp. 80–81
63 Ralph Barker, *The Royal Flying Corps in World War One*, pp. 89–93
64 H. A. Jones, *The War in the Air*, Oxford, 1928, p. 199
65 This was Franklin Juler who had lost his own brother in the early months of the war. See *Plarr's Lives of the Fellows*, Royal College of Surgeons website (accessed 6 November 2023)
66 TNA WO 339/31427
67 The personal papers and photographs of his Commanding Officer Major J. S. D. Berrington are in the Imperial War Museum
68 IWM Photographs of Major J. S. D. Berrington, Ref. 2005-06-08
69 Robert de Ropp, *Warrior's Way*, pp. 4–5
70 Charles Fisher would be killed at the Battle of Jutland, 1916, when his ship HMS *Invincible* blew up in a scene witnessed by his brother William, who was the captain of HMS *St Vincent* (Fisher papers at Churchill College, Cambridge).
71 TNA KV 2830/1 Folio 22
72 Extract from a letter sent by Friedrich von der Ropp to the German Foreign Ministry on 3 September 1930. Privately held by the Böttcher family
73 It is interesting that Grey was the only senior member of the British Cabinet to support President Woodrow Wilson's 1916 peace initiative. So Ballin's hunch may have been valid. See David R. Woodward, 'Great Britain and President Wilson's effort to end World War I in 1916', *Maryland Historian* (1970)
74 Andrew, op. cit. pp. 182–4
75 Ibid. pp. 185–6
76 Ibid. p. 187
77 Jaime Reynolds in *Journal of Liberal History* 47, Summer 2005
78 Ibid. p. 174
79 TNA KV 2/2830 and 2831
80 TNA HO 144/1402/273161
81 TNA KV 2/2830 and 2831
82 *London and China Telegraph*, 2 December 1902, p. 4
83 *Army and Navy Gazette*, 30 May 1903
84 J. Lee Thompson, 'Lord Northcliffe in the USA', *Journal of Contemporary History*, Vol. 34, No. 2, April 1999, pp. 243–62
85 TNA T/12212/41059
86 *Daily Mail*, 28 October 1957, p. 4

87 Eberhard Demm, 'Propaganda at home and abroad', *International Encyclopaedia of the First World War*, June 2017

88 During the war von Maltzan served as a lieutenant in the Mecklenburg Dragoons, but in the spring of 1917 was transferred to diplomatic duty as representative of the Wilhelmstrasse (German Foreign Office) at general headquarters and later represented the Chancellor on the eastern front, where he made himself so thoroughly unpopular by opposing the militarists that he was transferred to The Hague, Netherlands. See his obituary in *Time* magazine, 3 October 1927

89 Extract from a letter sent by Friedrich von der Ropp to the German Foreign Ministry on 3 September 1930, Privately held by the Böttcher family

90 F. von der Ropp, *Zwischen Gestern und Morgen*

91 See for example the *Journal de Genève*, 30 June 1916

92 *Morning Post*, 29 November 1916

93 Pearson, *The Sealed Train*

94 TNA KV 2 2830/1 Folio35

95 TNA KV 2830/1 Folio 28

96 Simon Robbins, *British Generalship on the Western Front in the First World War, 1914–1918*, PhD thesis, 2001, p. 145

97 Churchill quoted in Hansard on 17 March 1920

98 Robert de Ropp, *Warrior's Way*, pp. 5–6

99 Jeffery, *MI6*, p. 295

100 Landau, *All's Fair*, pp. 96–7

101 Ibid., p. 228

102 Smith, *Foley*, pp. 3–18

103 Ibid., pp. 111–41

104 Jeffery, pp. 267–71

105 Ibid., p. 154

106 See Spitfires of the Sea website. (accessed 13 November 2023)

107 Brook-Shepherd, *The Iron Maze*, pp. 145–6

108 *The Oregon Daily Journal*, 19 April 1919, p. 4

109 TNA FO/371 4381. Report No 12, 11 July 1919

110 Armistice Agreement with Germany. Clause XII. Available on Census.gov (accessed 17 April 2024)

111 Robert Foster Phillips, 'British policy in the Baltic region – 1919', (PhD thesis, Oregon University, 1957)

112 Crozier's colourful military career is told by Charles Messenger in *Broken Sword: The Tumultuous Life of General Frank Crozier 1897– 1937*, Barnsley, 2014

113 *Dictionary of Irish Biography*: Crozier, Frank Percy

114 This comes from a quote by Sir Henry Wilson: 'Our real danger now is not the Boche but Bolshevism', Jeffery, p. 172. In the Baltic States in 1919 it was both.

115 Nigel Nicolson, *Alex*, pp. 47–66

116 TNA FO/371 3609 Folio 179

117 Eberhard Demm, *Friedrich von der Ropp and the Lithuanian question*. There had actually been an earlier plot: this was Friedrich's second and much more serious attempt.

118 Paul Schiemann, Wikipedia entry (accessed 17 November 2023)

119 This letter is dated 29 December 1919 but was clearly referring to events a few months earlier.

120 Northcliffe, who already owned the *Daily Mail*, had bought *The Times* in 1908.

NOTES

121 This is a very truncated version of Marina von Wildemann's account of events in 'Chronicles'.
122 Ibid.
123 A more detailed account of the coup plotting can be found in *Documents on British Foreign Policy 1919–1939* First Series Vol 3, pp. 141, 167–71, 193–4, 203, 241
124 TNA FO 371 3609 Folio 280
125 TNA KV 2/2830/2 Folio 43
126 Gediminas Vaskela, 'The Land Reform of 1919-1940: Lithuania and the Countries of Eastern and Central Europe', *Lithuanian Historical Studies*, Nov. 1996, pp. 124–5
127 Smith, *Six*, pp. 16–17
128 Ibid. p. 16. Smith thinks this man is George Rollo but Bernard's profile as a top banker better fits the description.
129 TNA BT 31/32434/168401
130 Gilbert died in 1932 and Bernard in 1935. The company was wound up between 1936 and 1938
131 Post Office London Directories 1919–1923
132 Bennett, *The Zinoviev Letter*, p. 254
133 Smith, *Six*, p. 308
134 Bennett, *The Zinoviev Letter*, pp. 26–8
135 TNA FO 371/10478 Folio 145. The initials MW are clearly visible
136 Bennett, '*A Most Extraordinary and Mysterious Business*', pp. 91–2
137 Gill Bennett's notes indicate that she was not shown Bill de Ropp's file (12821) during her visits to the MI6 archive. Her email to the author, 18 December 2022
138 Bennett, '*A Most Extraordinary and Mysterious Business*', pp. 91–2
139 West and Tsarev, *Crown Jewels*, p. 42
140 Ship's manifest and list of passengers (accessed on the Ancestry website)
141 Jim de Ropp in conversation with the author 30 January 2023
142 Robert de Ropp, *Warrior's Way*, pp. 1–19
143 TNA KV 2/2830 Folios 1–6. Letter from Gerard Clauson to Vernon Kell dated 28 July 1926
144 TNA CO 962/1 and CO 962/2
145 Report of the East Africa Commission, HMSO, 1925
146 Archibald Church papers at Cambridge University Library. Add. 9560 File 13
147 Elspeth Huxley. Introduction to *The Night of the Hyaena* by E. A. T. Dutton. Microfiche Acc 587. The Bodleian, Oxford
148 TNA KV 2/2830/2 Folios 1-5. Gerard Clauson to Vernon Kell dated 28 July 1926 marked Secret
149 TNA KV 2/2830/1 Folio 6
150 TNA KV 2//2830/2 Folio 29–31. PCO Berlin letter dated 1 April 1924
151 Ibid. Folio 33. Menzies to Ball, dated 5 April 1924
152 Ibid. Folio 27. Ball to Menzies, dated 6 May 1924
153 Ibid. Folio 26. Menzies to Ball, dated 15 May 1924
154 Ibid. Folio 28. Home Office minute copied to MI5, dated 10 April 1924
155 Ibid. Folios 8–9. Metropolitan Police letter dated 11 January 1926
156 TNA FO 371/10478 Folios 132–3
157 Ibid. Folios 118–9
158 Ibid. Folios 115–7
159 Chester et al., pp. 106–8
160 Whitwell (Nicholson), *British Agent*, p. 65
161 Bennett, *The Zinoviev Letter*, p. 53
162 Ibid., p .193

163 Farina may have been involved in another mystery. Alan Sargeant explains in his *Murder on the Hastings Express*, available online via www.academia.edu
164 Mistakenly called Charles in many books, including by Bennett
165 William Lewis Blennerhassett, Great War Forum (accessed 20 November 2023)
166 Foreign Office List for 1921
167 Savile Club Registers. Proposal of A. M. van Ostveen of 109 Ebury Street. April 1922 (consulted 8 March 2023)
168 Bennett, *The Zinoviev Letter*, p. 134
169 TNA BT 32434/168401
170 Robert de Ropp, *Warrior's Way*, p. 18
171 MI6 could have cut a corner by producing just the translation, which might explain why the alleged original could not be found
172 Bennett, *The Zinoviev Letter*, p. 138
173 Chester et al., pp. 201, 204–6
174 Ibid., pp.97–107
175 West and Tsarev, pp. 40–1
176 Lord Kinnock in an email to the author 25 September 2024
177 Alumni Cantabrigienses, Roy Francis Truscott, p. 238
178 Europeans in East Africa website, Roy Francis Truscott
179 *The Sphere*, 16 July 1927
180 Robert de Ropp *Warrior's Way*, p. 6
181 The diary is in Cambridge University Library GBR/0012/MS Add.9560. File 13
182 The Siemens-Schuckert Shannon Power Scheme document is on the JSTOR website
183 Robert de Ropp *Warrior's Way*, p. 19
184 Ibid.
185 Edith Fisher's will and probate
186 Big Brother Movement website (accessed 30 November 2023)
187 *The West Australian*, 23 February 1929, p. 18
188 Robert de Ropp, *Warrior's Way*, pp. 29–33
189 *The Register* (Adelaide) 3 January 1931
190 *The Advertiser* (Adelaide) 3 and 10 January 1931
191 Robert Vansittart, *The Mist Procession*, p. 458
192 Pavel Sudoplatov, *Special Tasks*, p. 91
193 Hugo Dewar, *Assassins at Large*, Marxists Internet Archive (accessed 30 March 2024)
194 Ibid.
195 Letter of Friedrich von der Ropp to the German Foreign Ministry dated 3 September 1930
196 TNA KV 2 2830/1 Folio 10
197 Kathleen Sissmore (better known as Jane Sissmore, and after her marriage in 1939, Jane Archer) became the first female officer in Britain's Security Service, MI5, in 1929 and was still their only woman officer at the time of her dismissal for insubordination in 1940. She had been responsible for investigations into Soviet intelligence and subversion. She went on to MI6, where her abilities were recognised by her head of section, Kim Philby. She eventually returned to MI5.
198 TNA KV 2 2831/1 Folio 34
199 Author's discussions with Christoph and Fritz Boettcher, October/November 2023
200 *Outlook*, 7 August 1926,'The problem of East Africa'; 4 September 1926, 'The Portuguese failure in Africa'; 2 October 1926, 'The British in Tanganyika'
201 *Outlook*, 13 September 1926, 'Germany inside the League'

NOTES

202 Archives of the Bristol Aeroplane Company at Filton (accessed 15 December 2022)
203 Jeffery, *MI6*, p. 199
204 IWM 62/218/1 Sqn Ldr C. J. W. Darwin, Folios 42–50
205 TNA KV 2/2830/2 Folios 18 and 19 dated 22 February 1926
206 TNA KV 2 2830/1 Folio 11
207 Hooton, *Phoenix*, p. 33
208 *Outlook*, 13 November 1926, pp. 469–70
209 *Outlook*, 20 November 1926, pp. 490–1
210 Wikipedia page on the Junkers G-24 (accessed 1 December 2023) and Hooton, *Phoenix*, p. 55
211 Hooton, *Phoenix*, p. 56
212 TNA KV 3/12 contains CX/2760 dated 1 January 1929 and CX/1743 of 19 February 1929
213 For more on Voigt see *The Guardian*, 12 July 2021, 'Nazis, fear and violence'
214 *Manchester Guardian*, 3 December 1926, p. 9
215 *Yorkshire Post*, 7 December 1926, p. 6
216 Winterbotham, *Nazi Connection*, p. 23
217 See, for example, p.184 of *Colonel Z* by Anthony Read and David Fisher, and p. 83 of *Elizabeth Wiskemann* by Geoffrey Field
218 *Outlook*, 2 October 1926, pp. 309–10
219 Ibid., 27 November 1926, p. 511
220 Ibid., 16 April 1927, pp. 401–2
221 NYPL, John L. Balderston papers, T-Mss-1954-002
222 *Outlook* 5 February 1927, pp. 123–4
223 Stephen Roskill, *Hankey*, Vol. 2, p. 507
224 Ibid., pp. 506–8
225 Jeffery, *MI6*, pp. 295–7
226 Two former MI6 officers speaking in 2023 but who prefer not to be identified
227 TNA WO 208/4475
228 *Daily Mail*, Monday 28 October 1957, p. 4 'I Spied on Hitler'
229 Ibid.
230 Ibid.
231 See Andrew, *HMSS*, p. 348 and Nicholson/Whitwell, pp. 40–2
232 *Daily Mail*, Monday 28 October 1957, p. 4, 'I Spied on Hitler'
233 Ibid.
234 Cecil, *Myth of the Master Race*, pp. 3–20
235 *Daily Mail*, Tuesday 29 October 1957, p. 4, 'I Meet Hitler, Then he Flies into a Rage'
236 Ibid.
237 Ibid.
238 Ibid.
239 Ibid.
240 Quoted by Cecil, p. 5
241 Discussion between the author and Professor Keith Jeffery 2009
242 Yad Vashem website: 'Extracts from *Mein Kampf* by Adolf Hitler' (accessed 31 November 2023)
243 Gilbert, *Auschwitz and the Allies*, London, 2001, p. 13 quoting *Mein Kampf*, p. 553
244 United Nations website. The Question of Palestine (accessed 12 November 2023
245 *Daily Mail*, 29 October 1957, p. 4, 'I Meet Hitler'
246 Winterbotham, *Nazi Connection*, pp. 17–18
247 Sisman, *Hugh Trevor-Roper*, p. 90

248 Ibid., p. 92
249 Reilly, papers, Bodleian, pp. 6–8
250 Winterbotham, *Nazi Connection*, pp. 21–2
251 Ibid., p. 23
252 TNA KV 2/952/2 Folio 70
253 Ibid., Folio 37
254 *The Journals of A. L. Kennedy*, pp. 86–7
255 Dawson to H. G. Daniels, 11 May 1937, quoted in Wrench, *Geoffrey Dawson*, pp. 360–1
256 Dawson to H. G. Daniels, 23 May 1937, quoted in Gannon, *The British Press and Germany*, p. 114
257 Gannon, *The British Press*, p. 68
258 Ibid., p. 69
259 There is a well-researched Wikipedia page on Locker-Lampson
260 *The Graphic*, 12 December 1931
261 Heiden, *Der Führer*, pp. 339–40
262 Ibid p. 165
263 Lüdecke, *I Knew Hitler*, pp. 403–24
264 *The English Review*, February 1932, pp. 142–8
265 Preliminary Examinations, Vol. I, p. 100. Dr Sack's (counsel for one of those accused of arson) extracts from the 32 volumes of preliminary examinations
266 Fritz Tobias, *The Reichstag Fire*, p. 181
267 Lüdecke, *I Knew Hitler*, p. 569
268 *Western Daily Press*, 10 May 1933, p. 12
269 *Daily News*, 8 May 1933, A. J. Cummings' report
270 *Reynold's News*, 7 May 1933, p. 1
271 *The Scotsman*, 15 May 1933
272 *Daily Herald*, 15 May 1933, p. 2
273 *The Times*, 15 May 1933
274 Heiden, *Der Führer*, p. 482
275 Rosenberg, *Diary*, p. 24
276 Ibid., p. 26
277 Ibid., p. 28
278 Ibid., p. 69
279 TNA 2/3427 Folio 23
280 *Daily Mail*, 28 October 1957, 'I Spied on Hitler'
281 *Daily Mail*, 30 October 1957, 'The Nazi Carve-up'
282 Heiden, *Der Führer*, p. 385
283 *Daily Mail*, 30 October 1957, 'The Nazi Carve-up'
284 This report entitled 'Germany and Colonies' is held by the Woollcombe family. It was to be circulated to the Foreign Policy Committee of the Cabinet
285 European Royal History website. Life of Fredrich-Franz IV; (accessed 14 March 2024)
286 *Daily Mail*, 31 October 1957, p.4, 'Permit me, said Heydrich'
287 Jeffery, *MI6*, p. 296
288 TNA KV 2/953/3 Folio 24
289 Ibid., Folio 23
290 Ibid., Folio 23
291 Another report on Thost's activities in London from Bill de Ropp can be seen on Folio 92 of KV 2/952/1

292 There is nothing on Thost's MI5 file to suggest that MI5 was behind this approach. Thost's post-war account can be found on Folio 67 of KV 2/954/2. For MI5 to use a Hungarian diplomat to entrap or recruit a Nazi journalist would have been politically risky.
293 *The Scotsman*, 11 November 1935, p. 13
294 Richtofen.eu website: 'Herbert v. Richthofen (1879–1951) – ein Diplomat im Auswärtigen Dienst des Deutschen Reichs'
295 Herbert von Richthofen was arrested by the Russians in 1945 and died in the Lubyanka prison in 1951.
296 Ernst Woermann has a well-sourced page on Wikipedia (accessed 14 March 2024)
297 Herbert von Dirksen has a well-sourced page on Wikipedia (accessed 14 March 2024)
298 TNA FO 1093/86. Views of the German Ambassador, 13 March 1939
299 IWM Oral history project, Winterbotham Reel 7 00.00 to 16.48
300 Winterbotham, *Nazi Connection*, p. 47
301 Ibid., p. 43
302 Rosenberg, *Diary*, p. 20
303 The author's meeting with Christopher Andrew, Cambridge, 11 May 2023
304 IWM Oral history project, Winterbotham Reel 7. 16.48 to 26.07
305 Hanfstaengl, *Unknown Hitler*, pp. 228–9
306 Winterbotham, *Nazi Connection*, p. 80.
307 Ibid.
308 IWM Oral history project, Winterbotham Reel 9 10.38 to 20.34
309 Winterbotham, *Nazi Connection*, pp. 8–4.
310 I am grateful to Major-General Mungo Melvin, the biographer of Field Marshal Erich von Manstein, for much of this paragraph.
311 Heinz Guderian, *Panzer Leader*, p. 13
312 Winterbotham, *Nazi Connection*, p. 57
313 Ibid., p.87.
314 The author has not found this telegram in the National Archives. If it was copied to the Palace it may not yet have been released. It is interesting that Phipps copied it to the Palace, as this must indicate interest being shown in the Nazis by one or more of the King, the Prince of Wales, the Duke of Kent and the Duke of Connaught.
315 IWM Oral history project, Winterbotham Reel 9 05.15 to 06.47
316 Ibid., Reel 10. 00.00 to 03.00
317 Ibid., Reel 10. 03.00 to 04.21
318 Ibid., Reel 10. 04.21 to 09.15
319 Wesley Wark, 'British intelligence on the German air force', *The Historical Journal*, September 1982, p. 634
320 Martin Kalb. *Environing Empire*, pp. 186, 231, 253, 254, and 266
321 Steven Press, *Blood and Diamonds*, Harvard, 2021
322 Tilman Dedering, 'Prisoners of War and Internees (Union of South Africa)', *International Encyclopedia of the First World War* (July 2015)
323 Avon, *Eden Memoirs*, p. 71
324 TNA KV 2 343/2 Folio 76
325 TNA KV2/344/3 Folio 14. Another version is that Treviranus escaped by aeroplane.
326 Nigel West claims he was recruited by Claude Dansey of MI6 with the codename Speaker. (*MI6*, p. 70)
327 Savile Club bedroom book for 1934

328 IWM . MGH-4907. Hendon Air Display 1934. Film shot by Lancelot House
329 Winterbotham, *Secret and Personal*, p. 118
330 Lüdecke, *I Knew Hitler*, p. 680
331 Rosenberg, *Diary*, pp. 37–43
332 Cecil, *Myth of the Master Race*, p. 172
333 Robert Harding in the Savile Bulletin XIV
334 Ibid., XIV
335 Ibid., XIV
336 *Daily Mail*, 29 October 1957. p. 4
337 Obermüller's successes can be viewed on the uboat.net website. One of the ships he attacked, the HMT *Aragon,* carried the author's grandmother, a nurse, who was one of the survivors.
338 KV 2/1740/3 Folio 25
339 Rosenberg, *Diary*, p. 52
340 John Hanbury Williams, *The Emperor Nicholas II as I Knew Him* (originally published 1922)
341 Ukrainians in the UK website: Anglo-Ukraine Committee
342 Obituary, Lord William Percy, Wiley Online library, 1963, p. 568
343 *Buckingham Advertiser*, 27 March 1937, New Labour candidate
344 History of the BBC, BBC website (accessed 12 January 2024)
345 Karina Urbach, *Go-Betweens for Hitler*, Oxford, 2015, p. 187
346 *Gloucestershire Echo*, 13 September 1934, 'The Real Germany of Today'
347 G. E. O. Knight, *In Defence of Germany*
348 *The Scotsman*, 17 August 1935
349 Rosenberg, *Diary*, p. 51.
350 *Gloucestershire Echo*, 12 August 1938, p. 8, 'Bishop of Gloucester chides Labour Party'
351 Rosenberg, *Diary*, pp. 51–2
352 Ibid.
353 In 1984 Winterbotham gave a different account to the IWM Oral History project, in which he mistakenly suggested that Bill de Ropp saw the Prince of Wales (the future Edward VIII). Catalogue no 7462, Reel 6
354 Rosenberg, *Diary*, p. 62
355 Philip Ziegler, *Edward VIII*, London, 1991, pp. 200–2
356 Karslake papers; letter Menzies to Karslake, 24 July 1936, IWM 02/41/2 Folder 8
357 Karslake was the author's grandfather's commanding officer in Quetta. Both grandparents survived the earthquake.
358 Europeans in East Africa website: Eric Dutton
359 Winterbotham, *Nazi Connection*, pp. 152–60
360 Winterbotham mentions this same moment in the *Nazi Connection*, p. 154
361 Winterbotham, *Nazi Connection*, p. 158
362 Ibid. p. 15.
363 *Daily Mail*, 31 October 1957, p. 4, 'Permit me, said Heydrich'
364 Karslake papers, IWM 02/41/2 Folder 8
365 Karslake, draft letter to unidentified field marshal, IWM 02/41/2 Folder 8. It is not clear if it was ever sent.
366 Rosenberg, *Diary*, pp. 94–5
367 *Cheltenham Chronicle*, 12 December 1936, p. 7
368 *Daily Mail*, 31 October 1957, p. 4, 'Permit me, said Heydrich'
369 Ziegler, *Edward VIII*, pp. 386–92

NOTES

370 Robert de Ropp, *Warrior's Way*, pp. 108–13
371 Hesse, *Hitler and the English*, pp. 85–6
372 Dick White would become Director General of MI5 in 1953 and then Chief of MI6 in 1956.
373 Andrew, *Defence of the Realm*, pp. 195–213
374 Bower, *Perfect English Spy*, pp. 26–8
375 Andrew, *Defence of the Realm*, p. 201
376 von Schweppenburg, *Critical Years*, pp. 51–2
377 Winterbotham went to great lengths to cultivate 'Charlie' Bömer, as he called him. The young man tended to be rather ebullient after a few drinks and may have been usefully indiscreet. This was his eventual undoing. When he was working for Goebbels in May1941 he hinted to some Bulgarians that Germany might move against Russia. He was sentenced to two years in prison. On his release he went to the Russian Front where he was killed in 1942. *See* Winterbotham (*Nazi Connection*), Howard Smith (*Last Train from Berlin*, p. 168) and Longerich (*Goebbels*, pp. 476–7).
378 The association did not do Gage's career any damage. He would be ambassador to Thailand and to Peru in the 1950s.
379 TNA KV 2/3427 Folio 20
380 F. von der Ropp, *Zwischen Gestern und Morgen*, p. 261
381 TNA KV 2/2831/2 Folio 26
382 Ibid., Folio 35
383 *Edinburgh Evening News*, 25 February 1937, p. 9
384 *Essex Newsman*, 17 April 1937, p. 1
385 The Civil Service Christan Union paper *Service*, Vol. 8, No. 1, January 1937
386 National Library of Wales: Esther Waldegrave to Tom Jones, letters 29 July and 13 September 1937
387 Reinhard Bollmuss, *Das Amt Rosenberg*, p. 244
388 Vansittart, 7 April 1934. Churchill College Archives
389 Henderson, *Failure of a Mission*, p. vi
390 TNA FO 371/23006
391 Smith, *Foley*, p. 269
392 Franklin Gannon, *The British Press*, pp. 123–4.
393 George Ward Price, *I Know These Dictators*, p. 376
394 TNA FO 371/18861 Folios 164-186 and 260-261
395 *The Aeroplane*, 22 January 1930, p. 130
396 Andrew, *HMSS*, p. 383
397 Vansittart Papers, VNST 1/14 Folio 15
398 TNA KV 2/3289 Folio 31
399 Ibid., Folio 45
400 Schellenberg, *Memoirs*, p. 55
401 Vansittart Papers, VNST II Folio 5
402 National Library of Wales, A. J. Sylvester papers. (B1990/42) B54. Lloyd George meeting with Hitler
403 National Library of Wales, A. J. Sylvester papers. Letter Lloyd George to Ribbentrop 19 September 1936
404 National Library of Wales, Thomas Jones papers. Class E, Vol. 1. Germany 1918–1939
405 *Daily Mail*, 30 October 1957, p. 4, 'The Nazi Carve-up'
406 Winterbotham, *Nazi Connection*, p. 153

407 Thorsten Kalijarvi, 'The problem of Memel'
408 John Wolf, 'Memelland'
409 *Hartlepool Northern Daily Mail*, 21 December 1934
410 *The Times*, 11 March 1935, p. 11
411 *The Times*, 27 March 1935, p. 14
412 *Melbourne Argus*, 21 May 1934, p. 10, 'Baroness commits suicide'
413 Private conversation with the author, 9 October 2023
414 TNA FO 1093/86
415 TNA KV 2/661 Folio 60
416 Ibid., Folio 63–5
417 Rosenberg, *Diary*, pp. 44 and 53.
418 TNA KV 2/661 Folios 50–5
419 More of Bill de Ropp's reports on Korostovetz can be found on TNA KV 2/2574/2 Folios 45, 60 to 64
420 TNA KV 2/1239/1 Folios 83–7
421 Ibid., Folio 94
422 TNA KV 2/879/2 Folio 83
423 TNA KV 2/1239/1 Folios 55–8
424 Ukrainians in the UK website (accessed 17 January 2024)
425 TNA KV 2/661 Folio 62
426 TNA KV 2/340/1 Folio 35
427 Ibid., Folio 38
428 TNA FO 371/21659 Folios 59–64
429 TNA FO 1093/86
430 Rosenberg, *Diary*, 22 April 1939, p. 155
431 Ibid., 25 April 1939, p. 160
432 Ibid., p. 20
433 Winterbotham, *Nazi Connection*, p. 52
434 AVM Ron Dick, 'Confronting Complacency', *Air Power History*, Spring 1994, pp. 23–9
435 Leo McKinstry, *Spitfire*, London, 2007, p. 88
436 Hansard, 10 November 1932
437 Smith, *Foley*, p. 83
438 *Bristol Review Engine*, nos. 1–11, 1931–1936
439 Winterbotham, *Nazi Connection*, p. 100
440 Rosenberg, *Diary*, pp. 19–20
441 Ibid., p. 52
442 Ibid., p. 44
443 TNA AIR 2/2797 Medhurst to DCAS 28 January 1937
444 Von Schweppenburg, *Critical Years*, p. 48
445 Ibid.
446 TNA AIR 2/2797 Medhurst report dated 1 December 1936
447 TNA FO 371/19947 CID paper 1 September 1936
448 Ibid., CID paper 1 April 1937
449 Gunston, *Fedden*, p. 203
450 Ibid., p. 9
451 TNA CAB 64/17 Fedden's June visit to Germany
452 Ibid., Fedden's September visit to Germany

NOTES

453 Bennett, *Churchill's Man of Mystery*, p.167
454 Hinsley, *British Intelligence*, Vol. 1, pp. 64–5
455 IWM, Fedden Papers 1/15-2/3 22716c Box 289
456 Ibid., 1/15-2/3 22716c Box 301
457 John Christopher, *The Race for Hitler's X-planes*, London, 2013, Ch. 8
458 Aviation History website for the DB600 range of engines
459 Fedden Papers, October 1938 visit, p. 22, University of Warwick. MSS.242/SW/3/2
460 Hinsley, *British Intelligence*, Vol. 1, p. 61
461 *Daily Mail*, 1 November 1957, p. 8, 'The Führer was Terrified'
462 The album is in the possession of the de Ropp family
463 *Daily Mail*, 31 October 1957, p. 4, 'Permit me, said Heydrich'
464 Winterbotham, *Nazi Connection*, pp. 174–5
465 For further detail on the highly contentious C. H. Ellis case, see Peter Wright, *Spycatcher*, pp. 325–30, and Chapman Pincher, *Their Trade is Treachery*, pp. 192–205
466 Fink, *The Eagle in the Mirror*, pp. 77–9
467 *Daily Mail*, 30 October 1957, p4, 'The Nazi Carve-up'
468 Jeffery, *MI6* p. 296
469 Malcolm Muggeridge, *Chronicles of Wasted Time*, London, 1973, Vol. 2, pp. 130–1
470 Cecil Insall's memoir is privately owned
471 Georg Perlmann wrote a book, *Indemnisation in Wartime German East Africa 1921–1926*, for the Reichs Kolonial Amt, so he may have known Bill de Ropp from Africa in 1924–5
472 Undated interview with Bill de Ropp published in the *Hereford Times* and republished in *Flashback II* by Nigel Heins
473 Quoted in Larson, *In the Garden of Beasts*, p. 47
474 Winterbotham, *Secret and Personal*, pp. 23–4.
475 *Daily Mail*, 29 October 1957, p. 4
476 Ibid.
477 Winterbotham, Oral testimony, IWM Tape 6 at 0151 mins
478 Conversations in Peterchurch, Herefordshire in 2022 and 2023. See Preface.
479 Winterbotham, Oral testimony, IWM Tape 11 at 0243 mins
480 *Gloucestershire Echo*, 29 March 1935, p. 4
481 Wiskemann, *The Europe I Saw*, London, 1968, p. 177
482 Field, *Elizabeth Wiskemann*, p. 158
483 Dilks, *Cadogan Diaries*, p. 208
484 Anthony Mockler, *Haile Selassie's War*, London, 1984, pp. 22–4, 185–7
485 *German Foreign Policy*, Series D, Vol. 7, p. 81
486 Volker Ullrich, *Hitler*, London, 2020, Vol. 2, p. 134
487 Howard, *Spying on the Reich*, p. 189
488 Helen Fry, *Spymaster*, London, 2021, pp. 140–50
489 Schellenberg, *Memoirs*, p. 102
490 Ibid., p. 228
491 Ibid., p. 337
492 Ibid., p. 119–20
493 Jeffery, *MI6*, p. 296
494 TNA CAB 104/43
495 Shirer, *Third Reich*, pp. 404–7
496 TNA FO 1093/86

497 *Daily Mail*, 1 November 1957, p. 8, 'The Führer was Terrified'
498 Templewood, *Nine Troubled Years*, p. 323
499 TNA CAB 21/540 Folios 60–4
500 John Darwin, diaries and letters, IWM 62/218/1
501 Ibid., IWM 62/218/1
502 TNA FO 1093/86
503 Schorske, Carl, 'Two German Ambassadors: Dirksen and Schulenburg', pp. 477–511, *The Diplomats 1919–1939*, ed. Gordon A. Craig and Felix Gilbert, Princeton, 1953, p. 494
504 TNA FO 1093/87 Folios 27–31
505 James Knox, *Robert Byron: A Biography*, London, 2004, p. 420
506 *Documents on German Foreign Policy*, Series D, Vol. VII, pp. 81–2
507 Ibid., p. 82
508 Rosenberg, *Diary*, p. 83
509 Watt, *How War Came*, p. 443
510 Dilks, *Cadogan Diaries*, p. 201
511 Dilks, *Cadogan Diaries*, pp. 199–203
512 Winterbotham, *Secret and Personal*, pp. 185–6
513 *Documents on German Foreign Policy*, Series D, Vol. VII, p. 163
514 Insall, Memoirs
515 *Daily Mail*, 1 November 1957, p.8, 'The Führer was Terrified'
516 Ibid., p. 158
517 Goodman, *History of the JIC*, p. 10
518 Ibid., p. 24
519 Ewan Butler, *Amateur Agent*, London, 1963, p. 14
520 The Georg Bell story is complex and mysterious with no entirely reliable sources. See for example, Glyn Roberts, *Life of Deterding*, pp. 298–318
521 Spicer, *Coffee with Hitler*, pp. 268–9
522 *Evening Standard*, 8 February 1911, p. 9
523 Read and Fisher, *Colonel Z*, p. 172
524 Ibid., p. 174
525 Northern Mining Research Society: Hugh Elliot Charles Whittall
526 Read and Fisher, *Colonel Z*, p. 174.
527 Ibid.
528 Read and Fisher, *Colonel Z*, and Wikipedia: Frederick Augustus Voigt (accessed 13 March 2024)
529 IWM Papers of Sqn Ldr C. J. W. Darwin Ref 22281
530 Reilly, papers. MS Eng Box 6918. Folios 207-209, Bodleian, Oxford
531 TNA CAB 127/376. *The Hankey Review*, pp. 10–11
532 Pincher, *Their Trade is Treachery*, p. 202
533 Dilks, *Cadogan Diaries*, p. 128
534 Ibid., pp. 94–5
535 Ibid., p. 202
536 Ibid., p. 227
537 *Documents on German Foreign Policy*, Series D, Vol. VIII, p. 134 dated 25 September 1939
538 Rosenberg, *Diary*, pp. 165–6
539 *Documents on German Foreign Policy*, Series D, Vol. VIII, p. 258
540 Ibid., p. 259
541 Ibid., p. 260

542 Ibid., p. 262
543 Savile Club Registers. Daniels had written *The Rise of the German Republic* in 1927 and *The Framework of France* in 1937.
544 Rosenberg, *Diary*, p. 169
545 *Documents on German Foreign Policy*, Series D, Vol. VIII, p. 363–8 undated
546 Rosenberg, *Diary* p. 174
547 Boyle, *Montagu Norman*, p. 303
548 Ibid., p. 304
549 *Documents on German Foreign Policy*, Series D, Vol. VIII, pp. 333–7
550 Ibid., p. 367
551 Londonderry, *Ourselves and Germany*, p. 170
552 Michie, *Portrait of an Appeaser*, p. 134
553 Avon, *Eden Memoirs*, pp. 182–6
554 Ibid., pp. 479–95
555 Ibid., p. 486
556 Air History website, Spitfire, Production charts (accessed 28 April 2024)
557 M. G. Christie papers, Churchill College, CH1 27–28
558 Ibid., Christie's additional notes on 25 September 1939
559 Colville, *Fringes of Power*, pp. 50, 52, 68
560 Rosenberg, *Diary*, p. 189
561 Douglas Hamilton, *Rudolf Hess*, pp. 28–9, foreword by Roy Conyers Nesbit
562 TNA KV 2/755. This is Jahnke's MI5 file, comprising three volumes
563 Douglas Hamilton, *Rudolf Hess*, p. 52
564 Ibid., p. 141
565 Ibid., p. 161
566 Ibid., p. 202
567 Adolf Hitler's speech to the Reichstag 19 July 1940: iBiblio.org
568 Douglas Hamilton, *Rudolf Hess*, p. 204
569 Ibid., p. 206
570 Rosenberg, *Diary*, pp. 245–7
571 Ibid.
572 Hanfstaengl, *Unknown Hitler*, p. 249
573 Schellenberg, *Memoirs*, p.199
574 Ibid., pp. 200–1
575 Ibid., p. 202
576 Douglas Hamilton, *Rudolf Hess*, p. 249.
577 Ibid., p. 123
578 TNA FO 1093/11 Folios 18 and 19
579 Haushofer had been a close friend of her late son Patrick Roberts, a British diplomat. Roberts knew Bill de Ropp's friend Archibald Church and had invited him to meet 'a young German', who was almost certainly Haushofer, in May 1932. (Church papers in Cambridge University Library; Add. 9560 Folder 12. Folios 23 and 24).
580 Douglas Hamilton, *Rudolf Hess*, pp. 181–3
581 TNA FO 1093/11 Folios 1-5
582 Ibid., Folio 33
583 TNA FO 1093/11 WSC to AC 16 May 1941, Folio 121
584 Schellenberg, *Memoirs*, p. 203

585 Ibid., p. 201.
586 Von Hassell, *Diaries*, p. 194
587 TNA KV 2/2839 Vol. 1 Folios 49 and 77; Vo.l 2 Folios 33-37 and 99.
588 Lonsdale-Bryans was an old Etonian with close connections to German sympathisers such as Lord Brocket, the Duke of Buccleuch, Fitzroy Fyers and Guy MacCaw. On the shutting-down of the channel he wrote bitterly 'The appeaser-mongers of yesterday are the war-to-the-finishists of today.' (KV 2/2839 Vol 2 Folio 119)
589 TNA FO 1093/249
590 Ibid.
591 Douglas Hamilton, *Rudolf Hess*, pp. 311–12
592 TNA FO 371/26542, quoted by Peter Padfield, *Hess, Hitler and Churchill*, London, 2013, p. 140
593 Douglas Hamilton, *Rudolf Hess*, pp. 329–31
594 TNA KV 2/755/2 Folios 30–33
595 TNA KV 2/965/1 Folios 20–28
596 Richard Deacon, *'C': A Biography of Sir Maurice Oldfield*, London, 1984, p. 87
597 TNA KV 2/755 Vol. 1 Folios 37–42.
598 Schellenberg, *Memoirs*, p. 269
599 Ibid., p. 304
600 TNA KV 2/2831/1 Folios 9–15.
601 Sadly, the draft letter has not survived in either the family or the IWM archives.
602 Robin MacWhirter, letter to F. W. Winterbotham dated 18 September 1987; in private hands
603 Jeffery, *MI6*, p. 296
604 Reilly, papers, Bodleian Library. MSS. Eng. c. 6918. Folios 223–9
605 Wilfried Strik-Strikfeldt, *Against Stalin and Hitler 1941–1945*, London, 1970, pp. 96, 192
606 Rosenberg, *Diary*, p. 165
607 Jeffery, *MI6*, p. 379
608 A full copy is available on the Hoover Institution website under 'Die Sonderfahndungsliste G.B.'
609 TNA KV2/9151 Folio 57
610 Hermann Freiherr von Harder und von Harmhove, *Lebenserinnerungen*, Vol. 5, pp. 759–60
611 See *Documents on German Foreign Policy*, Series D, Vol. VIII, pp. 257–63
612 R. V. Jones, *Most Secret War*, p. 68
613 *Daily Mail*, 1 November 1957, p. 8, 'The Führer was Terrified'
614 TNA FO 1093/206
615 Martin Gilbert, *Second World War*, pp. 243, 255
616 Howard K. Smith, *Last Train from Berlin*, pp.59–76
617 Dilks, *Cadogan Diaries*, p. 406
618 Ibid., p. 410
619 Winterbotham, *Ultra Spy*, p .243
620 Stephen Roskill, Letter to Eric Keen, 29 July 1976, Winterbotham Papers, IWM
621 Samuel Mitcham et al., *Hitler's Commanders: Officers of the Wehrmacht, the Luftwaffe, the Kriegsmarine, and the Waffen-SS*, Lanham, Maryland, 2012
622 Beevor, Antony. *Stalingrad*, pp.51–2
623 Diplomatic documents of Switzerland BAR E 4320(B)1968/195/, 77; C.2.10094 / 2 March 1945
624 Hans-Heiri Stapfer, 'Ende einer Dienstreise', *Cockpit Magazin*, July 2017, p. 36–7
625 TNA KV 2/99/2 Folio 20
626 Braunschweig, *Secret Channel*, p. 249

NOTES

627 Swiss Federal Archives E4320B 266/755 Consulat Britannique Genève 1941–47 and 29/327 Englischer Spionagedienst 1941–59
628 Compton Mackenzie, *First Athenian Memories*, London, 1931, pp. 241, 388
629 Field, *Elizabeth Wiskemann*, p. 94
630 'We went after a lot of military intelligence, order of battle things, and we weren't too occupied with what would happen after the war, just what we had to do to win the war at the moment. Whereas Allen [Dulles] saw his mission as much more encompassing.' Van den Heuvel quoted by Field, p. 116
631 TNA KV 2/99/1 Folio 63
632 Braunschweig, *Secret Channel*, pp. 136, 150–1
633 OSS Memoranda for the President: Japanese Feelers in 1945, CIA website
634 TNA WO 204/12814. Allied Forces HQ Note on Eggen dated 29 September 1945
635 Neal H. Petersen, *From Hitler's Doorstep: The Wartime Intelligence Reports of Allen Dulles, 1942–1945*, Penn State University Park, 1996, pp. 396, 537, 546
636 TNA KV 2/99/2 Folio 1
637 Ibid.
638 TNA KV 2/96/1 Folios 49–51
639 TNA KV 2/143 Vol 2 Folios 5 and 6
640 Ulrich von Hassell, *Diaries*, p. 213. Hassell refers to him as Danfeld
641 Jesse Fink, *Eagle in the Mirror*
642 TNA KV 2/963/3 Folio 32
643 TNA KV 2/143 Vol. 1 Folios 21–31
644 Daufeldt letter to Stallforth of 23 August 1950, pdf. 21 of CIA papers on Archive.org
645 For more on Harry Carr see Jeffery, *MI6*, pp. 371–3, 515–8, 551–4
646 There are extensive records on Daufeldt available on the CIA website
647 Note from Chief of Munich Operations Group, 10 September 1962, pdf. 26 of CIA papers on Archive.org
648 Schellenberg, *Memoirs*, pp. 428–54
649 Hartman, *Erinnerungen 1874–1962*, p. 239
650 F. von der Ropp, *Zwischen Gestern und Morgen*, pp. 269–70
651 Hartmann, *Erinnerungen 1874–1962*, p. 255
652 Ibid., p. 256
653 Von Harder, *Lebenserinnerungen*, Vol. 6, pp. 990–1032.
654 Alfred Rosenberg's Memoirs. Available on the Internet Archive
655 TNA WO 205/1225
656 TNA WO 208/4494
657 TNA WO 208/3802
658 Ibid.
659 Cecil, *Myth of the Master Race*, p. 229
660 Office of the US Chief Counsel for the Prosecution of Axis Criminality. Document 1144-PS
661 John Brown Mason, *The Danzig Dilemma*, Stanford, 1946, pp. 352–3
662 TNA FO 371/57594
663 Richard Griffiths, *Fellow Travellers of the Right*, London, 1980
664 The aeronautical punditry of C. G. Grey: WW2 aircraft net website (accessed 23 March 2024)
665 Avalon Project, Yale Law School. Document No. 003-PS
666 Ibid., 15 April 1946, pp. 452–3
667 Ibid., 16 April 1946. p. 481

668 Ibid., 17 April 1946, p. 560
669 Ibid., p. 563
670 Ibid., p. 570
671 Ibid., p. 576
672 Ibid.
673 Ibid., Judgement; Sentences
674 Reilly, papers, pp. 216, 243
675 Evelyn Sinclair, letter to Eileen Woollcombe dated 16 February 1968
676 Harold Gibson, letter to Malcolm Woollcombe dated 1 July 1944
677 Stewart Menzies, letter to Eileen Woollcombe dated 18 February 1968
678 Rear Admiral K. H. Farnhill of the MoD, letter to F. W. Winterbotham dated 9 April 1974, IWM 84/40/1
679 Dr David Owen to the House of Commons 12 January 1978, Hansard, pp. 829–30
680 William Stevenson, *Intrepid's Last Case*, pp. 251–2, and Chapman Pincher, *Their Trade is Treachery*, p. 203
681 Norman Taylor, Encyclopedia of Australian Science and Innovation (eoas.info accessed 24 March 2024)
682 Eva Morgan to the author, Peterchurch, 20 November 2022
683 Eva Morgan to the author, 10 November 2023
684 *Leamington Spa Courier*, 26 July 1961
685 Bill de Ropp, four letters to Sue Hunstman, 1967–70
686 Ruth de Ropp to Jim de Ropp, 9 January 1973
687 Vansittart, letter to Malcolm Woollcombe dated 14 December 1936; in private hands
688 Walter Schellenberg, TNA KV 2/94, 95, 96, 97, 98 and 99, each comprising several volumes; Carl Marcus, TNA KV 2/964 and 965; Wilhelm Höttl, TNA KV/2/412; Hans Daufeldt, TNA KV/2/141, 142 and 143; Richard Protze, TNA KV 2/1740; Hermann Giskes, TNA KV 2/961, 962 and 963; Horst Kopkow, TNA KV 2/1500 and 1501; Hans von Chappuis, TNA KV 2/3427 Hans Thost, TNA KV 2/952, 953 and 954; Fritz Hesse, TNS KV 2/915
689 National Archives Collection of Foreign Records Seized (RG 242). NARA, US archives
690 Lüdecke, *The Hitler I Knew*, p. 601
691 John Charmley *Churchill: The End of Glory*, London, 2009
692 Outrage at Clark's attack on Churchill: *The Independent*, 3 January 1993
693 John Colville, *Fringes of Power*, Vol.1, p. 44
694 Ibid., p. 521
695 Ibid., p. 64
696 History of Sir Austen Chamberlain. Gov.uk website (accessed 21 April 2024)
697 Erik Goldstein, 'Neville Chamberlain', *Diplomacy & Statecraft*, 1999, p. 286
698 Templewood, *Nine Troubled Years*, p. 367
699 Spicer, *Coffee with Hitler*, p. 241
700 Paul Stafford, 'Select Political Autobiography and the Art of the Plausible: R. A. Butler at the Foreign Office, 1938–1939', *The Historical Journal* December 1985, pp. 908, 920
701 Private email to the author, 8 May 2024

INDEX

Abetz, Karl 225
Abwehr 14, 194, 195, 268, 280, 300
Achtung Panzer (H. Guderian) 185
Adelaide Advertiser 41
The Aeroplane 357–8
Africa, German plan for 169–70
Agar, Augustus 68–9
Air Ministry, British *see* British Air Ministry
Alexander, Lieutenant-Colonel Harold 75
Alexander, Major William 104, 119–20
Alfthan, Bertil von 39
Allen, William 239
Alliance of Red Front Fighters 129
Allied Powers 2, 124, 125, 232
Anglo-Baltic Merchants Ltd 81–2, 83, 104
Anglo-German Brotherhood 221
Anglo-Ukrainian Committee 240–1
Anschluss 229, 265, 266, 283, 286
Antinori, Marchese Francesco 274
Apsley, Lord 156, 207, 212–13
ARCOS raid (1927) 12
Ashton-Gwatkin, Frank 10, 17, 19
Asquith, H. H., 1st Earl of Oxford and Asquith 57
Aue, Captain W.C.R. 173
Auersperg, Major Alois 344
Australia 8, 40–1, 114–15, 287
Austria 58, 229, 242, 265–6, 276, 283, 286, 296, 329, 358
aviation intelligence and developments, German 123, 124–5, 126–8, 225–6, 245–6, 248–54, 261–3, 339
Axis forces 18, 19

Baku oilfields, Soviet Union 162, 297
Balderston, John 121, 129–30, 324
Baldwin, Stanley 9, 86, 104, 156, 188, 248
Balfour Declaration (1917) 144
Ball, Joseph 94–5, 100, 102, 104, 105
Ballin, Albert 52, 53, 54, 56
Barlow, Alan 162, 167
Bartlett, Ken 122, 248–50
Bath Chronicle 40
Battle of Britain 263
Battle of Switzerland (1940) 339–40
Beaverbrook, 1st Baron 58
Beck, General Ludwig 280, 300
Beer Hall Putsch (1923) 129
Belfast Newsletter 5
Bell, Clive 46
Bell, Georg 296
Bellegarde, Madame 102
Bennett, Gill 88, 101, 102, 107
Beresford, John 228
Berliner Tageblatt 127
Bermondt-Avalov, General Pavel 74, 82–3, 91
Bernadotte, Count Folke 347

Berthold, Hans 188–9, 190, 192
Best, Sigismund Payne 300
Bethel Foundation, Bielefeld 36
Between Yesterday and Tomorrow (*Zwischen Gestern und Morgen,* F. von der Ropp) 34, 51, 52, 60, 367
Big Brother programme, Australian 114–15
Bismarck, Otto von 200–1
Bistram, Baron 76–7
Black, Captain 88, 90, 101, 105, 107
Bland, Sir Nevile 20
Blennerhassett, William 103
Bletchley Park 21, 288, 365
Blitzkrieg concept 185
Blomberg, General Werner von 182, 189, 191, 213, 219
Blue Shirts 156
Bohle, Ernst 134, 283
Bolshevik Russia 67, 68, 69, 124, 128, 137, 197, 320–1
  see Bolshevism; Communism; Soviet Union
Bolshevism 70, 94, 100, 128, 158–9, 220, 230, 285, 290, 304, 308, 309
  see also Bolshevik Russia; Communism; Soviet Union
Bömer, Karl 220, 221
Bormann, Martin 2, 4, 312, 316, 350, 359
Bosch, Robert 225
Bose, Subhas Chandra 175
Böttiger, Theodor 219
Boyle, Captain Archie 57, 156
Bradley Dyne, Aminta 103
Brandis, Cordt von 74, 76–7, 79, 82–3
Brecknock, Earl of 198
Briand, Aristide 126
Bristol Aeroplane Company 122–3, 124–5, 248–9, 254, 255, 288, 357
Britain
  British Empire/Commonwealth of Nations 8, 17, 285, 287–8, 293
  German invasion of Poland 218, 235–6, 252, 286–7, 290–3
  German peace efforts 300–1, 311–25, 342, 343–6, 347, 349
  Hitler's pre-WWII view of Anglo-German relations 158–9, 215, 284, 285, 286–7, 288
  Nazi sympathisers 23, 193, 199–200, 203–4, 224, 228, 356–8
  rearmament 18–19, 130, 188, 279, 285, 307
  relations with France 235–6, 281, 284, 285, 291
  see also government, British; MI5; MI6; Royal Air Force and British aircraft development
British Air Ministry 26–7, 57, 123, 148, 150, 166, 168, 179, 187, 204–5, 247, 248–50, 251–2, 253, 254, 255, 261, 290, 291, 299, 301–2, 304, 305, 307, 329, 358
British Electric Transformer Company 42
British Embassy, Berlin 173, 180, 186, 222–3, 227
British Military Mission, Berlin 63, 64–5, 70–1, 134
British Union of Fascists (BUF) 27, 193
Brown, Lieutenant Colonel 48
Browning, Freddie 106
Bruckmann, Bruno 259
Brüning, Heinrich 111, 119
Burckhardt, Carl 235, 320–2, 343, 356
Burmester, Admiral Sir Rudolf Miles 207
Butler, Ewan 290
Butler, R.A. 291
Byron, Robert 290

Cadogan, Alexander 7–13, 19–20, 21, 218, 222–3, 244, 279, 281, 286, 289, 294, 298, 301, 319, 321, 333–5, 336–7
Campbell, John Ross 100
Canada 8, 287
Canaris, Chief Admiral Wilhelm 194, 226
Canterbury, William Temple, Archbishop 344
Carr, Harry 346
Catholic Church 32, 37
Chamberlain, Neville 9, 19, 25, 26, 168, 216, 218, 223, 274, 279, 280–1, 285, 288, 291, 301, 305, 306, 313–14
Chappuis, Hans von 173, 219
Chetwode, Roger 199
Chicago Daily Tribune 69
Christie, Group Captain Grahame 134–5, 224–7, 253, 281, 296, 308–9
Church, Major Archibald 92, 111–13, 190, 304, 348
Churchill, Randolph 344
Churchill, Winston 25, 63–4, 187, 298, 304, 307, 311, 314, 318–19, 320, 322, 325, 344, 346
City of London 26–7, 305, 307
Clauson, Gerard 91–2
College of Electrical Engineering, London 42
Collier, Laurence 10, 17, 19
Colville, John 309, 346, 380
Colvin, Ian 223
Committee for Imperial Defence (CID) 9, 130, 253, 262
Communism 64, 68, 74, 100, 108, 128, 130, 129,

INDEX

156, 182, 186, 202, 203, 211, 239, 320
see also Bolshevik Russia; Bolshevism; Soviet Union
Communist International (Comintern) 67, 85, 98–100
Communist Party of Great Britain (CPGB) 85, 98–100, 106, 108
Conference of Nationalities (1916), Switzerland 59–60
Connaught, Duke of 198, 200–1, 204, 205, 211, 358
Conservative Party, British 86, 92, 94, 102, 107, 119, 240
Corsica 275, 291
Courland, Latvia 32, 137, 367
Crabb, Commander 29
'Crisis and Aftermath: Tendencies and Reactions', MI6 report 280–3
Croft, Sir Henry Page 119
Crossman, Richard 319
Crowe, Sir Eyre 99–100, 118–19
Crozier, Brigadier Frank 75
Cumming, Captain Mansfield 66–9, 81
Cunliffe-Lister, Philip 307
Curzon, 1st Marquess Curzon of Kedleston 9, 73
Czechoslovakia 18, 19, 217, 227, 237, 268, 279, 283, 286, 287

Dahlerus, Birger 301
Daily Herald 90, 101
Daily Mail xvii–xviii, 29, 57, 77, 85–6, 104, 106, 107, 121, 136, 168, 224, 269, 365, 369
Daily News 23, 23, 27–8, 369
Daniels, Harold Griffith 121, 304, 309, 342
Dansey, Claude 296–7, 299, 327–9, 330, 340–1, 342, 344, 346, 361, 377
Danzig, Poland 235–6, 284
Darwin, John 123, 288–9, 298
Daufeldt, Hans 345
Dauzogir estate, Lithuania 32–3, 34, 37, 51, 52, 54, 78, 113–14
Davidson, J.C.C. 104
Davis, Norman 161
Dawson, Geoffrey 152, 154, 155, 167
de Graff, Johann 67
de Haas, Walter 111
de Ropp, Baron Bill xvii, 57, 115–16, 138, 194, 289, 373–82
adoption of de Ropp surname 42
agent number 12821 14
army application referees 46
and Arno Schickedanz 137–8, 168, 231, 239, 266, 355
in Australia 40–1
Austria with Rosenberg (1938) 265–6, 361
aviation journalism and intelligence 57, 123, 124–5, 126–8, 152, 250, 251, 254–5, 262, 339
Bristol Aeroplane Company 122–3
British Military Mission, Berlin 63, 64–5, 70–1, 134
British propaganda 57, 58, 134, 289–90
childhood in Dresden and Dauzogir 34, 38
and Claude Dansey 327–8, 341, 346, 377
contacts in German Foreign Ministry (AA) 173, 175–6
'Crisis and Aftermath: Tendencies and Reactions' 280–3
Daily Mail xvii–xviii, 29, 77, 107, 121–2, 136–7, 168, 269, 369
Daily News — News Chronicle articles 23, 27–8, 369
defence of Jews 141, 272
and Duke Friedrich-Franz 170
education 38, 39, 42
engagement and wedding 40
English Review article on Hitler 159
and Ernst Röhm 189, 192–3
establishing connections with the Nazi Party 136–45
estrangement from brother Friedrich 120
on faltering German invasion of Russia 334–7
family background 32–8, 43, 234–5
first wife's death 65
and Francesco Antinori 274, 341–2
Fred Winterbotham visits Berlin 180–1, 183, 184, 186, 188, 246, 267
and Gauleiter Erich Koch 167, 168, 188, 208–9, 231–2, 266, 329
and General Franz Ritter von Epp 168–70, 282, 284, 329
Germans in Memel, Lithuania 233–4
Germany and Danzig, Poland 236
Germany and the Ukraine 237–40, 242–3
'Germany: Factors, Aims, Methods etc.' report 242–3, 283–6
the Great War 45–6, 48–51, 56–7, 58, 61, 134, 142–3
and Hans Berthold 188–9, 192–3
and Hitler xvii, 26–7, 28, 29, 129, 133, 136–7, 140–5, 159, 170, 181, 205, 209–10, 213, 215–16, 229–30, 246, 263, 265, 281, 286–7, 304–5, 306, 355

and Hugh Whittall 297, 335, 340
intelligence gathering at the Kaiserhof Hotel 171–2
intelligence reporting precautions 269–72
interviewing German PoWs 58, 63, 134
and Jacob Makohin 238–9
Japanese activity in Berlin 239–40
joins MI6 65–6
joins the army/British citizenship 46, 48, 82
leaves Germany before outbreak of WWII 293–4, 295–6
life post-WWII 368–71
linguistic ability 42–3, 48, 57
Lithuanian German Baltic heritage 31–2, 38
and Major Archibald Church 111–13
meets with Prince George, Duke of Kent 204–5
meets with the Duke of Kent 205–6, 357
MI6 cover – Anglo-Baltic Merchants Ltd 81–2, 83, 104
MI6 in the Baltic States 69–71, 75, 81, 82
MI6 role uncovered by Germans 329–30
Nazi Party Foreign Affairs Bureau (APA) 26–7, 173 (*see also below* and Rosenberg)
Night of the Long Knives 192–3, 194
Nuremberg Rally (1936) 206–10
opposition to communism/Bolshevism 64, 100, 128, 130, 203, 230
Outlook magazine articles 121–2, 124, 128–9, 130, 152
peace efforts from Switzerland and Hermann Harder 301–8, 309, 316, 331–2
and Reinhard Heydrich 168, 170–1, 266
retired by MI6 361
as RFC Balloon Officer 48–9, 143
and Rosenberg 5, 26–7, 28, 29, 133, 138–40, 141, 142, 144–5, 147–8, 151, 152–4, 155–7, 164, 165–8, 172, 176, 192, 195, 204–5, 229–30, 237–8, 241, 262, 263, 265–7, 268–9, 280, 290–2, 293–4, 304–5, 306, 309, 316, 329, 355, 357, 361
and Rudolf Hess 312, 324–5
Savile Club, London 5, 16, 50–1, 81, 91, 95, 103, 121, 162, 167, 190, 193, 194, 208, 274, 301, 304, 306, 324
scares and threats to cover 171, 194–5, 266–7, 268–9, 277
and Schellenberg's peace efforts 343–4
second wife's tactical sexual liaisons 273–4
summoned to Rosenberg's trial 355
'What Should We Do?' report 15–20, 21, 242, 279, 292
the Zinoviev Letter 85–96, 97–108, 109, 116
see also de Ropp (née Woodman), Marie Winifred; de Ropp, Robert 'Bob'; de Ropp (née Fisher), Ruth; Ropp, Friedrich von der
de Ropp, Jim 370, 371
de Ropp (née Woodman), Marie Winifred 'Jimmy' 110, 115, 140, 192–3, 269, 271–4, 295–6, 367, 370–1
de Ropp, Robert 'Bob' 50, 65, 91, 104–5, 111, 113–14, 216, 281, 369–70
de Ropp (née Fisher), Ruth 27, 39–42, 65
de Ropp, Ruth M. 27, 65, 111, 368–9, 370–1
de Ropp, Stefan 235
Delahaye, Lieutenant Colonel James Viner 199
Delmer, Sefton 319
Der Tag 137
Deruluft 124
Deterding, Sir Henri 162, 237, 241, 297, 356
Deverell, General Sir Cyril 223
Devereux, Colonel Wallace 257, 259, 262
Dewar, Hugo 117
Dirksen, Herbert von 176, 289
Dodd, Thomas 360
Domville, Admiral Barry 200
Dresden, Germany 33–4, 38
Dukes, Sir Paul 50, 68
Dulles, Allen 341, 342–3, 344
Dunderdale, Biffy 116
Dutton, Major Eric 93, 208, 212
Dvina River, bridge across 75

East Africa Commission 92–4, 104, 122
East African Standard 110
Ebbutt, Norman 121, 154–5, 223–4
Ebert, Friedrich 75
The Economist 54, 55–6
Eden, Anthony 9–10, 247, 307, 321, 325
Edward VIII, King 25, 205, 206, 356
Eggen, Hans 343–4, 345
Eichenpomusch estate, Lithuania 32–3, 37, 78, 113
Eire 287
Ellington, Air Chief Marshal Edward 307
Ellis, Dick 268, 300, 365
Elze, Hildegarde 352, 353
'English Party' 26, 305, 307
English Review 159
Enigma machine 21, 185
Epp, General Franz Ritter von 168–70, 282, 284, 329
Ewer, William Norman 90
executions, Nuremberg Trial 1, 4–5

INDEX

Farina, Rafael 103, 105
Farr, Walter 29
Farrer, Philip 199–200
Fedden, Sir Roy 122, 254–7, 258–9, 261–2
Féronce, Freiherr Albert Dufour von 220, 221
Fisher, Edith 39, 40, 42, 65, 111
Fisher, Mary 46
Fisher, Sir Warren 20
Foley, Captain Frank 67, 95, 223, 248, 269, 272, 293, 324, 371
Footman, David 364
Foreign Affairs Bureau (APA), Nazi Party 26–7, 160, 168, 173, 191, 192, 219–20, 221, 231, 239, 243, 282, 302, 354
France 18, 61, 125, 158, 170, 176, 211, 216, 217, 232, 233, 235–6, 268, 275, 281, 283, 284, 285, 291, 303, 314
Franco, General Francisco 19
Friedrich-Franz, Hereditary Grand Duke of Mecklenburg-Schwerin 170
Freikorps 74, 76–7, 79–80
Fyers, Major Hubert Fitzroy 198, 200–1, 204, 205

Gabrys, Juozas 74, 76–7, 80
Gambier-Parry, Brigadier Richard 288–9
Genny, Ada 39
George V, King 25, 204–6
George VI, King 213
German Air Ministry 248, 250–2
German Communist Party 202
German Documents (Documents on German Foreign Policy) 24, 25–7, 29
German Embassy, London 161, 162, 173, 193, 198, 217–19, 280–1
German Foreign Ministry (AA) xvii, 51–2, 56, 59–60, 111, 113, 117–19, 173, 175–6, 289, 323
see also von der Ropp, Friedrich
German Protestant School, Dauzogir 33
Germany
- annexation of Austria (Anschluss) 265–6, 283
- aviation developments 122, 123–7, 129, 225–6, 245–6, 248–54, 261–3
- British foreign policy 8, 9, 10–21
- claim to Danzig, Poland 235–6, 284
- the Great War 43, 55–6, 79
- invasion of Britain postponed 334, 336
- invasion of Czechoslovakia 19, 227
- invasion of Poland 218, 222, 235–6, 252, 283, 284, 286–7, 290–3
- invasion of the Soviet Union 350–1
- and Italy 268, 274, 282, 284, 285
- joins the League of Nations 122
- Molotov-Ribbentrop Pact (1939) 37, 81, 243–4, 283, 289, 306
- Munich Crisis and Agreement (1938) 19, 259, 280–2, 285
- Night of the Long Knives (1934) 182, 190–2, 193–4, 225, 242, 283
- Nuremberg rallies 197–213, 259, 303
- Party Day celebrations (1937) 170–1
- peace efforts 300–1, 311–25, 342, 343–6, 347, 349
- plans to take down the Soviet Union/Operation Barbarossa 182, 184–5, 186, 187, 229–30, 242, 282, 284, 314–15, 319, 334–8
- in the post-Great War Baltic States 73, 74, 75–6, 79, 80, 81, 82
- pre-WWII National Socialism 36, 93, 127–8, 129, 130–1, 133–7, 154, 157–8, 159–61, 164, 165, 167, 173, 175, 182, 190, 210–12, 222–4, 242–4, 281, 313 (*see also* Foreign Affairs Bureau (APA), Nazi Party; individuals by name)
- RAF bomb Berlin 350
- Reichswehr Ministry 126–7, 169, 182, 189–90, 194
- Russo-German aviation collaboration 124, 125–7, 129, 245
- Treaty of Brest-Litovsk (1918) 60, 73, 79
- and Ukraine 236–40, 242–4, 283, 359–60
- undercover rearmament 125, 130–1, 187–8, 205, 252, 253
- withdrawal of Allied occupation force 122, 130

'Germany: Factors, Aims, Methods etc.', MI6 report 242–3, 283–6
Gestapo 14, 160, 168, 192, 194–5, 275–6, 296, 308, 330
Gibson, Harold 364
Glasenapp, Otto von 52
Gloucester, Arthur Headlam, Bishop of 203–4
Gloucestershire Echo 201
Glyn, Sir Ralph 305
Godfrey, Admiral John 298
Goebbels, Joseph 4, 133, 135, 139, 154, 155, 164, 165, 166, 168, 190, 192, 230–1, 241, 272, 273, 276, 282, 284, 312, 352
Goerdeler, Dr Carl 225, 300
Goltz, General Rüdiger von der 74, 75, 80, 82–3, 203

Göring, Hermann 4, 134–5, 154, 160, 161, 164, 165, 179, 183, 190, 192, 194, 219, 225, 241, 251, 273, 282, 290, 293, 296, 308–9, 312
Gough, General Hubert 63, 75
government, British xviii, 313–14
  Foreign Office 7–21, 61, 64, 68, 74–5, 99, 119, 152–3, 166–7, 172, 187, 218, 251–2, 262, 280, 283, 285–6, 287–8, 292, 294, 299, 307, 320
  German peace efforts 300–1, 311–25, 342, 343–5, 347, 349
  German policy 8, 9, 10–21, 279
  Hitler's peace offer 314
  Home Office 46, 56, 82, 95, 98
  Munich Crisis and Agreement 259, 280–2, 285, 300
  the post-Great War Baltic States 74–5, 81
  Ten-Year Rule repealed 130
  War Office 13, 14, 136, 166, 167, 187, 188
  see also Chamberlain, Neville; Churchill, Winston
Government Code and Cypher School (GC&CS) 98, 283
The Graphic 157
Gravina, Count Manfredi 355–6
Graziani, General Rodolfo 273–5
Great War 8, 10, 11, 13, 14, 43–61, 63, 78, 139, 214, 246, 340
Greenley, Lieutenant Colonel W.A. 199
Gregory, John Duncan 'Don' 103
Gregory, Maundy 240–1, 297, 330
Grey, Charles 357–8
Grey, Sir Edward, 1st Viscount Grey of Fallodon 53, 56
Griffith, Sanford 128
Groebe, Peter 259
Grubbe, Brudenell Hunt 40, 46
Guderain, General Heinz 185
Gulbin, Lithuania 33, 37
Guriev, General Syvester 32

Hailsham, 1st Viscount 161
Halder, General Franz 314, 336
Halifax, 1st Earl 9, 17, 19, 222–3, 227, 289, 320
Hall, Admiral Sir Reginald 106–7
Hamilton, Duke of 317–18
Hanfstaengl, Erna 344
Hanfstaengl, 'Putzi' 134, 182, 267, 316, 344
Hankey, Sir Maurice 9, 107, 130, 241, 299
Harder, Hermann Freiherr von 302–4, 305, 309, 316, 331–3, 337, 350
Hartmann, Woldemar 347–9
Hassell, Ulrich von 320, 322–3, 345
Haushofer, Albrecht 313–14, 317–18, 320, 321–2
Haushofer, Karl 313
Hebbert, Stanley Benbow 95, 123
Heiden, Konrad 157–8, 163–4, 169
Henderson, Arthur 97, 98–9
Henderson, Sir Nevile 222–3, 276, 285, 287, 289, 293
Henlein, Konrad 225, 226
Hess, Rudolf xviii, 133, 135, 182, 209, 252, 311–25
Hesse, Fritz 218
Heydrich, Reinhard 168, 170–1, 195, 230–1, 266, 295, 300, 313
Heyking, Baron Igor 54, 259
Himmler, Heinrich 4, 135, 160, 165, 170, 190, 194–5, 230–1, 241, 276, 282, 312, 313, 343, 345, 347, 351, 352, 366
Hindenburg, Paul von 59, 60, 130, 159, 169
Hirst, Francis 54, 55–6
Hitler, Adolf xviii, 4, 8, 9, 19, 129, 135, 136, 154, 159–60, 169–70, 176, 189, 193, 214, 221, 313, 343
  annexation of Austria (Anschluss) 265
  and de Ropp xvii, 26–7, 28, 29, 129, 133, 136–7, 140–5, 159, 170, 181, 205, 215–16, 229–30, 246, 263, 281, 286–7, 301–2, 304–5, 306, 355
  Duke and Duchess of Windsor 213–14
  German plots against 280–1, 300, 301, 342
  'Germany: Factors, Aims, Methods etc.' MI6 report 242–3, 283–6
  hatred of Jews 141, 143–4, 210, 211, 285
  invasion of Poland 252; 286–7
  meeting with David Lloyd-George 227–8
  meeting with Fred Winterbotham 181–2, 245–6, 357
  Molotov-Ribbentrop Pact (1939) 243–4
  Munich Crisis and Agreement 280
  Nuremberg Rally (1934) 201
  Nuremberg Rally (1936) 209–12
  peace offers to Britain 314
  plan for Africa 169–70
  plans to take down the Soviet Union/Operation Barbarossa 229–30, 284, 242, 314–15, 319, 338
  on pre-World War II Anglo-German relations 158–9, 215, 284, 285, 286–7, 288
  and Rosenberg 26–7, 28, 135, 139, 140, 142, 144, 160, 205, 212, 229–30, 245–6, 291, 301–2, 304–5, 351, 354–5

and Rudolf Hess's flight to Scotland 316–17, 319
suicide 351
Hoare, Sir Samuel 186–7, 287, 307, 343, 358
Hodson, Rev. Harold Victor 199, 201, 203, 354
Hoesch, Leopold von 166, 167, 217
Hoffman, Gustav 275
Hohenlohe, Max von 225, 226, 301, 308–9, 343
Hotblack, Colonel Frederick Elliot 223

Im Thurn, Donald 103–4, 106
India 8, 9, 175
Industrial Intelligence Centre (IIC), British 257–8, 262
Insall, Cecil 270–2, 293
Inskip, Sir Thomas 256, 259, 307
Institute of Inventors 42
International Committee of the Red Cross (ICRC) 320
International News Service 4
Irish Free State 112
Ismay, Major General Hastings 280
Italy 18, 19, 128, 158, 175, 233, 268, 274, 282, 284, 291, 319

Jahnke, Kurt 312–13, 323–4, 345
January Club 193
Japan 18, 158, 175, 239–40, 284, 319, 344
Jebb, Gladwyn 17, 20, 285–6
Jeffery, Professor Keith xvii, xviii, 16, 269–70, 328, 330
Jews 37, 156, 163, 166, 210–11, 227, 303, 307
Alfred Rosenberg 1–4, 201, 354
British Passport Control and visas 67, 224, 272
Communism 202, 211
G.E.O. Knight's changing views 202–3
Hitler questions de Ropp's position on 141, 143
Hitler's hatred of 141, 143–4, 210, 211, 272, 285
Jean-Marie Musy's rescue efforts 345
Kristallnacht (Night of Broken Glass) 272
and Palestine 18, 67, 144, 282
widespread European anti-Semitism 143
Joint Intelligence Committee (JIC), British 294
Jones, Tom 228
Joyce, Mr W. 'Lord Haw-Haw' 193
Junkers 124–5, 127

Kaiserhof Hotel, Berlin 171–2
Kaltenbrunner, Ernst 5, 343, 345
Kapp, Wolfgang 189
Karslake, General Henry 206–7, 208, 210–12, 281
Keitel, Field Marshal 4–5, 367
Kell, Colonel Vernon 56–7, 91–2, 94, 153
Kendrick, Thomas 276
Kennedy, A. L. 154
Kent, Prince George, Duke of xviii, 205–6, 239, 356–7, 358
Kesselring, Air Commodore Albert 179, 183, 186
KGB 88, 90, 116–17
Kilmarnock, 4th Baron 64
Kindelberger, James Howard 297–8
Kinnock, Neil (Baron Kinnock) 108
Kirkpatrick, Ivone 318
Kitchener, 1st Earl 204
kite balloons, British 48–9
Knight, G.E.O. 200, 202–3
Koch, Gauleiter Erich 166, 167, 168, 172, 188, 208–9, 231–2, 266, 329, 352, 359–60, 365
Kohlerausch, Lisette 2, 192
Kolchak, Admiral Alexander 80
Konovalets, Yevhen 238
Kordt, Erich 280, 300–1
Kordt, Theo 218, 280–1, 300–1
Korniyev, General 90, 101, 105, 107
Korostovetz, Vladimir 238, 239, 240, 241
Koutrik, Folkert van 268, 275
Kreisler, Fritz 192
Kries, Wilhelm von 123
Kristallnacht (Night of Broken Glass) 272
Krüger, Dr Karl 275
Kurfürstendamm, Berlin 272
Kutyepov, General Alexander 116

Labour Party, British 12, 86, 90, 92, 97–8, 108, 113, 118, 119, 203–4, 239
Landau, Henry 66–7
Latvia 69–70, 73, 75
Lawrence, Peter 24–8, 301, 305, 369
Lawrence, Sir Geoffrey 359–60
Le Queux, William 42
League of Nations 122, 144, 235, 282
Leeper, Rex 76
Legge, Robin 50
Lenin, Vladimir 60, 69, 290
Liberal Party, British 92, 240
Lindbergh, Charles 254
Linfield, Frederick 92
Lithuania 31–3, 37–8, 43, 51, 59, 60, 70–1, 73–4, 166
British support for independence 74, 75, 81
German government 80, 81, 82

German landowners and Freikorps post-Great plot to overthrow the government 74, 75–7, 78, 79–81, 82–3
Land Reform Law (1922) 80–1
Memel 166, 232–4, 236
nationalists 74, 75, 79, 80
and Poland 74, 75, 79, 80
post-Great War German troops in 74, 75–6, 79, 80, 81
Russians and Bolshevik supporters 73, 74, 75–6, 79, 81
White Russian forces 74, 79, 80
Lloyd George, David 57, 58, 204, 227–8, 240
Locker-Lampson, Oliver 156
Lody, Karl 55
Loehner, Kurt 259
Loerzer, Bruno 183
Londonderry, 7th Marquess of 187, 193, 307
Long, Tania 356
Lonsdale-Bryans, James 320
Loxley, Peter 320
Lucht, Colonel Rulof 252–3
Lüdecke, Kurt 158–9, 161, 165, 172, 190
Ludendorff, General Erich 54, 129, 140
Lufthansa 124
Luftwaffe and German aircraft development 22, 123–7, 129, 183, 226, 245–6, 248–54, 261–3, 292, 304, 307, 308, 336, 339, 353
Lutheran Protestants 32, 33, 36

MacCaw, Captain Guy Hardy 198, 204, 357
MacDonald, Ramsay 86, 97–8, 100–1, 113, 161–2, 166, 167, 188, 192, 356
Mackenzie, Compton 50
MacWhirter, Robin 325
Magor, Captain Arthur 45–6
Magor (née Fisher), Dora 45, 111
Makohin, Jacob 238–9, 240
Malcolm, Major General Neill 63–4, 66, 69, 70, 134, 140
Malone, Cecil L'Estrange 238–9
Maltzan, Adolf von 59
Manchester Guardian 126, 152, 223–4, 274
Markau, Karl 323
Marlowe, Thomas 104, 106
Masson, Colonel Roger 340, 343–4
Matheson, Hilda 228
Medem, Walther von 75, 137
Medhurst, Wing Commander Charles 252–3
Mein Kampf (A. Hitler) 2, 143, 186, 315
Memel, Lithuania 166, 232–4, 236
Menzies, Colonel Stewart 13–15, 21, 65, 71, 77, 95, 99–100, 102–3, 105, 133–4, 142, 150, 206–7, 214, 289–90, 292, 294, 298–300, 320–1, 327, 328, 333–5, 346, 355, 364, 371
MI5 21, 46, 56, 68, 123, 153, 217, 237, 323, 324, 377–8
de Ropp intelligence reports 171–4, 176, 237–40
German Embassy, London 218–19
interest in von der Ropp family 56–7, 60–1, 95–6, 119–20, 220–1
and Maundy Gregory 240–1
Zinoviev Letter 91–2, 94, 98, 101, 103, 104, 105
MI6 xviii, 29, 60, 112, 120, 122, 123, 133–6, 150, 151–2, 170, 187, 194, 217, 226, 237, 240–1, 288–9, 311, 319, 366, 371
aviation intelligence 123, 125–6, 127, 245–6, 248–51, 262–3
Claude Dansey and Z Organisation 296–8, 327–9, 330, 341, 342, 344, 346, 361
'Crisis and Aftermath: Tendencies and Reactions' report 280–3
de Ropp advises war time propaganda 289–90
de Ropp and Hermann Harder peace talks 332–4
de Ropp cover – Anglo-Baltic Merchants Ltd 81–2, 83
de Ropp, Hitler and Rosenberg xvii, 133, 136–7, 142, 143–5, 148, 150–4, 155–6, 164, 176, 192, 206–7, 241
de Ropp in the Baltic States 69–71, 75, 81
de Ropp intelligence reporting precautions 269–72
de Ropp report on military situation in the Soviet Union 334–7
de Ropp's *Daily Mail* articles xvii–xviii, 136–7, 168, 269
and Dr Karl Krüger 275
and Friedrich von der Ropp 60, 95, 120
'Germany: Factors, Aims, Methods etc.' report 242–3, 283–6
government disdain of the secret service 11–12
the Great War 50, 56, 60
Hankey Review 299
and Hugh Trevor-Roper 149–50
infiltrated by German intelligence 268
Nuremberg Rally (1936) 206–7, 212, 214
operatives uncovered in Germany 275–6
Passport Control Office (PCO) 68, 136, 224, 293, 297, 298

retiring de Ropp 361
Secret Writing equipment 270
Soviet Union/Bolshevik Russia 67–9
in Switzerland 298
Venlo Incident 299–300, 342
'War Station', Bletchley Park 288
wartime relations with Switzerland 339–40
Western Front train-watching system 66
'What Should We Do?' report 15–20, 242, 279, 292
Zinoviev Letter scandal 86, 90, 98–108, 116
see also de Ropp, Baron Bill; Menzies, Colonel Stewart; Sinclair, Admiral Sir Hugh; Winterbotham, Fred W.; Woollcombe, Malcolm
MI9 2
Milch, Erhard 225, 251, 252, 255
Miller, General Yevgeny 116, 117
Missouri Synod 33, 36, 370
Molotov-Ribbentrop Pact (1939) 37, 81, 243–4, 283, 289, 306
Montgomery, Bernard, Field Marshal 351
Morning Post 60–1
Morton, Desmond 102–3, 187, 241, 257–8, 262, 299
Mosley, Oswald 27, 193, 200, 239
Mounsey, George 12, 99, 285–6
Muggeridge, Malcolm 270
Müller, Karl 55
Munich Crisis and Munich Agreement (1938) 19, 259, 280–2, 285, 300
Mussolini, Benito 19, 128, 274, 275
Musy, Jean-Marie 345
Myth of the Twentieth Century (A. Rosenberg) 1, 2

Nadolny, Rudolf 59
Namier, Lewis 64, 70
Neave, Airey 2–3
Neumann, Dr Ernest 234
Neurath, Baron Konstantin von 160, 167
New York Herald Tribune 128
New York Times 356, 358
New Zealand 8, 287
Newall, Sir Cyril 150
News Chronicle 24–8, 223, 369
Nicholas II of Russia, Tsar 37
Nicholls, Helen 41
Nichols, Philip 10–11, 17, 19
Nicholson, Captain Randolf Gresham 297
Nicholson, Jack 101–2
Night of the Long Knives (1934) 182, 190–2, 193–4, 225, 242, 283
Noel-Buxton, 1st Baron 319
Norman, Montagu 305
Norman, Nigel 156
Northcliffe, 1st Viscount Northcliffe 57–8, 61, 65, 77, 94, 134
Nuremberg War Crime Trials 1–6, 135, 352–61
Nuremberg Rally (1934) 197–206
Nuremberg Rally (1936) 206–11, 212–13
Nuremberg Rally (1937) 211–12, 259
Nuremberg Rally (1938) 303

Obermüller, Horst 168, 191, 197, 198, 219, 251, 297, 358
Office of Strategic Services (OSS), US 341, 342–3
Okamoto, Brigadier Kiyatomi 344
Oldfield, Sir Maurice 323
Operation Barbarossa (1940) 314, 319, 324, 334–8
Operation Sealion 336
Operation Ultra 21
Oregon Daily Journal 69–70
Organic Statute of Memel (1924) 232
Orlov, Vladimir 90
Ormsby-Gore, William 91–4, 104, 122
Oslo Report 333
Oster, Colonel Hans 280
O'Sullivan, H.D.E. 51
Outlook magazine 121–2, 124, 128–30

Palestine 18, 67, 144, 282
Pallavicini, Count 172, 173
Passport Control Office (PCO) 68, 95, 136, 224, 272, 293, 297, 298
Peace of Riga (1921) 237
Percy, Colonel Lord William 199
Perkins, Bobby 156
Perlmann, Dr Georg 272
Petrie, Sir Charles 128
Petrov, Waldemar von 345
Phipps, Sir Eric 180, 186, 222
Piggott, Henry Howard 82
Pokrovsky, Ivan 88, 90, 101, 103, 104, 105, 106
Poland 26, 37, 59, 70, 74, 80, 125, 185, 233, 237, 244, 282, 284
German invasion 218, 222, 235–6, 252, 283, 286–7, 290–3
Propaganda Department, British 57–8, 94, 134
Protocols of the wise men of Zion 2

Rauschning, Dr Hermann 225
Raven-Hill, Leonard 46
Red Army 129
Reichenau, General Walther von 179, 182–6, 187, 188, 231, 321, 323, 337–8
Reichsleiter Dienst 168
Reichstag fire (1933) 160
Reichswehr Ministry 126–7, 169, 182, 189–90, 194
Reilly, Patrick 150, 299, 328
Reilly, Sidney 69, 102
Reiswitz, Alfred von 35, 37
religion 32, 33, 36, 119, 130, 220, 221, 366, 370
Reynold's 162
Rhineland, remilitarisation of 242, 283
Ribbentrop, Joachim von 4–5, 155, 164, 175, 193, 217–18, 219, 226, 227, 241, 243, 282, 283, 284, 287, 289, 306, 312–14, 323
Ribbentrop-Molotov pact (1939) 37, 81, 243–4, 283, 289, 306
Richthofen, Herbert von 175
Riga, Latvia 69–70, 73
Ritter, Hans 225, 226, 301
Robb, Eustace 200
Roberts, Violet 318, 320
Röhm, Ernst 134, 135, 168, 189–90, 191, 192, 312
Rollo, Bernard Francis 81
Rollo, Gilbert de St Croix 81, 82
Romania 237, 284
Rommel, Erwin 185
Ropp, Alexander von der 36, 42
Ropp, Baron Wilhelm Sylvester von der *see* de Ropp, Baron Bill
Ropp, Bishop of Mogilev, Edward von der 71, 234–5
Ropp, Christoph von der 329
Ropp, Dietrich von der 329
Ropp, Dorothea von der 235
Ropp, Elizabeth 'Elli' von der 77, 78
Ropp, Elizabeth 'Lili' von der 52–4, 55, 77, 112–13, 347–8
Ropp, Friedrich von der 34, 36, 37, 45, 51–5, 59–61, 69, 74, 75–8, 79–80, 82, 94, 95–6, 100, 105, 107–8, 112–13, 117–20, 220–1, 330, 347–9, 366–7
Ropp, George von der 329
Ropp, General Baron von der 57
Ropp, Guillaume Alexandrowich von der 32–3
Ropp, Hanno von der 233–4
Ropp, Helene von der 35, 37
Ropp (née Guriev), Lydia von der 32–3, 35–6, 38, 370
Ropp, Margaretta von der 35
Ropp, Maria 'Marusch' von der 35, 36
Ropp, Paul von der 37, 77–8, 81, 113
Rosenberg, Alfred 'the Sphinx' 166, 167, 209, 212, 231, 240, 250–1, 256, 282, 312, 315, 333, 350, 365
  the Anschluss 265–6
  and de Ropp 5, 26–7, 28, 29, 138–40, 141, 142, 144–5, 147–8, 151, 152–4, 155–7, 164, 165–8, 172, 176, 192, 195, 204–5, 229–30, 237–8, 241, 262, 263, 265–7, 268–9, 280, 290–2, 293–4, 301–2, 304–5, 306, 309, 316, 329, 355, 357, 361
  diary entries 165–7, 191–2, 203, 204–5, 243–4, 250, 290–1, 302–3, 315–16, 329, 350–1
  and the Duke of Kent 356–7
  final Political Testament 352–3
  fleeing Berlin and capture 350–4
  and Hitler 26–7, 28, 133, 135, 139, 142, 144, 160, 205, 212, 229–30, 241, 245–6, 291, 301–2, 304–5, 309, 350, 352–3, 354–5
  London visits 152–4, 155–7, 160–4, 359
  Molotov-Ribbentrop Pact (1939) 243–4
  Night of the Long Knives (1934) 190, 191–2
  Nuremberg Rally (1934) 198, 203–4
  as Reich Minister for the Occupied Eastern Territories 231, 284, 354
  and Rudolf Hess 315–16
  trial, testimony and execution 1–6, 353–61
  Winterbotham's visits to Berlin 179–82, 186, 245–6, 267–8, 356–7
  see also Foreign Affairs Bureau (APA), Nazi Party
Royal Air Force (RAF) and British aircraft development 8, 91, 191, 246–7, 252, 254–5, 256–7, 259, 263, 292, 308–9, 318, 350, 257, 359
Royal Dutch Shell Group xviii, 162, 237, 297
royal family, British xviii, 25, 204–6, 213–14, 356, 358
Royal Flying Corps (RFC) 48, 49, 91, 64, 110, 123, 138, 224–5
Royal Navy (RN) 8, 75
Rudenko, Roman 359–61
Rumbold, Sir Horace 130–1, 222
Runciman Mission 10
Russia 4, 37
  Great War 59–60, 61
  Orthodox Church 32, 33, 36, 370
  Revolution 37, 61, 78–9, 139

INDEX

Russian Consulate 46–7
Treaty of Brest-Litovsk 60
Tsarist Empire 32
Russo-German Air Traffic Co. 124

SA (Sturmabteilung) 189–90, 194, 272, 312
Sachse, Helmuth 250, 254, 255, 259
Saloman, Franz Pfeffer von 312, 323
Sass, Pastor Theodor von 234
Sassoon, Sir Philip 172, 187
Savile Club, London 5, 16, 50, 81, 91, 93, 94–5, 103, 104, 121, 162, 167, 193, 194, 274, 304, 306, 324
Schacht, Hjalmar 111, 280
Schellenberg, Walter 195, 226, 276–7, 300, 313, 316–17, 319, 323, 324, 330, 343–4, 347
Schickedanz, Arno 137–8, 139, 168, 219, 231, 239, 266, 350–1, 355
Schiemann, Paul 77
Schleicher, General Kurt von 190, 237
Schlözer, Leopold von 34–5
Schmidt, Paul 280
Schnee, Heinrich 111
Schröders Bank xviii
Schubert, Carl von 117–18
Schweppenburg, Baron Geyr von 219, 252
The Scotsman 5, 162–3, 203, 356, 358
Scott, Sir Gilbert 9
Scrase Dickins, Guy 95–6
SD (Sicherheitsdienst) 14, 195, 226, 276, 300, 313, 330
Second World War 21, 23–4
Secret Service, British *see* MI5; MI6
Seekht, General von 126–7
Seibert, Dr Theodore 173, 220
Seidel, Dr 259
Seitz, Theodore 111
Seraphim, Hans-Gunther 28
Serebryansky, Yakov 116
Shannon Power Scheme 112
Shell *see* Royal Dutch Shell Group
Shirer, William 280
Shmidkoff, Artur 101
Siemens 125, 249
Simon, Sir John 161, 166, 181, 222, 233, 246–7, 318–19
Sinclair, Admiral Sir Hugh 11–17, 20, 21, 99–100, 123, 148, 152–3, 179–80, 187–8, 218, 241, 275, 277, 279, 288, 289, 292, 298
Situation Report Centre, British 294
Skoropadsky, Pavlo 236–7, 238, 239, 240, 241
Skorzeny, Otto 339
Smith, Howard 335
Smith, Joseph Kingsbury 4
Snow, General Thomas 49
Solf, Wilhelm 52, 54
South Africa 8, 189, 287, 367
Soviet Union 10, 12, 17, 116, 122, 158–9, 162, 240, 253, 320
invasion of Germany 350–1
the KGB 88, 90, 116–17
and MI6 67–9
Molotov-Ribbentrop Pact (1939) 243–4, 283
Nazi plans to take down/Operation Barbarossa 182, 184–5, 186, 187, 229–30, 242, 282, 284, 314–15, 319, 334–8
Nuremberg Trials 359–61
and post-Great War Baltic States 73, 74, 75–6, 80
Russo-German aviation collaboration 124, 125–7, 129, 245
the Ukraine 3, 162, 236–43, 244, 359–60
Spain 10, 18, 19
Spanish Civil War 18
Spanish flu pandemic 65
Spencer, Colonel Frank 111
Spencer, Herbert 68
Sprent, Colin 38–9, 46
Squire, John Collings 193, 194
SS (Schutzstaffel) 14, 170, 176, 190, 194, 195, 219
Stahlhelm 129, 137, 189
Stalin, Joseph 303
Stallforth, Federico 322–3, 345
Stennes, Walter 189
Stevens, Richard 300
Steward, George 218
Stewart, Colonel Reginald 48
Stralendorff, Joachim von 35, 170, 329, 367–8
Strang, William 10, 12, 17, 19
Strasser, Gregor 134, 135–6, 190, 192, 225
Strasser, Otto 225
Stresemann, Dr Gustav 126
Sudetenland 18, 280, 284
Sudoplatov, Pavel 116
Suez campaign (1956) 29
Sunday Times 102
Supermarine 308
Swinton, Major-General Ernest 208
Sykes, Commander Percy 'Pay' 138, 179
Synod, Missouri 33
Tallents, Colonel Stephen 75

Tanaka, Colonel 239–40
Tatler 193
Technische Hochschule, Dresden 38
Teutonic Knights 31
The Times 57, 61, 121, 127–8, 150, 152, 153–5, 163, 166, 167, 203, 223–4, 234, 290, 298, 304, 318
Thoma, Dr Alfred 3, 5, 355, 359
Thomson, Sir Basil 241
Thost, Dr Hans 153, 161, 162, 172–4, 220, 330
Toynbee, Arnold 267
Treaty of Brest-Litovsk (1918) 60, 73, 79
Treaty of Rapallo (1922) 107–8
Treaty of Versailles (1919) 123, 125, 140, 158–9, 161, 204, 232
Treviranus, Gottfried 111, 119, 190
Trevor-Roper, Hugh 149–50, 299
Truscott, Roy 109–10
Tsarev, Oleg 88, 90, 101
Tufnell, Louis 241
Turkey 18
Tyrrell, 1st Baron Tyrrell 119

Udet, Ernst 255, 336
Uiberreither, Dr Siegfried 266
Ukraine 3, 162, 236–43, 244, 359–60
Ultra operations 21, 328, 346, 364, 365
United States Counter Intelligence Corps 324
United States of America 18, 42, 57–8, 61, 165, 254, 341, 345
Universal Aunts 115
Urban, Gotthard 265
Ustinov, Klop 218–19, 281, 300

van den Heuvel, Frederick 297, 339, 341, 361
Vansittart, Robert 2, 9–10, 12, 116, 130–1, 134, 152, 161, 179–80, 218, 222, 224, 226, 227, 251, 253, 281, 289, 300, 301
Vaughan-Williams, Adeline 115
Vaughan-Williams, Ralph 46, 115
Venlo Incident 299–300, 342
Vitzthum Gymnasium, Dresden 37, 38, 170
Vivian, Valentine 105, 120, 171, 173, 237, 239, 241
Voigt, Frederick 126, 127–8, 224, 274, 298
Volkischer Beobachter (VB) 137, 153, 161, 169, 172, 191, 219, 220
Walker DSO, Colonel C.W.G. 92
Ward, Lieutenant Colonel Richard Barrington 75
Ward Price, George 224
Wehrmacht 182, 218–19, 281, 300
Wenninger, Ralph 173, 183, 219, 248, 252–3, 290
West, Nigel 90
'What Should We Do?' report, MI6 15–20, 242, 279, 292
White, Dick 218
White, Herbert 60–1
White Russian forces 69, 74, 79, 80, 116, 237
White, Sir George 122
Whittall, Hugh 297, 335, 340–1
Wildemann, Bernhard (Benno) von 35–6, 76–7, 78–80, 82, 367
Wildemann (née von der Ropp), Gertrud von 35–6, 77, 78–9, 370
Wildemann, Marina von 36, 78–9
Willans and Robinson 42
William II, Kaiser 54, 60
Wilson, Harold 108
Wilson, Sir Horace 9, 218, 223
Wilson, Woodrow 204, 235, 290
Windsor, Duke of 213–14
  see also Edward VIII, King
Winterbotham, Fred W. xviii, 5–6, 11–12, 148, 150–2, 155–7, 164, 179–88, 191, 204–5, 207, 208, 214, 231, 231–2, 248–51, 267–8, 272–3, 288, 292, 293, 299, 308, 333, 355, 358, 364–6, 371
  meetings with Hitler 181–2, 245–6, 357
Wiskemann, Elizabeth 341–2
Witzleben, General Erwin von 280
Woermann, Ernst 175
Wood, Kingsley 291, 307
Woodman Hunter, Gertrude 110
Woollcombe, Malcolm 13–20, 21, 101, 102–3, 104, 133–4, 142, 152, 179, 218, 240, 269, 282, 284, 285, 286, 299, 328, 363–4, 371

Z Organisation, MI6 296–8, 305
Zeitschel, Carl Theo von 176
Zeppelin airships 50
Zimmermann, Arthur 52
Zinoviev, Grigory 85
Zinoviev Letter scandal (1924) xvii, 12, 85–96, 97–108, 109, 116
Zog of Albania, King 235
zu Putlitz, Wolfgang 218